PROMISED LAND

Ace Books by Connie Willis and Cynthia Felice

WATER WITCH
LIGHT RAID
PROMISED LAND

PROMISED LAND

CYNTHIA FELICE   CONNIE WILLIS

ACE BOOKS, NEW YORK

PROMISED LAND

An Ace Book
Published by The Berkley Publishing Group
200 Madison Avenue, New York, NY 10016

The Putnam Berkley World Wide Web site address is
http://www.berkley.com/berkley

Make sure to check out *PB Plug*, the science fiction/fantasy newsletter, at
http://www.pbplug.com

Copyright © 1996 by Cynthia Felice and Connie Willis

Book design by Maureen Troy

First edition: February 1997

Library of Congress Cataloging-in-Publication Data

Felice, Cynthia.
    Promised land / by Cynthia Felice and Connie Willis.
        p.   cm.
    ISBN 0-441-00405-9
    I. Willis, Connie.   II. Title.
    PS3566.E466P76   1997
    813'.54—dc20   96-31436
                                                  CIP

Printed in the United States of America

10   9   8   7   6   5   4   3   2   1

● ●

For Sheba and Gracie,
utterly loyal, and to Laura
For bridging the collaboration Format gaps

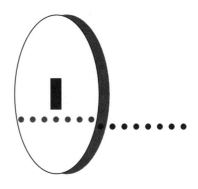

There was no one waiting for her.

Delanna stood at the bottom of the shuttle ramp shading her eyes against bright sunlight shimmering off the silvery ribbon of runway. At the other end, where the runway faded into blue-green grass, she could see a solitary shuttleport building, and an unimaginative blue rectangle that had to be the shuttleport warehouse. There was a dirt road that cut straight across the featureless landscape to a row of shiny particolored buildings of the town of Grassedge that seemed perched on the edge of the horizon. She pushed her hair back away from her face and turned her back to the sun. Nothing. Just a sea of grass stippled with dominolike dots that must be irrigated farm fields, and somewhere out there in the east were the mountains, so distant she couldn't even see the snow-capped peaks she remembered.

"No one here to meet you?" the shuttle pilot said as he came down the ramp.

"A neighbor was supposed to come, but maybe he's waiting at the terminal."

"Not likely. People only use the terminal to camp in until we can shuttle them up to the ships."

Delanna nodded, vaguely remembering snuggling up

against her mother in a sleeping bag while they waited for the ship to come to take her to school. Then her mother had put her in the shuttle, and it wasn't until the door closed between them that Delanna had realized her mother wasn't coming along. She'd cried all the way into orbit, and hadn't been mollified until someone had given her ice cream. She didn't remember much else—riding in a solaris for what seemed like days and days, and seeing a brush fire—she had only been five years old. Grassedge and the plains around it looked only very vaguely familiar. The landscape was as barren as her mother had described it in her letters. "A sorry excuse for a planet," she'd written of Keramos. "I hope you never have to come back here."

And now she was back, but only for as long as it took to settle her mother's estate.

"Maybe the neighbor boy *is* camped out at the terminal," Delanna said hopefully to the pilot. "He couldn't know exactly when the ship would arrive, could he?"

"Not exactly," the pilot agreed. "But there wasn't anyone camping there when I left at dawn."

"Still, I'd better take a look."

The pilot shrugged indifferently and gestured toward a half-mile-distant lump of green ceramic at the edge of the field. Even now she could make out the long shadow better than the terminal building itself. "Just follow the yellow line."

"You mean walk?" Delanna said, staring at him. She knew services, even in Grassedge, the largest settlement on Keramos, were limited compared to Gay Paree, the tiny city on Rebe Prime where The Abbey was located. Her mother had told her Keramos was primitive, but this was ridiculous.

The shuttle pilot shrugged. "Gilby has already gone home," he said. "Gilby's usually here to look after passengers when we have any, but sometimes he doesn't make it past the bars."

"Surely there's someone else."

The pilot shook his head. "Just me and Gilby until the cash crops in the fall," he said, then added thoughtfully, "For those that have cash crops."

"What about you?"

"We try to please," he said, in a tone that didn't convince Delanna at all, "but I have to get the first load off the shuttle before sundown. The pallet is solar-powered, and as you can plainly see, it's almost sundown."

Delanna stared at the huge golden blob above the horizon, feeling, just for an instant, as lost and forlorn as she had been when she first went to Rebe Prime, five years old and in a strange school in a strange city on an even stranger planet. She had been all alone then and she was all alone now. Her friends were back in Gay Paree, her mother was in a grave somewhere near Milleflores Lanzye and had been for almost ten months. But she was no longer a little kid. She took a deep breath.

"I'm not walking in these," Delanna said, pointing down at her ribbon-laced highups. Surely the pilot could see walking was out of the question.

"Well, I guess if you don't mind riding on the pallet, I could take you on over to the cargo dock on it."

Delanna eyed the pallet warily, and finally nodded. Anything would be better than walking.

The pilot ducked under the stubby wing of the shuttle and went to the cargo-bay door. Delanna watched him pull a lever and step out of the way as the first pallet descended. Like all pallets, it was sealed, but this one had oxygen tanks attached, and a makeshift sign that said "Livestock! Protect from extreme temperatures." She could hear muted honking. Wonderful. She would be sharing her ride with a crate of geese. She had shared taxis in Gay Paree with stranger companions, and some of them had sounded almost like this.

She perched on the metallic crate and clutched her travelwallet and carryit while the pilot walked alongside, guiding the pallet with a tether. When the pallet rolled off the runway, the ride became bumpy, and she had to hold on to the cranehook in the center of the crate.

She closed her eyes against the stream of sunlight and relaxed against the cranehook. The sunlight felt warm on her face, and the air smelled wonderful, full of dust and the scent of freshly mowed grass. She felt almost like a traitor enjoying it; her mother had hated everything about Keramos, had wanted more than anything to escape but hadn't succeeded. I'd hate it, too, if I were stuck here, Delanna thought, but right now the fresh air and the warmth and the space felt wonderful after the stale-smelling, cramped ship.

Abruptly the sunlight disappeared, and she opened her eyes. The pilot had steered the pallet into the shadow of the warehouse. Its blue ceramic tile exterior was so dark that at first she didn't notice the black gap of an open cargo door. Then two men stepped out of the shadows, and waved.

Delanna waved back. "Maybe that's him," she said eagerly. One man was older, white-haired with a brightly flowered shirt and a paunch hanging over his pants. The other was a handsome dark-haired man. She remembered the Tanner boy having been fair-haired when he was ten or eleven. He would have grown up by now, and his hair could have darkened.

The pilot was waving, too. "That's the port veterinarian, Doc Lyle. The one with him is the prairie caravan captain, Jay Madog. The vet will be wanting blood samples from these geese, and Jay probably wants to check the bills of lading to see how much cargo space he needs for the next train east. I think he has some software licenses to sign for, too."

"Oh," Delanna said, disappointed.

They pulled up even with the men. ". . . see any Royal Mandarins last time you were up that way?" the vet was saying.

"Not a one," the younger man said.

They both turned to look at the pallet.

"You have the geese in there?" the vet called as he reached around the edge of the black hole, apparently for a light switch, for the depth of darkness was suddenly flooded with light. Inside were a few crates, far too few to fill the vast recesses of the warehouse. "Where are their importation papers? I'd like to get home in time for dinner for a change."

"I've got them here," the pilot said. "You got anybody in there waiting for a passenger?"

"Nope." The vet came forward to meet the pilot, who handed him a sheaf of papers without stopping. "Go ahead and uncrate them," he said, already examining the papers. "I'll be right in."

The pilot stepped through the low doorway ahead of the pallet, ducking his head. Delanna realized that she'd never clear the overhang without getting scraped.

The younger man, Jay Madog, his dark hair falling rakishly over his forehead, stepped up to the moving pallet. "And who might you be?" he asked, holding his arms out to her.

Delanna hesitated, looking at the approaching door, then jumped down into his arms. Madog caught her around the waist and pulled her away from the pallet. He held her a moment too long once she was down, his wrists tight against her breasts. Then he let go, reached up to the top of the crate, and got her carryit and travelwallet. When he handed her wallet over, he asked again, "And what's your name, little lady?"

"You're missing paperwork," the vet cut in. "There aren't any importation papers on this pig."

"It's on the bottom," the dark-haired man said, then returning to Delanna, added, "Allow me to introduce myself. I'm Jay Madog. And this guy over here giving me a hard time with my paperwork is Doc Lyle." His smile broadened, a very pleasant smile, Delanna decided.

She shook the hand he offered. His grip was firm, but not painful like some of the boys' back on Rebe Prime.

5

The boys had always been showing off. Somehow, she didn't think Jay Madog ever needed to show off. "How do you do, Captain Madog," she said in her best school manner.

"Everybody calls me Jay," he said, leading her through the doorway into the warehouse, her carryit still in hand.

"Hrrrumph," she heard the veterinarian say, and she turned to find him peering at her over the sheaf of papers. "He's called Mad Dog, and with good reason."

Jay still didn't let go of her hand. "Don't believe anything about me you haven't seen with your own eyes," he said. "I don't," the veterinarian replied, and returned to his papers.

"And don't you," Jay said to Delanna. She turned to look at him. He was smiling. "Lanzye folk gossip entirely too much, but you can't hold it against them because there just isn't anything else to do."

"And I can just imagine that you love it," Delanna said as she reached over, trying to take her carryit from him. She didn't have time for the local Lothario, even if his friendliness was refreshing. And she didn't want anyone else holding her carryit and what was in it.

Jay held on to the carryit and pointed to a bench near a livestock pen. "But what can I do?" he asked with exaggerated innocence.

"I'll bet you could think of something if you tried," Delanna said, following him over to the bench, "but from what I remember of Keramos, you'd be doing the entire population a disservice."

Jay laughed. "A woman who understands me. And a beautiful redhead, to boot. Where have you been all my life? And now that I've found you, where are you staying?"

"I'm not," she said, eyeing the carryit. "I'm leaving tomorrow afternoon."

Jay glanced over at the pilot, who nodded. "It's true. She's reserved space to go back up to the *Scoville* tomorrow afternoon. Didn't even bring a trunk down."

Jay looked crestfallen. "But why would anyone come to Keramos for a day?" he asked.

"My business should only take a few hours," Delanna explained. "But a better question would be, Why would anyone want to stay on Keramos for anything more than a day?"

The veterinarian, who had followed them in, harrumphed again.

"I only came here to see a lawyer," Delanna said, reaching for the carryit again.

Jay stuck it behind his back. "Well, then, if there's only the one night," he said, leaning close to her, "we've got a duty to make the most of it."

"Jay!" Doc Lyle said. "Stop pestering the tourists and go check your cargo. Or come help me with these geese."

"We'll go right to the lake for a picnic, Delanna," Jay continued, ignoring the vet. "And maybe a midnight swim if it's not too cold."

"Aren't you supposed to be on the midnight train?" Doc Lyle asked.

"An *evening* swim," Jay amended. "Or we might build a bonfire and watch the stars."

Delanna laughed and shook her head. "Sorry," she told him. "I've got to be at the lawyer's first thing in the morning," and this time got the carryit away from him. She slung the strap over her head so he couldn't grab it again, and went over to the vet and the pilot, who were opening the crate full of geese. They were honking in alarm.

Jay followed her. "Then I'll take you to the hotel."

"Not till you've checked that cargo," the vet said. "I'm not staying around here all night. And don't you have some software licenses you need signed before the shuttle takes off?"

"I want to get back, too," the pilot put in.

"I'll go get the licenses," Jay said. "Till tonight," he whispered to Delanna, winked, and went outside.

7

The pilot and vet had the crate open and were herding the honking geese into a pen.

"Someone was supposed to meet me here," Delanna said.

"In a minute," the vet told her, grabbing for a goose in the corner of the crate. He caught hold of it, and it honked like it was being slaughtered.

Delanna backed away from the flapping goose, found a bench near the pen, and sat down. She opened the carryit cautiously, looked inside, and then shut it again, watching the vet and the pilot. The goose had gotten loose again and was fluttering wildly around in the crate.

"There, there," Doc Lyle said comfortingly, "I won't hurt you." He lunged and grabbed it by one leg. Its wings flapped against his face. He got one wing tucked under his arm, but the long-necked bird was struggling so frantically that it took both his hands to control it. "Give me a hand, here, will you, Wilbur?" he asked the pilot.

The pilot frowned and shook his head. "I tried to help you with that filly last month, and got kicked right in the—" He caught himself and glanced red-faced at Delanna.

"This isn't a filly, it's a goose," the vet said, trying to pin the wings against the goose's body. "Come help me."

"I gotta go sign those licenses of Jay's," the pilot said, and scurried outside.

The vet looked up at Delanna. "You. Come here and help me."

"Me?"

"Yes, you."

Delanna got up from the bench. She slid the strap of the carryit off and looked around for a place to put it.

"Now!" the vet said. Delanna tucked the carryit under the bench and came over to the pen. She let herself in and took the frantic goose from the vet, pinning its wing firmly with the crook of one arm while supporting its chest with her hand. She controlled the long neck and head with her

8

other hand. ''Hush now, you silly thing,'' she said to the goose.

The vet straightened and took a vial out of his pocket. ''Looks to me like you've done this before,'' he said.

''I have,'' she said. ''Not for a long time, though.''

The vet brushed aside some feathers on the goose's back, and stuck the vial against the skin.

I was supposed to meet someone here,'' Delanna said, trying again. ''Mr. Tanner. From Milleflores Lanzye. Do you know him?''

''These are his geese,'' he said. He withdrew the vial from the goose feathers. ''Hold on. I've got to do something else.'' He reached in his pocket. ''If it's Sonny Tanner you're waiting for, he'll be here. He's gotta pick up these geese.''

''This afternoon?''

Lyle pulled another vial, larger than the first one, from his pocket. ''He'd better. These geese have got to be on that midnight train, too.'' He pressed the vial against the bird's neck. ''Hold her. That's good. Where'd you learn to handle geese?''

''My mother kept geese.'' And Delanna had taken a class in animal husbandry at school, which her mother had had a fit about. ''Don't waste your time on classes like that,'' she'd written Delanna. ''I want you learning to live in a city, not on a farm.''

''Funny,'' Doc Lyle said, pulling a long tube out of his pocket. ''You don't think about been-tos keeping geese.''

''Been-tos?''

''Off-planeters. Hand me her wing.''

''I'm not exactly a 'been-to,' '' Delanna said, readjusting the goose to free its wing. ''I was born on Keramos.''

Doc Lyle took hold of the wing and held up the tube. ''Vegetable dye,'' he said, ''so I know which ones I've done,'' and sprayed the wingtip green.

The goose hadn't struggled at all at the two vaccinations,

but the dye sent her wild. She gave a hysterical honk and nearly got away from Delanna.

"Don't," Delanna said, trying to get a grip on the bird.

She finally got it quieted. "Put it in here," Doc Lyle said, pulling a clean cage over. She poked it in, cornered another one in the crate and picked it up.

Doc Lyle was looking at her speculatively. "You're meeting Sonny Tanner . . . your ma kept geese . . . You're Serena Milleflores' girl that went off to school, aren't you?"

"You knew my mother?" Delanna asked.

"Back in the old days I knew everyone in the world," he said. "Of course, there was only five hundred of us in the first landing. And I saw her quite a bit a few years back. There was a pair of nesting Royal Mandarins on Milleflores Lanzye then." He smiled for the first time. "Beautiful pair. Beautiful lanzye, Milleflores. I don't think your mother ever liked it much, though."

That was putting it mildly.

He pulled out a vial. "So you're here to take over Milleflores, you and Sonny?"

"I'm here to settle my mother's estate," Delanna said, pulling back the feathers so he could give the vaccination. "And then I'm going on to Carthage."

"Ooh, the big city," he said, giving the second vaccination. "That's a pity. Keramos has got a lot to offer."

"I can imagine."

"You sure are your mother's daughter," he said, splaying out the wing. "Did you ever see a Royal Mandarin while you were at Milleflores?"

"I don't remember," Delanna said, bracing the goose for the dye. "I was only five when I left."

"Beautiful birds," he said. "All the colors of the rainbow. Hardly any left now, and most of those aren't breeding pairs. There were thousands of them when I first came to Keramos."

Delanna was still holding the wing out, but the vet had

apparently forgotten all about spraying it in his enthusiasm over the Royal Mandarins.

"The dye," Delanna said.

"Sorry," he said, coming to himself. He sprayed the wing, took the goose from her, and shoved it in the cage. "It's my job to protect the animals on Keramos, and I guess I get a little carried away when it's a beautiful specimen like the Royal Mandarin. That's what all these vaccinations are for, to keep imported animals from bringing any infections onto Keramos."

"When do you think Mr. Tanner might get here?" Delanna asked, hoping it would be soon. The geese smelled terrible. Her mother's birds and the ones in her husbandry class had smelled bad, but "loose as a goose" took on a whole new meaning when geese had been cooped up on a ship for two months.

"I expected Sonny before this," Doc Lyle said. "Hand me that one over there."

She obediently grabbed up the next goose and they went through the routine again, the vet talking the whole time about the Royal Mandarins, the dangers of off-planet infections, Milleflores. "It's a beautiful lanzye. All those flowers."

Good, Delanna thought, then I'll get a good price for it.

"Pretty run-down, though, of course."

Of course.

"I do believe your mother was the first one to hatch goose eggs on Keramos," he said, vaccinating the last goose. "Toulouse geese, gray like these Junos."

"I don't know if they were first or not, but I remember them being huge. I had to feed them every day," Delanna said. "I hated them."

He fumbled the feathers apart. "The hatred doesn't seem to have lasted."

She wrinkled her nose. "As badly as these geese smell, it could return very quickly," she said, but she held the goose snugly while the vet sprayed its wing.

When all thirteen geese had green swatches on their left wings and were safely stored in clean cages, Delanna followed the vet out of the pen. He picked up the sheaf of papers and started working on it, initialing each sheet.

Delanna went to the door of the warehouse and looked outside. There was no sign of anyone coming, or of Jay Madog and the pilot either. She went back inside, pulled out a sack of feed from the overhead on the goose crate, and took it over to give it to the caged birds. The food dispelled all pretense of shyness on their part. They clustered and honked and snatched the grains as they came out of the bag. Crouching, Delanna spread the feed as she remembered doing so many years ago, making a long trail of it along the edge of the cages so that all the geese could eat, not just the bigger ones.

"Good. You're still here," Jay Madog said. "And that friend of yours isn't, which means I can give you a ride into town and"—he leaned over her—"then out to that lake I told you about."

Doc Lyle looked up from his initialing. "I think you ought to know that that friend she's waiting for is Sonny Tanner," he said.

"Really?" Jay strode over to the bench, reached under it, and got Delanna's carryit. "You know Sonny Tanner? He's a good man."

"I think you ought to also know that this is Delanna Milleflores," Doc Lyle added.

"Delanna—" Jay said, clearly taken aback. "You're Serena Milleflores' daughter?" He looked surprised and something else Delanna couldn't make out.

"Just thought you should know," Doc Lyle said, sounding amused. "Before you took her off on that moonlight swim. Not that that'll stop you."

Delanna looked bewilderedly at them, wondering what this was all about.

"I thought you said you were only staying till tomorrow," Jay said, holding the carryit out to her.

"I am," she said, but before she could take the carryit from him, it let out a loud roar.

Jay almost dropped it. "What the devil do you have in there?" he said.

Delanna grabbed the carryit and hastily set it down to open it. It roared again.

"Yes, just what is in there?" Doc Lyle asked, stepping out from behind the crate.

"It's okay," Delanna assured them. "It's just Cleopatra, my scarab. She's getting hungry."

Delanna pulled the scarab out and cuddled her close, the soft underside molding itself to her chest while the fuzzy muzzle rubbed against her chin. Cleopatra immediately started purring when she realized she was safe in Delanna's arms.

"What is that?" Jay asked, standing well back. "Some kind of big bug?"

"It's a scarab," Doc Lyle said, putting the sheaf of papers on a corner of the crate and holding his hands out to Delanna. "I've never seen one up close before. It *is* a scarab, isn't it?"

Delanna nodded and put her cheek against Cleopatra's shoulder plate to pin her; Cleopatra had seen the veterinarian's outstretched hands and didn't want to go. "He won't hurt you," she whispered, and to Doc Lyle she said, "She'll probably roar again."

He took the scarab from her anyhow, his grip firm but gentle. Cleo ducked into her plates, but she didn't roar. "You must spend a lot of time polishing these plates," Doc Lyle said admiringly. "She looks like a basket of jewelry."

"I didn't have much else to do on the trip. Besides, Cleo's plates have beautiful markings, don't they?"

He nodded and stepped over to show the scarab to Jay Madog, who stood stiffly. "It's not an insect at all," Doc Lyle said, carefully turning Cleo over to expose her belly. "It's a member of the genus *Scaraeoptera*. From Rebe Quarto. There aren't any scaraeoptera on Keramos." Toenails of all six feet stood out like needles and Cleopatra snarled to discourage the examination. But the veterinarian was unconcerned. He pulled at one of her feet, and being much stronger than the scarab, was able to extend it to the knee. "It should extend more," Doc Lyle said, looking over at Delanna. Jay Madog stepped away, suddenly interested in the papers on the crate. "But it hinges, doesn't it? I don't want to hurt her."

Delanna reached over to unhinge Cleopatra's knee, and extended the fuzzy leg fully. "She's waist-high when she stands up all the way, but Cleo's lazy, and she's never had anything higher than a curb to look over. She rarely extends. Skittering low to the ground is her normal gait."

Cleo tucked the leg back in as soon as Delanna let go, but she poked her nose out. The compound eyes above the nostrils glittered like jewels, and upon recognizing Delanna, the nictating membranes on the fore-eyes also opened.

"Interesting specimen," Doc Lyle said, looking at Delanna. "I'm afraid I'll have to impound her."

"Impound her!"

"No animals are allowed on Keramos except those certified as hatchlings, or birthed en route in sealed environments. We haven't got the resources to do any other kind of disease control, and even less for pests that might ride in on a mature animal."

"She doesn't have pests," Delanna protested, starting to fumble through her travelwallet. "I have her health certificate. She's had all her vaccinations."

Doc Lyle shook his head. "She's a mature animal. I can't allow her on Keramos."

"But—can I send her back up on the shuttle, then?"

"It's already left," Jay said.

The vet looked at her. "Imported animals are a threat to the animals of Keramos."

"Couldn't I just keep her in the carryit?" Delanna asked, holding out her hands. Cleo extended her forelegs and roared softly. "It has a lock, and I promise I won't let her

14

out. She'll sleep the whole time anyway. And I'll keep her away from other animals.''

''Sorry. Rules are rules.'' Lyle turned away, carrying the scarab.

''What are you going to do with her?'' Delanna said, following him. ''I didn't know I wasn't supposed to bring her down with me. Nobody on the ship said anything about it being against Keramos's laws, and it never occurred to me . . .''

There was a row of cages alongside the wall. The vet opened one and set Cleo inside. The scarab tightened up until she looked like a jeweled ball in the middle of the cage. The vet snapped the lock in place, slipped the key in his pocket, and started toward a large metal box with a control panel on the front.

''It isn't as if I'm trying to import her,'' Delanna argued. ''I'm only going to be here one day.''

Doc Lyle looked thoughtful. ''You're going back up on the shuttle tomorrow?''

''I thought you said this was Delanna Milleflores,'' Jay put in.

''I am,'' Delanna said. ''But I'm just here to sign some papers. I won't even be here a whole day. And Cleo doesn't have any diseases or mites or anything. She's been sterilized and everything. See, here's her health certificate.'' She thrust it at the vet.

He didn't take it. He reached above the metal box to a cabinet, and pulled down a thick notebook. He began looking through it, turning pages intently.

''You said you didn't have any *scaraeoptera* on Keramos,'' Delanna went on urgently. ''I learned in school that diseases aren't cross-genus, so she can't infect any of the animals.''

''I'd leave it be,'' Jay said softly, taking her arm. ''Arguments don't count with Doc Lyle, only rules.''

I hope he finds a rule that lets Cleo stay then, Delanna thought.

Apparently he did. After a few minutes, he put his finger on a passage and said, "The animal isn't considered to be officially imported until it's been processed and left the shuttleport. Processing of the animal must be completed in twenty-four hours. Until then, the animal hasn't been imported or denied import status." He looked up. "You sure these papers you have to sign won't take more than twenty-four hours?"

"I'm sure," Delanna told him.

"Then so long as the animal stays here and isn't processed, there's nothing in the rules that says you can't take it back up with you to the *Scoville*." He took the key out of his pocket and unlocked Cleo's cage.

"Oh, good," Delanna said.

"I'm going to put her in an isolette, just in case," Lyle explained, opening the cage. Cleo stayed in a tight little ball. "That way there won't be any chance of her exposing anything else." He carried her over to a clear-sided cage with a number of dials on the front and put her in.

"All right," Delanna said, watching Cleo. She hated leaving her, but she didn't want to press her luck, and with luck, she could meet with the lawyer first thing in the morning and be back before midday. She went over to the cage and put her hand up to the clear side to comfort the scarab. Cleo stuck one paw out of her carapace, then another, and eventually poked her head out, too. She reached for Delanna's hand, felt the barrier, and ducked back in. Delanna sighed.

"Don't worry," Jay said, coming up behind her. She felt his hands on her shoulders. "It'll be fine. Doc Lyle'll take good care of it."

But Delanna shook her head. "She'll stay rolled up until I come back, poor thing. She's frightened." Sighing again, Delanna stood there a moment, hating to leave the scarab. "It's just until tomorrow," she said, giving the side of the cage a final pat. She started to turn around, but Jay's hands were still on her shoulders.

"You ready for that ride into town now?" he said, giving her shoulders a final squeeze before letting go. When she turned, she found him standing with her carryit in his hands. She nodded and reached for it, but he held on to the bag.

"I'll carry . . ."

"Yeoh!" came a shout from outside.

They all turned to see a man silhouetted in the doorway.

"Those my geese?" he said, sounding happy. He stepped into the warehouse lights, a tall, thin figure in baggy pants rolled up at the cuffs and an orange flowered shirt. He carried a suit jacket over his shoulder and wore a red cap on his head. "Did all twelve come through?" he asked, handing a sheaf of papers to the vet and hurrying to the pen, for he couldn't help but know exactly where the geese were with all their honking. "Look at that," he said after just a moment. "The bonus egg hatched, too! Thanks, Doc, for recommending Juno geese to me. Never would have believed all thirteen would make it."

"That's why it didn't tally," Jay said, shaking his head. "You only reserved room for six of them on the *Mad Dog.*"

"That's all right," the man said. "I can take all thirteen. I bought a new wagon, and I brought my solaris over from the lanzye. It's over at Grayson's having a motor fixed. I'll carry the other seven in the wagon and we'll put the rest of my freight in your rig."

"You're going to need seven more permits," Doc Lyle said. "I can't release these geese without importation permits, and you've only got six."

And rules are rules, Delanna thought, even when it was just eggs.

"I'll get them from Maggie when I go into town," the man said, looking up. He saw Delanna, and his jaw dropped.

"Is this Mr. Tanner?" Delanna asked doubtfully. She hoped he wasn't. He didn't look anything like the fair-haired boy she remembered, and he was so grubby and brainless-looking. He was still gaping at her.

"It is, Delanna. Don't you recognize your own—" Doc Lyle began.

The man cut him off. "You can't be Delanna," he said stupidly. "You're over at the terminal."

"Guess again," Jay said. "She's right here."

"How do you do?" Delanna said in her best school manner. "I'm Delanna Milleflores. You must be Tarleton Tanner."

"Tarleton?" Jay echoed, grinning.

"Everyone calls me Sonny," he said, flushing slightly as he wiped his hand on his baggy pants and stuck it out. When Delanna hesitated, he wiped it on his pants again. "I haven't touched the geese," he said, apparently trying to understand why she wouldn't shake his hand.

"*I* have," Delanna said, grasping his hand firmly.

Sonny smiled shyly as he squeezed her hand—too hard! "Sorry!" he said quickly when he saw Delanna wince, and snatched his hand back like he'd been shocked. He shook his hand and flexed the fingers. "I didn't mean . . . Whew! You were in with the geese, weren't you?"

"I had a lot of time to kill," she said coolly, "so I helped the vet."

"Yeah," Doc Lyle said, bringing over a sheaf of papers for Sonny to sign. "Good thing you showed up when you did. Jay Madog was about to make off with your—"

"I was just offering Delanna here a ride into town," Jay cut in. "Where have you been?"

"I had to pick up the wagon before the dealer closed. I was going to go to the terminal to get Delanna just as soon as I was finished checking the geese, so we'll save some time now because I won't have to go to the terminal."

"Right," Delanna said, "because I'm right here, right?"

"Right!" he said, almost beaming.

Behind him, Jay was shaking with laughter.

Doc Lyle didn't smile. "You ought to take Delanna into town now, Sonny," he said, looking at the signed paperwork. "She's had a long day and is probably tired. You can bring me the permits after you've got her settled at the hotel."

"The hotel," Sonny said, first nodding, then shaking his head. "Your letter said you wanted to see the lawyer first thing." He looked confused.

"I assumed we'd see the lawyer first thing in the morning."

"This evening," Sonny said.

It took a moment for Delanna to realize he meant barrister access was available around the clock, just as it was on Rebe Prime. She had assumed all public vega terminal centers in Grassedge would shut down at sunset, like everything else did. Except the bars, she reminded herself, and the dance hall. But if the lawyer could see them tonight, so much the better. She could get back to the warehouse, and Cleo, sooner.

Finally Sonny spied the carryit in Jay's hand. "This yours?" he said to Delanna, reaching for the bag.

"I could still take you over to the hotel," Jay offered, resisting Sonny's attempt to take the bag from his hand.

Delanna almost agreed, but then shook her head. "My business is with . . . Sonny," she said, certain now after meeting him that she'd need every available minute to make sure this yokel understood that he needed to be at the lawyer's, too.

Jay released the carryit. "Well then, until we meet again," he said, clearly disappointed.

"That's not likely to happen," she said pleasantly.

"I'll be in mourning for thirty days," Jay said, his eyes sparkling.

"Thirty minutes, I'd wager," she responded, with a laugh. Jay shrugged.

"Let's go," Sonny said, turning abruptly. He walked out of the building with short, quick steps, carrying her bag and pushing one of the goose cages out through the shadows into the sunlight. Delanna glanced longingly toward Cleo, who was still curled up in a tight little ball.

"Thanks for your help, young woman," Doc Lyle said. "I'll see you tomorrow. Don't worry about your scarab. I'll take good care of her."

"You're sure you won't change your mind about staying?" Jay asked, catching her hand in his. "We need more beautiful redheads around here." She felt something pass from his palm to hers.

"I'm sure," she told him. "Goodbye," she said to both of them, and turned to follow Sonny, who was already out of sight.

She paused in the middle of the doorway to see what Jay had pressed into her hand. It was a business card, made of real paper, like the bills of lading.

JAY MADOG
CAPTAIN OF THE *MAD DOG* PRAIRIE CARAVAN
CALL 5373 DAY OR NIGHT IN GRASSEDGE
IF NO ANSWER, TRY FREQUENCY 139 ON THE HAM.

She hurried out the door.

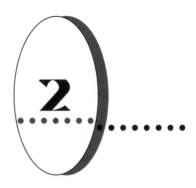

Sonny was waiting for her outside the warehouse, still holding on to her carryit. Delanna looked at the card again, memorizing the number, and stuck it in her pocket.

"I wouldn't get mixed up with Jay Madog if I were you," Sonny said.

Just let me get through the next half hour, Delanna thought. Let me get the money in my hands, and I'll kill him.

"I want to see the lawyer as soon as possible," she said aloud. "Have you made an appointment?"

"Appointment?" he repeated, as if he had no idea what the word even meant, and then stood there looking stupid.

"Yes. An appointed time when she'll see us."

Instead of answering, he disappeared suddenly around the corner of the building and came back pulling a large wagon. The cage with the geese in it was propped at an angle in the wagon, and Delanna's carryit was crammed in on one side on top of Sonny's jacket. The geese were honking wildly.

"You have to come, too, to sign the papers," Delanna told him. "We need an appointment."

"Miz Barlowe'll see us whenever we get there," he said,

lifting the wagon tongue and giving it a yank that set the geese to honking even louder. "So let's go."

"You're not taking that thing with you to the lawyer's, are you?"

He looked surprised. "It's either this, or make 'em walk, like us. Grayson said the solaris won't be fixed till tonight, and I figure their feet aren't used to rough ground. They were ship-born, you know."

He gave another honk-provoking tug and started off toward the cluster of buildings to the south. Delanna debated telling him she was going back into the warehouse to ask Jay Madog for a ride into town. Sonny would probably look at her with one of those stupid open-mouthed expressions and ask her why she couldn't walk, and she wanted to get this over with, see the lawyer and get everything taken care of in time for the shuttle tomorrow. She started after Sonny.

"Rough ground" was putting it mildly. The dirt road was alternately muddy and as hard as the rocks that stuck up out of it, but apparently the idea that her feet might be as tender as the geese's hadn't occurred to him.

"How far is it to town?" she asked, struggling to keep up with him.

"About a mile," he said. "If I was a woman, I wouldn't trust Jay Madog as far as I could throw him. He has lady friends all the way from Grassedge to the mountains and every stop in between."

Which I'm sure is more than you can say, Delanna thought. She had remembered Tarleton Tanner as a smart, nice-looking boy who would sometimes read her stories and play games with her when he wasn't working in the orchards with his father. Which just went to show how right Mother had been about this planet. It took every ounce of spirit and intelligence out of people and made them into nothing but work animals. Sonny might still have been nice-looking if he wasn't wearing that ridiculous outfit, the overly bright shirt and the pants with the cuffs rolled above the ankles. But Delanna didn't think that a change of clothes would alter the fact that he seemed barely able to answer a simple question.

"Are you sure the lawyer will see us without an appointment?" she said.

"Yep."

"And she's got the paperwork all ready for us to sign?"

He didn't answer that, just trudged on with the cart full of geese. After a while he said, "You don't remember much about Milleflores, do you? You left when you were no bigger than a timarine."

Delanna didn't know what a timarine was, but she thought she could see where this was heading. Her mother had warned her that people would try to talk her into keeping the land. "I won't have you trapped on some forsaken lanzye like I was," her mother had written. "I'm working with the lawyer to straighten out some technicalities so that you never have to come back to Keramos." But things hadn't been straightened out, and her mother had died. The lawyer had said she'd have to come to Keramos to protect her interests.

"I remember enough about Keramos to know I don't want to live here," Delanna said. "I've already told the lawyer to sell the land, and I assume she's lined up a buyer."

He didn't say anything to that either, just plodded ahead at a steady pace Delanna was having trouble keeping up with. She had dressed in a conservative business outfit for the meeting with the lawyer, a simple short skirt with a tailored blouse and vest, but her ribbon-laced highups with their high metal heels and open toes were ill-suited to the rutted road. She was out of breath after only a few minutes, and the town didn't look any closer than it had before.

The sun was setting on the flat horizon, reddening the fields and the air. There was a low haze several miles off. "What's that?" she asked, stopping to point and hoping Sonny would stop, too, so she could catch her breath.

He shaded his eyes with his hand. "Smoke."

"Smoke? You mean a prairie fire?" Her mother had told her about roaring fires that could rip across hundreds of miles of grassland.

"Yep," he said, sounding completely unconcerned. "Probably fire monkeys." He picked up the wagon tongue again.

Her mother hadn't written about fire monkeys, so they probably weren't too big a problem. Sonny wasn't worried about them anyway, and even if he were he wouldn't bother to tell her.

"How are your brothers?" she said to get another minute of standing still. "Did they come with you?"

He shook his head. "Summer," he said, which she supposed meant summer was a bad time for them to leave the lanzye. Oh, he really wasn't worth trying to talk to, even if it meant a chance to catch her breath. She struck out ahead of him, trying to find a rut wide enough for her heels, but Sonny pulled even with her immediately.

"We'll have a good crop if the weather stays dry," he said. "Two hundred barrels of fresh."

"That's nice," Delanna responded, although she didn't know whether two hundred barrels was a good crop or not. Her mother had hardly ever written about the cannonball orchards except in passing references.

"Wilkes and Harry fixed up your mother's cottage," Sonny went on.

"Good," she said. "That should help with the sale value."

"They put in a pump, too. It's real pretty this time of year. Lots of flowers."

Delanna didn't answer. She was having all she could do to keep up with him, and she had no idea what he expected her to say to something like that. He couldn't possibly be laboring under the delusion that she was planning to come visit.

"It's really important that the lawyer see us this evening," she said, in case he still hadn't grasped the fact that she was leaving tomorrow. "I definitely want to be on that shuttle tomorrow."

He stopped in the middle of the road and turned to face her. Though she was standing in her highups on one of the bigger lumps of dirt, he still towered over her. "Your mother never liked Milleflores," he said in that slow drawl that made him sound half-witted, "but your father loved it. He would have done anything to keep it."

Here it comes, Delanna thought. The big pitch. "And?" she prompted, her jaw set stubbornly.

He looked down at her for a long couple of seconds. "And nothing," he said disgustedly, and yanked on the handle of the wagon so hard the geese shrieked. He didn't say anything the rest of the way into town.

By the time they got there, Delanna was exhausted by the ever-faster pace Sonny had kept, and he wasn't even breathing hard.

The sun seemed to hover motionless on the horizon, only the deepening bronze on the dark grasses indicating that it was setting. Grassedge didn't have a definite beginning. They passed a prefab, then a field, then a wreck of a Quonset hut that had shed piles of mismatched ceramic tile. After they passed a neatly tiled silo that was set far back from the road and another field, the buildings gradually got bigger and closer together till they turned into a straggling line.

The geese had more or less settled down on the trek into town, but as soon as they were even with the first real building they started honking again. Sonny stopped in front of a clapboard structure. On the roof was a painted wooden sign that read "Billy's." On either side of the sign was a row of ceramic monkeys. The statues each had a raised right arm, and Christmas lights had been strung between them so that each monkey looked like it was holding a green or blue or red torch.

The front of the building was plastered with beer and liquor signs, most of them cut from the cardboard boxes the liquor came in and nailed up. A hand-carved sign said

"Ambrosia," and there was a large, glittering plasequin Watney's Ale sign obviously brought in on the shuttle. It had to be a bar or saloon or whatever they called it here.

"Be right back," Sonny said and left her standing there while he went inside. Wonderful. Her mother would have considered this homecoming appropriate. "There isn't an ounce of intelligence or manners on the whole planet," she had complained in one of her letters.

Well, perhaps her mother had been wrong about that. Jay Madog had been very polite, and the lawyer must be intelligent. Her letter had been well-written if unsatisfyingly vague, and obviously neither of them would have left her sitting in the middle of the street with a gaggle of geese.

She sat down on the edge of the wagon and waited, glad of the rest. The sun dipped lower, and the row of colored lights stood out brighter against the building. She wondered if Sonny intended to leave her here while he got drunk.

He appeared on the porch, turning to speak to someone inside. "Thanks," Delanna heard him say. "I couldn't bear to think of leaving those extra hatchlings behind. I'll pay you back after the harvest, when we press the fresh." He stuck a wad of bills in his pocket and came over to the wagon. "I borrowed some money to spring my geese I left behind," he explained to Delanna, and started off again.

His mention of the geese he'd left behind made her think of Cleo. She hoped her scarab was all right.

She's fine, Delanna told herself. Every time she'd put Cleo in her cage on board ship, she'd curled up into a ball and slept till Delanna came back. But on board ship there hadn't been honking geese to wake her up. What if she got frightened?

We'd better be on our way to the lawyer's office, Delanna thought. And we'd better have an appointment. And she'd better have those papers ready, so I can sign them and go rescue Cleo.

Sonny had stopped again. "Take me to—" Delanna began, but he had already disappeared again, this time into a big barn of a place with a small plasticlight sign that read "Sakawa's Metalworking." It had a row of monkeys, too, metal ones with what looked like flashlights in their hands.

What was Sonny doing? Borrowing more money? Or doing his shopping? At this rate it would be midnight before they managed to get to the lawyer's. Which was probably the idea. He didn't want her to sell—he'd made that plain with his talk of her father loving Milleflores.

She looked down the street, trying to see where the lawyer's office might be. She couldn't spot any building that remotely resembled an office complex, but she could surely ask someone. "In words of one syllable," Delanna muttered, pulling her carryit out of where it was wedged next to the geese's cage, "because every single person on this planet is a moron."

She peered up and down the street, wondering where to go to ask directions. Except for Sakawa's Metalworking, the town seemed to be made up entirely of bars, all with monkeys and cardboard signs. She hesitated, and was looking dubiously at the one next to Sakawa's, when Sonny came out of the barn with a short, round man who was wearing a baseball cap.

"It's beautiful," Sonny was saying. "I'll come get it as soon as I'm done with this lawyer thing."

"I heard about that," the short man said. "She coming in on the shuttle tomorrow?"

"No. She's already here."

"Already here?" the other man said, pushing his hat back off his forehead. "Well, hell, where is she? The whole town's been wanting to get a look at your new—"

"I gotta go," Sonny said. "We got an appointment with the lawyer." He bounded across the street, calling over his shoulder, "I'll come back as soon as I can." He came up hurriedly alongside the wagon, saying "Come *on!*" to Delanna, as if she'd been the one making *him* wait.

He set off at a pace that frightened the geese into silence, oblivious to the fact that Delanna was lugging her carryit.

"Wait up!" a woman's voice called from behind them. Sonny glanced around and then started walking even faster. The geese set up a rebellious muttering. "Sonny Tanner!" the woman shouted, "You wait for me! I want to talk to you!"

Delanna turned around. A woman in a big floppy hat was standing in the middle of the street half a block back, making no attempt to catch up with Sonny that Delanna could see. She was standing perfectly still with her hands on the hips of very tight pants. She was younger than Sonny, and her hair, what Delanna could see of it under the hat, was blond.

"Sonny Tanner, there's a few things you neglected to tell me!"

"Oh, for gosh sakes," Sonny said. He dropped the wagon tongue and turned around. "You stay here," he said to Delanna. "I'll be back in a minute." He hurried back to her. "What are you doing here, Cadiz?"

She came forward to meet him, her hands still on her hips. "What am I doing here? What the *hell* are you doing sneaking off without even telling me what you're doing?"

"I told B.T. to tell you what was happening, and . . ."

"B.T.," she said, nearly spitting the words. "You didn't have the courage to tell me yourself, so you sent your idiot brother."

"Now don't be mad at B.T. over all this. It wasn't his fault."

"B.T.? Why would I waste an ounce of strength being mad at B.T.?" Cadiz suddenly crossed one arm across her chest and started examining the fingernails on her other hand. "It would never occur to anyone as dense as B.T. that you might need the people you love at a time like this."

"So you came," Sonny said, lifting the baseball cap so he could run his fingers through his hair. "How'd you get here?"

"Jay Madog brought me," she said, tossing her head.

''And under the circumstances you've got no right to be jealous.'' She waved her arm in Delanna's direction. ''Is that her?''

''Yes,'' Sonny said, trying to steer her off toward one of the bars. ''Now you just calm down, Cadiz.''

Delanna couldn't hear the rest of what their conversation. Sonny seemed to be doing most of the talking, which was a surprise, but whatever he said, it didn't seem to calm Cadiz down. At one point she took off her hat and flung it on the ground.

''I want to meet her,'' Cadiz said loudly enough for Delanna to hear, snatched up her hat, and sauntered over to her. ''So you're Serena's kid,'' she said, walking around Delanna, slapping her hat rhythmically against her leg. ''I don't know what I was worried about.''

Sonny said rapidly, ''Cadiz, this is Delanna Milleflores. Delanna, this is Cadiz Flaherty. She's a neighbor. Her folks live on the next lanzye over.''

''How do you do?'' Delanna said, offering her hand. She was surprised. Cadiz was actually quite nice-looking, in spite of the hat. She had short yellow hair and large blue eyes. Delanna had always heard that women were in short supply on planets like Keramos. If that was true, she couldn't imagine why one as pretty as Cadiz was tagging around after somebody like Sonny Tanner.

''So you're the kid Serena spent all that money on, getting you educated off-planet?'' Cadiz said, glancing with distaste at Delanna's extended hand. ''Doesn't look like she got much for her investment.''

''At least I learned manners,'' Delanna said, taking her hand back.

Cadiz stopped, hooked her thumbs in her pants, and spit into the dirt at Delanna's feet. ''Are those things on your feet shoes? You wouldn't sell them to me, would you? I need something to scare the monkeys with.''

''We have to go see the lawyer, Cadiz,'' Sonny broke in.

Cadiz spat again, and put her hat back on. "I figure she'll last two days if the fire monkeys don't get her first," she said to Sonny. She sauntered across the street toward Billy's and stepped up on the porch. "I've seen fire monkeys tear people limb from limb for a box of matches, let alone something like those shoes," she called out to them, and disappeared through the door.

"Fire monkeys don't really kill people," Sonny said to Delanna.

"I insist on seeing the lawyer *right now*," Delanna said from between clenched teeth.

"I think that's a good idea," Sonny agreed. "Just a minute." He ran across the street and into a bar that had a Coors Newbeer sign on it with a rippling waterfall. The geese set up their deafening honking the second he was out of sight.

"Oh, shut up," Delanna said. Amazingly, they did. "You realize you're the only creatures who listen to me on this godforsaken planet?" She stuffed her carryit back in the wagon. "I hope the lawyer isn't like everybody else on Keramos or I'll never get my money."

A boy had appeared in the door of the saloon. He looked about fourteen years old. "You talkin' to them geese?" he asked, and turned to Sonny, who was right behind him. "You didn't say nothin' about havin' to talk to 'em."

"All you have to do is watch them, Buck," Sonny said. He jumped down off the porch and beckoned to Delanna. "Come on inside."

"Look," Delanna said, "you may have all the time in the world, but I don't." She practically shouted the word *don't*. It set the geese off again.

"Well, what are you waiting for, then? Come on." He turned to the boy. "You just hang onto the wagon handle and don't let anybody pester my geese." He walked back into the saloon.

Absolutely Neanderthal, Delanna thought. She stomped across the street and started up the steps, angry enough now to drag him away from his Watney's or his Coors and demand that he take her straight to the lawyer's.

She put her foot on the second step and went straight through. Clutching at a post to keep her balance, she looked down. The steps had apparently been constructed of liquor boxes, too. The second one was slatted—the heel of her highups had gone right through.

There was a wild outburst of sound from behind her. She twisted furiously around. The boy was doubled-up with laughter, and the geese were obviously following his lead. "Shut up!" she shouted. "And you, Buck or whatever your name is, if you want to get paid, you'll watch the geese like you were told to."

She gave a mighty upward heave on her foot, but it was stuck fast. She bent over and undid the ties, trying to keep her balance. This sent the boy off into fresh gales of laughter, as did her finally getting her foot out of the shoe. Standing on one foot, she took hold of the shoe with both hands and yanked it free.

"Where you been?" Sonny said, appearing in the doorway. He was apparently oblivious of the fact that she was wearing only one shoe. "Come on. The lawyer's waiting," he said, and stepped back inside.

The boy thought that was unbelievably funny. Delanna wasn't about to provide him with more entertainment by putting on her shoe. She hobbled up the last two steps and into the saloon. It was so dark inside she couldn't see anything except a tubelight Seagram's sign.

"Welcome to Maggie's, honey," a woman said, appearing out of the gloom. She was a large woman with an untidy mass of hair piled on top of her head and stuck there with a flower. She was wearing pants with the cuffs rolled and a flowered shirt like Sonny's, and a glittering necklace. "Come on in and have a drink. What'll you have?"

"Nothing, thank you," Delanna said, trying to get away from the woman's hand on her arm. "I'm looking for Sonny Tanner. He was supposed to—"

"He's right here waiting for you," the woman said, leading Delanna toward a bar of stacked liquor boxes, apparently the only building material on Keramos. Reaching behind the boxes, she brought up three squat ceramic cups and a brown bottle. "How do you like Grassedge so far?"

Delanna felt a sudden impulse to brain this woman with the shoe she still held in her hand. "I don't like it," she said, glaring at Sonny, whom she was beginning to be able to make out in the gloom. "I want to see the lawyer this instant," she hissed at him, "and then I want to leave this mudhole of a planet."

"You're looking at the lawyer," he said. "Maggie Barlowe, this is Serena's daughter. Delanna, this is Maggie Barlowe, the lawyer."

"I'd have known her anywhere," Maggie said, not even squinting in the near-darkness, "Even though I haven't seen her since she was grass-high. She was a pretty little thing then, too."

"You're Margaret Barlowe," Delanna said, disbelievingly. This was like a bad dream. She had pictured the lawyer as an outpost of sanity in this wilderness, and here she was, tending bar and swigging down ambrosia.

"Sure am," Maggie said. "Want a drink? Tried our ambrosia?"

"No, thank you."

"I suppose you're anxious to get on with this," Maggie went on, sounding almost lawyerlike, "so why don't you come on back into my office and we'll take a look at the will?"

"I'd like to take care of all the paperwork as quickly as possible," Delanna said. "I have to catch the shuttle back tomorrow."

Maggie looked at Sonny. "How much have you told her?" she asked him.

"You're the lawyer. I thought you could explain things better."

"You haven't told her anything?"

Sonny squirmed under her glare until Maggie picked up the brown bottle. "I think you'd better have some ambrosia, Delanna," she said, pouring a reddish-gold liquid into one of the ceramic cups. "It'll make things go a mite easier."

"No, thank you," Delanna said firmly. "Shall we go into your office?"

"Sure thing, honey," Maggie agreed, and led the way to the back of the bar, carrying the bottle and cups with her.

Delanna had given up hoping that the office would look like an office and that the will and all the paperwork would be in a neat printout folder. She'd be happy if the room had a light. It did. It also had two green-topped tables and a vega terminal.

Maggie set the cups and bottle down on one of the felt-covered tables and rummaged in a beer crate. Delanna sat down in a straight-backed chair and put on her shoe. Sonny sat down two chairs away from her and stared at the table. He seemed to be studying the circles left on the felt by various beer bottles.

Maggie came up out of the crate with, wonder of wonders, a neat printout folder. Then, seating herself, she put on a pair of pink-tinted glasses and peered up at Delanna. The effect was almost reassuring. "How much do you know about Milleflores Lanzye, Delanna?"

"I know that half of it belonged to my mother," Delanna said, determined to get this off on the right foot, "and that she left her half to me. I wrote you that I wanted to sell my half."

Maggie was looking worried behind the pink glasses. "You got my letter, didn't you?" Delanna said.

"I did." The lawyer peered at Sonny. He was rubbing his finger around one of the beer bottle circles.

"Well, you've sold my half for me, haven't you? It took me almost three months to get here. Surely you were able to line up a buyer in that time."

Maggie poured ambrosia into her cup, to the brim, and drained it. "Let me give you some background on Keramos and Milleflores," she said. "Keramos' first generationers were mostly unhappy settlers from New Heaven and Starbuck. They'd seen those planets get bought up by big megas and speculators, and they were determined not to let that happen on Keramos. I come from Starbuck myself, and let me tell you, the first crop was hardly in before the speculators were there, buying up land that wasn't worth anything yet from people who'd gotten worn out and discouraged or who couldn't make a living off of it."

She adjusted her glasses. "The first-generationers knew if they made it harder to sell, the speculators would just up the ante, so they set it up so the land couldn't be sold at all. It could be passed on, or you could marry into it, but you couldn't sell. If you wanted out, you walked away with nothing to show for all your hard work, and to keep people from getting any bright ideas about forcing their neighbors out and then buying up their land, abandoned land couldn't be worked for ten years after the owner forfeited."

That explained why Delanna's mother had stayed on Keramos all these years when she hated it. It didn't explain why Maggie felt the need to go through all this, or why Sonny was looking so unhappy. "My mother stayed on the land, didn't she?" she asked, feeling almost panicky at the thought of what they might say.

"She stayed on the land," Maggie said. "She died in her own bed at Milleflores." She picked up the will and plucked at its edge, then put it down. "The first-generation laws worked pretty well for the inland farms, but not as well for the lanzye ranges, which need nearly ten times as much land to be profitable. It didn't work at all for the orchards.

"They need to have enough natural cannonball groves to supply saplings for orchards—you just can't get into a natural grove with harvesting equipment because of how the trees and limbs twist so badly when they're crowded—

and you need some mature forest to provide a reliable supply of staves for barrels to age the ambrosia. And of course you have to have a water supply that won't be drying up on you in droughty years, and some bottomland for cash crops until the orchards produce well enough. Your father and Douglas Tanner had a partnership that put all those elements together. But of course their partnership wasn't legal, and if either of them died, they'd just have to hope whoever inherited would keep the agreement. How old were you when your father died, Miz Milleflores?''

"Five," Delanna said.

"You weren't old enough to remember much about monkey fever, were you?''

"No.'' Actually, when Maggie mentioned the name, she did remember something about the illness. Her mother in a room they wouldn't let Delanna into, and somebody saying something about monkeys. They had taken her to stay at the Tanners' house, and she had been happy about that; she loved playing with Tarleton. "I know both my parents had it, and it killed my father.''

"Your mother got it first," Sonny said, looking up for the first time. "They thought sure she was going to die. Your father didn't have it half as bad when he got it.''

"There wasn't a vaccine for monkey fever, and people were dying like flies," Maggie said. "Only the adults. Children didn't catch it. Your father was afraid that if both he and his wife died, off-planet relatives might remove you from the land and then you wouldn't be able to inherit. You had no relatives on Keramos. If they took you off-planet to live with them, the lanzye would be forfeit, the Tanners couldn't work it for ten years, and Milleflores would cease to exist. The same thing would be true if the Tanners died of the fever and left Sonny and his brothers.''

Delanna had been trying to put all this together, but she couldn't figure out what Maggie was getting at. Her mother hadn't died of the fever, and neither of the Tanners had even contracted it. She fastened on something Maggie had said about her relatives. "You said if my relatives had taken me off-planet to live, I would have forfeited Milleflores. You're not saying that because I went away to school I don't inherit, are you?" In spite of her best efforts, her voice had risen on a note of fright at the end of her question. Her mother had told her she had inherited. She never would have sent her off-planet if it had meant she would lose her inheritance.

"No, of course not," Maggie said. "Your mother was the owner of the lanzye. She was the one who had to occupy the land, which she did. You definitely inherit."

"Then what is all this about?" Delanna said, unable to stand the suspense any longer. She looked from one to the other. Sonny stared glumly at the table. Maggie stared glumly at the will. "Obviously something is wrong here. What is it? Can't my half be sold?"

"It can be sold," Maggie said. "The laws have changed a lot, mostly due to the outlanders. A lanzye owner can sell so long as he occupies the land until the sale is completed."

That must be it. She would have to stay here on Keramos a week, two weeks, even a month, till the sale went through. She felt relieved, in spite of the fact that she had hoped to leave tomorrow and in spite of the fact that a few minutes ago she'd thought she couldn't stand another second on Keramos. The way the two of them looked, all these ominous hints, she had thought it was something catastrophic rather than just a delay. She didn't have enough money to stay two weeks, but surely she could get an advance of some kind from the lawyer.

"If a lanzye is jointly owned, as in marriage," Maggie went on, "and one partner wishes to sell, the remaining partner has first option on the land. He has up to a year in which to buy out his partner, after which time the half can be sold outright. The partner wishing to sell must occupy the land till the sale is completed."

A year! "But my land isn't jointly owned," Delanna said. "You said my mother left Milleflores to me outright."

"At the time of the monkey fever epidemic, your father and Sonny's father decided to ensure the continuation of Milleflores Lanzye by combining the two lanzyes into one. At the death of all parents, the lanzyes would become legally one."

"I thought you said they couldn't do that, that they could only pass the land on to their children."

Maggie poured another drink into her ceramic cup and tossed it back. She picked up the cup Delanna had refused earlier, and offered it to her again. "You sure you don't want one of these?"

"I'm sure," Delanna said impatiently.

Maggie set the cup down. "Your pa and Sonny's pa had the two of you legally betrothed during the epidemic, to become final when all four parents died. That way the two lanzyes became one, jointly owned."

"Betrothed?" Delanna repeated, staring at Sonny. "Betrothed?" She picked up the cup of ambrosia and drained it in one searing, wretched-tasting gulp. It didn't help. "You mean I'm *engaged* to you?"

"Nope," he said, and reached for the bottle. "She means we're married."

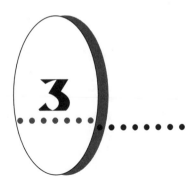

"Married!" Delanna squeaked. She shook her head and cleared her throat. "Married," she said again. "I didn't come to Keramos for a wedding. I came to pick up my money from the sale of my mother's land. I'm supposed to go on to Carthage tomorrow."

Sonny refilled her cup, then his own. "No wedding."

Delanna started to sigh with relief, but it stuck in her throat when she saw Maggie's face.

"He means," Maggie said, "you're already married. You have been from the moment your mother died."

"Even if I had the money to buy you out..." Sonny began.

"Which he doesn't," Maggie put in.

"I can't," Sonny finished. He drank some of the ambrosia. When he put his cup down, he leaned back in his chair and stretched his legs out under the table.

"At least not for a year," Maggie explained when she realized Sonny wasn't going to, "because the law forbids it."

Delanna drank down more of the ambrosia. It still burned, and this time she could taste it. It was horribly bitter and had a nasty aftertaste. "If you think I'm going to wait a year in Grassedge to get a divorce and my money, you're crazy.''

"Not in Grassedge," Maggie said. "On Milleflores. You're the owner now. You have to stay on the land to protect your claim while the case is being decided. And you need to get there as soon as possible. There's a limit to establishing residency. There's a train—''

"I'm not going to Milleflores," Delanna interrupted. "I'm not going anywhere until this ridiculous situation is resolved.''

Sonny frowned. "You have to.''

"Who do you think you are to tell me I have to do anything?'' Delanna said furiously.

"What he means,'' Maggie interjected, "is that if you don't, you lose everything. Honey, there's no other way. My official advice as your lawyer is for you to go to Milleflores as quickly as you can so that you don't jeopardize your claim before we get it straightened out in Circuit Court.''

"Wilkes and Harry fixed up your mother's cottage,'' Sonny reminded Delanna. "The flowers are real pretty this year, too.''

Delanna ignored him. "You're appealing to the Circuit Court?'' she asked Maggie hopefully.

"Of course,'' Maggie said, a trifle indignant. "I'm your lawyer, and your instructions were very clear. I'm just sorry your mother didn't explain everything to you, that you had to find all this out when you got here. I appealed to the Council of Worlds Circuit Court the moment we were turned down in Keramos Statute Enforcement Court.''

Delanna nodded as she thought about her mother's letters. She'd mentioned legalities that needed straightening out, but she hadn't said what they were, just gone on for pages about how glad she was Delanna was safe in Gay Paree because Keramos was no place for a daughter of hers to grow up. "When will we know?''

"Circuit Court orbits about harvest time. We should be

early on the docket, since we were one of the first to file after planting time.''

"Circuit Court orbits?" Delanna said dubiously.

Maggie nodded. "Twice a year. Harvest time and planting time, the *Justice* arrives and goes into synchronous orbit with Grassedge.''

"Outrageous," Delanna muttered. "Stupid backwater planet."

"That sounds like your mother. In fact, I think I've heard her say those very words. Keramos is considered progressive by many pioneer worlds' standards," Maggie said, not unsympathetically. "At least Circuit Court comes twice a year now. And harvest time is only five weeks away."

"Meanwhile I'm married to a Neanderthal," Delanna said.

Sonny paled.

Good! Delanna thought. I didn't expect him to know that big a word. "What if Circuit Court rules against me?" she said aloud.

"Then we appeal," Maggie told her, "but I don't think that'll be necessary."

"By then I'll have a crop," Sonny said, "and I can give you the profits as a down payment for your half of Milleflores.''

"And if the crop fails?"

"I won't let it fail," Sonny said.

"But if it does. What then?"

"There's next year's crop."

"Or a third-party buyer," Delanna said desperately.

But Sonny shook his head. "I can't agree to that. It wouldn't be right."

"What isn't right is that I can't leave this godforsaken planet tomorrow either," Delanna protested, pushing her chair back from the table. It not only wasn't right, it wasn't even possible. Grounded and stuck with Sonny Tanner. *Married* to Sonny Tanner.

"Yes, but your not being able to leave is the law,"

Sonny said. "A third-party sale just wouldn't be right."

"What he means," Maggie explained, "is that your parents spent their lives developing Milleflores, and it would be a shame to sell it off, especially now when it looks like there's a chance for big profits for the first time. But I'm not so sure I agree with Sonny on this. You might be better off to take what you can get before the Milleflores ambrosia exports have a chance to fail."

"Won't fail," Sonny said stubbornly.

"We've talked about this before," Maggie said to him, "and you know there's a risk. Now, I'm not telling you two what to do, but I think you ought to spend the time till harvest getting acquainted and discussing all the possibilities. You two have to spend the next month together anyway, and usually when people talk things over, they can come to a common agreement."

And just how was she supposed to talk to Sonny Tanner, Delanna wondered, when practically everything he said had to be interpreted by Maggie? She got up from the felt-covered table, threaded her way between it and the jumble of chairs to look out the window. There was no view, just the blue ceramic wall of the building next door, and that was barely visible. Maggie's windowsill was lined with the same blue tile as the wall. It was getting dark. Delanna stepped back, feeling trapped. She hugged herself with her arms and turned her back to the window.

"And you're saying that's my only option?" she asked. "To go to Milleflores and wait till harvest time?"

"You can forfeit your entire claim to the estate, *and* Sonny's claim," Maggie said, looking grim, "and go back out to the shuttleport and up to the *Scoville* and anywhere you like."

No, I can't, Delanna thought. She'd left Rebe Prime with only her last month's allowance and the ticket to Carthage. She hadn't even paid up her school account. She had only a hundred and twenty-five credits of her allowance left.

Without the money from the estate, there was no way she could go on to Carthage.

She had to face it. She was stuck here. "How long do I have to take up residency?" she said stiffly.

"There's a train tonight," Sonny said.

Delanna looked at Maggie. "I can't leave tonight," she said, feeling as if things were getting totally away from her. "I have to get my trunk from the *Scoville*." And Cleo. She'd forgotten all about Cleo. She'd have to get her out of quarantine, make arrangements to take her to Milleflores, get some sort of importation papers for the vet.

"Sorry, honey," Maggie was saying. "The train tonight's the only connection for Milleflores for a month. If you don't take it, you won't make it in time to establish your claim. I'm going to work all the angles for you, including one that just might get us a third-party sale."

"But Maggie . . ." Sonny started to say.

"I know it's not what you want, Sonny, and I don't think there's much hope for pulling it off, but I can give it a try. Whatever happens, you," she said, looking pointedly at Delanna, "must protect your rights by being at Milleflores. You'll lose everything sooner than later if you don't go."

Someone knocked hard on the office door.

Maggie ignored it. "It's two and a half hours till train time. You need to go down to the station—"

"But I *can't* leave," Delanna said desperately. "Not without—"

"Your trunk can come on the next caravan."

"You don't understand—" Delanna began.

Jay Madog stood in the doorway, towering over Maggie for half a second before he leaned over to kiss the lawyer on the tip of her nose. "Sounds like I'm just in the nick of time," he said, brushing past Maggie so quickly after the kiss that her admonishing slap missed. "I can arrange to retrieve your trunk, Mrs. Tanner," he said pleasantly. "And I'll see what I can do about getting a refund on the unused portion of your fare. I take it you've decided to stay?"

"She's going to Milleflores," Maggie said. "I've already booked her passage."

"Wonderful!" Jay said. "I'm delighted. And I'd be delighted to retrieve her trunk."

"And charge you a handling fee for doing it," Maggie said to Delanna.

"A *small* handling fee," Jay said, "which is a good deal, especially considering that your transport contract has no transfer or refund provisions."

Hearing that, Maggie went over to the vega terminal and began touching icons. The screen flashed green, then erupted into a rainbow before displaying black print scrolling over a blue background. Maggie put her finger on the screen to stop the scrolling. She read for a few seconds, then shook her head. "You shouldn't have signed a contract like this, Delanna. They'd be within their rights to take your trunk all the way to Carthage, ship it back and charge you freight rates for doing it. You could sue, but . . ."

"I know," Delanna said hopelessly. "We'd have to take it to Circuit Court, and by the time the matter was settled, they'd have declared my trunk abandoned or something, and sold it."

"You see," Jay said, smiling again. "I'm offering a bargain. No pain or anguish of a law suit, no freight bill if you lose. Just a trunk delivered to your door at Milleflores."

"Just don't start telling us how you'll accomplish all of this," Maggie said, "or I'm sure we'll both regret it."

"Tsk, tsk, Maggie," Jay admonished, his grin smug. "You'll have Mrs. Tanner thinking I'd do something underhanded or . . ."

"Just shush, Jay," Maggie said, her voice suddenly stony. "I don't play games with the law."

"There's something else I need," Delanna said.

Jay turned to face her, smiling rakishly. "At your service, Mrs. Tanner."

"I'm *not* Mrs. Tanner," Delanna said. "I'm Delanna Milleflores."

He nodded wisely. "I know a lot of you been-tos keep your own names when you get married."

"I'm *not* married," Delanna said, exasperated. "This is all some kind of legal mixup."

"My feelings about marriage exactly," Jay said, grinning. "And I'm glad to hear you feel the same. Was that what you wanted to tell me?"

"No, of course not," Delanna said. She beckoned him over to the window. Turning her back on Sonny and Maggie, she whispered, "Because of this mixup I need to stay on Keramos longer than I thought. So I need to get Cleo out of quarantine."

"That little bug of yours?" Jay said, his smile fading. "I don't know. Dealing with Doc Lyle isn't like dealing with Copperfield Transport Company about a trunk. In fact, I came here to make sure Sonny got his paperwork on the other seven geese worked out. Doc Lyle would cross the Salt Flats on foot to confiscate a goose that didn't have its importation papers. I suspect he'd get even more excited about a creature from off-planet."

"But if I leave Cleo behind, he'll put her on the shuttle tomorrow and send her on to Carthage without me."

Jay was shaking his head. "He wouldn't send her back up to the *Scoville*, not without transport papers. It'd be against the rules, and Doc Lyle's a stickler for following rules."

"But she can't stay in quarantine for a whole month."

"You're right about that," Jay said, frowning.

"What do you mean?" Delanna asked.

"The thing is, you brought this cleo thing in without importation papers. That's against the rules. And Doc Lyle's—"

"A stickler for the rules. So what does that mean?" Delanna asked again, starting to feel frightened.

"It means you better tell Maggie about this."

"What? What happens to animals that don't have their importation papers? What's the vet going to do to Cleo?"

Delanna had raised her voice. Maggie was watching them, frowning, and Sonny said, curiously, "What's a cleo?"

"Doc Lyle locked up Delanna's little pet," Jay said, "a bug of some kind. She brought it down from the *Scoville* in her carryit. Doc Lyle stuck it in quarantine."

"You have to get it out," Delanna said to Maggie, but the lawyer was frowning just like Jay.

"You didn't have importation papers?" Maggie asked.

"She'd had all her shots before we came on the *Scoville*," Delanna said. "She has all her passage papers."

Maggie was still looking worried.

"She's not a pet," Delanna tried to explain. "I've had her since my first year at school. I can't leave her behind. You have to get her out."

"You don't understand, honey," Maggie said placatingly. "Keramos' laws—"

"Are completely unfair," Delanna cut in and burst into tears.

Jay handed her a flowered handkerchief. "Can't we wangle some importation papers for it, Maggie?" he said, patting Delanna's shoulder.

"You know better," she said. "It'll take twenty pages of paperwork just to get Doc Lyle to approve those hatchlings of Sonny's, and they weren't smuggled down here in a carryit. You know how he is about following the rules to the letter. He's not going to go for an after-the-fact set of importation papers. I can draw up a restraining order so Doc Lyle can't"—Maggie stopped short, glanced at Delanna, and then went on—"make a determination on the animal for thirty days, but that's about all I can do."

Delanna wiped her eyes with the handkerchief. "I'm not going anywhere without Cleo, and that's final," she said, looking around at everyone.

Maggie was frowning again, and Sonny looked unhappy.

Jay smiled reassuringly. "It'll be all right. A restraining order's good for thirty days, and by that time Maggie'll come up with a legal loophole, won't you, Maggie, smart lawyer like you?"

Delanna didn't think Maggie looked very convinced, but Maggie said, "There might be something in the original planet by-laws. I'll start looking into it as soon as you leave for Milleflores."

"I'm not—"

"You don't have any choice, honey," Maggie said. "It's either catch that midnight train or forfeit the estate. And if you do that," she added shrewdly, "how are you gonna pay Cleo's legal fees?"

Delanna knew she was defeated. "And you're sure Cleo will be all right?"

"'Course she's sure," Jay said. "I'll be back before the thirty days are up, and I'll go out and check on her. Maggie, write out that restraining order, and I'll deliver it to Doc Lyle in person. Then I'll come back and escort you to the train, Mrs. Tanner."

"She's going with me," Sonny said. "Do you have the importation permits for my extra geese ready?"

"Yep." Maggie turned to the vega terminal, touched a few icons, and a sheaf of papers dropped into the basket. She handed them to Sonny, tapped another icon, and another sheaf, thicker than the first, emerged.

"Is that the restraining order?' Delanna asked.

"Not yet," Maggie said, tapping icons and watching papers drop. "These are still Sonny's hatchling importation permits."

Delanna's heart sank. They were obviously right about the vet and his insistence on the rules. And all this material was just for eggs that had hatched after the *Scoville* lifted off.

Maggie handed what looked like a whole ream of paper to Sonny, then turned back to the terminal and began tapping icons again, a lot of them. She paused, reading the screen, tapped several more icons, and pulled a single sheet out of the basket. She handed it to Jay. ''That's good for thirty days—care, feeding, and full liability.''

''Good,'' Jay said, folding the paper up and sticking it in his shirt pocket. ''Come on, little lady,'' he said to Delanna, placing his arm around her waist.

Sonny got to his feet. ''Come on, Delanna, let's go. I'll walk you over to the train station.''

''I'm not going with either of you,'' she said, pointedly removing Jay's arm from her waist. ''And don't call me 'little lady.' ''

''Sonny and Mad Dog, you get out of here before I go find my broom and chase you out,'' Maggie said, snapping the vega terminal off. ''There's no point in her going with either of you. She can stay with me till train time, and I'll take her to the station. You two go tend to your business.''

With a wink at Delanna, Jay left. Sonny stopped at the door and started to say something, then went on out, leaving whatever it was unsaid.

''Now,'' Maggie said when they'd gone, ''we've got two hours and a half till train time, and I'll bet you're bushed.'' She sat down and poured herself another shot from the ambrosia bottle, then gestured toward a dusty-looking couch at the back of the office. ''Why don't you lie down and catch a little shut-eye? I'll wake you in plenty of time for the train.''

''I want to see another lawyer,'' Delanna said.

Maggie put her cup down and stared at Delanna, tapping the table with her hand. It occurred to Delanna that alienating the only person who had taken any interest in her at all was probably a bad mistake, but she was past caring. If this was where having Maggie look after her interests had gotten her, she could hardly do worse with her as an enemy.

''There *is* another lawyer in this one-horse town, isn't there?'' Delanna said, staring back at Maggie.

''There are five, matter of fact.'' Maggie got up, walked over to the door, and opened it. ''Philo!'' she hollered into the bar, which was now quite noisy. "Can you come here a minute?"

"Sure thing, Maggie honey," a deep voice yelled back.

"Are there any lawyers here who aren't drunks or saloonkeepers?" Delanna asked, knowing the minute the words were out how insulting they sounded.

"Philo!" Maggie bellowed.

"I'm coming, I'm coming," he said impatiently. "Just let me finish this hand."

"Never mind. I don't need you after all!" she shouted. "I need Buck. Somebody go out front and get him," she said and shut the door.

"Seems to me you don't know much about drunks or saloonkeepers," Maggie noted quietly, still standing by the door. "Or about lawyers." There was a tap on the door. She opened it, and Buck, the boy who'd been watching the geese, came in. He was grinning the way he had when Delanna caught her heel in the step. He tipped a big hat and said, "Congratulations on your wedding, Mrs. Tanner!" and grinned even wider. Delanna hoped his face would split in two and fall off.

"Go fetch me Lydia Stenberg," Maggie said and shoved him out the door before he could ask any grinning questions. "Lydia Stenberg's not a drunk or a barkeep," she said, sitting down heavily in her chair. "What she is, is the only other lawyer in this town right now. Happens we've got *five* in this one-horse town, but one's out doing circuit prep for the orchards, one's over at the mines, and you already said you didn't want Philo." She regarded Delanna calmly. "Lydia's not going to tell you anything different than I did."

"We'll see about that," Delanna replied. "I refuse to believe that I can be forced into a marriage and required to sit on this planet for a year so I can inherit what my mother left me."

"Suit yourself," Maggie said. She leaned forward and poured herself another drink. "Your mama filled you full of a lot of poison about Keramos, didn't she? Wrote you a lot of negative stuff?''

''She obviously wasn't nearly negative enough,'' Delanna said. ''You force people into marriage, you steal their scarabs.''

That silenced Maggie. She sat in her chair, sipping ambrosia brandy, until Buck came back with Lydia Stenberg, who was wearing a suit and highups and looked about fifteen years old.

''My consulting fee's fifty credits an hour,'' she announced. ''How many hours can you afford?''

I can't afford any, Delanna thought, mentally counting her hundred and twenty-five credits, but she said, ''Two hours' worth. Only it shouldn't take you that long. This whole thing's a mistake.''

''Two hours,'' the lawyer said, sitting down at Maggie's computer. ''So tell me about this mistake, Maggie.''

Maggie told her. Lydia Stenberg interrupted her several times to ask intelligent-sounding questions, and began scrolling through the will and making notes on a window-pad before Maggie was even halfway through with her explanation.

She called up precedents and statutes, scrolled through the entire file, and typed in all kinds of directives, tapping her fingernails impatiently on the keyboard while she waited for the answers. Delanna began to feel hopeful.

The computer began beeping while Lydia Stenberg was waiting for something to appear on the screen. She turned the computer off immediately and turned to Delanna. ''Sorry,'' she said, scooping up the hardcopies she'd littered the table with and shuffling them together.

''What do you mean, sorry?'' Delanna asked.

''I mean, your father's will is unbreakable. I could tell that five minutes into it, but you'd paid for two hours . . .'' She shrugged. ''That'll be one hundred twenty-four credits.''

Delanna counted out the credits twice. "You told me fifty credits an hour."

"Plus sales tax and flowback," Lydia Stenberg said matter-of-factly. She held out her hand. "Are you going to appeal to Circuit Court?"

"Yes," Delanna said.

"Well, you're wasting your time and your money. Circuit Court will rule the will valid." She extended her hand a little farther.

Delanna put the money in it, thinking, That's it. I'm marooned on this planet with no money and no legal rights.

"Your fee just went down to forty-eight an hour," Maggie said, snatching three bills out of Lydia Stenberg's hand. "Take the flowback out of what I could have charged for computer time." She handed the bills back to Delanna. "You gotta pay for your train ticket."

Lydia Stenberg looked irritated, but she put the rest of the credits in her briefcase, snapped it shut, and left.

Maggie shut the door behind her. "You want me to get the drunk for you? You still got half an hour till train time."

"And have him tell me the same thing and charge me my last credit? No thanks."

"I'll give you a ride to the station," Maggie said without any expression in her voice at all. She swept up the three cups off the table and went out the door.

Delanna looked around for her carryit, then realized she must have left it in the wagon with the geese. She hoped Sonny would remember to bring it to the train. As if it would do her any good. All she had in it was a pair of pajamas, some underwear, and her cleanupkit. Plenty for an overnight stay, she thought bitterly. She'd have to buy some more clothes from the vendors at the station. If she had any money left over after paying for her train ticket. She followed Maggie into the bar.

There were several patrons in the saloon now, young

men and women in bright floral shirts at the bar and clustering around the game tables.

"Hey, Maggie. Who's your friend?"

"Would you like to dance, cupcake?" a young man in a pink-and-red flowered shirt said to Delanna.

"She doesn't look like much to dance with," a woman said, stepping in front of the young man. Her arms were chalky, and Delanna could see streaks of white powder on her neck. "I bet you don't even know how to dance, do you, honey?"

Maggie had placed the three cups on the end of the bar, and now she grabbed Delanna's hand and pulled her through the crowd; a gale of giggles and laughter followed them out the front door.

"Miners," Maggie said in disgust. They were on the wooden porch and it was dark out now. "I hate Friday nights. Probably have the place torn up by the time I get back."

Maggie hurried down the steps, her flat-heeled boots making hollow sounds. At the bottom of the stairs, Buck stood, looking expectantly at Delanna as she started down. His face fell when she made it down without getting her heel stuck. Delanna thrust her chin in the air as she walked past him to follow Maggie around the corner of the saloon.

They went through an unlighted passageway that was so black Delanna thought she'd stepped into a cave. The back of the building wasn't much better, but she could make out the shape of something light that she took to be Maggie's solaris. Maggie reached it, and suddenly the area brightened to reveal a courtyard and the solaris, a tiny wheeled vehicle with lights all around the bottom of the chassis and the cockpit canopy. The lawyer was holding the canopy open for Delanna. She squeezed into a narrow seat, her knees almost to her chin, then Maggie slipped in front of her in the other seat. The solaris chittered with life when Maggie slammed the canopy shut. It had a noisy little motor that needed new bushings so badly it caused the whole chassis to vibrate, and there were audibles all trying at once to give Maggie a status report.

"Hush," the lawyer said. "I know what you need, but you're not getting it tonight. Just tell me if your brain can figure out how to get to the train station."

"I can drive us to the train station."

It was the almost male tone of a computer, a voice deliberately modulated to be recognized as mechanical. "I was beginning to think Keramos didn't have audibles until I got in this vehicle," Delanna said. "At least something is familiar." She tried to lean back, but the seat wouldn't give.

"Give Keramos a chance, Delanna. I know your mama didn't think well of it, but it was more her fear for you than dislike of our world."

"Sure," Delanna said.

The solaris started moving toward the passageway they'd just come through. Delanna didn't think it would fit, but it did; its lights flooded the space and made the ceramic walls gleam.

"Someone's barring our way," the audible announced as the car slowed. "Shall I begin evasive maneuvers?"

"It's not a fire monkey, you stupid piece of silicon. It's Philo. Stop and open the window." Maggie ordered. The solaris stopped at the end of the passage, where Buck was standing.

"Sonny Tanner said to give this to you, only I forgot before," he said to Delanna, handing her little carryit through the window. He was grinning imbecilically at her bare legs.

Delanna tried to tug the short skirt down past her thighs. Philo stared. She snatched the carryit out of his hands and balanced it on her knees. "Thank you," she said coldly.

"Is that your trousseau in there?" he asked, smirking lewdly. "I heard you and Sonny Tanner got hitched. Not much of a suitcase. Of course, how much do you need for a honeymoon?"

"Close the window on Philo's hand," Maggie said to the computer. The solaris did its best to follow the order. Philo snatched his hand back, still grinning.

"Resume journey," Maggie said. "As I was saying, in spite of the local morons, Keramos isn't so bad, and it's really very pretty, too. Tourists are even starting to come here just to see the Salt Flats, and if they like the Flats, wait to see what happens when they discover the mountains. I like the foothills the best, especially where Milleflores—"

"Maggie, if you gave me a ride just to see if you could change my mind about staying on Milleflores, you're wasting your breath. I'm not interested in endless grasslands or mountains. I prefer cityscapes myself, the kind where the buildings are taller than the mountains, not where the whole place looks like the inside of an overheated sauna. But what I really want is civilization. Farmers who think they can tell me who I can or can't ride to the train station with are almost as bad as bourgeois miners who call me 'cupcake.' "

They rode silently for a few minutes. Delanna stared out the window. There were more ceramic boxes lit with strings of multicolored lights, and the street was lined with ceramic light fixtures, too. When the solaris turned from the dirt road onto a paved one, she guessed the pavement was ceramic. Except for the liquor crates, it seemed the entire town of Grassedge was built of ceramic.

Marooned on a planet made of bathroom tile, with no money, no clothes, and no legal rights.

"You're worrying about your trunk, aren't you?" Maggie said. "We got some extra time. I'll run by my place and loan you a few things to get you by till your trunk comes."

"No, thank you," Delanna said, thinking, If you really wanted to help me, you'd have gotten me out of this trumped-up marriage and off this planet. "They wouldn't fit me," she added cruelly.

"Suit yourself," Maggie said. They drove quietly for a while.

"Don't be so hard on Sonny," Maggie said at last. "He's as good as they come. Not much polish, but there's a reason for that." She paused and then went on. "He worked himself practically to death trying to make something out of Milleflores, and nobody to help him after his pa died."

"My mother," Delanna said.

That silenced Maggie for a long minute. "I know he's not very well-spoken, like Jay Madog, but he wasn't trying to order you around when he told you to come on. He's used to giving orders to his brothers. He just didn't think before he spoke."

"I haven't seen any signs that he thinks at all," Delanna said. "He's a bumpkin."

Again Maggie fell silent. Ahead was a huge, brightly lighted structure that not only dwarfed the buildings around it, but was different from them in shape. Circular, tall in the center, with each story forming promenades, it looked like a wedding cake. Ornate railings encircled it, like ribbons of frosting. The solaris pulled up in front, where light splayed out from huge double doors. Inside them was another pair of doors.

"Is this the station?" Delanna asked, feeling more hopeful. "Yes," Maggie said.

Delanna nodded in approval. She had thought the railway terminal would be even more rustic than the shuttleport, maybe nothing more than a shack with a bench.

"Open door," Delanna said to the solaris. The canopy popped, but didn't swing out of the way. Delanna pushed it open with her carryit. "You want me to go in with you?" Maggie asked.

"No," Delanna said.

"I'll keep you posted on your case over the ham radio. Sometimes the storms and sunspots play havoc with the transmissions, so I'll call when I can. If you don't hear from me, you can call in.''

''Storms,'' Delanna said dully. ''Great!'' She stuck her legs out of the solaris and wriggled the rest of her body free. As she started toward the brightly lit station, Maggie called to her. Delanna paused and looked back.

''If you won't give Keramos a chance, at least be good to Sonny. You owe him a lot.''

''I don't owe him anything,'' Delanna said, but Maggie had closed the canopy and the solaris was already turning around.

The Grassedge terminal didn't look like a Gay Paree transport concourse, but it did appear more promising than anything she'd seen so far in Grassedge. She walked up the mosaic path to the outer tier of the wedding cake, slightly surprised to realize it was exactly the same mosaic as in the remodeled section of the concourse back on Gay Paree, where vendors had used it lavishly to mark the paths to their doors.

She looked at her watch. She had twenty minutes till train time, plenty of time to find a clothing vendor. Maybe with luck one of them would take Visacredit. This far out, they wouldn't have instantaneous statusread and would have no way of knowing her cards were past their limit. She could buy a whole new wardrobe.

4

The ticket counter was the first thing inside the door, not inside the station proper, but stuck in the little hall formed by the two sets of doors. It wasn't even a real counter, just a trestle with a plank over it and a schedule board tacked up on the elaborate ceramic wall behind. A metaphor for this whole planet, Delanna thought, right down to the low-lifes standing in line in front of it.

They were all men, all at least a week away from their last shave and a month away from their last bath, and they all turned to look at Delanna when she came in, as if she'd be overjoyed to see them. She went to what she assumed was the end of the unruly line, keeping as much distance as she could between herself and the men.

"You go on ahead, little lady," the man in front of her said, waving her forward with a blackened hand. The line wavered and separated, and she found herself at the ticket counter, wondering if this was the local brand of chivalry or if they were suddenly going to close in around her.

"Where to?" the ticket agent said. His question made her realize she had no idea where she was going. Mille-flores wouldn't have a train station of its own, and she had no idea of the nearest town with a depot. There hadn't even been a train on Keramos when she left for school, and she couldn't remember her mother ever writing about a station going up.

She scanned the board behind the ticket counter, hoping to see a familiar name from her mother's letters. Si Chrome Lode, China Dome, Richmond Furnace, Last Chance, Cermet Summit. She didn't recognize any of them except Last Chance.

"Can't make up your mind, little lady?" a grubby-looking miner with a real beard instead of just stubble said. "Whyn't you come out to the Anaconda?"

"Yeah," his buddy, obviously the worse for too much ambrosia, said. "We'll show you a real good time."

"You don't want to go with those ore-eaters," another one broke in. He was covered from head to foot with blackish-gray dust. "You want gentlemen, you just come on out to the Matchless. I was gonna take me a week's R and R, but hell, I'll go back with you right now and show you the way. Name's Frank Fuller. What's yours, little lady?"

"I want to go to Milleflores," Delanna told the ticket agent, trying to keep her voice down. "What's the nearest station?"

"Nearest station?" the agent said blankly. "To Milleflores?"

"Milleflores?" the one who'd said his name was Frank Fuller said. "You're going the wrong way, little lady. There's nothing that direction except dirt and salt and more dirt, in that order. You don't want to waste your charms on a bunch of fruit mashers. You come on out to the Matchless."

"I need a ticket to Milleflores or the nearest station to it," Delanna hissed at the agent.

He still looked blank.

"Seems like you can't go to Milleflores anyway," the bearded miner said, "so why don't you just come along with me and—"

Delanna shoved her money at the agent. "*Give me* a ticket to Milleflores," she said.

He blinked at the money, gaped at her, then suddenly brightened. "You're Sonny Tanner's wife, aren't you?"

No, Delanna thought, absolutely not. "Yes," she said.

The agent held up a red folder. "Here's your ticket. Jay Madog said you'd be by for it." She tried to give him the money, but he pushed it back at her. "Mad Dog already paid for it. So you're Sonny's new wife. Boy, I bet Cadiz Flaherty is steaming. She's been trying to catch Sonny for three years, and couldn't. And then he goes and marries you, just like that. You must've hit him hard."

I'd like to hit him hard, Delanna thought, him and you and a bunch of others. She grabbed for the ticket folder, but he held it out of reach. "You've been on Rebe Prime, right? How'd you two fall in love with him here and you going to school?"

"We didn't," Delanna snapped, and knew immediately that was the wrong thing to have said in front of this gang of thugs. None of this was any of their business, but she couldn't say that either. What she needed to say was something that would satisfy the agent so he'd give her her ticket and let her get out of here.

"You didn't?" the agent said, looking as blank as when she asked him about Milleflores.

"I mean, I didn't have to fall in love with him. I knew him when I was a little girl, and I guess I just always loved him." He still looked blank. "And, of course we corresponded." Even blanker, if that was possible. "We wrote letters back and forth. I've got to hurry. Sonny'll be here any minute." She lunged for the ticket and got it. "Thank you," she said rapidly and started through the crowd of men. "Excuse me, pardon me, excuse me."

"Did you say you're Sonny Tanner's wife?" Frank Fuller asked, planting himself directly in front of Delanna.

"Sonny Tanner'd never get married," the bearded one

objected, "and if he tried it, Cadiz Flaherty'd have something to say about it."

"I guess I don't have to ask how you went about catching Sonny," the drunken one said. He looked pointedly at Delanna's short skirt.

"She says she wrote him letters," the ticket agent offered.

"Whoee, then somebody get me a piece of paper!" the bearded one said. "I want me a wife, too!"

"What did you say in those letters?" somebody asked, Delanna didn't even see who.

"I'll bet I know what she said," the ticket agent hooted, "and it wasn't 'Dear Sonny'!"

"That's it!" Delanna shouted, slamming her carryit down on the plank counter. "I've had about enough of this hellhole you call a planet, and I've had enough of you scumgrates! I came here to buy a ticket and catch a train, not be harassed by a lot of filthy, ignorant yahoos! So shut the hell up and get the hell out of my way!"

"Now, we were just having a little fun, Mrs. Tanner," the ticket agent said.

"And *don't* call me Mrs. Tanner!" she yelled. "Or little lady!" She grabbed up the carryit, prepared to swing it into somebody's stomach if she had to. Frank Fuller stepped back, his dusty hands up in front of him and a maddening grin on his face.

Delanna stomped past the miners and through the inner door.

"Where to?" a man in a conductor's cap said, cringing a little. Good. He'd obviously heard what she said.

She didn't want any more blank looks when she told him, "Milleflores." She thrust the ticket at him.

He opened up the folder and looked inside. "You go through the gate marked Last Chance," he said in a voice actually approaching politeness, and pointed through another set of doors.

She snatched the ticket back from him and pushed the

doors open. Behind her, she heard somebody say, ''Poor Sonny. Somebody oughta warn him. He's written himself into a lot of trouble.'' The doors swung shut behind her, and she was in the station.

It wasn't, as it had looked from the outside, made of tiers of floors. It was one vast space, the ceiling narrowing every ten meters or so till it culminated in a skylight far overhead. The whole thing was tiled in an incredible red and chartreuse, with tiled flames and lumpy trees in a border around the second level, and a series of arches with lettering above them in a hideous turquoise and the same names as on the board—Si Chrome Lode, Last Chance, Richmond Furnace, Cermet Summit—which obviously led to the trains.

And that was it. There were no restaurants, no vendors, no banks, not even any benches to sit on. Over by the arch marked Anaconda, a cluster of ragged-looking men sat on the floor against the wall, and out in the middle of the vast tiled floor an old man was sleeping with his mouth open, snoring snores that bounced off the skylight.

Wonderful, Delanna thought. Not only am I married to a moron, stuck on this godforsaken planet, and heading out into an even more godforsaken wilderness, but I'm doing it in highups and a skirt that leaves me prey to every lowlife and drunken miner on the planet. This is not happening to me.

One of the men sitting against the wall looked up and whistled at her, and the whistle echoed wildly in the immense tiled space. He started to get to his feet.

Delanna walked rapidly through the gate marked Last Chance and down a long, only sporadically lit tunnel tiled in yellow, her heels sounding like rifle fire on the ceramic floor. She wondered if she had to change trains at Last Chance and what station her ticket was for. The way her luck had been going, the train wouldn't go within fifty miles of Milleflores and she'd have to walk the remaining distance with Sonny and thirteen geese. She didn't know which was worse.

She wished she hadn't thought of the geese. They reminded her of Cleopatra. Poor Cleo, all alone out there at the shuttleport with no idea why Delanna had left her. She should have insisted on going out to the shuttleport herself. She should have insisted that Maggie give the restraining order to her, and taken it out to the vet right then. Surely she could have talked him into letting her take the scarab with her, or done something. At least she could have seen Cleo, reassured her.

The tunnel ended abruptly at the train, with barely room beside the tracks to walk. Delanna handed her ticket to another man in a conductor's cap. He glanced at it, said, ''Last car,'' and handed the ticket back to her. She stuck it in her carryit and started down the narrow walkway. The train was an older model monorail but more modern than she'd expected. There were only four passenger cars, but behind the last one stretched a long string of flatcars, loaded with plastic-covered boxes, and larger, less-definable objects, all strapped down with binders and rope. She hoped the conductor hadn't really meant the last car on the train.

She climbed on the last passenger car, found the compartment marked on her ticket, and sat down in the first comfortable seat she'd had on Keramos. It came to her just how tired she was—the long trip down on the shuttle, that ridiculous trek into town, the frustrating hours at Maggie's. No wonder she was tired. Maybe, if Sonny Tanner would leave her alone, she could get some sleep on the way to Milleflores.

Somebody whistled in the passage outside the compartment. ''Whyn't you come on out to the China Dome, little lady?'' an artificially deep voice said, and the young woman Delanna recognized as Cadiz sauntered in, wearing her floppy hat and lugging two huge duffels. ''I hear you told those miners off good! Frank Fuller was still shaking when I got there. I didn't know off-planet schools taught language like that!''

This is all I need, Delanna thought. "What are you doing here?" she said.

"Me?" Cadiz said innocently. "Why, I'm just going home. I was going to stay in Grassedge a week or so, but then I thought, Why not go home with Sonny and his new bride and keep them company? I thought, What could be more fun than going on a honeymoon?"

"Oh, really," Delanna said. "I'd have thought the 'real good time' out at the Anaconda was more your speed."

"Ooh, Frank was right. Your tongue could slice right through a cannonball rind." Cadiz hoisted her duffels into the overhead compartment and tossed her hat after them. "Where's the blushing groom?" she asked, fluffing out her short blond hair.

"I don't know," Delanna said.

"Bad sign," Cadiz commented, peering out the window at the tunnel. "Bridegroom running off on his wedding night and all. You sure he's coming back?"

The train lurched suddenly, knocking Cadiz almost off her feet. Delanna hadn't realized monorails *could* lurch. Cadiz sat down on the seat opposite Delanna and shook her head sadly. "Your groom's gonna miss the train if he doesn't get here in about five seconds."

The outside door of the car opened, and they both turned toward the sound. Jay Madog came into the compartment.

"Oh, good, Delanna, I was afraid you might . . . What the hell are you doing here, Cadiz?"

"I'm going home," she said, smiling wide-eyed at him. "With you."

"The hell you are. This trip's booked."

"Sonny's got room. He said it would be okay."

"I'll bet he did," Jay said. The train lurched again and began to creep forward.

"Where's Sonny?" Delanna asked anxiously. He *was* going to miss the train.

"He's catching up with us at Last Chance," he said

thoughtfully, as though he was worried about something. "He ran into some trouble."

"Trouble?" Delanna said, thinking of Cleo. "With the vet?"

"No, he got the geese cleared in no time," Jay said, still frowning. "With some equipment he bought. He didn't want to entrust it to the train."

I can see why, Delanna thought as the train picked up speed. It swayed heavily from side to side and lurched periodically as if somebody were switching gears, except that monorails didn't have gears.

"I say he lit out," Cadiz said.

"Did you give Doc Lyle the restraining order?" Delanna cut in to ask Jay.

"Yeah," he said abstractedly, and then seemed to come to himself. "Yeah. No problem there. And your bug's fine. I checked on it myself. Doc Lyle said he'd take good care of it."

"You're sure Cleo's all right?" Delanna said anxiously.

"Who's Cleo?" Cadiz asked. "Your daughter? Don't tell me Sonny's got a wife *and* kid I don't know about."

"Cleo is my pet scarab," Delanna told her. "She's in quarantine now, but my lawyer is going to get her out and send her to me."

"Sure, and the Salt Flats're going to turn to sugar," Cadiz retorted.

Jay shook his head sharply at her.

Cadiz ignored him. "Doc Lyle's never let anything go that didn't have importation papers. Not even those funcats the whorehouse ordered that time." She imitated the vet's voice: " 'Rules are rules. I can't do anything that would endanger Keramos.' Sorry, honey."

The train shot forward with a whoosh past a blur of darkened buildings and darker fields.

"What do you mean?" Delanna asked. "What does she mean, Jay?"

"Nothing," he said, with another severe glance at Cadiz.

"I told you. Your bug's fine. I gave him the restraining order. He can't do anything to her for thirty days."

"Do anything—what will he do after thirty days?"

"Torch her," Cadiz said, stretching out on the seat. "Your little pet's fire monkey fodder."

"Is that true?" Delanna demanded of Jay. "Is it?" He looked uncomfortable.

"Of course it's true," Cadiz said. "Doc Lyle's got orders to incinerate anything without importation papers. If Sonny hadn't come up with those waivers for the extra hatchlings, we'd be eating roast goose right now. What did Jay tell you, that he could talk Doc Lyle into letting you have your pet back?" She clasped her hands behind her head. "Listen, the first thing you got to learn is that Jay Madog'll tell a woman anything so she'll do what he wants her to."

"Like get on a train?" Delanna said, looking at Jay.

He had his hat in his hands. "Look, I got a caravan to run, and you've got to get to Milleflores. I said I'd get your trunk, and I said I'd try to get your bug out of quarantine." He turned the hat in his hands. "The restraining order's for thirty days. Doc Lyle'll obey it, you can count on that."

Rules are rules, Delanna thought.

"I'll be back before the thirty days are up," he said. "I'll go see Maggie as soon as I hit Grassedge. I'll do everything I can to save your bug, ma'am. Everything," he said again emphatically. "I gotta go check on the piggybacks," he said. "You ladies enjoy the scenery."

He left.

"I'm going with you," Cadiz said. She snatched her hat off the overhead rack. "You can count on me to do everything I can to save your precious pet, *ma'am*," she said to Delanna, turning it in her hands. "You're a mighty fast worker, *ma'am*. You've only been on Keramos a couple of hours, and you've already got yourself a husband *and* a boyfriend." She tossed the hat in the air, caught it, and stomped out.

Delanna turned and looked out the window. It was dark. The train passed a few houses lit by ceramic lampposts, but they got fewer and farther between, until she couldn't see anything. She leaned her head against the window, wishing she could sleep, but Cadiz would probably be back any minute.

Oh, Cleo, she thought. All alone on a strange planet with nobody to take care of you, with no idea what's going to happen to you.

• • • • • • •

When she woke up, the train had stopped. Cadiz was in the opposite seat, her arms folded over her chest and her hat down over her eyes. Delanna sat up. "Is this Last Chance?"

"It's Vira's," Cadiz said. She tipped her hat backward. "We're picking up supplies."

It was still dark outside, but there was a thin line of gray along the flat horizon. Delanna yawned. "How long are we going to be stopped here?"

"About—" Cadiz began, and the train lurched forward. "Not long," she finished, and pulled her hat back down over her eyes.

Delanna looked out the window at the crawling landscape. It wasn't light yet, but she could make out shapes. There wasn't much to make out: small, square fields bordered by wide, bare strips of dirt. She wondered if they were firebreaks. A long way to the north she caught a glimpse of reddish light that might be a fire.

She wanted to ask Cadiz how far it was to Milleflores, but Cadiz appeared to be asleep, her head resting against the back of the seat and her arms once again folded across her chest. She looked uncomfortable.

Good, Delanna thought sleepily, I hope she gets a crick in her neck.

• • • • • • •

When Delanna woke up again, it was full daylight. The square fields with their careful borders had given way to uneven patches of green surrounded by scrub and sand. There were no buildings anywhere.

Cadiz was glaring at her.

"Where are we?" Delanna asked, rubbing her neck. It had a terrible crick in it.

"About ten miles out from Bismuth," Cadiz said. "You slept right through the stop. You slept through lunch, too. You resting up for your wedding night?"

Delanna ignored that. Her watch said four-thirty, which couldn't be right, but it obviously wasn't midday. What shadows there were in the barren landscape were already getting long. The strain from going planetside must really have caught up with her.

"How far are we from Milleflores?" she asked.

"Five thousand miles," Cadiz said, looking out the window. "Give or take a couple hundred."

Delanna had been stupid to think she could get a straight answer from Cadiz. She needed to go find Jay. She went out into the corridor and ran right into Sonny. "What are you doing here?" she said, surprised.

"I caught up with the train sooner than I expected." He looked down the corridor and then glanced behind him. "I've been driving like crazy to get here," he said. He didn't look as if he'd been driving a full night and a day. He looked wide-awake and happy about something. His face was flushed with excitement, and for a moment, Delanna thought he looked like the boy she remembered.

"Come back in the compartment," he said softly, taking hold of her arm.

"But—" Delanna began, but he already had the compartment door open and was pushing her inside.

"Delanna, I've got to talk to you," he said urgently. "I've—"

"Well, if it isn't the long-lost groom," Cadiz said, sitting up and pushing her hat to the back of her head. "I thought you were meeting us in Last Chance."

"What are you doing here, Cadiz?" Sonny said, looking surprised.

"I'm going home," she said.

"Not on this caravan, you're not."

"It's Mad Dog's caravan, not yours," she said, standing up to face him, "and he invited me to come along."

Cadiz didn't even glance in Delanna's direction when she told this outrageous lie. Delanna had to admit she was good at this.

"You're just doing this to make trouble and you know it, Cadiz," Sonny said, and Delanna was pleased that he actually saw through her.

"Make trouble?" Cadiz shouted. "Make trouble? Who married a highupped been-to? Looks to me like you're the one making all the trouble."

The train lurched, and Cadiz reached out to regain her balance and cracked her head on the window. I hope it knocks her senseless, Delanna thought.

"If Jay Madog invited you on this trip, why don't you go keep him company?" Sonny said.

"So you can talk to your blushing bride? 'Delanna, I've got to talk to you!' " she mimicked in a silly, romantic voice. "As a matter of fact, Jay told me he can't stand to be alone without me for even a minute, but I guess he'll just have to. I want to see this 'equipment' you couldn't trust to the train in Grassedge. You're trusting it to the train at Bismuth, though. How come?" She flounced out past him.

Sonny hesitated by the door, looking after her. "Delanna, look, I've got to talk to you, but . . . ." The train lurched again. "I've got to go look after my equipment. Cadiz is liable to . . . Don't worry," he added cryptically, and left.

Don't worry, Delanna thought. Right. There was obviously nothing to worry about. She was stuck on a strange planet with no money, and if her watch was right, she was going to miss the shuttle back to her ship in about five minutes, after which time she would really be stuck. *And* she was sharing a compartment with her 'husband's' jealous girlfriend, on a train apparently heading straight out of what passed for civilization on this forsaken planet.

The scraggly fields turned into browning patches and then petered out altogether. Even the scrub began to look more stunted and farther apart in the dusty landscape.

She wondered what it was Sonny wanted to talk to her about. It was too much to hope he'd found a loophole in that ridiculous will—he'd probably found a way to push the Circuit Court hearing up to a mere four weeks from now instead of five.

The door to the compartment opened. She looked up expectantly, but it wasn't Sonny. It was Jay Madog.

"Sonny's on the train," he said.

"I know," Delanna said. "I saw him."

"Where's Cadiz?"

"She said she was going to go find you. She said you couldn't stand to be alone without her for even a moment."

"Oh," he said, as if he hadn't heard Delanna, and left, but he was back almost immediately, carrying a large paper sack folded down from the top. "Philo gave me this to give you," he said and left without waiting for her to open it.

Maggie must have sent her some clothes after all, even though Delanna had acted worse than Cadiz. She started to open the bag.

Cadiz slammed in, took a sandwich and a piece of greenish-yellow fruit out of her duffel, and sat down. "You hungry? We'll get supper at Last Chance, but that's still an hour away. What's that? Sonny bring you a wedding present?"

"No, this is from Jay," Delanna said. A sudden thought struck her. Jay had said Philo gave him the sack, but if so, why had he waited all this time to give it to her? And why had he waited till he saw there was no one in the compartment with her? *I'll do everything I can to get Cleo back*, he had said. *Everything.*

"Oh, a present from Jay," Cadiz said sarcastically. "I forgot, you've got a husband *and* a boyfriend." She pulled out a pocketknife and jabbed at the fruit. "Well, what is it?"

"It's some clothes," Delanna said, hastily refolding the top of the sack. "My trunk's still on board the *Scoville*. I needed some extra clothes." She stood up and put the bag on the overhead rack, pushing it to the back and jamming her carryit in front of it.

"Clothes, huh?" Cadiz said, prying a piece of greenish-yellow rind loose. "First time I've ever heard of Jay Madog giving a woman clothes. I've heard of him *taking*, mind you. To hear Sally Jane Parkiner tell it, she didn't have a stitch left by the time she made it across the Salt Flats with Mad Dog. Ripped them right off her back." She pried another piece of rind loose and worked a walnut-sized piece of pulp free. "Of course, I can see why he'd want to cover you up." She popped the fruit into her mouth. "What did he give you? A hood and a veil?"

Delanna wasn't listening. She was wondering what she could say that would make Cadiz leave. It obviously wasn't possible to insult her. She was debating whether to tell her Jay had been in looking for her, when Cadiz stood up again, grabbed another piece of fruit out of her duffel, and went out, banging the door behind her.

Delanna waited till she heard the outside door close, then waited another endless couple of minutes before standing up and getting the bag down. She laid it carefully on the seat and then went out into the corridor and looked both ways. There was no one in sight, but Cadiz had a disconcerting way of just appearing. She tried to lock the compartment but couldn't get the door to latch. The late afternoon sun was streaming in the windows. There were no shades.

She sat down, put the bag on her lap, and opened it. "Cleo?" she whispered, and reached in. There was a flowered shirt on top like the ones the miners wore and then a pair of wrinkled roughies and a wool shuttlecoat. Delanna pulled them out hastily. On the bottom of the sack was a heavy cardboard box. Delanna glanced anxiously into the corridor again, her heart pounding, and opened the box.

Maggie had sent her a lunch—sandwiches, a container of milk, and three of the same kind of fruit Cadiz had been eating—and a note. "I know all this has been hard on you, but it'll all turn out for the best. Sonny's one of the best men I know."

"Nice shirt," Cadiz said, flouncing in "You'll look just like Frank Fuller in that. We're pulling into Last Chance."

"We are?" Delanna said, trying not to let her tears blur her voice. *Everything*, Jay Madog had said, but he'd had no intention of rescuing Cleo. He had a caravan to run, and anyway, Cadiz had said you couldn't trust anything he said. Apparently she was right.

"What are you bawling for?" Cadiz said, hauling her duffels down. "The shirt's not that ugly. Those pants are, though."

Delanna closed up the box and piled the clothes on top of it in the bag. "How long are we stopped here?"

Cadiz looked blankly at her. "Till we get ready to go, I guess."

"Can I leave my things on the train?"

"Not unless you want them to go back to Grassedge. This is the end of the line." She maneuvered the door open and pushed her duffels through.

"But—" Delanna said.

"Last Chance, little ladies," Jay announced, leaning over the duffels to stick his head in the door. "You have a nice trip?"

"Do we change trains here?" Delanna asked him, and

got the same blank look. "Is this really as far as the train goes?"

"Sure is. We have to go by caravan the rest of the way."

"Caravan? You mean buses or something?"

"Solarises. Didn't Maggie explain that to you?"

There were all sorts of things Maggie hadn't explained to her. And how many did she still have to find out the hard way? "Solarises," she repeated. "How far is the rest of the way?"

"I already told you," Cadiz said.

Delanna ignored her. "How far is it to Milleflores, Jay?"

"Depends on which way we have to go."

"*About* how far?"

"I already—" Cadiz began.

"Oh," Jay said slowly, as if he was figuring it in his head, "if we don't run into too many dips and falloffs, and we don't have to go around any storms, five thousand miles."

5

"**Five thousand miles!**"

"What'd I tell you?" Cadiz said cheerfully. "Hey, you're looking a little green. Don't you think it's gonna be a fun trip?"

"How long will that take?" Delanna asked weakly.

"Depends," Cadiz said. "Three and a half weeks. Four. Five. Two months."

"Excuse me, ladies," Jay interrupted. "This train is carrying a lot of my cargo, and I'd like to jockey it off the flatbeds myself. Some of it's precious." He winked at Delanna. "I'll need your help with the geese. Sonny will be babysitting his Sakawa crate."

"And I'll be helping Sonny," Cadiz said, sashaying past them into the corridor.

"It's really killing you not to know what's in that crate, isn't it?" Jay said, following Cadiz.

Cadiz turned the corner, and an earsplitting train whistle drowned out her reply.

Five thousand miles.

Delanna sank back in her seat, staring out the window, trying not to cry. The platform was dusty, but behind it was a clean brick path that would have looked inviting except that it was lined with spindly saplings whose trunks were nearly bent back on themselves, pulled by massive red balls of fruit on the tips of the skinny branches. Some of the sad little trees bowed over a brick fence that formed a courtyard in front of a cluster of buildings that were faced with the inevitable ceramic, and all some shade of green: moss-green, olivine, aquamarine, malachite-green, bottle-green, apple-green, and emerald, each with a pimento-red tiled roof, like so many stuffed olives standing on end.

A few men had come out of the buildings and were walking down the brick path toward the train, each wearing brightly flowered shirts. A finger tapping on her window from the outside startled her. It was Jay Madog, pointing at her and then at the wagon of geese he had just pulled up. The geese were honking with excitement.

"I'm not Sonny Tanner's goose girl," she said angrily, but Jay had already turned away, shouting and waving to someone at the other end of the platform. He couldn't have heard her through the window, anyway. The geese continued honking wildly, several of them pecking at something in the corner of the cage. "They'll just have to honk," Delanna said to no one. "I don't give a damn if the noise drives everyone nuts. I hope it does. I hope—" She saw the flash of a rainbow and the pearly luster of claws on the bar of the goose cage. "Cleo!" That's why Jay wanted her to take care of the geese! Because he had hidden Cleo in the cage with them. Suddenly Delanna realized the men on the brick path were almost to the station platform.

She grabbed her carryit and the sack with the box lunch and the clothes in a single motion, then rushed through the compartment door. She ran down the corridor—and tripped going down the stairs to the platform, her high heels making it impossible to regain her feet before falling spread-eagled into the dust. The geese whooped and honked in response to the clatter. A man who looked like he could be Frank Fuller's brother was running toward her. She stood up, ignoring the pain in her ankle, shouting, "I'm fine.

Really, I'm just fine,'' and limped toward the goose cage, waving pants, shirt, shuttlecoat, and carryit at the man. She must have looked threatening. He stopped with one foot up on the platform. ''I'm fine,'' she repeated, clutching the carryit and clothes in front of her now.

''Fine.''

''You must be Sonny Tanner's wife,'' he said.

''Must be,'' she said, falsely bright.

''That explains it.'' He touched his hat and turned away, and followed the other men to the end of the platform.

Explains what? Delanna wondered briefly as she turned to the goose cage. She didn't see Cleo's toes any longer, but she could hear her growling. Goose feathers were flying and the fowl were trumpeting. ''Cleo,'' she said softly as she opened the latches to the wire door. She thought she'd find the little scarab in a state of panic, but Cleo was spitting with joy from her corner, perched on the sack of grain from which she'd obviously escaped. She had scattered some of the grain on the floor of the cage, and with her telescopic limbs was snatching the kernels away from the geese's bills. The stupid geese just looked around for another kernel, usually to have that one snatched away, too. The scarab had all six legs engaged in grain-snatching. ''Cleo, come here,'' Delanna ordered. She was so relieved to see the scarab safe that she didn't have the heart to scold her for teasing the geese. Cleo blinked her nictating membranes, pulled in her legs, and skittered across the floor of the cage to Delanna's extended hands. The geese attacked the grain.

''All this time I thought you were balled up in fear,'' Delanna said, chiding gently as she hugged the little scarab against her chest. But Cleo was glad to see her now. She extended her spidery limbs around Delanna and pressed her warm belly against Delanna's neck, lying there under her chin like a jeweled pendant. For everyone to see. Delanna pulled the flowered shirt on over her blouse; it didn't do much to hide Cleo. She pulled the baggy trousers on over her short skirt and cinched in the waist. "Into the pocket, sweetie," she said, unlocking Cleo's claws. The scarab rolled up into a ball, and Delanna dropped her into the pleated pocket. She fit neatly. Delanna put the lumpy fruit from Maggie's box lunch in the other pocket, making sure some of the greenish-yellow rind showed at the top. Cleo wasn't as lumpy as the fruit, but Delanna thought the bulges in her pockets didn't look too suspicious. And just in time. Cadiz, Sonny, and half the men on the platform were headed back toward the last car, with Jay Madog barking out orders as he led the way.

"Get the boxes out from under the seats in the last car," Jay was saying to the men, "and pull this crate of geese to the staging yard." He turned to Delanna. "How'd you get them to quiet down?"

"I fed them," she said. She put her hand in her pocket, cupping the balled-up scarab and smiling when she felt her begin to purr.

"Found the grain, huh?" Sonny said, glancing in the cage.

Cadiz peered idly into the cage. "Are they going to molt like that all the way home?" she asked.

"Put the goose wagon at the end of the caravan," Jay said to the man who had come to put his shoulder to the tongue of the wagon. "That way they can molt without getting feathers in the rest of the caravan." He glanced at Delanna. "If that's all right with you, that is. They seem to be getting to be your special pets." He grinned at her.

Delanna nodded happily. "I'll even feed them the whole trip," she said. "You know, take care of their grain my-self." And, she said to herself, stash Cleo whenever I need to, and no one, especially not Sonny, will be the wiser.

Jay Madog patted the man at the wagon tongue on the shoulder, signaling him to leave.

Cadiz was studying Delanna's outfit. "I do believe that shirt has put some color back in your cheeks," she said, slapping her floppy hat back on her head and pulling the brim down to shade her eyes from the long, slanting rays of the sun. "Those pants make you look hippy, though."

"Come on," Jay interrupted. "Let's get checked in. I'm hungry, and if I know Chancy, he'll have dinner on the table as soon as the sun drops under the horizon."

He held his arms out to usher everyone down the path. For the first time, Delanna realized a dozen other people had joined them on the platform, passengers from the train. She hung back until most of them had started up the brick path through the droopy trees.

"I didn't get to thank you properly," she said when Jay looked at her expectantly.

"What are you thanking Jay for now?" Cadiz said from fifteen or twenty feet in front of them. She must have ears like a cat, Delanna thought. "Oh, the shirt. He'd probably be glad to take back the pants, wouldn't you, Jay?"

Delanna ignored Cadiz. "I'm really grateful," she said to Jay, and stood on tiptoe to kiss him on the cheek.

"Are you coming?" Sonny asked, appearing from under the sagging boughs of the closest tree.

"Let's go," Jay said, "If delivering a little sack from Maggie makes you grateful enough to kiss me, I can't wait to see what happens when I deliver your trunk."

They walked up the path to the inn and into the greenest of the buildings. It was a lobby with a shining ceramic floor and a large desk. Behind it, a single clerk was pounding at a vega terminal between glances up at the new arrivals as they pressed their thumbs to the IDer. Numbered key tags still sizzling from being lasered with duplicate thumbprints dropped from a slot. Gingerly the clerk read the room number off the hot tags, tossed the tags to the guests, and directed them through the courtyard to their rooms.

Thank goodness, Delanna thought, we're finally someplace halfway civilized. She hoped the keys meant real rooms with baths and saunas, but at the least they meant a lock on the door so she could keep Sonny out.

"Cadiz," the clerk said when Cadiz pressed her thumb

to the IDer. "Weren't expecting you, but I think we can manage to squeeze you in."

A tag dropped out of the slot. Cadiz grabbed it before the clerk could stop her. "Fifty-three," she said. "I know the way, Chancy."

Chancy nodded agreeably and then looked up. "Sonny and Mrs. Tanner," he said, smiling broadly. "The wedding suite, I presume?"

"We want separate rooms," Delanna said coldly.

"Ha, ha," Chancy said. "That's a good one. Separate rooms for the bride and groom. Heard on the ham she was a real character. Now, you just put your thumb on the IDer, too, Mrs. Tanner, and I'll get you fixed up with another tag."

She turned to Sonny. "This is not funny."

"It's been a long day for the lady," Sonny said. "I'd like her to have a separate room, so she can get some rest."

"Well, I'd like to oblige," Chancy said, looking bewildered, "but the wedding suite's the only room left. And whatever spat you two newlyweds have been having—"

Delanna pressed her thumb to the IDer, snatched the tag that fell out and Sonny's as well, which had been cooling in the basket. "You can sleep with the geese," she said to Sonny, brushing past him.

"Now just a minute," Sonny started to say.

"Or maybe Cadiz will take you in," Delanna added brightly.

Cat-eared Cadiz, who had not yet gone off to her room, turned and grinned.

"I'll sleep in the solaris," Sonny muttered.

Delanna didn't care where Sonny or anyone else slept as long as she could have a long, hot bath and a bed to herself. She walked into the courtyard, surprised to find that it was actually filled with nice-looking greens, living greenery, not garish ceramic. She found the door with the number matching the two tags in her hand, pressed the IDer, and the door swung open. The wedding suite had a heart-shaped bed with shiny white linens and lacy pillows. There was no other furniture in the room. Windows that looked out onto the courtyard were covered with heavy drapes that had been thoughtfully closed. For the honeymoon couple, Delanna thought with irritation. She slammed the door, pulled Cleo out of her pocket, and sank onto the bed.

"We don't need anything except a bed, do we, Cleo?" she said to the balled-up scarab. Cleo didn't even poke her nose out. Playing with the geese must have tired her out, and of course she would feel safe enough to sleep in Delanna's pocket. Delanna wished she felt that safe. She didn't think she would ever feel safe on Keramos with its crazy laws and crazier people. She pulled one of the lacy pillows to the center of the bed and put Cleo on it. The scarab stretched one claw lazily, caught it up in the lace, and just left it there.

The speaker above the bed crackled, and Chancy's voice could be heard announcing, "Dinner is being served in the main dining hall." The speaker snapped off, and then on again. "Come and get it."

For a moment Delanna looked enviously at the sleeping scarab, but she knew if she put her head down even for just a minute she wouldn't pick it up again until morning, with her empty stomach growling all night long. She hadn't had anything to eat since she'd come down on the shuttle. Sighing, she padded into the bathroom, which had a tub, but no sauna, splashed water on her face from a heart-shaped ceramic sink, and dried herself with a thick hearts-and-cupids towel. She ran her brush through her hair; it needed washing to look good again, but she didn't care. There wasn't anyone she wanted to look good for, except maybe Jay Madog. After all, he had thought enough of her to rescue Cleo, which was more than she could say for Sonny Tanner. Sonny probably didn't have *any* thoughts, let alone the inspiration to steal Cleo out of Doc Lyle's cage.

She took a little wavefoam from the carryit and rubbed it into her hair, and brushed it again. Her red curls shone nicely against her cheeks. Satisfied, she straightened the flowered shirt and fastened the front, letting it hang down over the baggy pants. She'd almost forgotten she had her skirt on underneath; she sure couldn't tell by the looks of the pants. Reaching inside the waistband, Delanna tugged at the skirt until it was all scrunched up around her waist, then pulled the seam open to get it off. She stuffed it in her carryit and headed for the door, pausing at the bed to make certain Cleo was still sleeping, which she was. Delanna opened the door and stepped outside.

During the few minutes she'd been in the room, the sun had set, leaving the courtyard dark except for the luminescent leaves of the plants bordering the walks. Delanna followed the plants back to the lobby of the inn, where she thought she'd glimpsed a dining room. She had. The tables were covered with big green leaves that kept the plates and utensils from clanking against the ceramic tabletops, and each had a centerpiece of bright yellow flowers that might be kin to the garden dandies that grew on the campus of The Abbey. Half of the tables were already filled with diners. She wondered where she was supposed to sit. Spotting Chancy on the far side of the dining room putting a flower in a woman's hair, Delanna started over to ask him.

''Would you like an escort?'' she heard Jay Madog whisper from behind her.

She turned to find him wearing a white dinner jacket over his khaki pants. His hair was freshly combed and he smelled of cologne. ''I didn't know we were supposed to dress for dinner,'' Delanna said, looking down at her baggy pants in dismay.

''You'll find that on Keramos a lady has only to put a flower in her hair to be dressed for any occasion,'' Jay said, and with a gallant flourish, produced a spray of creamy white flowers attached to a hair clip. ''These ladyfans need red hair to set them off. Will you allow me?''

''Sure,'' Delanna said, smiling through the tiredness she felt. His fingers brushed her cheek as he pinned the flower in her hair, and she thought his hand lingered long past when she was sure the flowers were secure. She looked up at him and met his eyes. "What would I do without you?"

"Probably be sitting at the table eating already," Cadiz said from the courtyard door. She had her floppy hat tucked under her arm and was bent over trying to pin a flower behind her ear. Finding she couldn't do it and still hold the hat, she put the hat on the table just inside the door. "I almost forgot that Chancy likes the ladies to be dressed at his dinners," she said, finally getting the flower pinned. "There. That will have to do." She bounced up to Jay and hooked his arm under hers. "You wouldn't make me wait to have Chancy seat me, would you?" she said, tugging him along.

Jay stopped, nearly upsetting Cadiz, and offered his other arm to Delanna. "Two beautiful little ladies," he said. "What riches!"

Delanna started to take his arm.

"Delanna, wait!" someone called.

She glanced back and saw Sonny come skidding into the lobby, gesturing wildly to her.

"Sonny Tanner, you can't come in here without a jacket," Chancy said, stepping between Sonny and the dining room. "You know better'n that. And on your wedding day, too."

"I've got to talk to Delanna," Sonny said.

"Your wife already start putting stuff where you can't find it?" Chancy asked, grinning.

"No, it's . . ." Sonny was whispering frantically to Chancy, but Chancy shook his head.

"Sorry. No exceptions, Sonny. No, go on. Run get it."

Sonny looked like he was going to argue, and then took off in the direction of the rooms.

"Delanna?" Jay said, softly touching her hand and dropping Cadiz's to do it. Delanna looked up at him, saw his rakish grin, and smiled back. "The table over there," he said, gesturing.

Jay seated Delanna while Cadiz tapped her foot, and then he seated her, too. Cadiz stuck both feet up on the fourth chair. ''I'll just save this for Sonny,'' she said.

Delanna thought Jay was just as unhappy about that as she was. The thought of trying to make even polite dinner conversation with Sonny Tanner seemed like hard work, and Delanna was sure she was too tired even to try.

Sonny returned in time for the main course, wearing a jacket with sleeves a bit too short, his hair looking no different than it had before, and his expression still harried. He was carrying Cadiz's hat by both sides of the brim.

''You forgot your hat,'' he said to her, but before Cadiz could take it from him, he set it down under the table and pulled his chair up, nearly upsetting Cadiz, who still had her feet on the chair.

''Sonny, you don't look before you do anything, do you?'' Cadiz said, barely getting her feet off the chair before Sonny sat.

Sonny didn't answer. He reached past Delanna for a ladleful of vegetables, nearly upsetting his goblet of ambrosia in the process. Then he reached past Delanna again, for his portion of the main course still on the platter. She quickly moved her goblet of ambrosia out of his way so he wouldn't knock it over.

He's a moron, she thought. Not only can't he talk straight, he doesn't know how to eat, either. She was sure of it when Sonny started wolfing his food down. Even Jay and Cadiz were staring.

Delanna returned to eating the last morsels on her own plate, trying not to watch Sonny from the corner of her eye. No manners at all. Her mother had told her he and his brothers were practically animals, and she'd been right. At least Jay Madog had nice manners. She smiled over at him, but he wasn't eating. He was staring at the door.

''What's Doc Lyle doing here?'' Jay said, as he wiped the corner of his mouth with his napkin.

Cadiz looked over the rim of her ambrosia goblet. Sonny

kept his head down, still wolfing his food like a starved animal. Delanna froze, fork midway between plate and mouth.

The veterinarian was standing in the doorway arguing with Chancy about something, pointing over at their table. Delanna dropped her fork; it clattered onto her plate, but she didn't even notice. She knew why Doc Lyle was here in Last Chance, where he wasn't supposed to be. He'd found out Cleo was gone, and he knew just where to look for her, too. Oh, she should've put Cleo in the carryit. Was he telling Chancy that he had a warrant for her arrest? Or was he demanding a key to her room?

No. Apparently his lack of a dinner jacket was the cause of the heated discussion with Chancy, for the argument ended with Chancy giving Doc Lyle his own jacket. The sleeves were too long, but apparently it satisfied Chancy's dress code. Chancy nodded and let Doc Lyle enter.

Jay looked worriedly across at Sonny, who was still eating. "Is there something wrong with those geese permits of yours?" he asked Sonny. "Doc Lyle's headed right toward us, and he looks mad. Evening, Doc," he ended sweetly.

"You come all this way to help with the wedding festivities?" Sonny asked, wiping his plate with a piece of bread. "That was mighty nice of you. Wasn't it, sweet-love?" he said to Delanna.

Doc Lyle ignored him.

"Which one of you took that scarab?"

"Which scarab?" Sonny asked.

"The only one on Keramos," Doc Lyle said. "Her scarab," he added, pointing to Delanna.

"Did you lose it?" Jay asked him. "Delanna's scarab? That's pretty serious, Doc. Maggie's restraining order makes you responsible for its well-being for the next thirty days." He *tsked* admonishingly.

"I know one of you took it," Doc Lyle said, the veins on his forehead bulging.

"One of *us!*" Cadiz said dramatically. "I resent your accusation. I'd no more steal a bug than a bridegroom. Unlike *some* people."

"Not you, Cadiz. Him," the vet said, pointing to Jay Madog. "Or him," pointing now to Sonny. "They were the only two who could have gotten into the pens last night. One of them busted the seal on the isolette and took it."

"You have proof of that?" Sonny asked, looking up at long last from his plate, which was now as clean as everyone else's at the table. "Could'a been one of those miners out at China Dome. They'd steal anything they could get their hands on. Or somebody from Grassedge."

"No proof, but I know what I know. You took that scarab and you've got it here. I bent the rules to hold that animal for twenty-four hours. I should have destroyed it when I found it in her carryit," Doc Lyle said, shaking a finger at Delanna. "I will destroy it when I find it this time. And after I do, I'm charging whichever one of you stole it with illegally importing a dangerous contraband animal onto this planet and thereby seriously endangering the indigenous Keramos flora and fauna."

"Now, we both know that's not true," Sonny said. "The scarab'd had all its shots. And it's a *scaraeoptera*. There isn't anything on Keramos it could even give the sniffles to, and you know it."

"Rules are rules!" Doc Lyle insisted, his face getting very red. His clenched knuckles were white. "I trusted you, trusted the both of you, have for years, and look what you've gone and done. You've broken the laws of Keramos, and you're going to pay for it. I'll find that animal if I have to search every room in this inn and every solaris in your caravan. And when I do, I'm charging you both with attempted murder." He turned and stalked out.

"And breaking the rules," Cadiz said softly. "Which is even worse in Doc Lyle's book. One of you is in a lot of trouble."

"Room-by-room search is going to take him half the night," Jay said.

"Do something," Delanna pleaded, looking frantically at Jay. "Please!"

"Yeah, Jay, why don't you go help Doc Lyle?" Sonny chimed in. "You know if he doesn't find what he's looking for, he's going to make you unpack every crate in the caravan."

"Damn," Jay muttered. "We'll be here three days." He stood up. "Unless of course he finds what he's looking for. Is he gonna?"

"Hope so," Sonny said. "Wouldn't want ol' Doc in suspense for too long. Mess up the caravan's schedule."

"I've got to get Cleo," Delanna said, starting to get up in a panic. Sonny's hand was on her thigh, pushing her back. "Jay, help me," she said, mad with fear for Cleo. "Sonny's going to undo everything you've done. Just so he can get back to his precious Milleflores." She jerked up in her chair, but Sonny pushed her down again.

"Sit down," he said, "and keep your voice down. Doc'll find something, all right," he said to Jay, "unless he gets distracted by all this squealing. There are some scarab scales in Chancy's kitchen. Right next to the garbage disposal."

"You've killed Cleo," Delanna said, horrified.

"Nope. Chancy's cook did," he said to Jay. "Found her in a load of chicken feed, took a cannonball cleaver to her, and put her down the disposal just to make sure. Nothing left of her but a few scales." He turned back to Delanna, who'd pressed her hand to her mouth. "It cost me every credit I had, too, and twenty more. I told Chancy's cook you'd pay him when the caravan left. I figured it'd be worth it to you not to have Doc Lyle following us halfway to Milleflores."

"It's worth more than that," Jay said, looking toward the kitchen. "You're sure Chancy's cook's got his story straight?"

Sonny nodded.

"Story?" Delanna looked at the two men bewilderedly.

"And you're sure Doc Lyle won't accidentally find something else before he gets to the kitchen?" Cadiz asked.

"Positive," Sonny said. "But keep it under your hat."

"My hat," Cadiz said, looking down at her hat. "Sonny Tanner, you don't mean to tell me you put that awful thing in my hat?"

"Keep it *down*," he said. "You're as bad as Delanna, and why don't you look at the hat, too, Jay, or maybe make an announcement to the whole dining room?" Sonny said, sitting back in disgust.

"Cleo's in the hat?" Delanna whispered, making an effort not to look down at it. "She's not dead?"

"She *is* dead," Sonny said. "Chancy's cook axed her, and you'd better remember that, or she *will* be. Doc Lyle means business. He'll destroy her if he finds her. So take a drink of that ambrosia and look like you're enjoying yourself." Casually he picked up his own goblet and sipped.

Cadiz leaned across the table and whispered to him, "What possessed you to bring that bug here?"

"Well, I couldn't very well leave her where Delanna left her, right in the middle of the bed."

"That's not what I meant and you know it," Cadiz hissed.

Sonny ignored her. "Not a very smart place to put a fugitive, Delanna. From now on you're going to have to keep her out of sight. And don't worry, I didn't hurt her. I just picked off a few loose scales to leave around the disposal so Doc Lyle would believe the cook's story."

"How'd you know she was in my room?" Delanna asked. "How did you get in my room?"

"Where else would you take her? It's my room, too."

"But how'd you even know I had her?"

"Where else would you put her? You said you found the grain, and that's where I'd hid her. Like to never got all those legs in the sack," he added, shaking his head.

"You? But I thought—" Delanna looked at Jay Madog, who smiled, but looked confused. "You stole her from the shuttleport, Sonny?" Delanna asked.

"*Nobody* stole her," Sonny said. "We don't even know what Doc Lyle's talking about. Do we?" he added, looking at Cadiz and Jay.

"Nope," Jay said. "Maybe I should go help Doc Lyle." He edged away from the table, pushing his chair as far from the hat as it would go. "Maybe I can divert him to Chancy's kitchen before he starts on the caravan packs." He rushed past the tables toward the lobby.

"I better help him," Cadiz said. "Jay Madog's as transparent as a fiddle-bug's web full of dew. Just keep the hat, you two. Think of it as a wedding present from me to you."

Delanna watched Cadiz thread her way past the tables, her well-shaped backside silhouetted against the lobby lights attracting more than Delanna's stare. Only Sonny wasn't looking. He was still sipping his ambrosia, watching Delanna.

"Don't look now, but your hat is moving," he said softly. "And please don't reach for it."

Meekly, Delanna nodded. She slid her feet over and spiked both sides of the hat rim with her heels. "Go to sleep, Cleo," she whispered, fervently hoping the scarab would at least stop moving around. She felt Cleo push at the hat a few times before she pulled in her limbs. Sonny was still looking at Delanna, both elbows on the table now, his plate pushed forward, his fingers threaded around the stem of the ambrosia goblet. Delanna bit her lip. All the while she had believed Jay Madog had rescued Cleo, Sonny had been the one. And then he'd rescued Cleo again, and she hadn't even thanked him. "Thank you," she said. "I don't know what I would do without Cleo."

"Your smile was thanks enough," Sonny said.

"Was I smiling?"

Sonny nodded. "Before. By the train. When you first found her. You smiled."

"At the wrong guy," she said.

Sonny shrugged. "I saw it. That was enough."

He had nice eyes, Delanna thought, of a clear gray color. She started to reach for her ambrosia, then thought better of it. It looked just like the stuff that had burned her throat at Maggie's yesterday. Was that already yesterday? She sighed and leaned back in her chair, watching Sonny sip his ambrosia.

"Dessert, you newlyweds?" Chancy asked.

Delanna jumped. Neither of them had heard him approach.

Chancy didn't wait for a reply before putting two mounds of pink froth in front of them. "We were going to bake you a wedding cake," he said, "but we had a little accident in the kitchen."

"Really?" Sonny said.

Delanna picked up her spoon, carefully keeping her eyes down, and took a bite of the froth.

"Cook killed some kind of bug, and Doc Lyle had a fit. You know how he is about animals."

"Yeah," Sonny said. "Is he still out there?"

"Yeah, yelling at my cook," Chancy said. "He wanted to take the disposal apart, but I told him if he couldn't put it back together, I'd make him pay to import another one from Carthage. How's your dessert, Mrs. Tanner?"

"Good," Delanna said. She hadn't even tasted the spoonful she'd eaten.

"After Doc Lyle leaves," Chancy went on, "we'll bake you a cake to take with you."

"Thank you," Delanna said.

"And you take care of your bride, Sonny," Chancy said, and dropped a wad of crumpled paper in Sonny's lap. "From Jay," he whispered conspiratorially, then turned away to deliver desserts to the next table.

"What's the note say?" Delanna asked, picking at the dessert. It was tangy but sweet. Good.

"It says for us to stay here until Doc Lyle leaves."

"You didn't even read it yet," she said.

Sonny rolled the crumpled ball of paper over to Delanna. She opened it. "You're right. It says to stay here until Doc Lyle leaves."

"Really?"

"Close enough. Actually it says, 'He bit. Stay put.' I think he doesn't want Doc Lyle around Cadiz's hat. How'd you know what the note was going to say?"

Sonny shrugged. "Made sense. Didn't need to read it. Jay's got some sense . . . sometimes." He reached across the table to put his hand on Delanna's. "Don't look up now, but Doc Lyle's standing in the doorway."

Cleo bumped against the hat.

"Your hand is cold," Sonny said, spreading his fingers over hers.

"I'm frightened. Cleo wants out," she whispered.

"Got her secure?" he asked.

She nodded.

Sonny scooted his chair closer and put his arm around Delanna. "I—" She started to protest, and realized he'd put his foot down on the hat brim.

"Give me your other hand," he said. "We don't know anything about Cleo. We're on our honeymoon."

"But we aren't," she said, but he'd already taken hold of both her hands.

"This is just for Doc Lyle's benefit," he said. "You don't want him over here asking why we're standing on Cadiz's hat, do you?"

The hat bumped suddenly between Delanna's ankles, and she felt a foreleg brush against her toe. "No," she said, and let Sonny raise her hand and rub it against his cheek.

"Is he gone yet?" she whispered.

He looked up at the door. "Uh-oh," he said.

"Uh-oh, what?"

"Don't look," Sonny said. "Look at me."

She looked straight into his eyes. They were more green than gray, with lots of light in them.

After a long minute, she said, "I think we've convinced him," and pulled her hands away, making sure she kept her eyes averted. She looked over at the door. "There's no one there," she said accusingly.

Sonny took her hand again, then relaxed and reached out for the full goblet at Delanna's place. "Are you going to drink this ambrosia?"

"I don't think he was ever there," she said, wondering why she had ever believed Sonny in the first place.

"He wasn't," Sonny said, gulping down the ambrosia. "Got to stay warm somehow. Don't dare use the solaris's batteries for heat, or there won't be enough energy tomorrow for the trip."

"Are you talking about drinking my ambrosia or tricking me into holding your hand?"

He wasn't even listening. He was watching Chancy, who was standing by the door talking to three men. "Put the hat on," Sonny told her. "I'm walking you to your room."

"What is it?" she said, anxious all over again. Chancy and the men were leaning toward each other conspiratorially.

"Just keep the hat on," Sonny said. He reached under the table, scooped up the hat, and put it on Delanna's head with the same surprisingly deft motion he had used when he put it under the table. Cleo's toenails dug into her hair.

Sonny stood up and pulled out Delanna's chair. She got up, trying to resist the impulse to hold onto her hat with both hands. She stuck one hand in her pocket. Sonny took hold of the other one.

"Is that absolutely necessary?" she whispered sharply.

"For Doc Lyle's benefit."

Chancy and the three men stopped talking as soon as she and Sonny approached, and Chancy said, "We cleared up that little problem in the kitchen, Sonny, and Doc Lyle left in a huff, but not before he'd fined my cook twenty credits for not turning a contraband animal over to the authorities.

So now you and your bride can get on with your honeymoon.''

"Thanks, Chancy,'' Sonny said, and pulled Delanna along the path.

The three men and Chancy started talking again the minute they were past. Delanna's heart began to pound, but no one followed them through the shadowy green courtyard.

Delanna reached for her key. Sonny was already opening the door. "Where did you get that?'' she demanded.

"Chancy gave it to me,'' Sonny said, walking into the room ahead of her. "He said he hated to see newlyweds fighting.''

"We're not newlyweds,'' she said. They were standing just inside the. "I want to thank you for saving—''

Sonny put his finger to his lips.

"For bringing me my hat. You know how much it means to me.''

He grinned. "It looks real nice on you, all right.''

She opened the door. "Well, good night,'' she said.

"I've gotta talk to you about some things,'' Sonny said, shutting the door.

"What things?'' She took Cadiz's hat off and reached up for Cleo. The scarab grabbed Delanna's ear with one of her claws and dug in. "And don't tell me you have to stay here for Doc Lyle's benefit, because he left.''

"This isn't about Lyle,'' Sonny said, prying two of Cleo's claws loose from their grip on Delanna's hair. "See, on Keramos, when you get married . . .'' He unhooked Cleo from Delanna's ear.

"We're *not* married,'' Delanna said emphatically, trying to untangle a lock of her hair from a hinged joint. "And I don't want to hear about your local marriage customs. In fact, I don't want to hear one more word about this godforsaken planet. I've already heard and seen way too much.''

Cleo suddenly retracted all her limbs and curled into a

ball. Sonny lifted her off Delanna's head and handed her over.

"Whatever else you've got to tell me," Delanna said, "like we're sitting on a fault line or that monkeys sacrifice brides, it can wait until morning. I'm going to bed." She put Cleo down on the bed. The scarab scuttled to the center and started making a nest in the lace pillows.

"Well, actually, going to bed's what I needed to talk to you about. See, on Keramos, when people get married—"

"We're *not* married," Delanna repeated, "and if you have any idea about claiming your conjugal rights—"

"Shh," Sonny said, tilting his head to one side. He went over to the front window and pulled the drapes aside a fraction of an inch.

"And don't try to pull that 'Doc Lyle's coming back' routine on me again. You already tried that in the dining—"

"Shh." Sonny left the front window and went around to the other side of the bed. He pulled the drapes back from the window on that side and ran his hand along the sill.

"Is that why you rescued Cleo?" Delanna said. "Did you think I'd be so grateful that I'd collapse in your arms?"

He stopped whatever he was doing at the window. "I didn't think anything," he said. "I was thinking of you. I—"

"I'll bet. You were thinking of how you could weasel your way into my room. 'Shh. There's somebody at the window. Maybe I'd better stay the night.' Well, it won't work. You were crazy to think it ever would."

Sonny opened the door. "I'll be out in the solaris if you decide you need me."

"I won't," she shouted after him, and slammed the door.

"What's the matter, Sonny?" a man's voice said outside the window. It sounded like Chancy's. "You two have another spat?"

Delanna pulled the drapes cautiously aside and looked out. Chancy and the three men she'd seen him talking to were standing in the center of the courtyard. Delanna locked the door and then looked around for something to push against it.

Cleo had sprawled over and through the pillows like a lace-weaving spider. Delanna lifted her gently off them, grabbed all but one pillow, and filled the space between the door and the bed with the pillows and all the towels. Then she opened her carryit, took out her nightgown, and jammed the carryit between the pillows and the bed. Cleo had crawled onto Delanna's pillow. Delanna pushed her aside and got into bed.

Someone knocked on the door. "Go away," Delanna shouted, and then suddenly thought, What if Doc Lyle really is out there? Her heart began to pound. "Who is it?" she asked.

"It's me, Mrs. Tanner, Chancy. Come on, let Sonny back in. He's sorry, whatever he did."

"Or didn't do," another voice said. There was more laughter than two men could generate. Who all was out there? Delanna sat up in the bed, the lace covers pulled up to her neck, looking dubiously at the door and wondering whether she should try to move the bed.

"Maybe Mrs. Tanner'll soften up if we sing her a song or two," a third voice said when the laughter had subsided.

"Good idea," Chancy said. "Mrs. Tanner, I don't know if you know this or not, being new to our fair planet, but when people get married on Keramos, we got a custom of singing them to sleep. Now, we know you and your new husband have had a little falling-out, but after you've heard us sing, we know you'll make it up. One and two and . . ."

There was a horrible cacophony from outside Delanna's window. She thought she recognized a bangle drum and a triphone. Or maybe the geese had gotten out and someone was slaughtering them. Cleo tried to crawl under the covers. Delanna put her hands over her ears. At least it can't get any worse than this, she thought. The triphone beeped with what she supposed was the tune, but it couldn't be. It sounded like an ancient Christmas carol.

They started to sing. It *could* get worse.

"Hark, the bride and groom are wed!
 Glory, now they've gone to bed!"

"Come on, Mrs. Tanner," Chancy shouted. "Don't that
make you want to forgive him?"
Deanna put her head under the covers. It didn't help.

"Late in time they hit the hay,
 While we sing another lay.
 Hark, their marriage has gone wrong,
 So we'll sing another song!"

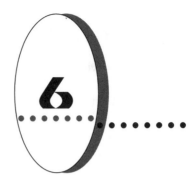

6

Delanna got exactly three hours' sleep. She knew it was only three hours because even with her head under every lace pillow in the room she had still been able to hear a sprightly rendition of ''Three o'clock\In the morn'\Won't you let him in?'' to the tune of ''Jingle Bells,'' and then Chancy was banging on her door shouting, ''Six o'clock. Time for breakfast.''

She was too tired even to think about eating, but she was afraid last night's serenaders might come to roust her out with ''O Come All Ye Newlyweds'' and lyrics about eggs and bacon. She got up and put on Maggie's pants and flowered shirt and dragged a comb through her hair. She looked like she'd had about ten minutes' sleep.

At some point during the night Cleo had crawled under the bed and curled herself up into a fist-sized ball in the least reachable corner. Delanna shimmied in under the bed on her stomach. ''You poor baby, they scared you to death with those awful carols, didn't they? Poor little sweetie.''

She grabbed for the scarab. Cleo scrunched herself even farther into the corner. ''I know, I know, sweetie. Don't be scared. Those awful men are gone.'' She managed to get hold of a folded leg. ''You get to go for a ride in the hat again.'' Delanna began backing out, keeping a firm grip on the hinged joint so Cleo couldn't extend the leg and scratch her. ''How would that be? A nice ride in Cadiz's hat. It looks a lot better on you than it does on her.'' Delanna, holding fast to Cleo's leg, wriggled out from under the bed.

Sonny was standing there, looking down at her.

She scrambled up, keeping an iron grip on the scarab and getting nipped for her pains. ''What are you doing here?'' she demanded.

''I came to get your scarab. I need to put her in with the geese.'' He held out a grain sack like the one Cleo had eaten her way through the day before. ''You stay here. I'll come back and take you to breakfast.''

''You're not taking me anywhere,'' Delanna said angrily. ''I can take care of myself.''

''Not on Keramos, you can't. You don't know how determined the boys can be.''

She stepped back so he couldn't get Cleo. ''I suppose this is all part of the 'full treatment,' along with having caterwauling drunks outside all night.''

''Afraid so,'' he said. He clucked at Cleo like she was one of his geese. ''Come on into the sack.'' Cleo began to unfold her legs. ''I know a sack isn't traveling in style, but as soon as we've got a few miles between us and Doc Lyle, you can get out.'' The scarab extended one foreleg, unsheathed her toenails, and gripped the open top of the sack.

''Come on, that's right,'' Sonny said, still clucking. ''Into the sack. It's nicer than under the bed.''

Delanna watched him, amazed. He hadn't uttered this many sentences in the entire time since she'd met him. Cleo climbed into the open sack and promptly curled herself into a ball again.

Sonny tied the sack shut with a length of cord from his hip pocket. ''Be right back,'' he said. ''Or better yet, come with me out to load the geese.''

''I told you,'' Delanna said, ''I have no intention of going anywhere with you.''

"Suit yourself," Sonny said, and slung the sack over his shoulder. "They're still out there, you know. I walked in here in full view of Chancy and his carolers. If I walk back out now by myself I can't answer for what they might do."

"I'm coming," Delanna said. She put her highups on, fastened the ankle straps, and hurried after him.

He had waited just outside the door for her. When she came out, he took her hand.

"Aww," a deep bass voice said, and a young man carrying a bangle drum came out from behind the brick fence. Two other men, carrying homemade-looking instruments, followed him. "You two finally make up?"

"Yep," Sonny said. The bass started tuning up his drum. "Come on, sweetlove," Sonny said, gripping Delanna's hand, and led her out of the courtyard almost at a run.

He let go of her hand as soon as they were out of the courtyard and shifted the grain sack to his other shoulder. "I was afraid they were going to start up again," he said apologetically.

"So was I," Delanna admitted. "I don't think I could have stood another chorus of 'We Three Gents of Keramos Are.' "

Sonny grinned and took off down the sapling-lined path. The drooping red fruit looked even heavier than it had yesterday. About the way I feel, Delanna thought. They came out onto the platform where the train had pulled in the day before. On the platform, front wheels pulled up over its edge so that their panels were at an angle, were dozens of solarises. Behind them were a jumble of cloth-covered wagons, some of them already hooked to the backs of the solarises, some of them still being loaded or pulled into place.

Sonny led the way through the maze to the geese's cage. The minute he and Delanna came in sight, the geese set up an excited honking.

"You have this same effect on everybody?" Cadiz asked. She was coming from the direction of the train platform, carrying a bedroll. "I never heard a ruckus like that one last night. I had to go bed down with the livestock to get any sleep.'' She looked at the geese, which had crowded into the corner of the cage closest to Delanna and were craning their necks through the bars. ''Actually, the geese sound a lot better than Chancy's carolers.'' Cadiz stared pointedly at Sonny's sack. ''Hiding the evidence, huh?''

''Yep,'' Sonny said, unruffled. He slung the grain sack off his shoulder and laid it in the farthest corner of the cage. Delanna expected Cleo to immediately begin engineering her escape, but there was no movement from inside the sack. Poor Cleo, Delanna thought. She's probably sound asleep on that uncomfortable corn.

Delanna could understand that—she herself had visions of falling asleep on the breakfast table, dishes and all, while she waited for Sonny and Cadiz to finish hooking up the wagons, but when they finally got to breakfast there wasn't even a table. Chancy stood by the door of the dining room pouring what looked like coffee and passing out paper pokes.

''I knew you two newlyweds would patch it up if we just kept on singing,'' he said, handing Delanna some kind of vegetable sandwich. ''Nothing like a good song to make a person feel romantic. Isn't that right, Sonny?''

Sonny took a swallow of the ''coffee,'' set the cup down, and stuck his sandwich in his pocket. ''I've gotta go check my cargo,'' he said and took off.

Chancy frowned. ''You two aren't still fighting, are you?'' he asked Delanna.

''No,'' she said, looking nervously around for lurking carolers. She took a swig of the brown liquid, hoping it might wake her up. It definitely wasn't coffee, and it was too sweet to be ambrosia. It tasted like hot peach juice.

''The boys and me usually only sing a couple of songs to honeymoon couples, kind of like lullabying them to sleep, but when we saw your husband stomping off to sleep in the solaris, I just said, 'We can't have that. Boys,' I said, 'we gotta keep singing till she lets him back in.' "

Wonderful. If she'd let Sonny stay a few minutes, the carolers would have gone off and left her in peace. "We're married, and there's certain traditions on Keramos," Sonny had said. It occurred to Delanna suddenly that he had been trying to tell her about the carolers instead of trying to claim his conjugal rights. Well, if he had been trying to tell her, why hadn't he just told her, instead of wandering around the room messing with the windows? Maybe he had intended climbing out the window so the carolers wouldn't know he'd gone, she thought ruefully, and she had to admit she hadn't given him much chance to tell her anything. Well, he should have tried harder.

"Which song did you like the best?" Chancy was asking.

They had all been equally awful. "It's hard to say," Delanna murmured, sipping her peach juice.

"My favorite's 'Good King Wenceslas,' " Chancy said, and burst into a scarifying tenor. "Come and listen, all you folks/ To this song of bedding!/ They were wed, oh, just today/ I went to their—"

"The caravan's leaving without you," Cadiz said, sashaying in in with her floppy hat and Delanna's carryit. Delanna had never been so glad to see anyone in her life.

"Coming," she said, put down her mug and untouched poke, and took the carryit from Cadiz.

Cadiz tried to hand her the hat, too.

"It's your hat," Delanna said.

"Not anymore, it's not. I got a thing against bugs."

"Brightly shone the moon that night," Chancy warbled.

It was no time to argue. Delanna took the hat and started for the solaris.

"On the happy couple/ When the singers came in sight . . ."

Chancy's voice faded mercifully away when they turned the corner. "It's a real talent, that's what it is," Cadiz said. "I can't wait to see what effect you have on the fire monkeys. Far as anybody knows, they're mute, but then again, they haven't seen you yet.''

"Cleo is *not* a bug," Delanna said, and tried to hand the hat back to Cadiz.

"Looks like a bug to me. Probably laid eggs all over the inside that'll hatch into brain-eating worms.''

"You'd have noticed scarab eggs," Delanna said, wanting to push the hat right into Cadiz's self-satisfied face. "They look like giant pearls. But Cleo's been sterilized.''

"Well, you figure out a way to sterilize my hat, and I'll take it back. Until then, I'll get another from my duffel." Cadiz said. She stopped next to a solaris hooked to four large covered wagons and the open cage of geese. "This here's where we ride.''

"We? I thought you were hitching a ride with somebody.''

"I am. Sonny. I was gonna ride with Jay, but he didn't have any room. Speaking of Jay, there he is.'' She waved. "Jay!''

He was squatting next to a covered wagon, peering at the underside and talking to a short, pudgy man with a red flowered shirt and an even redder face. Jay looked up, said something to the man, and hurried over to Delanna. "You're looking prettier than ever this morning, Mrs. Tanner," he said.

Cadiz snorted.

"I heard the carolers gave you a rough time last night," he went on. "I had to go up to Joriko's to pick up some supplies, or I'd have seen to it they left you alone. Are you okay? Is there anything I can do for you?''

"You can get *me* another wagon," the pudgy man said. He came up, his face looking even redder. "That bottom'll split first dip we hit. I'll have seedlings all over the place.''

"We won't hit any dips today," Jay assured him. "The scout's soundings just came in. Blue sky and solid all the way to Whitewater. We'll reinforce that bottom tonight.'' He turned back to Delanna. "We're gonna have a real easy trip. You can sleep the whole way to Milleflores.'' He glanced at the little solaris. "Soon as we get into the Salt Flats, you can come ride with me.''

"I thought you didn't have any room,'' Cadiz said.

"He doesn't,'' the now purple-faced man said, "because if that bottom splits, Jay's gonna be the one carrying my seedlings.''

"You need anything, Delanna, you just holler,'' Jay said and went on to check the other wagons.

"Open door,'' Delanna said to the solaris. The canopy didn't so much as pop.

"No voice response left on the Tanner solaris,'' Cadiz said, banging the cockpit canopy up. "Wilkes can't get them to work anymore.''

"Does the highway chauffeur work?'' Delanna asked, worried now that they wouldn't be able to keep up with the caravan.

"Don't have one,'' Cadiz said easily. "Highway, that is. The automated chauffeur probably works. Probably never been turned on. Hmm, I wonder . . .'' She leaned into the cockpit and pressed something on the panel.

"The highway guides are not registering,'' the audible said. "Please resume manual control.''

"The road doesn't have any automated guideposts?'' Delanna asked.

"What road?'' Cadiz said. "Come on. Get in.''

The inside didn't look big enough for Cleo, let alone three people. Especially when two of the people were Sonny Tanner and Cadiz.

"You sit up front next to your new husband and I'll get in the back,'' Cadiz said. "Go on, get in. Don't stand there wasting energy.''

Delanna wriggled into the tiny front seat.

"I gotta go see about some seedlings,'' Cadiz said, and slammed the cockpit canopy down practically on Delanna's head.

There was no room at all in the solaris. Delanna's knees

were squashed against the dashboard, and her feet in the highups were jammed against the floorboards. With the canopy down, there wasn't even room to sit up straight. She had to hunch her shoulders forward, and that put her knees practically in her face. She tried to move her legs into a more comfortable position, and in the process managed to get her heel wedged in the narrow space next to the gearshift. It took her the whole time till Cadiz got back to get it unstuck.

I can't go five thousand miles like this, Delanna thought. She wondered how Sonny had managed to sleep the night before. Her neck was already starting to cramp.

''I want to sit in the back,'' she said when Cadiz returned, and then had to suffer the humiliation of trying to get out of the front seat and into the back. When she finally managed it, it was even worse. The space between the seats was too small to sit facing forward, and the seat was too narrow to lie down on. She could just barely lie on her side and stay on by wrapping one arm over the back and digging in her nails like Cleo.

Cadiz pulled the panel down within inches of her ear.

''Can't we keep it open till we leave?'' Delanna asked.

''And waste energy?'' Cadiz scoffed. She had maneuvered herself into a sort of lotus position in the center of the front seat and looked maddeningly comfortable. ''These solarises don't run on shade, you know.''

The heel of one of Delanna's shoes was digging into her other foot. She tried to move it. ''Why don't they make them bigger?'

''They do. You heard Jay. He's got plenty of room.''

Delanna's hands were going numb from clutching the back of the seat, and she couldn't feel her feet at all. She pushed the canopy open and tried to stand up.

''Thanks,'' Sonny said, and got into the driver's seat. ''You two all set?'' He pulled the panels down and fastened them. ''The scout says it's going to be blue sky all day.

We should make it to Whitewater.'' He flipped a switch and started the vehicle up.

The whirring drone of the motor was louder than it had been in Maggie's solaris, and seemed to be coming from somewhere right under Delanna's right ear. Sonny backed the solaris off the platform with a thunk, turned it, and started forward. Delanna made one more attempt to get comfortable, failed, and turned her face into the now-vibrating seat back. She was almost instantly asleep.

She woke up to the sound of voices. At first she thought the solaris must have stopped, though she was too drowsy to open her eyes and see, but the motor was still whirring. The man's voice speaking wasn't Sonny's, though.

''. . . down at Honeycomb with a whereat. I'm looking for Trader Kearney. Anybody knows where he is, tell him I've got a crop of cannonballs I want to sell on spec.''

Another voice, a woman's this time, cut in. It had a different quality, not fuzzy or unclear, but distant, as if it were coming from much farther away. ''Think you'll get stormed out, huh? Kearney's up at New McCook with''—there was a burst of static—''but I don't think it's cannonballs he's looking at. It's Nance Fremont.''

Delanna supposed it was some kind of radio bulletin board. Maggie had mentioned something about getting in touch with her over the ham radio. This must be what she meant. She lay there with her eyes closed, listening.

''He's crazy to think Nance'd pay him the time of day,'' the voice went on, punctuated by static every third word or so. ''Not with York Chantsall around.''

Correction: it wasn't a bulletin board. It was a back fence for the old biddies to gossip over.

There was another burst of static, and then an entirely different voice said, ''Speaking of marriage, have you heard about—''

Sonny reached across and flicked off the radio.

''What'd you do that for?'' Cadiz demanded.

"We're not listening to the ham in this solaris," Sonny said.

"Why not?"

"You know why not."

"She's asleep," Cadiz said.

"No," Sonny said.

There was a moment's silence, and then Cadiz said, "You're worried about her feelings, I suppose. Funny, you being so worried about her feelings. Too bad you couldn't spare a little concern for your family and friends. You know how I found out? From the ham. That snoop Liz Infante out at Blue Rug put out a whereat. On me! 'Sonny Tanner found a bride in Grassedge today, and *whereat* does that leave Cadiz Flaherty? I hear she had her wedding garland all picked out!'" Cadiz sounded more indignant than hurt.

"Sorry," Sonny muttered. "I didn't know till I got to Grassedge if she'd stay or not."

"From the looks of things, you still don't. She's not exactly acting like the happy bride. She's acting like somebody who thinks they made a big mistake."

"She's tired," he said. "She didn't get any sleep last night, thanks to that caroling party. I suppose you're the one who brewed that up."

"Me?" Cadiz said. "I was down with the livestock crying my eyes out because it wasn't me they were singing to."

"I'll bet," Sonny said. "You were crying your eyes out because you can't use me to fire up B.T. and make him jealous anymore now that I'm married."

"B.T. Tanner can dry in a dip," Cadiz said. "Your little bride can't hear the ham. She's asleep. She's been snoring away back there all morning."

Delanna heard the flipped switch, and the same voice that had been cut off before blared forth. ". . . threw him out. Right in the lap of the carolers. He spent the night in his solaris."

Another voice came on, not cutting in but just carrying on a conversation. "That's what always happens with those been-tos. Remember that time Willy Schell came back from Starbuck married to that little black Pursoor, what was her name?''

"Well, but Sonny's wife was *born* here. Of course, she went all those years to that sniffy school, what was it called?''

A new voice said, "*I* heard the first thing she did when she saw Sonny Tanner was to go find a lawyer and try to get a divorce.''

"Then you must have heard wrong,'' a girl's voice cut in. What was this? Delanna wondered. Some kind of radio conference call? "Anybody that doesn't think Sonny Tanner's the cutest thing east of the Salt Flats's got to be crazy.''

"Yes, well, Lizabeth,'' the first voice said. "We all know how you feel about Sonny. Too bad his new wife doesn't feel the sa—''

Sonny cut the radio off in mid-word. "Don't they have anything better to do than get on the ham and gossip?'' he said angrily.

"Well, you gotta admit it's interesting,'' Cadiz said. Delanna would have bet she was wearing that self-satisfied smile. "I mean, her going to see Maggie *and* Lydia Stenberg, and you sneaking her bug out of quarantine, and then her pitching you out on your wedding night.''

"You haven't told anybody on the ham about the scarab, have you? I told you and Jay not to tell a soul.''

"I know. I was there. You don't have to worry. I haven't blabbed and Jay's not going to tell. He doesn't want Doc Lyle traipsing after us and confiscating cargo. It *is* romantic, though, you taking a risk like that for your new bride, and her throwing you out on your ear. There hasn't been anything this exciting since Jay Madog got caught dandling both the Spellegny twins. You never told me Lizabeth Infante had a crush on you.''

"Why should I when you can find out every blessed thing about everybody on Keramos from the ham?''

The solaris suddenly jerked to a stop. Delanna nearly fell off the back seat.

"Jay's got the flag up," Sonny said. "I better go see what's up." He pushed the panels open to a blast of hot, dusty air and climbed out.

Delanna sat up. She must have been asleep several hours. The sun was already straight overhead, and the landscape had completely changed. The neat farms and tiled irrigation ditches were gone, and in their place was a flat brownish-gray scrub. She couldn't tell whether that was the natural color of the plants or whether they were coated with the brownish-gray dust that filled the air.

Sonny came back coughing. "The dust's bad up ahead," he said, leaning on the window, "and the scout's out doing soundings. I'm gonna ride lookout for Jay. Cadiz, you'll have to drive. Stay right behind the Hansens."

"What about Cleo and the geese?" Delanna asked, looking back anxiously. The dust was so thick she couldn't see the cage.

"I've got a tarp I'll put over them," Sonny said.

"Can't Cleo ride with me?"

"Not while I'm driving, it can't," Cadiz said. She stood up on the front seat and stepped over onto the driver's side. "I don't want no bug climbing up my neck."

"She's not a bug," Delanna snapped.

Sonny reached in behind the back seat, pulled out a wrinkled tarp, and walked back to the cage. He disappeared almost immediately into the heavy dust. Cadiz reached up to pull the panels down. Delanna stopped her.

"I'm getting in front," she said. Her foot had gone to sleep. She pitched forward onto the canopy and then got her heel caught again. Cadiz watched her, smirking.

Sonny dumped Cleo in Delanna's lap, pushed the panels into place, and disappeared into the dust again. Cadiz switched on the ham and floored the pedal so hard, the solaris would have leaped forward if it had been fossil-fueled.

". . . stole it right out of quarantine," a man's voice was saying. "The vet was madder than a burned monkey. He torched it right there at Chancy's, in front of everybody."

Another man asked a question that came across as nothing but static, but apparently the first speaker understood him.

"No," he said. "Some animal I never heard of. Some kind of a bug."

"I told you it was a bug," Cadiz said, scowling at Cleo, who was climbing up Delanna's shirt.

"This is Markie Woodward down at Shelter Lanzye. I just heard Sonny Tanner got married. Who to?"

"A snippy little redhead who likes bugs." Delanna recognized that voice. It was Lizabeth Infante, the one with the crush on Sonny. "And *I* heard she's not happy about being married. Soli Hansen said when she was in Grassedge she went to see Maggie Barlow about getting out of the marriage."

"I can't imagine anybody not wanting to be married to Sonny," Markie said.

"Me neither," Lizabeth agreed. "You can tell that redhead for me that if she doesn't want him, I do."

Cadiz grinned at Delanna. "You get that?"

Delanna wouldn't give her the satisfaction of answering. She stroked Cleo's carapace and looked ahead at the dust. It got thicker and then abruptly thinner, and they emerged into blue sky and scrub again. The trailer they were supposed to be following was only a few feet ahead.

"You can also tell Sonny Tanner if he'd married me," Liz continued, "he wouldn't have spent his wedding night in a solaris. What did she think, that he needed to charge up his batteries?"

There was apparently nothing sacred or secret on Keramos. Delanna remembered Sonny telling her that the settlers on the lanzyes gossiped a lot, but she had assumed he meant face-to-face, not over the air.

"This is B.T. Tanner at Milleflores with a whereat. I'm

looking for Cadiz Flaherty. Anybody who knows where she is, I got an answer board set up.''

Delanna looked inquiringly at Cadiz. ''That's you, right?'' she said.

Cadiz gripped the steering wheel and stared straight ahead.

''If you're out west, I got an enhancer set up.'' B.T.'s tone of voice changed from matter-of-fact to angry. ''Cadiz, I don't know what you're up to, but if you went traipsing after my brother like a lovesick goose, it's my duty as a friend to tell you you're making a public fool of yourself. You want them talking about you on the ham?''

Cadiz punched off the radio so hard Delanna figured she'd broken it. Her face and neck were a bright scarlet. ''It's my duty as a friend,'' she mimicked. ''Well, B.T. Tanner, it's *my* duty to tell you you're the biggest fool on the planet. 'You want them talking about you on the ham?' I didn't hear my name mentioned *once* this morning, but you can bet they'll mention it now. You've seen to that, you big lummox. You're even dumber than your big brother.''

She turned and glared at Delanna. ''I suppose you're getting a real kick out of this.''

Delanna didn't answer. She was trying to remember which of the brothers B.T. was. The second oldest, she thought. All but one were a lot younger than Sonny because they'd been born after she left Keramos, and her mother had hardly ever mentioned them in her letters. But Delanna seemed to remember that their names were Wilkes and Harry. B.T. must be the second oldest.

''Fine time he picks to take an interest,'' Cadiz said. Cleo flattened herself against Delanna. ''Never as much as gave me a look before, and now all of a sudden it's his duty as a friend. A friend! And Sonny goes off without a word to anybody and gets married!'' She braked savagely. The solaris lurched to a stop. The trailers crashed into it, one by one, and the geese began honking hysterically. ''This is all your fault!'' she yelled at Delanna. ''You stole Sonny Tanner away from me, and when you get to Milleflores you'll probably try and steal B.T. too!''

Cleo climbed halfway up Delanna's neck, trying to get away. Delanna was suddenly furious. ''All right,'' she said, disentangling toenails from her collar. ''If you want to have it out, we'll have it out.'' She tried to put Cleo in her lap, but the scarab made a sudden dive for the floor and grabbed hold of Delanna's ankles. ''Anything's better than the ambushing you've been doing ever since I met you.''

''Ambushing?'' Cadiz shouted. ''What do you call stealing Sonny Tanner out from under my nose?''

''Now get this straight. I didn't steal your boyfriend. I don't even want him. You want him, you take him.''

Cadiz's mouth was open, but nothing came out. ''What did you marry him for then?'' she said finally.

It was Delanna's turn to stare. ''I didn't,'' she said. ''Didn't he tell you about the will?''

''What will?''

''The will his father and my father signed. They wanted to keep the lanzye intact, and according to the crackpot laws of this godforsaken planet, they could only make sure it wasn't broken up by betrothing the heirs. When my mother died, the marriage automatically became legal.''

Cadiz shook her head as if to clear it. ''You're kidding!'' she said. ''A seal will? No wonder Sonny didn't tell me.'' She looked speculatively at Delanna. ''That's why you had all those meetings with Maggie and Jezabel Stenberg. But I still don't understand. If the will's the only reason you're married, why didn't you just stay in Grassedge and get a divorce?''

''Because if I did, I'd lose my mother's estate and Sonny would lose Milleflores. The estate can't be settled till Circuit Court comes, and in the meantime, I have to be in residence at Milleflores.''

''Boy, I hope that doesn't get out on the ham,'' Cadiz said, then murmured, so that Delanna barely caught it,

"Poor Sonny." In a louder voice she said, "I guess it's just as well Sonny didn't tell me. I would've been even madder."

"You've got no reason to be jealous," Delanna told her. "I don't want to be married to Sonny, and he doesn't want to be married to me."

"I wouldn't bet on that," Cadiz replied. "He's talked about you ever since I can remember. When I heard about it, I figured he'd finally talked you into coming back and marrying him."

"But I thought he was your boyfriend."

Cadiz looked sheepish. "Oh, that," she said. "He took me to the harvest-do last year."

"When B.T. wouldn't?" Delanna asked.

There was a tapping overhead on the canopy. They both jumped. Cleo dug herself farther down between Delanna's ankles. Cadiz popped the canopy.

"What happened?" Sonny demanded, towering over them. "Is something wrong with the solaris?"

"No, why?" Cadiz said blankly.

"Because the caravan's clear up in the next quadrant, that's why."

Delanna looked out at the gray-brown horizon. There was nothing to be seen of the caravan except Jay's rig. Jay leaned in the other side.

"We thought you got lost in the dust storm," Sonny said.

"Or killed each other," Jay added. "I didn't figure we'd find anything left except claw marks."

"We were talking," Delanna said.

"That's right," Cadiz chimed in. "Delanna was telling me about some interesting customs. They were so interesting we just forgot to keep up."

Sonny and Jay looked bewildered.

"Well, I'm glad the solaris is okay," Jay said. "Delanna, how'd you like to come ride with me for a while? I got a bunk you can take a nap on."

"No, thank you," Delanna replied. "I think I'll ride with Cadiz."

"That's right," Cadiz said, smiling sweetly. "We have a lot to talk about."

7

Cadiz refused to relinquish the driver's seat to Sonny, so he climbed into the back, leaning forward with his chin on his knees so that he could see out the canopy and, no doubt, listen to them talk. But they were silent now. Cadiz occasionally glanced at Sonny and chuckled to herself, which would bring a scowl from Sonny, but no comment.

His gaze was focused intently on the distant horizon, light eyes with lashes that were almost sooty they were so thick, a hint of stubble along the set jaw and chin. Then something changed in his expression, and even though his eyes had not moved, Delanna knew his attention was on her. He leaned back slightly and smiled at her. Delanna felt herself flushing, and she quickly turned away.

"What?" Cadiz said, leaning forward to look around at Sonny. "Oh, she can smile. Honey, you should do that much more often. That ol' frown you been wearing all day makes you look like a prune."

Delanna stared out the window, letting the brown brush and occasional leafless trees blur past her eyes until she felt the heat of the blush fading. It doesn't matter what he looks like, she told herself sternly. All that matters is getting your inheritance and getting off this planet.

"More speed, Cadiz," Sonny directed.

Délanna risked a glance, and sighed gratefully at realizing his attention was once again focused on the horizon.

"There *is* no more speed. It's wide open," Cadiz said.

"But you're dropping behind again," Sonny told her.

"I can see that," Cadiz answered. She was looking at the gauges on the dashboard. "Sucking sunbeams out of the battery too fast. I better call Jay."

"Not yet," Sonny said as he reached forward and flipped a rocker switch back and forth.

"I already had solar direct on," Cadiz said, sounding annoyed.

But Sonny wasn't listening. He was squeezing between the seats to put his hands on the shaft that ran through the middle of the floor. "Try downshifting. This gear shaft is hot."

Delanna watched Cadiz push a lever on the steering pod with her thumb, and the solaris lurched a bit. The motor whined louder, even though the solaris had slowed some more.

They followed a path of crushed grass over and around gently rolling hills that cut them off from seeing the rest of the caravan ever more frequently as time passed.

"Pull up, Cadiz. This shaft is getting hotter."

"I better call Jay," Cadiz said. "Can't even see the high flag anymore."

"Let me try opening the chassis first and getting some air cooling underneath."

Cadiz sighed, but she halted the solaris. Sonny popped the latches on the canopy, got out and undid more latches on the chassis, then raised it so that it was open a few inches all around. When he got back in and refastened the canopy, Cadiz had to stretch to see over the raised top. They made it up over a big hill, safely down the other side, and were halfway up the next hill.

"What's that smell?" Delanna asked, suddenly realizing

there was a new acridity in the dry and dusty air.

"A motor," Sonny said glumly.

"Or maybe both of them," Cadiz said. "Can I call Jay now?"

"Call, and stop the damn motors. You're burning them up."

"I'm burning them up?" Cadiz said. "You're the one who didn't want me to stop half an hour ago."

Sonny just shook his head.

"I guess he thought downshifting and opening the chassis would help," Delanna said.

Sonny nodded slightly and reached past her to flip the latch on the overhead. When Cadiz brought the solaris to a halt, he pushed it up and stepped over Delanna to get out. He threw his hat down on the ground, then crawled under the solaris.

"Jay, you listening up?" Cadiz was saying into the mike.

"Yes, I'm listening." They heard Jay's voice through both sides of the stereo speakers. "How far back are you? You gals get to talking again?"

"We've got a problem here, Jay," Cadiz said. "We're sucking sunshine as fast as we can get it in and our drive shaft is hot."

"Number-one motor's froze up," Sonny said as he climbed out from underneath the solaris. He was looking up at the sky, Delanna thought primarily at the sun just above the western horizon. He shook his head. "I just had it fixed in Grassedge."

"And we've lost the number-one motor," Cadiz added into the mike.

They heard Jay whistle. "Stay put," he directed. "I'll be back to give you a tow."

Sonny rearranged the solar panel so that it was perpendicular to the sun, then stood with his hands in his pockets, leaning on the solaris. Cadiz climbed out, and Delanna followed her, carrying Cleo, grateful for the opportunity to stretch her legs.

Delanna breathed deeply. Without the rest of the caravan around to stir up the dust, the air was almost sweet, though a bit hot and dry. The grass beneath her feet was brittle and broke with a crunch with every step she took. Behind them, the gently rolling hills were brown; no trace of the green, irrigated fields she'd seen from the train window yesterday.

For want of something to do, she started to walk on the crushed grass to the top of the hill, but her highup heels were too awkward to get that far. Sitting down where she was, she looked back at the solaris. Its slender body was tapered to cut into the wind, the wheels swept back on delta struts, its overall appearance something like a flying insect at rest. Even the wagon it pulled had some aerodynamic considerations, long, slender, and tapered. Sonny must have pulled the tarp off of it, for the geese were poking their bills out from behind the bars. Had anyone fed them? she suddenly wondered. Reluctantly, she got up and started back to check on them, taking Cleo with her. After she'd fed the geese, she stuck her in the grain sack.

When Jay appeared in his big caravan outfitter, the two men made short work of attaching a tow bar to the little solaris. All of them climbed into the cab of the outfitter with Jay. Even with four, it was roomy enough to stretch out. Jay took cups from a compartment and pulled a spigot down from a ceiling panel, filling their cups with one hand and steering with the other. Plain water, but icy cold and very refreshing. Delanna drank all of it down, and he filled her cup again.

"Do you have a spare motor?" Jay asked Sonny.

"Won't help," he replied glumly.

"Something's making the drive shaft hot," Delanna explained. "Replacing the motor won't help unless Sonny can find whatever it is that's making the transmission work so hard. Another motor would just burn out."

"You going to be able to fix it?" Jay asked.

"Gonna try," Sonny said, but Delanna thought he sounded doubtful.

114

They had just topped another hill, and Delanna saw a startling change in the terrain before her. The gentle hills ended abruptly in a rock outcropping overlooking a flat pan of dry, baked dirt broken only by a serpentine line of low, dusty green shrubs that could not hide the sparkle of running water. The rest of the caravan had stopped near the creek, all the solarises with their solar panels perpendicular on masts, looking like lizards lined up to take in the last of the day's sunshine.

Jay stopped at the end of the line and got out to help Sonny unhitch the wagon, and then the solaris. (Cadiz and Delanna climbed down and watched them.) As soon as the solaris was unhitched, Jay got back in his rig and drove up to the head of the line and parked. Sonny pulled up the chassis the rest of the way and his torso disappeared under the solaris.

"Gonna be a long trip," Cadiz said, stretching.

"How far is it to the inn?" Delanna asked.

"Inn?" Cadiz looked puzzled. "What inn?"

"The one where we're going to stay tonight." The water Jay had given them had satisfied Delanna's thirst, but she was dusty and still very tired. A bath would be very welcome right now.

"Oh, you mean the campzye. Sun will be down in an hour, so I guess this is it for the night." Cadiz cocked an eye at her. "Sonny didn't tell you that we'd be camping until we got home?"

"No," Delanna said. "He didn't mention that. I naturally assumed . . ."

"You gotta stop assuming, honey. This is Keramos."

"I haven't forgotten," Delanna said. "Do we at least have a tent?"

"I think all Sonny has is a one-person cocoon. Two can use it in a pinch." Cadiz giggled. "B.T. has a cocoon, too. I forgot mine when he and I went up to check the east blossom set last spring."

Delanna looked at her with interest.

But Cadiz just shrugged. "B.T. gave me his cocoon, and I scooted over as far to one side as I could." She stopped and frowned. "In the morning I was still scooted over and B.T. was still outside. The Tanners can be so damn noble."

"Wish I had known that last night," Delanna remarked. "I might have been able to get some sleep."

"Don't tell me you were worried about Sonny," Cadiz said, and then laughed because Delanna didn't deny it. Suddenly she sobered. "Then again, if I was you, I'd have reason to worry." She smiled. "Maybe then we'd see if B.T. is still just a friend."

"What is this, Cadiz?" Delanna asked. "You can't get B.T. to notice you, so you try to get Sonny's attention in hopes that B.T. will get jealous?"

"Why would I care what B.T. thinks?" Cadiz said sullenly. "He's just a friend. At least, that's what he tells me and everyone else on Keramos."

"It's a better start than some," Delanna said.

"Like your marriage, you mean," Cadiz said.

"It's not a marriage."

"Does Sonny feel that way, too?" Cadiz asked.

"Yes," Delanna said. "It's a business arrangement."

"You sure about that? He's spent a lot of years talking about you."

"I can't imagine Sonny talking about anyone, let alone me. Even if it were true, I can't imagine why."

"Well, I guess it's not quite true he talked about you. He talked about the little girl he remembered you as, always curious about what he was doing, following him around all the time. He can talk, Sonny Tanner can, but it takes a bit of ambrosia to loosen his tongue."

"I did follow him around a lot. I remember that. And he was nice to me when I was a little girl. But that was then and this is now. We don't want the same things anymore."

"What do you want?"

"To get off this godforsaken planet and back to civilization where I can take a bath whenever I want to."

"There's a shower at Milleflores," Cadiz said kindly.

"Thanks, but that's hardly enough to make me want to stay. It's the horrible customs, the primitive laws. I'm married to a man I don't even know. Did anyone ever stop to think that maybe I regard marriage as something sacred and personal when they made these laws?"

"Did you ever stop to think maybe Sonny does, too? That maybe all of us do?"

"All Sonny cares about is his precious lanzye and his crop."

"It takes an unconditional commitment," Cadiz said. "He knows that."

And Sonny Tanner sure had that—for his land and crop. Frustrated, Delanna shook her head. Cleo poked her nose out from under her jeweled scales.

"It's moving," Cadiz said, scooting away from Delanna. "Your bug is moving."

Cleo isn't a bug, Delanna wanted to say, but she was too tired to argue. She turned away from Cadiz. Sonny still had his torso under the chassis of the solaris, and she couldn't see Jay anywhere among the line of solarises.

The scarab had climbed out of Delanna's arms and was headed toward the creek. Delanna snatched her up. "You're traveling incognito, Cleo," she said. "You can't go down there."

Cleo struggled against her, all of her forelegs flailing, trying to get down. She obviously wanted some exercise, after being cooped up all day in the the solaris and the geese's cage, but Delanna couldn't risk anybody seeing her. They'd immediately broadcast it on the ham, and Doc Lyle would show up again.

"Just a minute," Delanna said and got her carryit out of the back of the solaris. "This is just till we're past the caravan," she told Cleo as she stuffed her inside and shut it. "Then I'll let you out." She started up the row of standing solarises. She stopped when she thought she saw Jay ahead, but it was another man, and he was frowning at her.

"Haven't you got anything better to do than to cast your shadow on my solar panel?" the man said.

"She don't know no better," said his companion, the red-faced man she'd seen this morning. "She's Sonny Tanner's new wife." He grinned at Delanna. "When you stand in front of the solar collectors, they can't charge up, little lady. They've got to have sun."

"Sorry," Delanna said, and moved out of the way.

"Going somewhere?" the first man said, grinning now, too. He pointed at the carryit.

"For a walk," she said, and was instantly sorry. She could hear them on the ham tomorrow. *You should have seen her. Can't even go for a walk without taking her luggage along.*

"So, how's married life?" the red-faced man asked.

Delanna ignored him and walked rapidly down the line of solarises and over to the creek. She looked back to make sure no one was watching, especially the two men who'd spoken to her, and then let Cleo out of the carryit.

The scarab scuttled out onto a flat rock and extended her forelegs. Delanna sat down next to her and pulled off her shoes. The water was cool, running swiftly over her toes. She splashed some on her arms, and the coolness felt wonderful. Cleo, however, disengaged, scrambling up over Delanna's neck, down her back and onto the bank where she stood watching her mistress.

"What's the matter, Cleo?" she asked, for the scarab usually liked water as long as it wasn't too cold. However, Cleo had never encountered water in a creek before, only in nice calm pools with stone steps and railings she could hold onto. Come to think of it, Delanna realized, she herself hadn't encountered running water since she was a little girl on Keramos. She remembered she hadn't needed railings and marble steps back then, so she didn't need them now.

Delanna stepped out a little farther, letting the water creep up over the baggy pants. The water was the color of tea, and not muddy except where her feet stirred the bottom.

She stepped out still farther, debating whether to take off her clothes. She looked back toward the caravan. The man who'd told her to stop blocking his solar collector was watching. So was a woman she took to be his wife, and at least a half dozen other people.

"Never seen anybody take a bath," she muttered. "Probably they only wash twice a year."

She wasn't about to give them a show by taking off her clothes, and her clothes could probably benefit from a bath as much as she would. She waded out farther, letting the baggy pants drag in the water, which already felt warmer. When she was hip deep and already in the middle of the creek, she held her nose and dunked herself. The current grabbed her and pulled her along the rocky bottom, tumbling over onto her back. She let go of her nose to right herself, banged into a rock and gasped in fright.

She came up sputtering, choking, a ghastly salt taste in her mouth and her eyes burning. From the bank, Cleo was shrieking, but Delanna couldn't open her eyes to see why. Her eyes stung like fire.

"Cleo . . ." she called to the scarab, and started coughing. Water ran down her face from her dripping hair and into her mouth. "I'm . . ." She choked again. "I'm coming."

"Delanna, what the hell are you doing in there?" she heard Sonny shout.

She pushed her hair back and groped for the bank, trying to get her eyes to open.

"Come out of there, Delanna!" Sonny yelled.

She squinted her eyes open against the terrible burning. He was a blur on the edge of the bank, a blur with a jewel in his hand. He was talking to the jewel.

"It's okay, Cleo," he said. "She's not hurt . . . Are you?"

Dumbly, Delanna shook her head, too proud to tell him how badly she'd banged her elbow on the rock. She struggled toward shore, making progress but feeling incredibly clumsy and stupid now that someone was watching her.

Cleo reached out for her, extending one foreleg to grab the wet flowered shirt, but she let go instantly. She wiped her claw on Sonny's shirt, whining as she always did when she encountered something unpleasant.

"That's a salt creek," Sonny said.

"I found out," Delanna said.

"That salt's going to make you real itchy," he added.

"Great. I wasn't miserable enough just being dusty." She reached for Cleo, but the scarab scurried around to the back of Sonny's neck. "Traitor," she muttered, and whirled around and stalked down the creek, furious with them all.

It wasn't just the salt. It was that man being so snippy about his precious sunshine and the red-faced man being so condescending, and it was Cadiz, talking about Keramos and Sonny as if Delanna had no right to be mad, and what business did a wretched creek have being full of salt smack in the middle of a continent? Her mother was right about Keramos. It *was* a godforsaken planet.

She stubbed her toe and stopped because the pain was too great to take another step. And just where did she think she was going, anyhow? Back to Last Chance? Fat chance. It would take days of walking. She looked back. Sonny was still standing at the creek's edge, watching her. He was holding the carryit; he must have put Cleo in it. She glanced over at the camp; everyone else was watching her, too, a few of them standing on their solarises to get a better view. Great! As if she didn't have enough notoriety already, she'd also sound like a complete fool when this got on the ham.

"Haven't you ever made a stupid mistake?" she shouted at them, her hands defiantly on her hips.

They were probably too far away to hear her clearly, but whether it was her posture or they just got bored, the gawkers drifted back to whatever they had been doing before. She looked back at Sonny. He glanced down at his boots, then turned to walk back to the camp with the carryit. Delanna slipped her hands into her wet pockets and pretended to stare at the brilliant golds and reds in the western sky as the ball of gold started to slip below the horizon; then she started to walk back to camp.

Sonny was back under the chassis and Jay squatting on his heels next to the solaris when she got back. Cadiz had a fire going, and Cleo was apparently back in the geese's cage. There were wild honks emanating from it. Delanna grabbed a brush from her carryit, and sat down by the fire. Cadiz had a pot of something hanging over the fire and she was stirring it with a long-handled spoon.

"Did you enjoy your bath?" Cadiz asked, grinning from ear to ear. "Boy, I wish I'd been there when you figured out what you were swimming in."

"You could have warned me, Cadiz." The salt on Delanna's arms and legs had already dried into white rime, and the flowered shirt and baggy pants felt sticky.

"Truth is, no one thinks like a been-to except maybe another been-to, which I definitely am not," Cadiz said, pulling the spoon out of the pot to take a sip. "Needs salt," she said. "Why don't you just jump in?" She started to laugh. "No, that'd make it too salty. How about just sticking your head in?" She went off into gales of laughter.

Delanna ignored her and continued grimly trying to pull the hairbrush through the sticky tangles.

Jay got up from whatever he was doing by the solaris and came over to her.

"I have a sonic cleaner in my rig," he said. "You're welcome to use it."

"Oh, that sounds—"

"We've got water she can use to clean up," Sonny said, cutting Delanna off as he appeared out of the darkness behind Jay.

Water sounded even better than a sonic. Delanna was about to say so, when Cadiz asked, "*What* water? Our drinking water?"

"She's my wife," Sonny said, not to Cadiz but to Jay. "She doesn't need your sonic."

"I'd love to use your sonic," Delanna said, glaring at Sonny. "Thank you for offering, Jay. Cadiz, do you have some clothes you can loan me?"

"Yeah," Cadiz said warily. She handed Sonny the stirring spoon and began poking through the sack she'd brought.

With a frown, Sonny stuck the spoon in the pot and stirred. Broth slopped over the edges and sizzled in the fire.

"Stir, Sonny. Don't whip it," Cadiz said without looking up. A second later she handed Delanna a bundle of clothing.

"Thanks," Delanna told her, and turned toward Jay's rig. "This is so nice of you," she said to Jay, fully aware that Sonny and Cadiz were listening. "I couldn't stand going all the way to the lanzye caked with salt. It isn't really five thousand miles, is it?"

"More like four thousand five hundred now," he replied. Even though the sun had set, Jay walked behind the solarises with their raised sails. Or perhaps he'd chosen the way that was least lighted by campfires.

Four thousand five hundred. They'd only come five hundred miles today. "It will take us ten days at this rate," Delanna said, feeling almost as discouraged as she had in the morning.

"More like twenty. We can only make half that in the Flats. If it doesn't rain."

He stopped, his foot poised on a rock, his hand extended to help her up a series of ledges to the top of a flat, rocky outcropping where his rig was parked. The rocks were bone-dry.

"Rain?" Delanna repeated incredulously, taking his hand so she could test the ledge surface before she put her full weight onto her bare feet. "It's hard to believe it ever rains out here."

"We got word on the ham of a big line of storms east

of here. Look out there,'' he said, pointing to the east as she stepped up onto the narrow ledge. ''Can you see it?''

As she turned and teetered a bit, Jay let go of her hand and grabbed her hips to steady her. Delanna looked where he'd pointed. The sky was a pale pink, the stars already coming out overhead. Near the horizon was a line of darker pink. She had noticed it on their walk through the caravan and hoped it might be the mountains where the lanzyes nestled.

''See that line of cloud there?'' Jay said, finally stepping up onto the ledge with her. ''It's raining out there, which means trouble on the flats.''

''Why?'' she said. He still hadn't let go of her hips. ''Is it the mud?''

He laughed. ''I wish mud was all we had to deal with. No. That whole plain out there is underlaid with salt rock. When it rains, the water washes out all kinds of crevasses and sinks that you can bury a solaris in. We have to take soundings and run subsurface erosion checks, and it slows us down. I hoped we could get north of it, but it doesn't look like it.''

''No,'' she said, looking at the narrow line of cloud. It was red now, the sky above it a pinkish-orange. Two stars stood out, close together, pale against the bright color.

''The sky's beautiful, isn't it?'' Jay said, leaning closer.

''Yes,'' she agreed. She turned so she was facing west, pulling away as she did so. ''Look at that sunset!'' She moved to the far lip of the ledge. ''What's that?'' she asked, pointing at a dark smudge far behind them. ''Is that a storm, too?''

''No.'' He came up beside her and put his hand on her shoulder. ''It's only a fire. Probably one the damn fire monkeys set.''

''The fire monkeys?'' she said, thinking of what Cadiz had said about them setting fire to her hair. ''They're dangerous, aren't they?''

''They're a *damned* nuisance, stealing settlers' wood,

starting fires. Someday they'll start a brush fire and burn up the Flats all the way to the lanzyes." His hand slid across her shoulder. "They don't come out this far. Delanna . . ."

There was nowhere to go except off the ledge. "Why do they start the fires?" she asked hastily.

"They're reptiles. Cold-blooded. They start the fires at night to keep their body temperature up." His arm tightened around her. "You don't have to worry about fire monkeys or anything else when I'm around, Delanna."

Except you, Delanna thought, remembering Cadiz's story about Miller's bride and the Spellegny twins. She scratched at her arm. "I'd better go have that shower before I itch to death," she said, and clambered up to the next ledge.

"You're right." Jay scrambled past her and then turned to help her up the last few feet. He opened the door to the rig and stepped back to let her enter before him. She climbed up, and Jay followed her. "A relaxing sonic," he said, waving his hand toward a curtained corner of the rig, "dinner, a little ambrosia . . ."

She had told Cadiz she could take care of herself, but now she wondered. Jay's rig was small but luxurious, with not only a sonic, but a chemical cleaner for clothes and dishes, a cooking unit, and a real bed. And it was obviously designed for seducing settlers' wives. The bed filled almost the whole interior. It was covered with bright red fur. Delanna wondered if it was from fire monkeys. A small table with built-in decanters was pulled up cozily next to it. A relaxing sonic, a little ambrosia . . .

"You can throw your clothes in the chemical cleaner. Just flip the rocker," Jay said, edging around the bed to a cupboard. "Cadiz's clothes are going to be too small for you." He tossed a robe to her. "You can wear this till your clothes come out."

He went over to the terminal that was built into the wall opposite the sonic, sat down, and switched it on. "I'll check out that storm and then see about dinner," he said, pushing icons. The screen washed with color, but the configuration didn't look anything like a map.

Delanna, holding the robe and Cadiz's bundle of clothes against her as if she'd already undressed, went over to the sonic closet. She pulled the curtain across. It was made of clear plastic. *I'll just check out the storm.* Right, she thought, and wondered how many other dusty women he'd invited in for a *relaxing sonic and some ambrosia.* Both Spellegny twins? Lizabeth Infante?

She pushed the curtain back. "Jay, I think—" she started.

He turned around. "You want a little privacy?" he asked, smiling sardonically at her. "Hang on a minute, and I'll go make the rounds." He turned back to the terminal. "I just got this new program, supposed to interpret soundings, and I can't even get it to tell me how far away this line of storms is." He pushed a few icons, frowned, and shook his head. Then, with a sigh he stood up and went over to the door. "I'll be back in half an hour." He pointed at the keypad by the door. "You can lock yourself in if you want," he told her, and winked. "I'll be back."

"That won't—" Delanna began, but he'd already gone out. She stood glaring at the door. The men on this planet were so maddening. Sonny saw her as a piece of property, Jay as another conquest, and worse, one he was completely confident of. *I'll be back.*

She stomped over to the door and hit the lock, and then went back to the sonic closet and began taking off her clothes. She stepped inside, pulled the curtain closed, and put on the sonic mitts.

She switched on the power pack and started with her hair. Warm air rushed in from above as she rubbed her scalp. It wasn't water, but it was better than nothing, and a nice touch for what really amounted to nothing more than a portable unit. She scrubbed the salt crust off and then rubbed her skin until it glowed pink and she felt clean, even if not refreshed. When she was done, she hung up the mitts and looked doubtfully at the clothes Cadiz had given her. Jay was right; Cadiz was a lot smaller than Delanna, but, she realized as she picked up the underwear, he hadn't counted on Cadiz selecting so well. The underpants and chemise stretched easily, and the skirt was a wraparound, a little short but serviceable. The top stretched over her, too, a bit more snug than Delanna liked, but not that uncomfortable. Cadiz had stuck a hairbrush in with the clothes. Delanna brushed her hair and then stepped out of the closet, threw her dirty things into the chemical tub, and set the dial for clothing.

She looked around for somewhere to sit. There was nothing but the bed and the stool in front of the terminal. Delanna edged back around the bed and sat down at the terminal. Jay had gotten the map to come up. It was just a return beam display from a satellite, but Delanna could distinguish what must be the salt pan on the map, a dull gray circle in the middle of the continent, with a "handle" spiking to the north. She fingered the edge of the map for the touch panels, found them, and pressed the locator. A yellow dot flashed at the southwestern edge of the salt pan. She moved her fingers down to the alphanumerics and started spelling "lanzye." Another yellow dot flashed as soon as she touched the Z. They were about as far as Jay had said; which was not very far at all.

Disgusted, Delanna saved Jay's map in a window, and called up the false color image of the surface features with the satellite multispectral scans. Now she could see the ludicrously cool blue fireline obstructing the most direct path between the two yellow dots and the line of thunderstorms hanging like a curtain across the salt pan. Any other route and they'd need boats to get across those green inland seas. The salt pan was the only way.

She did a quick search of Jay's database for sounding data, found datapoints only three weeks old, and pulled that in to the data set she was working with. It showed a dotted line winding around the magenta pockmarks, apparently the most recent route through the eastern edge of the salt pan. The rest of the salt pan had washed saffron-yellow, indicating there was no data. The closest yellow dot was nothing more than a pale speck. Jay hadn't been kidding about the dangers. Delanna thought about taking a look at the subsurface images, but she should go see if her clothes were done. She released her queries and pulled Jay's map back out of the window.

"You look beautiful," Jay said.

Delanna twisted around on the stool. He was standing in the door, watching her. So much for locking the door, she thought. "If that's what that sonic can do, I got a bargain on this rig," he said.

Delanna stood up. "Thank you for letting me use it," she told him. "*And* the chemical cleaner." She gestured toward where her clothes were still spinning. "I feel much better."

"You *look* lovely." He started around the bed toward her. "Did you know your hair's even brighter than that sunset we just saw?"

"I really should be going," Delanna said, starting for the chemical cleaner. "My clothes should be nearly done."

He got there first. "Nope," he said with only a glance at the controls. "Another half hour at least. Plenty of time." He opened a wall panel above the chemical cleaner. "What would you like to drink? Ambrosia?"

"No, thank you," she said. "I don't like the taste."

"Some monkey juice, then." He pulled out a ceramic cup and poured a clear liquid into it from a large blue enameled jar. He handed it to her and reached down a second cup.

"Monkey juice?" Delanna said, peering doubtfully into the cup.

"It's a sparkling mineral water with a touch of fruit flavor added," he told her, pouring a cupful for himself. "It's called monkey juice because the fire monkeys live around the hot springs in the winter, not because there's ground-up monkey in it."

Delanna took a dubious sip. It might have come out of

a hot spring but it was cool, and she hadn't realized how thirsty all that salt water she'd swallowed had made her. She drained the cup and held it out for more. "It tastes like roses," she said.

He poured her a second cupful, putting his hand around hers to steady the cup. "And you look like a rose," he said, his eyes meeting hers. He touched his cup to hers. "Here's to roses and sunsets and romantic dinners . . ." He leaned toward her. "And to whatever comes after them . . ."

"Speaking of dinner," Sonny said.

Delanna whirled around. He was leaning against the doorjamb.

"It's about ready," he said. "Dinner, I mean." He shrugged at Jay. "The door was open. Come on, Delanna."

"I'm not ready to come," she said. "I'm waiting for my clothes to finish."

"You can come back for them after dinner," Sonny said cheerfully. "Or Jay can bring them over when they're done. Isn't that right, Jay?"

Delanna looked at Jay, expecting him to say, I've invited Delanna to dinner, but instead he nodded and said, "Sure. I'll bring them over later."

"Great," Sonny said. "Come on, Delanna."

"I prefer to wait till they're done," Delanna told him.

"Oh, okay," Sonny said, still cheerfully. He came away from the door and sat down on the bed.

"There's no need for you to wait," she said frostily. "I can find my way back perfectly well."

"That's okay," he said. "I'd hate to have my wife fall in the creek again."

"I am *not* your—" Delanna began, outraged.

"I think I'd better go see what that storm's doing," Jay cut in, and sidled out the door.

"I'm *not* your wife," Delanna finished as soon as he was gone. "And you had no right to come after me."

Sonny stood up. "The law says you're my wife," he

said, "and everybody on this caravan thinks you are. What do you think they're saying about your coming up here alone with Madog? He's seduced every unmarried woman on Keramos and half the married ones. He's a fast talker, Delanna. I don't want you falling for . . ."

"I don't need your advice or your protection," Delanna said. "Jay's invited me to dinner, and I intend to stay."

"Fine," Sonny said, and sat back down on the bed. "Then I'm staying, too." He grabbed a pillow, plumped it up, and leaned back against it.

"You—" Delanna glared at him, so angry she couldn't even speak. But then she did and said the first thing that came to mind. "You are leaving right *now*."

He put his hands behind his head. "When we get to our lanzye, you can act any way you want," he said, "but till we do, I won't let you be the laughingstock of the ham. And I won't let you make me a laughingstock either."

Jay came back in, looking wary.

"Delanna says you invited me and my new bride to dinner," Sonny said. "That's mighty nice of you. How's the storm?"

There was a knock at the door. Jay opened it.

"Why is it you can never get anybody to the table when dinner's ready?" Cadiz said. She came in, lugging the pot of stew. She looked pointedly at Sonny, lounging on the bed, and then at Delanna. "Since I couldn't get *any*body to come to dinner, I decided to bring it to you."

"Great," Sonny said. He got up off the bed. "I'll help you set the table." He took the pot from her and set it on the little table. It completely covered it. He started opening wall panels.

"Nice rig, Madog," Cadiz said, looking around appreciatively. "How come you've never invited me over to take a sonic? Have you seen that line of storms over there? How far north does it go?"

"Too far for us to go around it," Jay replied.

Sonny handed Jay a bowl of stew and a spoon. "How much will it slow us down?" he asked.

"A lot, if it's as big as I think it is. A couple of extra weeks maybe, if we don't have to go south to the bridge. A month if we have to."

I cannot stand a month more of this, Delanna thought. They were all sitting on the bed now, Cadiz cross-legged in the middle, eating stew and discussing the merits of giving up right now and going south to the bridge, whatever that was. Jay and Sonny both seemed to have completely forgotten about her.

"I've got a new program that's supposed to integrate the sounding data with satellite data and run probabilities to give us a route," Jay said, eating stew, "but the darn thing's too complicated. I can't even get it to give me a map that shows the storm." He handed his empty bowl to Cadiz and went over to the terminal. "Hey, the map's up." He sat down at the terminal. "The storm's not as big as I thought. Maybe we can go north around it after all."

Sonny went over and stood behind him, and Cadiz crawled across the bed to where she could see.

Delanna was still so furious with all of them, she could scarcely speak, but she wanted another look at the map. If the storm was small enough to go around, it mean that much less time she'd have to spend with all of them. She went around the bed and stood on Jay's other side.

"Is that the storm's position now?" Cadiz asked, kneeling on the bed and leaning on Jay's shoulders.

"Yes," he said. It's a direct satellite feed." He frowned at the keyboard. "I'm trying to get an inset-enlarge, but I can't . . ." He punched two icons, and the map froze.

"Push the OPEN WINDOW icon," Delanna said.

Jay looked at her as if he'd never seen her before.

"For a grid," she said. "Push the OPEN WINDOW icon and then feed in the coordinates for an inset-enlarge and touch ZOOM."

Now they were all looking at her as if she'd suddenly turned bright green.

"You know how to work this program?" Jay asked incredulously.

"Of course," Delanna said, frowning in surprise. "This is just a simple stats integration and interpretation program. Push the OPEN WINDOW icon," she said again.

He did, and a numbered grid appeared on the map. He ran his finger along the lines and then fed in the coordinates, and touched ZOOM. The map zoomed in on the section.

The storm covered nearly the whole section he'd enlarged, but Sonny pointed to the upper part of the screen and said, "Look at that. The cells aren't even connected."

"Can you get a density reading on the clouds?" Jay asked.

"Select the clouds, then push METRICS, and do an analysis selection," Delanna said, but Jay had stood up and was motioning her to his place in front of the terminal. She sat down and punched in the selections for a density reading.

"Look at that," Sonny said. "Point four five. Not enough for rain."

"We need the subsurface image," Jay said.

Delanna called up the menu and read the configuration for a subsurface density slicing. She brought up the image using the satellite data, superimposing it on the return-beam image. The salt pan looked more like cracked eggshells now, many of the cracks filled with green-imaged water, the directional flow indicated by rippling light. Delanna traced a thick green line with her finger and queried the vega for an interpretation.

"It's the underground river," Jay commented just as the terminal painted the answer. "That creek you jumped in runs underground until just a few miles from here. Looks to me like it's shifted again because of the lava flows."

Delanna could see the tendrils of lava spewing from east of the thunderstorms, crossing the main confluence of the rivers before it went underground. She was puzzled about how that could affect the underground flow of a river until she realized the water had been diverted into a region the computer was telling her was primarily gypsum and salt, both water soluble.

"We usually stay south of the salt pan," Cadiz explained, "but the fires are so big in the southeast that we either go through the salt pan or all the way to the bridge."

"No telling how far the river's bored through the salt and gypsum," Jay said. "At least, not from these images. I thought this was supposed to be such a great analysis tool, but this data's already two weeks old."

"It is?" Delanna said, for it looked like a live feed to her with its constant shifting.

Nodding, Jay reached past her to touch the date-source icon. She saw that he'd paid for a full database update from the satellite two weeks ago. Only the return-beam images were live, and free, she noticed, on the public broadcast. She'd been running the analysis programs the way she always had at school, where she was more familiar with the database content and sources. Now she turned on some basic status indicators so that she wouldn't be caught by surprise again. She froze the two-week-old density slicing data under the undulating return-beam image and frowned.

"If I had a good probablility tree, this program could show us how things probably look today," she mused aloud.

"There's a pretty good one in my database," Jay said. "If you can improve on that imaging, let's have a look."

It was a very good probability tree skeleton, which Delanna was able to trim to concentrate on the center of the salt pan. She zoomed in on the salt pan, set the underground river flowing into its probable path from two weeks ago, then added the thunderstorms.

"Give us an inset-enlargement of Spencer's Wagon," Sonny said, pointing to a gap of blue in an area of red elevation on the screen.

They kept her at it for over half an hour. A few minutes into it, Cadiz yawned, got off the bed, and said, "This has been a real romantic evening, Jay, but I've got to go." She picked up the pot and went out. The two men didn't even seem to notice.

"If the storm doesn't veer north tonight, I think we can go through at Spencer's Wagon," Jay said finally. "Delanna, can you feed in the soundings?"

She consulted the menu again and asked for the instructions. "Yes."

"Good. I'll send Nagle and Pierce up tonight to take preliminaries and we'll start for Spencer's Wagon in the morning. Thanks, Delanna."

She looked at him. "Are we done?"

"For tonight," he said. "I'll need you again tomorrow to feed in the preliminaries. I've got to go talk to Nagle and Pierce."

He left. Delanna switched off the terminal and sat there staring at the blank screen. Here's to roses and sunsets and romantic dinners, she thought. And what comes after.

"Ready?" Sonny asked. "Your clothes are bound to be done by now." He went over to the chemical cleaner and began pulling them out.

She tried to think of something devastating to say to him, failed, and walked out of the rig. It was completely dark outside, the stars fully out and Keramos' moons a third of the way up the sky. The storm stood like a black wall against the horizon. It looked closer than it had before, and as Delanna watched, lightning flickered and the middle part of the line lit up.

She started down the rocks, wishing she'd brought a light, skidded, and nearly fell.

"Steady there," Sonny said, catching her arm.

She shook his hand off angrily. "I don't need your help," she snapped. "I can take care of myself."

"Fine," he said. He dumped the load of clothes in her arms, jumped down the ledges, and disappeared.

"And I'm *not* your wife," she shouted after him.

They started for Spencer's Wagon as soon as the sun was up high enough to trickle-charge the solaris batteries. It was already hot, and there was a muggy, oppressive feel to the air. Cadiz switched on the air conditioner, but Sonny made her turn it off.

"The motor's still not fixed," he told her. "I don't want any extra strain put on it."

He had worked on the motor all night. He'd already been underneath the solaris when Delanna got back to their camp, with Cadiz holding a lantern for him. "My, what a romantic evening!" Cadiz said when Delanna stepped into camp. "Soundings and grids and undergrounds!" She clasped her hands together dramatically.

"Hold the lantern still, Cadiz," Sonny directed from under the solaris.

"I wish Madog would ask *me* to run a probability program," Cadiz said.

Delanna had ignored her and crawled in the solaris with Cleo and gone to sleep. When Cadiz woke her up, saying brightly, "I thought you might want to take another dip in the creek before we leave," Sonny was still at it.

He'd obviously fixed it enough that the solaris was able

to keep up with the rest of the caravan, but Delanna could hear the transmission catching every time they went up a rise, and Sonny bent tensely over the telemetry, checking the solar current, motor current and speed, and didn't respond to Cadiz's questions.

Cadiz switched the ham on, which apparently didn't run off the motor after all, since Sonny didn't tell her to turn it off, and began twisting the dial, trying to find a strong signal.

". . . so Sonny hauls her out, and she's dripping with salt water and spluttering like a hen in a rainstorm, and he says, 'What in the hell were you doing?' and *she* says, 'I wanted a bath!' Can you believe that? 'I wanted a bath!' "

"Turn that off, Cadiz," Sonny said.

"I'm trying to get sat-relay and see what they have to say about the storm," she said, turning the dial.

". . . cooking supper, and the next thing you know, she's in up to her ears. All that money to send her to some fancy school, and she doesn't even know enough to stay out of a salt creek. So Tom says—"

"That's Far Reach," Sonny said.

"I know." Cadiz was grinning. "News travels fast, doesn't it?" She inched the dial farther to the right.

"—nearly drowned—"

"—told Edgar, Sonny Tanner's got no business marrying a been-to. They've got no more sense than—"

"—swallowed enough salt to season a—"

Cadiz went all the way across the dial and back again, switching as soon as she'd identified the speaker or when Sonny said warningly, "Cadiz!" but it made no difference. It was on every band.

In assorted versions. She had tripped over her highups and fallen in. She had dived in headfirst. Sonny had dived in to save her. Cadiz had dived in to save her. It had taken six men to pull her out. Sonny had had to give her mouth-to-mouth resuscitation.

There was only one mention of her cleaning up in Jay's sonic.

"She knew better than to go to Madog's rig alone, didn't she?" a woman's voice cut in, sounding pleasantly shocked.

"I told you, she's a been-to," the other voice, also a woman's, said in a tone that clearly indicated a been-to wouldn't know better. "But Sonny wouldn't let her. He went with her. Sonny Tanner would never leave his wife alone with Madog like Emil Vanderson did."

The speaker then went off on a highly detailed story involving Emil Vanderson's wife and Jay and a haystack. Delanna sank down in the back seat, praying for a sunspot to cut out the signal, and plotting ways to kill Cadiz.

I won't let you be the laughingstock of the ham, Sonny had said. Well, she obviously was, but at least they weren't talking about her taking a sonic in Jay's rig. It wouldn't have mattered what really happened. These yokels were obviously capable of inventing any fact they didn't know. And blabbing it across the whole planet. She should be grateful that all they were saying about her was that she'd tried to take a bath in salt.

And Sonny was no doubt sitting up there in the front seat waiting to say, I told you so, waiting for her to thank him for protecting her reputation from a bunch of small-minded busybodies, waiting for her to say, You're right. I can't take care of myself. Thank you for saving me from a fate worse than death. *The smug, self-righteous—*

" 'You can't go swimming in there,' Sonny says," the first woman gossiped, "But does she listen to him? No. She takes off those fancy clothes of hers and—"

"Turn that off, Cadiz," Sonny said sharply. "I want to listen to the motor."

"I was just trying to find out about the storm," Cadiz protested, but she switched it off.

They both listened to the motor, which did sound uneven, for a minute, and then Sonny said, "Sorry, Delanna.

The settlers don't have much to do this time of year, and most of them live hundreds of miles away from each other. The ham's their only entertainment.''

He sounded genuinely apologetic, which had the effect of making Delanna even angrier.

Smug, condescending . . . she fumed inwardly. I am phoning Maggie Barlow when we get to Spencer's Wagon, and telling her I don't care about the inheritance. I want her to get me off this planet now! Signing an indentured servitude contract on the *Scoville* would be better than this.

She twisted around in the cramped back seat so she could see out the side window, and searched the horizon for signs of civilization, but there weren't any, and when Sonny pulled the solaris in alongside the rig ahead of it and parked, there still weren't.

The place they stopped looked exactly like the place they'd stopped yesterday, except it was hotter and there was no creek. There were no signs of life except for a thicket of dead-looking bushes a hundred meters off to the left.

''Nothing for you to fall into around here,'' Cadiz observed. She sauntered off to look at the storm still flickering on the horizon, and Sonny lifted up the solaris's chassis.

Delanna climbed out and went around to the front of the solaris to ask him how long before they'd reach Spencer's Wagon, but he had already disappeared underneath the vehicle. She fed Cleo and then got back in the front seat, determined not to do anything the local yokels could discuss on the ham.

Jay came up, bent over the solaris, and shouted to Sonny, ''Nagle and Pierce just got back. I'm taking Delanna up to my rig to feed in the preliminaries.''

Sonny muttered something that sounded like, ''Fine,'' and Jay took Delanna's arm and led her up to the front of the caravan. ''You look even more beautiful this morning than you did last night,'' he said.

''Thank you,'' she replied stiffly, angry with him for asking Sonny for permission to take her. They both treated her like property, and Sonny apparently no longer cared if she was talked about on the ham, since he'd made no move to follow them but had just let Jay walk off with her in full view of the whole caravan. "How far from here is Spencer's Wagon?" she asked.

"About forty miles and then another half a mile," he said, pointing over to where Cadiz and half the caravan were standing watching the storm. "Straight down."

"*Down?*"

"Yep. There are a lot of big sinks in through here. Rick Spencer lost a wagon down one of them a couple of years ago."

Spencer's wagon, Delanna thought. I should have known. "Are there any towns from here on?"

"Afraid not. But we'll be over this stretch and on our way to the panhandle in no time if this program does what it's supposed to," he said, opening the door to his rig.

He sat Delanna down in front of the terminal, handed her the preliminaries, and then squatted next to her, his cheek very close to hers as she fed in the data.

"Beautiful," Jay murmured into her ear as the picture started to take shape, but she couldn't tell whether he meant her or the picture.

She was hampered by the alphanumeric-only keyboard, so setting up the data dumps from the soundings data took longer than she would have expected. But finally she was able to fix last night's soundings data into something the probability process knew how to use, and the false color images began to wash over the screen.

"Beautiful," Jay murmured again, his lips almost brushing her cheek.

"Hi," Cadiz said. "I forgot my spoon." She came in, glancing at Delanna. "From the stew last night. I must have left it here."

"Your spoon?" Jay said blankly.

"Yeah. It must be here somewhere," she said, but instead of looking around, she came over to the terminal. "So how's it going?"

It was such a transparent excuse and Cadiz looked so irritated at being there that it was obvious Sonny had sent her. So, Delanna thought, he still cares about not letting me become another story on the ham about Jay's exploits. She felt obscurely pleased.

"It's going fine," Jay replied. "The seepage isn't bad so far." He pointed to the false color image on the screen. "I think we can cut across here," he said, tracing a path with his finger. "If *this* section holds." He pointed to a still unfilled-in section.

Delanna punched in the rest of the preliminaries and asked the computer to forecast the satellite density slicings. The picture shifted, showing the most probable multisensor readings, but the section Jay had pointed at stayed blank.

"I'll have to send Pierce and Nagle out again," he said, scribbling down the coordinates. "And I'd better send out a team to see how wide this is," he added, pointing at the narrowest part of the route he'd traced. "Delanna, you can stay here if you want, but it'll be several hours. Cadiz, you want to take her back to camp?"

"I can find—" Delanna began, but Jay had already left. "I can find my way back to camp by myself," she said to Cadiz instead.

"Sonny doesn't want you falling in any sinks," Cadiz told her. She waited while Delanna printed out a copy of the map and then went outside with her.

"Where are these sinks I'm not supposed to fall into?" Delanna asked as they started back.

Cadiz pointed in the direction of the storm. "They don't start for about a half-mile past where we're camped. We're still on shale here. Just don't wander off ahead."

"Anything else you haven't told me about? Fire monkeys? Poisonous plants? Tar pits?"

Cadiz shook her head. "The fire monkeys have more sense than to come this far out on the flats." She pointed in the direction of the thicket. "There are reddsie bushes and some salt palms over there, but nothing poisonous." She fanned herself with her hand. "Boy, it's hot!"

It was. The air was so thick and muggy it felt like they were swimming through it. Delanna stopped and looked back at the storm. "I wish it would come our way and cool things down."

"Don't even say that," Cadiz warned, "unless you want to spend the next three weeks sitting here or go all the way south to the bridge." She stared at the storm. "Do you think it's getting closer?"

"No," Delanna said. It didn't look any higher on the horizon, but the clouds seemed sharper, more defined, and after they got back to camp she thought she heard a faint rumble of thunder.

Cadiz went off to look at the storm from the front of the caravan. Sonny was still under the solaris, and Cleo was under one of the panels, lying with all her legs extended in the shade.

"I let her out," Sonny said, sliding out on his back for a minute. "It was too hot in the solaris. She seems content now that she has some shade. I don't think she'll wander off. Did you get the preliminaries fed in?"

"Yes," Delanna told him, and was about to add sharply that she didn't need a chaperone, but he'd already slid back under the solaris.

Delanna got in the solaris, but it was like an oven. She got out, sat down next to Cleo, and fanned herself with Cadiz's hat. She leaned back against the side and tried to sleep, but it was too hot to do more than doze, and an outraged sound of squawking woke her up.

She went back to the geese's cage and found Cleo pestering them, poking one of her forelegs through the wire of the cage. One of the geese had laid an egg; it was under-sized, but Cleo wouldn't care. Scarabs tried to hatch any egg they could get their forelegs on. She was trying to fish it out.

"You naughty girl!" Delanna scolded and scooped Cleo up in her arms. "Somebody might see you!"

She took Cleo back to camp and deposited her in the shade under the solar collection panel with orders to stay there, then went back and watered the geese, putting the water in shallow dishes on all four sides of the cage so they wouldn't crowd together and suffocate. Then she went back and sat down next to the solaris again.

The afternoon wore on. She saw Jay walking her way and stood up, brushing the dust off Cadiz's skirt, but he stopped two camps away, talked to the man who had yelled at her for blocking the sun, and went off with him toward the front of the caravan again.

Delanna walked up to the front of the caravan, thinking movement might produce some evaporation and she'd feel cooler, but it didn't. The storm looked perhaps a little farther away, its clouds brilliantly white in the afternoon sun. There were more people watching it than there had been before, but she didn't see Cadiz.

She walked back to camp, thinking even a salt bath would feel refreshing, got a drink, and filled a bowl with water for Cleo. She set it down next to the solar panel, but Cleo wasn't there.

Delanna squatted down and peered under the solaris. Sonny blinked at her, his face dirty and streaked with sweat. "Is Cleo under there with you?" she asked.

"Nope," he said and went back to unscrewing something.

She straightened up and looked around, worried. What if Cleo had wandered into one of the other camps and someone had seen her? She started down the row of solarises, looking and trying not to look like she was looking.

The camps were totally still, everyone stretched out in the shade of the solaris panels or up on the ridge, watching the storm, no shrieks or shouts, which was a good sign, but it might just mean nobody'd seen the scarab yet.

"Cleo," she called softly leaning under a wagon.

"Cleo!" The scarab was too shy to have wandered off looking for people, but she might have gone looking for eggs. Tom Torricelli, three rigs down, had chickens they were taking home from Grassedge. Delanna started toward their pen.

Behind her, there was a terrified squawk from the geese's pen.

"Cleo!" she said disgustedly, and walked back to the wagons. Cleo wasn't there, but it was obvious she had just left. The geese were huddled in the far corner of their cage, honking out an hysterical tale of terror and persecution.

Delanna looked around at the other wagons near the pen, and then toward Sonny's solaris, but Cleo was nowhere in sight. Surely she wouldn't have wandered away from the camp, even though the geese were looking that way. The scarab was still so traumatized by Keramos and its inhabitants, she retracted at every strange sound, and if she had wandered out across the plain, Delanna would have been able to see her bright carapace easily against the pale dirt.

"Cleo!" she called, hoping she'd appear between two of the wagons.

Delanna put her hand up to shade her eyes and scanned the dusty landscape. There was nothing between the geese's cage and the dead-looking thicket a hundred yards away, not even a rock. Cleo obviously hadn't gone that way.

"Where did she go?" she said to the geese, and half-turned to see if the scarab had crawled under one of the wagons. As she did, something flashed over by the thicket.

"Cleo!"

The scarab was nearly to the thicket, moving steadily and apparently fearlessly, her legs fully extended.

"Cleo, come back!" Delanna called, though there was as much point in talking to the scarab as to the geese.

She looked toward Madog's rig, but there was no one in sight, and Cleo was already disappearing into the bushes.

Delanna took off at a run, a mistake in the muggy heat. By the time she reached the thicket, she was panting hard and the blouse she'd borrowed from Cadiz was drenched with sweat.

The thicket looked even deader up close, the leafless branches of the dried-up bushes twisted into an impenetrable tangle she had to duck under.

She squatted down, peering into the shade, and called to the scarab, who had crawled into the exact center of the thicket and then stopped. Her new-found adventurousness having apparently deserted her, she had retracted everything into a tight little ball.

"Come here, Cleo," Delanna called. "Would you like a nice drink of water? Come here."

Cleo's plates didn't even quiver.

"I mean it, Cleo," Delanna said sternly. "Come *here*. I don't want to have to come in there after you."

It was clear that was exactly what Delanna was going to have to do. She stood up and walked along the edge of the bushes trying to find a way in through the tangle of branches, and then looked back toward the caravan. Sonny's legs were no longer sticking out from under the solaris. He must have gotten it fixed, or was off with everyone else, watching the lightning that never seemed to come any closer. It still flickered along the horizon, too far away to separate into strokes.

Delanna dropped back to her knees. Cleo hadn't moved. She leaned into the thicket, hoping Cadiz had been telling the truth and there weren't any nasty forms of local wildlife lurking inside. She could see the ground at least. There was no underbrush, only a couple of stray twigs that had died of the heat. Or a couple of snakes cleverly disguised to look like twigs.

"Cleo, come out this minute," she ordered severely. "Don't make me come in there after you," and went in.

There was just room enough to crawl on her stomach. Apparently there had been a breeze out in the open air, though Delanna hadn't been able to feel it, because it was at least twenty degrees hotter under the bushes. If Cleo had sought out the thicket thinking it would be cooler in the shade, she was sadly mistaken. That was probably why she was lying so still—she'd had heat stroke or something.

The low space under the branches got lower, so Delanna practically had her face in the dirt, and then ended a few feet in front of Cleo.

She stood up and looked around. From outside, she'd been able to see that Cleo was lying in an open space on some sort of dry grass, and she had expected an open glade, but instead she was in a grove of trees. The trees were tall and looked a little like palms, with thick, peeling trunks and a few whitish branches far overhead.

They cast scarcely any shade, and it was as hot as an oven here inside the enclosure the thicket made. Between the trees the ground was bare, with occasional patches of bluish grass. A little way off from Cleo the grass was charred black, as if someone had built a campfire there, although Delanna couldn't imagine anyone wanting a campfire in this heat. It was even more sweltering than it had been under the bushes, and completely airless. Maybe the grass had caught fire just from the heat. It certainly seemed hot enough for spontaneous combustion.

Delanna looked around, hoping for a quicker way out than the way she'd come, but the thicket formed a solid ring around the woods, and the bushes looked even more impenetrable from inside. She couldn't see the caravan over or through them, and they seemed to cut off sound as well as sight. She couldn't hear the geese or the thunder in the hot, airless silence.

"Let's get out of this place, you bad thing," Delanna said to break it, and scooped Cleo up in her arms. Cleo immediately opened out her forelegs and claws and clutched at Delanna's shirt.

"Were you scared?" Delanna said, wincing at the grip on her shoulder and trying to reposition Cleo's claws.

The scarab was trying to climb right over her shoulder.

"It's all right," Delanna said. "I'm here." She patted

Cleo's scales comfortingly. "Come on, we've got to go separate those geese before they suffocate."

She bent down, holding the scarab against her, to duck back under the thicket, when Cleo made a wild lunge for her head and tangled her claws in Delanna's hair.

"Cleo!" Delanna yelled, trying to free her hair. "What *is* the matter with you? You're pulling my hair! Stop it!" The scarab got an entire clawful of hair, and using it as a handhold, started down Delanna's back.

"Cleo! What are you doing?" Delanna twisted around, trying to get at the scarab's foreleg.

Three of them were standing in a semicircle around her, stooping forward so they were only a little taller than she was. "Ohh," Delanna squeaked, and took a step backward.

"Fire monkeys," she breathed, though they didn't look like monkeys. They didn't have red fur at all, but she knew instantly what they were by the vaguely primate features in their oval-shaped faces. They were the same color as the dead branches of the thicket, and they were obviously reptiles. The skin on their huge chests and haunches was thick and pebbly, and their hands were spikily clawed, like lizards'.

Cleo let go of Delanna's hair and made a sudden scrabbling dive over her shoulder and into her arms, wrapping her forelegs around Delanna's neck. Delanna clutched the scarab to her chest and took another cautious step backward.

And into the arms of another fire monkey. She jerked away from it and screamed, a bloodcurdling scream that should have brought the entire caravan running, but the sound was completely absorbed by the airless heat. It was as if the thicket had swallowed it whole.

Three more monkeys emerged from behind the palmlike trees and came forward, their orange-yellow eyes regarding her unblinkingly. The largest one was holding a stick in his clawed hand. Delanna looked frantically around for a weapon, but there was nothing, not even a leaf, on the dry grass. The one with the stick brought it up to his mouth and breathed on it, his throat puffing out like a frog's, and the stick began to glow a dull red.

"I didn't know this was your camp," Delanna said, edging toward the thicket. "I just came to get my scarab." She turned and shouted, "If anybody can hear me, I'm in the thicket! Help! Sonny! Somebody! Help!"

The sound reverberated off the bushes, and another fire monkey appeared, as if by magic, out of the bushes and joined the circle. The monkey with the smoldering stick slapped at his head with his free hand and took another step forward.

"Don't you come any nearer, I mean it," Delanna said, putting out one hand to fend him off and clutching Cleo with the other. "I *mean* it!"

She heard a rustling in the branches behind her, and she edged away from the thicket, afraid to take her eyes off the monkeys.

The one who had just appeared started toward her.

"You keep away from me!" Delanna said.

It extended its long arm toward her and touched Cleo with one of its claws. Cleo retracted so suddenly, Delanna nearly dropped her. She grabbed her like a caught ball.

The movement seemed to frighten the monkey, and it danced back, its forked tongue flicking rapidly in and out. The one with the stick handed it to the monkey next to him and moved forward, his hand reaching for Delanna's face. Delanna reared back. "You leave us alone!" she said and smacked him on the hand.

"Don't hit him," Sonny said behind her. "You'll scare him."

"Scare him?" Delanna said, relief flooding over her. She turned to look at Sonny. He hadn't crawled under the bushes; he'd crashed straight through them. "Scare *him*?"

"There's no reason to be afraid of them," he said. "They're harmless."

The one she'd slapped had withdrawn its hand, but it

was still looking intently at her. Its tongue flicked in and out.

She backed up against Sonny. "I don't care if they're harmless," she said. "Make them go away."

He clapped his hands, and the fire monkeys scattered, disappearing into the far reaches of the thicket, all except the one she'd hit. He stepped back, eyeing Sonny warily, and then started determinedly for Delanna again.

She nearly leaped into Sonny's arms, grabbing him around the neck with one arm and clutching Cleo in the other. "Get him away!" she yelped. "Get him away!"

"It's all right," he said, his arm going protectively around her. "He won't hurt you. They're not aggressive."

"Not aggressive?" she said, pulling away from him. "Not *aggressive*?!"

The fire monkey had stopped where he was when she flung herself at Sonny, but now he started forward again. Delanna shrank back against Sonny.

"I don't understand what he's doing. They usually run at the first sight of a human," he said, sounding puzzled. "With good reason. And it's obvious he's afraid." He took his arm from around Delanna and clapped his hands again.

The fire monkey flinched at the sound and paused, then took a half-sidling step toward her and reached his hand out. Delanna jammed her head against Sonny's chest.

"It's your *hair*," Sonny said. "He's probably never seen red hair—there are hardly any redheads on Keramos—he probably thinks it's on fire. Show him it isn't."

"What?"

He took hold of a lock of her hair. "Run your fingers through it," he said. "So he can see it's your hair."

She held her head to one side and combed her fingers through her long hair.

"See?" Sonny said. "Hair. No fire. No hot. Hair."

The fire monkey leaned forward till he was almost bent in half and peered at it.

"Let him touch it," Sonny ordered.

"Are you sure he's not dangerous?"

"I'm sure, so long as he doesn't have a box of matches."

She inclined her head further, and held a strand of hair out toward the fire monkey's outstretched hand. It took another tiny step forward and extended one spiky finger. He poked gingerly at her hair, scarcely touching it, and then jerked his finger back and stuck it in his mouth as if it had been burned.

Sonny laughed. He clapped his hands again, sharply. "Go. Get. Go."

The fire monkey disappeared behind one of the palms, moving so fast Delanna was finally convinced they were really reptiles.

"It won't come back, will it?" she asked fearfully. "No. They're afraid of sharp, cracking noises. And humans. They must have been really fascinated by your hair to even show themselves. Are you all right?"

"Yes," she said. It occurred to her suddenly that she was still clinging to him. She took her arms from around his neck and moved away. "They were so . . . Cadiz said there weren't any animals in the grove . . . They don't *look* harmless," she finished lamely.

"They don't," Sonny agreed, grinning. "The first time I ever saw one, I went straight up a cannonball tree, and it's got even fewer branches than these salt palms." He started toward the palm the big fire monkey had disappeared behind.

"Are you sure they're gone?" Delanna asked, following him, unwilling to let him get too far from her.

"I'm sure," he said, looking toward the bushes. "They'll hide till we go and then they'll leave the thicket. I hope."

"What do you mean, you hope?" She edged closer to him. "I thought you said they were harmless."

"*They* are," he said. "But there are a lot of people on this caravan would just as soon shoot them as look at them, including Jay Madog. If they find out they're here . . ."

Sonny turned and looked at her. "I want you to do something for me," he said seriously. "I don't want you to say anything about the fire monkeys when we get back. Nobody knows they're here. Cadiz thought she was telling the truth when she said there wasn't anything in the grove. Fire monkeys hardly ever come out on the flats and no one else will come out to the grove. We're about ready to pull out."

He put his hands on her shoulders. "They're harmless. They start a few fires, not nearly as many as they get blamed for, and they eat a few cannonballs. They're a nuisance, but they don't deserve to get massacred just because—"

"Because I was dumb enough to wander in here," she said ruefully.

"Because they were dumb enough to camp this close to a caravan route. Please," he said, looking earnestly at her.

"I won't say anything. Anyway," she added, turning her head away, "they'd just think it was one more hilarious story about how Sonny's wife can't take care of herself. They'd probably put it on the ham, how I screamed and made a complete fool of myself." She stopped and looked up at Sonny. "But what if somebody besides you heard me scream?"

"I didn't hear you scream," he said. "I was looking for you, and I saw you heading toward the grove." He hesitated. "I was coming to apologize for what I said last night."

"You mean for saying I couldn't take care of myself? You were obviously right. Or I wouldn't have gotten myself surrounded by fire monkeys and screamed for you to come rescue me."

He grinned. "For me, huh? Not for Jay Madog?"

She flushed. "I knew you were working on the solaris," she said and was immediately sorry.

"Right," he said. "I knew there had to be a sensible reason." He stooped and picked up Cleo. "Come on. The sooner we leave, the less chance there is somebody will come looking for us." He started for the bushes she'd crawled under, Cleo clinging to his neck.

Like I was a minute ago, Delanna thought. "Wait a minute," she said.

He stopped and turned.

"Thank you for coming," she told him. "I was really scared."

"You're welcome."

"And I want to apologize for the things I said last night, too. I listened to the ham this morning. I know you were just trying to protect me from them gossiping about me."

"They can be pretty hard, especially on the been-tos," he said. "One time during harvest I split my pants working the press and just about never heard the end of it." He smiled at her. "Come on."

He strode purposefully toward the thicket, carrying Cleo on one arm like a baby, and Delanna started to follow and then stopped.

"How did you get in here?" she said, looking at the unbroken circle of bushes.

"What do you mean?" Sonny asked, putting his hand out. "I walked, of course," he said, and the branches parted before him. "These are reddsie bushes." Red Sea bushes.

Delanna scurried after him, touching the sharp branches about as gingerly as the fire monkey had touched her hair. The twigs retracted, like Cleo's legs, into larger twigs, and in turn into the main branches, leaving her a clear path. She stared at them, fascinated.

"*Here* you are," she heard Cadiz say. "We've been looking everywhere for you. Pierce is back."

Delanna looked up. Sonny was already out of the thicket, holding out his hand to keep the path open for her, and Cadiz was standing beside him with her hands on her hips. "They're over here, Jay!" Cadiz called, waving her arms. "They're okay."

Delanna hurried out, glancing behind anxiously to make sure the fire monkeys weren't anywhere in sight, but she needn't have worried. The branches had already re-extended themselves. There was no sign anyone had ever passed through them.

"What were you two doing in *there*?" Cadiz asked, try-ing to peer through the thicket. "Jay's looking for you. He's got the new data."

"Delanna's scarab wandered off," Sonny said.

"Um hmm," Cadiz said skeptically. "Which explains what she's doing here, but not you. What's really going on?"

"I got caught in the bushes," Delanna said, looking straight at Cadiz. "I didn't know they parted, and I crawled under them. I got stuck, and I screamed for Sonny, and he came and rescued me."

"You're kidding," Cadiz said, laughing. "You crawled *under* Red Sea bushes! Oh, this is even better than you swimming in the salt creek. I can just see you, crawling along when all you had to do was—Wait till I tell Jay! This is great!"

She took off toward the caravan, presumably to find Jay.

"You didn't have to do that," Sonny said. "It'll be all over the ham by nightfall."

"I had to tell her something. I guess I'd better go find Jay and feed in the new data," Delanna said. "And put Cleo in the solaris so she doesn't wander off and get me in any more trouble." She reached to take Cleo from him.

"Yeah," he said, but he didn't release the scarab, "and I'd better see if the solaris will start." He handed Cleo to her. "Your hair really does look like it's on fire, you know. It's no wonder the fire monkeys are crazy about you."

Jay came rushing up. "Are you all right?" he said, look-ing from Delanna to Sonny. "I was worried sick when they couldn't find you."

"I'm fine," she said. "Sonny was with me."

When Delanna had finished re-running the probability analysis with the new data and Nagle, who'd gotten back the next morning, and Pierce had provided Jay whooped with joy as he ripped the film with the new map off the vega terminal.

"Look at that," he said, grinning widely. "Just about a straight line from Spencer's Wagon to Otherside."

The straight line on the map looked more like a dog's hind leg to Delanna, but the blank spaces from the satellite density slicings were filled in now and the underground river did not cross the dogleg anywhere.

Jay shooed her and Sonny out of the rig, ran up a bright yellow flag from the mast, and drove off to the front of the column to lead the way. Cadiz pulled up in Sonny's solaris, which sounded something like a banshee and had stunned the geese into absolute silence.

"This thing going to make it to Otherside?" Cadiz asked when she popped the canopy to let them in.

"I don't know if it'll make it as far as Spencer's Wagon," Sonny muttered. "I need to call B.T. He works on these things more than me. Maybe he knows what's wrong."

As Sonny motioned for Delanna to get into the back seat,

Cadiz grabbed the microphone and flipped it on. "Need a howdy-do for Milleflores," she said gaily into the mike. "Can you clear on ninety-six for me?"

Sonny folded his long legs into the front seat, pulled the canopy down, and gestured for Cadiz to drive on. The solaris squealed in protest, but it moved.

"Is that you, Cadiz?" asked a woman's voice. "You still in caravan or are you home now? 'Cause if you're home, you'll just have to wait to make your call until Kaylee comes back from diapering the baby. I'm teaching her to make wildroot ragout, and I want her to tell me how tender the blue-carrots are before I let her add the saffron."

"Yes, it's me, Mrs. Siddons, and I'm still in caravan."

"Then why are you calling Milleflores instead of home?" Mrs. Siddons asked sternly. "Are you just wanting to talk to one of those Tanner boys and using a caravan priority to get me off this channel? If Kaylee puts the saffron in too soon, the ragout won't be . . ."

Cadiz had quickly flipped the toggle and put the mike up to her mouth, but Sonny grabbed it away from her before she could say a word. "Mrs. Siddons, this is Sonny. Would you please clear ninety-six for a priority caravan call to Milleflores?"

Cadiz was following the dust of the caravan past the grove of Red Sea bushes until shortly they were serpentining past a series of sinks. The sinks didn't look as bad as Cadiz had led Delanna to believe they were, just circular depressions only inches deep with diameters of a few feet— nothing the big tires of the vehicles couldn't navigate. "I have never understood why when they're cooking they're always ready to think the worst of a body," Cadiz muttered as she drove over the rim of one of the sinks. The solaris bounced.

"Sonny, is that *really* you?" Mrs. Siddons asked, her tone suddenly saccharine.

"Yes, ma'am, it's me."

"If Cadiz has you in person, I don't see why she wants to talk to B.T., too," Mrs. Siddons said.

Cadiz grabbed for the mike, but Sonny dodged. "I'm the one who wants to talk to B.T., not Cadiz. She was just making the call for me."

"Well, I'll clear the channel for *you*, Sonny, but I don't think anyone's picking up at Milleflores. O'Hara at Winterset checked in with Markie Woodward with an all's-well after the rain and said Harry and Wilkes were going fishing."

"Baby's all dry again," said another female voice. "Now where were we? My, this ragout is boiling pretty hard."

"Sonny Tanner needs ninety-six for a caravan priority call to Milleflores, Kaylee, so we're going to have to stand by while he tries," Mrs. Siddons said sweetly. "Meanwhile, you just stick a fork in those blue-carrots."

"Is anyone holding open who can force the screamer at Milleflores?" Sonny said into the mike.

"You're gonna break their eardrums," Cadiz commented.

"B.T. doesn't like to fish," Sonny said, "and if he were in the cottage, every air-surfer who could patch to Milleflores would be telling him about Mrs. Siddons, and he'd have broken in by now."

"Sara Siddons is the bossiest woman in the world," Cadiz said over her shoulder to Delanna. "She likes Sonny, though, because he actually eats that green stew she sends over to him and B.T. and the boys."

"I'm forcing the screamer at Milleflores," came a male voice, "but if Harry and Wilkes are fishing, no one's gonna answer. B.T. put out a don't-worry two days ago."

Cadiz grabbed the mike from Sonny; this time she got it. "Where's he at?" she asked.

"The blue-carrots are tender all the way through," Kaylee announced.

"So you *did* want to talk to B.T.," Mrs. Siddons said,

with obvious disapproval in her voice. "Put in two pinches of saffron, Kaylee, and then . . ."

"No one in their right mind would want to talk to B.T., least of all me," Cadiz retorted, "but Sonny does like to know how his kin are doing when he's away."

". . . turn down the flame and put the lid on the pot," Mrs. Siddons said evenly. "B.T. is old enough for a don't-worry, and the little boys are just fine."

"Well, Mrs. Siddons, we're not. This solaris is barely limping along, and Sonny needs B.T. to help him fix it."

Cadiz's annoyance was apparent, no doubt even to Mrs. Siddons and anyone else who was listening. And it sounded to Delanna as if Cadiz was having to invoke Sonny's good name to get any cooperation at all.

"No one answering the screamer," the man's voice interrupted. "Tell Sonny I'll keep the screech going until someone picks up, and we'll get a patch back to you."

"I bet B.T.'s gone to see Mary Brigbotham," Kaylee chimed in. "I haven't heard from her in days."

"Why, neither have I," said Mrs. Siddons. "Now wouldn't they just make the cutest couple?"

"Mary!?" Cadiz almost shouted. She slammed the microphone back into the cradle and swung the solaris, still wailing like a banshee, around a sinkhole.

The sinks were getting deeper and broader, and now when Delanna looked out at the one Cadiz was swerving around, she realized the solaris was hanging over what seemed like a bottomless pit.

"Slow down, Cadiz," Sonny warned.

"I'm just trying to catch up to the others," Cadiz said, "but this darn machine just goes slower and slower."

"They aren't going to get far ahead of us this time," Sonny assured her. "They'll be stopped at the winchzye."

Cadiz slowed down, less because Sonny had asked her to than because the whole caravan was in view again. Jay's rig, with its bright yellow flag, had come to a halt, and the other solarises were lining up behind it. Cadiz pulled up behind the last one and stopped. Sonny popped the canopy and jumped out.

"Shut the motor off and let it cool down again," he said. "I'll go help them set the anchors."

Delanna watched as Sonny started to walk up the row of solarises, his long stride leaving a trail of dust behind him. He didn't look back, and she found herself vaguely disappointed.

"What are you looking so long-faced about?" Cadiz asked. "It's me the old biddies are gonna be talking about today on the air."

"I just hope that winches and setting anchors doesn't mean what I think it means," Delanna said, pulling her gaze away from Sonny. "When Jay said Spencer's Wagon was straight down, I assumed it was hyperbole."

"With Jay's rig, it's not too bad. Anchors are easy to set and his winch doesn't get hung up. It won't take more than two or three days to get this whole caravan down to Spencer's Wagon." She turned off the motor and leaned forward to pull off her shoes. "And I'm not going to help them unless they ask. And just see if I ever try to call B.T. for Sonny again." She started to lie down across the front seats, but then sat up with a start. "Where's your bug?"

"Cleo's right here with me," Delanna said, "and she's—"

"—not a bug," Cadiz finished for her. "I know that, honey, but she does look like one. B.T. will like her. He likes animals even more than Sonny does. B.T. and Wilkes think they've spotted a Royal Mandarin on Milleflores. Personally, I think it's wishful thinking. There are hardly any of them left."

Delanna remembered Doc Lyle talking about the Royal Mandarins while they'd vaccinated the geese. "What do they look like?" she asked.

"Well, according to Doc Lyle, they're a species of the *Mandarins* but they don't look anything like them. The

Royals have red and green and purple feathers, and the regular ones are just kinda grayish. Now to me, the gray ones taste just as good as the Royals once they're stuffed with breadcrumbs and spices, but there are people who say the Royals taste better. And of course gray feathers don't make pretty hats or anything, so they just go to waste. Royals are easier to spot, too, which is why they've just about been wiped out. Doc Lyle got a regulation passed saying they're endangered birds and you can't shoot them.

"Doc Lyle acts like they're his babies," Cadiz continued. "He'd probably kill anybody he caught shooting one, but there won't be very many of them even if people do stop. They lay their eggs on the ground, and the fire monkeys eat them. Do you suppose he tried to call me while Sonny had the radio turned off yesterday?"

"Who?"

"B.T. Who do you think we've been talking about all this time?"

Birds, Delanna thought, but now the conversation made a lot more sense to her. Somehow she hadn't been able to imagine Cadiz as a birdwatcher, and she wasn't. It was B.T. she was interested in, not Royal Mandarins. A thought struck her. "Doc Lyle wouldn't come out to Milleflores, would he? To see this bird B.T. and Wilkes think they've found?"

"Doc Lyle?" Cadiz said, obviously still thinking about B.T. "Oh, you're afraid he'll come out here and spot Cleo. I don't think so. The last time he was out was two years ago, and B.T. calls in all the sightings. If they found a breeding pair or something, he might come, I guess, but it's a long way."

A long way, Delanna thought. Let's hope Cadiz is right, and it's not just wishful thinking.

"Why wouldn't he tell me if he was going on a don't-worry?" Cadiz sat up and looked at Delanna as if she expected an answer.

B.T. had just been a little boy when Delanna left, but she doubted it would do any good to remind Cadiz of that. Instead she asked, "Does he usually tell you if he's going on a don't-worry?"

Cadiz thought a moment. "I don't think he's ever gone on a don't-worry, at least, not without Sonny." She frowned and nodded. "I better go ask him."

"Ask who what?"

"Sonny. If B.T. has ever gone on a don't-worry alone." Cadiz had already shoved her shoes on her feet and pushed them out under the canopy, hauled herself over the frame of the solaris and started walking toward the front of the caravan. "You coming?" she called over her shoulder.

Delanna shook her head. "I'll wait here to listen for any calls," she said. Or maybe make one myself to Maggie Barlow, she thought. She's had days now to work on the angles she'd said she'd pursue. Delanna climbed over into the driver's seat and put Cleo down on the passenger side. The scarab's nictating membranes flicked open and she stared at Delanna as she picked up the mike and turned up the volume.

"It needs to simmer all afternoon, and just before . . ." Delanna switched the channel halfheartedly, for she recalled that Cadiz hadn't found the air empty anywhere yesterday. She probably wouldn't either; Mrs. Siddons or someone just like her wasn't likely to get off the air for her as she had for Sonny.

"Grandpa Maitz is manning the screamer for . . ."

She kept turning the channel selector.

". . . but that nice Sonny Tanner grabbed the mike away before Cadiz could say . . ."

". . . Spencer's Wagon, and you know what happened there that time the O'Haras made the trip. Jay Madog took Ingrid O'Hara up to his rig and . . ."

". . . right in the salt creek, but Nagle says he's talked to her and she's nothing at all like her mother."

"Well, thank God for that!"

". . . if I had a bride, I sure wouldn't be hooking up with Madog's caravan . . ."

". . . had Cadiz make the call, so you can assume that new been-to bride of his doesn't know how to . . ."

Delanna turned the selector again, and amazingly she found an empty channel. Cadiz must not have had time to get on the ham to pass along the story of Delanna's adventure with the Red Sea bushes. That, she was sure, would have commanded more air time and attention than Sonny looking for B.T., and the worst thing they could say about Delanna today was that she didn't know how to operate a ham radio.

But they assumed wrong. She did know how to use a ham, and properly, too. She wiped the gritty face of the transmitter with her fingers until she could read the call letters she knew would be there. "This is niner-bravo-X-ray calling Grassedge alpha-dog-zulu, do you read?"

"That's Sonny Tanner's solaris, but it doesn't sound like him or Cadiz," a woman's voice said. Happily it did not belong to Mrs. Siddons.

"Who's alpha-dog-zulu in Grassedge?" another voice asked.

"Danged if I know."

"It's Maggie Barlow," Delanna said.

"You don't sound like Maggie," the first woman said.

"I'm *not* Maggie. I'm trying to reach Maggie," Delanna said, feeling exasperated. So much for proper protocol.

"Well, why didn't you say so in the first place?" the second voice asked.

"Maggie's out to the mines today," the first woman said. "Frank Fuller got caught in another scam. If that boy spent half as much time working as he does with his get-rich-quick schemes, he'd have enough to retire on Rebe Trium."

The geese had started honking, and Cleo extended herself partway to look back at them.

"Who would use one-oh-seven to call Grassedge?" the second voice asked.

The scarab put one foot on the frame of the solaris. Delanna leaned over to grab her leg, but she retracted all three on that side of her body, clinging to the frame with only one set of laterals, looking like a cantilevered ball of jewels stuck there for no good reason.

"Must be Sonny Tanner's new bride. She wouldn't know no better. You need to cut out now, Mrs. Tanner. This is a private conference call and we had this frequency reserved."

"I'm not—" But Delanna heard the mike click before she got out "*Mrs. Tanner!*" and knew she'd been cut off.

"Right now, please. This is the medical frequency, and this discussion is between me and my patient."

"Sorry," Delanna muttered. She wondered if the doctor and her patient were really the only two people on that channel, or did people eavesdrop there, too? As long as they kept quiet, no one would know. Probably some did, people like Mrs. Siddons and her ilk, and probably everyone knew exactly who they were. And the identities of the ones who wouldn't eavesdrop, people like Sonny, were well known, too. She found herself hoping that the doctor and her patient were enough like Sonny so that they'd forgive her interruption and just let it pass. She didn't want to embarrass him any more than she already had. Which meant she'd better not try to discuss the estate with Maggie on the ham unless they talked in code.

She put the mike into the cradle and got Cleo by the carapace just as she was about to heave herself out the window. "No goose eggs for you today," she said. She put Cleo on her head, and pulled Cadiz's floppy hat down over the scarab, and got out of the solaris.

There wasn't so much as a hint of breeze, and the air was even muggier than before. Delanna threaded her way around the solarises and wagons standing in a serpentine line that marked the way around and between sinkholes. The way was uphill and steeper than she'd thought, but at least she could see Jay's rig and everyone else at the top.

She kept going, her footsteps making puffs of gray powder around her ankles.

When she'd rounded the last sinkhole and got near the crest of the hill, the first thing she noticed was that the line of dark clouds seemed farther down on the horizon but went across the entire panorama. The storm was growing. The second thing she noticed was the sparkling white vista below her penetrated by deep shadows and craggy fissures. The salt flats were anything but flat. They were worn into steep hills and gullies, and she couldn't see how anything could possibly get through them, map or no map.

It was three days before it was their turn to be winched down to Spencer's wagon. On the afternoon of the third day, she went up to see how the work was progressing. Just beneath the yellow flag of Jay's rig, the men had a blue solaris tethered to a chain, which they were letting out from the winch much faster than seemed safe to Delanna. About a hundred feet below, Delanna could see that another solaris was already waiting at the edge of what might be a footpath leading through a couple of salt buttes. Surely they weren't going to drive along that.

"You want some monkey juice?"

Delanna jumped. She hadn't heard Sonny walk up behind her.

"Sorry," he said. "Didn't mean to startle you. I was just coming back to see if you wanted some of this instead of the warm water in our canteen, and I saw you standing here."

He was holding a lidded ceramic cup out to her. It matched the blue-with-gold-trim dishes in Jay's rig. Delanna accepted gratefully. Just sitting in the solaris, she drank more than Sonny or Cadiz did, and the trek up the hill had made her even thirstier. She unscrewed the lid of the cup and started drinking; the rose-flavored water felt wonderful going down. She was tilting her head back for the last drop when she felt Cleo moving under the hat. Hastily, she handed the cup and lid back to Sonny so she could grab Cleo. She pulled the scarab down into the crook of her arm and put the hat back on her head.

Sonny splashed a little monkey juice into the lid and held it out to Cleo. The scarab jabbed at it tentatively, tasting the droplets that clung to her pearly claws. Apparently she liked monkey juice, for she promptly grabbed the lid with her forelegs, and clenching Delanna's arm with her middle legs and hind claws stuck firmly to the waistband of Cadiz's skirt, she stretched out to suck from the lid. "Real acrobat, aren't you, Cleo?" Sonny said, stroking her carapace. Cleo arched into his touch and fanned the carapace so that he could rub the soft membrane. He smiled and stroked the full length of the carapace, amused by Cleo's quick intimacy.

"There you are, Sonny," Cadiz called, skittering down the hill to them. "They said you'd gone back to the solaris." She stopped up short. "Ugh. Is that *my* cup it's drinking from?"

"No, it's Jay's," Sonny said.

"Good. Now listen, has B.T. ever gone on a don't-worry without telling you?"

Sonny shook his head.

"Doesn't it make you worry that he's on one now?"

Again Sonny shook his head. "Harry and Wilkes will be back from fishing tonight and Wilkes might be able to tell me what's wrong with the solaris."

"I didn't mean because of the solaris," Cadiz said.

Cleo had disengaged her forelegs from the lid and settled back into the crook of Delanna's arm. Sonny started screwing the lid back on the empty cup.

"I know you didn't mean because of the solaris," Sonny said with a grin.

"Aren't you worried about your brother's having gone who-knows-where with a storm heading in?"

"Nope," he said, grinning even more broadly. "B.T.'s a grown man and I guess he can go where he wants and when he wants."

"Where do you think he went?"

Sonny shrugged. He looked up the hill and Delanna followed his gaze. Some of the solarises were pulling up to take their turn on the winches. They had two anchors in place now, and both winch chains were in use. "You two better go back and bring the solaris up," Sonny said. "I have to go up and get ready for my turn on the winch."

"What about B.T.?" Cadiz said, but Sonny was already striding to the rig.

"Maybe he'll call," Delanna said, sticking Cleo back under the hat.

Cadiz scuffed the dirt with her boot. "I don't know, Delanna. He does call if I tell him to call, but it just wouldn't occur to a Tanner to call on his own."

"I'm sorry you're disappointed."

"I'm not disappointed," Cadiz said hastily. "It's just that I've always kind of looked after the Tanners." She looked at Delanna and flushed slightly. "Well, someone has to. They can't look after themselves," she added dryly.

They started to drift back down the hill to the solaris. "What's he like?" Delanna asked, suddenly curious about this brother of Sonny's who had enough influence on the bright and bold Cadiz to make her worried just by not talking on the radio for a day or two.

Cadiz didn't ask who she meant. "Thinner than Sonny, but his hair is darker and his eyes are such a dark blue you almost think they're purple."

And he had dimples but wore whiskers, but Cadiz knew that the dimple on his left cheek was much deeper then the one on the right, so Cadiz had obviously been watching him since before he grew the whiskers. He was also a crack shot with her daddy's lase though he hunted on his own only with a homemade bow and arrow, with which he could bring down anything within fifty yards.

"You really think he might call?" Cadiz asked when the nose of the solaris was pointed straight down at the salt flat below.

"Steer, Cadiz," Delanna hissed. She had one hand braced against the dash, her body strained against the belts,

163

and was clutching Cleo under her other arm. The winching had looked pretty smooth from above, but in the solaris she could feel every link of chain being let out with a jolt.

"What if he went off to look for a Royal Mandarin and something happened to him? What if he fell off a cliff or something?"

Delanna didn't answer. She didn't even breathe till they were all the way down and unhooked from the winch and on their way again, several hundred feet lower.

"I just don't see what everyone sees in that Mary Big-bottom," Cadiz muttered. By now Sonny was back behind the wheel, steering gingerly between two salt pillars that were barely wide enough for the solaris to squeeze through. Delanna looked back at the wider wagon; the geese honked as the wagon shaved more salt off the pillars.

"Mary Brigbotham," Sonny corrected. There was no more dust trail to follow ahead, just tire tracks across crusts of dirty salt. "Watch as we make this turn, Delanna, and you'll see Spencer's Wagon."

Delanna looked out the window on the right and saw a couple of old tires under a mushroom of salt, a mushroom cut by running water. It wasn't hard to surmise that Spencer had been driving along on top of the mushroom when that had been ground level. The crust of salt had been too thin to hold the wagon, and it had caved in. What had happened to Spencer? Was he buried under the wagon? They turned again, and there was nothing but salt buttes around them, remnants of the old road. They had passed Spencer's Wagon; Delanna did not know what lay ahead, but she could imagine only too well the honeycombed salt crumbling beneath.

The caravan stopped in the late afternoon in an eerie garden of towering salt bridges. There were dirty water marks just under the spans, indicating that the water had rested for a while, dissolving the salt, until somewhere it had broken through again and fallen away quickly, as water drains from a tub. There were fissures in the bridge-garden floor, fissures scoured white and glistening by rushing water. Water that was somewhere beneath the caravan.

Delanna started to haul the rucksacks of food out of the solaris while Cadiz dug for the campstove; there'd be no friendly campfire tonight, not in this wasteland of salt where nothing grew.

"I don't know why you didn't bring a nuker, Sonny Tanner," Cadiz complained as she threw another sack out of the boot. "You sure the campstove is in here?" She stood up with her hands on her hips, looking at Sonny accusingly. "Maybe B.T. took it with him."

"It's in there," Sonny said easily.

Cadiz leaned back over the boot, disappearing to the waist as sacks, empty tins, broken ceramic, and pie tins came flying out. One of the pans sailed past Delanna's nose, getting her attention just in time to duck an old shoe. Delanna went around to the front of the solaris to help Sonny set the mast in place so that they could haul up the solar panels to catch the last rays of the sun. It seemed the safer chore.

Sonny slipped cotter pins into the mast bulwark, then started to fasten down the backstays. Delanna got the roll of solar paneling ready, and together they fastened it to the gaff and hauled on the lines. They were just finishing when Jay came up to them.

"How's the motor doing?" he asked Sonny.

"Seems all right this last leg," Sonny replied.

And it had been, Delanna suddenly realized. Ever since they'd winched down to Spencer's Wagon, the motor had run smoothly, no longer screaming, and the drive shaft had not scorched her leg either.

"That's a relief," Jay said. "I was thinking I'd have to tow you by tomorrow." He was looking past Sonny at Delanna, his expression not at all relieved. She wondered what excuse he would have made for Sonny and Cadiz to ride in the solaris while she rode in the rig with him. And was he going to ask now that she come to his rig to prepare another map?

"I'd sure appreciate it if you'd come run that program again for me tonight," he said to Delanna, "after dinner, of course."

When it's nice and dark? she thought. "Do you have new data since this morning, more soundings from Nagle and Pierce?" she asked him.

"No, but I think the storm has moved," he said. "We'll need to know if that's changed anything on your map."

"It makes more sense to check it in the morning," Delanna said. "That way we can pick up any change in the storm during the night."

Jay nodded easily enough, but clearly he was disappointed. Delanna wondered what kind of line he'd used on Ingrid O'Hara; she hoped it was more interesting than a probabilities run.

"Well, I'll be going now," Jay said, though he didn't turn to leave or look like he was going to do anything except soak up some shade from the sails. "I just wanted to make sure everything was all right back here."

Sonny reached into the solaris and came out with the lidded ceramic cup, which he tossed to Jay. "Take this with you," he said as Jay caught the cup. "Thanks for letting us use it."

"You're welcome," Jay said, finally straightening as if he were going to walk off. He actually took a few steps, but then turned and came back. He set the cup on the chassis of the solaris and rested his hands on the top of it, shaking his head. "I almost forgot," he said. "You have a whereat on frequency ninety-seven."

"B.T.?" Cadiz asked, standing up so quickly she slopped fuel out of the little campstove.

"No, it's for Delanna. Maggie Barlow's trying to reach her." He smiled at Delanna. "If it's about your trunk, just let me know and I'll have someone back at Grassedge take care of it." He waved jauntily and sauntered away, leaving

Sonny shaking his head as he went to help Cadiz with the campstove.

Delanna opened the door of the solaris, sat down, and grabbed the mike. "This is Delanna with a whereat for Maggie Barlow," she said, and flipped the switch open to listen. The microphone was crackling in her hand. Idly she picked up some salt grains and dribbled them over the call letters on the face of the radio. A few grains stuck.

"Delanna, is that finally you? Sorry I missed your call earlier, but one of the boys got in trouble out at the mines. If I hadn't gone out, he might have spent the night in jail. Probably deserved to, but maybe he's learned his lesson."

"Do you have any news for me?" Delanna asked, almost certain there would be none. If there had, Maggie would have called.

"Yep, I have news. You know that matter we discussed before you left?"

"Yes, the—"

"No need to say anything more *on the air*," Maggie cautioned, "if you know what I mean."

"I remember," Delanna said. So she'd been right about the private channel. People did listen in. "Yes. That matter we discussed."

"Well, I've been working on it as fast as I can, and it's looking pretty good, but these things take time."

"How much time?" Delanna asked.

"Only till Circuit Court gets here. And I know that must seem like forever to you, but I know if you'll just use the time to give Sonny half a chance, you'll find . . ."

"I will," Delanna said, cutting her off. She wasn't positive of what Maggie was about to say, but she was keenly aware that half the population of Keramos was probably listening in. She didn't think Sonny would appreciate their speculating on what Maggie Barlow meant either.

"Really?" The surprise in Maggie's voice was genuine. "I thought you might just come to your senses once you got to know him again," she said happily. "Didn't think even a been-to could overlook all those sacrifices he's made.''

What sacrifices? Delanna wondered.

"You're going to have to tell me all about that fancy school you went to some day when I have more time," Maggie continued. "Sure seems to have given you a solid education, at least in probabilities. Jay's real impressed with you. Sonny must be very proud. How are you enjoying the caravan? Bet you never saw terrain like that back in Gay Paree, did you?"

Delanna glanced at the long shadows that were threatening to reach the solar panels. "No, nothing like Spencer's Wagon," she said. "The scenery on Rebe Prime's mostly horizontal." She watched Sonny light the campstove and then step back while Cadiz set the big black pot on top. She ripped open packages and dumped their contents into the pot, then reached for the water jug and practically knocked it over. Sonny said something to her, and Cadiz shoved the jug at him, no doubt demanding that he pour. Sonny poured, but he was grinning, and Cadiz obviously didn't like that.

"Did you really crawl under some Red Sea bushes?" Maggie said.

Delanna stared at the microphone. When had Cadiz had time to put that one on the air? She'd been flailing around all afternoon, ever since she realized B.T. wasn't at home where she expected him to be. Delanna sighed. "It's true, I did it," she admitted.

Maggie laughed heartily. "Only a been-to could find a reason to explore a Red Sea grove on her hands and knees. What were you doing in there?"

"I . . ." She couldn't say *I went to find Cleo*, on the air, because Doc Lyle might hear about it. "I . . ." She couldn't say *I got caught by fire monkeys*, either because people might bring their lases on the next caravan. "I have to go eat dinner," she said lamely. "Bye."

"Bye."

Delanna put the mike back in the cradle, got up, and closed the solaris. Sonny had given up on helping Cadiz, who was whipping whatever was in the pot into some kind of froth. Delanna hoped it wasn't stew again; it would be in shreds.

"Everything all right?" Sonny asked her.

Delanna nodded and smiled. "She wanted to know if I'd really crawled under some Red Sea bushes."

"You didn't . . ."

"Of course I didn't say anything about the fire monkeys," Delanna assured him. "I was on the air."

He smiled approvingly. "Thanks."

"How's dinner coming?"

But Sonny was looking at the ceramic cup, which Jay had left on the chassis of the solaris. He picked it up. "Did you want to return this to Jay?" he asked. "Tonight, in the dark, and alone? I mean, I think that's what he's hoping."

"Maybe," Delanna said, taking the cup from him, and in so doing, she deliberately let it slip through her fingers. The cup shattered. "Oops," she said.

Sonny seemed surprised.

"He's so transparent," Delanna said, and Sonny grinned, a happy, more confident grin than she'd seen before. It made her smile, too.

Leaving the shards where they'd fallen, they went to help Cadiz.

• • • • • • •

Sometimes it seemed to Delanna that they could have gotten out and walked faster than the solarises could drive through the Salt Flats. The tires squeaked most of the time because they were constantly turning and probably also because the top layer of salt was so damp from the moisture-laden air. Usually it was dry in the Salt Flats, they had told her, but the storm stuck over there on the horizon was pushing a mass of warm, wet air before it, and the high pressure behind them was just holding it in place. So it could dissolve the very ground beneath them.

The nights were the worst part. She could feel the ground vibrate beneath her, vibrations that sometimes passed freely into the air, making an audible groan. She'd lie awake for hours listening to the noises, and then they would stop and she'd almost fall asleep, only to discover it was dawn and she had to get up and hurry to Jay's rig to run a new probability study so that the day's journey would be a safe one.

"If this holds true," Jay said on the fifth day as he smacked the new map against one hand, "we'll be to Otherside by tonight."

She told Sonny what Jay had said when they pulled out of a campzye of white salt dunes, the buttes and bridges a day behind them.

"That will cut two days off the best record ever through the Salt Flats," Sonny said. He was driving again, threading his way between the bases of two crusty dunes. Their party still brought up the rear of the caravan, though the solaris motor had not overheated since they'd been in the salt.

"Jay's gonna be real sorry to lose you, Delanna," Cadiz commented.

"It's not me," Delanna told her. "Anyone can do it with the right software, and he's got the right software."

"Yeah, but he can't run it, can he?"

"I'm not so sure about that," Sonny said, "not sure at all after his watching Delanna do it every day."

"I've watched her every day, too," Cadiz said sulkily, "and I couldn't do it. You have, too, most days, and I bet *you* couldn't either. B.T. would have picked up on it in no time, but he's no-one-knows-where."

Delanna suppressed a groan. Cadiz had been cranky since they got into the Salt Flats, and every once in a while she managed to bring the conversation around to speculating on where B.T. Tanner might be. No one had heard from him.

Sonny was past smiling when Cadiz complained about his brother. He just didn't answer her anymore, not even giving her the shrugs that so maddened Cadiz. She gave Sonny a scowl now and leaned forward to turn on the radio. She started flipping channels.

"... a new baby boy!"

"And Grandpa Maitz says last spring's was the best blossom set he's seen in thirty years ..."

"... so I told Bianca, 'You have no business getting involved with Jay Madog ... ' "

"With the storm just waiting over there in the east, I told Dominic it didn't make sense to grade the road until ..."

Delanna only half-listened as she stretched out in the back seat. She took out a stiff brush and started polishing the scales on Cleo's plates, which like everything else, were crusted with salt. After a while, she leaned up against the window, just watching the sparkling white dunes go by. At least they were moving faster now. Her eyes, heavy from lack of sleep, began to close. Maybe she'd sleep tonight, with real earth under her, bedrock that didn't creak because hunks of it were falling into an abyss dissolved out of the salt.

The solaris jolted and Delanna's eyes flew open. The salt dunes were not so tall here, and there was something green in the track they were following, smashed by tires and covered with rime, but green. Then there was another plant, this one off to the side because the dunes seemed to be parting like the Red Sea bushes, making way for the train of solarises. Their own motor was straining a bit, not like when it had overheated the drive shaft, but enough to indicate they were going uphill. Delanna sat up and took a look around.

She could tell that they'd gained lots of altitude, for behind them the salt dunes spread for miles, glistening like mounds of snow in the sun. Ahead was a new horizon, a green one softened by streaks of lacy yellow-green growth over dark branches that Delanna stared at until they brushed past the windows. Ahead, she could see the entire line of vehicles in the caravan with Jay's rig at the head.

"He'd better stop for supper," Cadiz said, "or there won't be any light for charging the panels left."

"Looks like he's making a run for the Little Dip," Sonny commented.

"What's the Little Dip?" Delanna wondered aloud. "A salt marsh?"

Sonny shook his head. "Freshwater pond," he said. "A tiny stream dammed up by . . . Hmm, look at that. Smoke coming from the grove. Did Nagle and Pierce go on out ahead this morning, too?"

"I don't think so," Delanna said, trying to remember. Then she shook her head. "No, I'm sure they didn't. Their scooters were loaded on the wagon, and they pulled out right behind Jay."

"Well, what kind of fool would be camping in Otherside?" Cadiz asked. "It's too far from anywhere for a picnic, and they'd have to wait a week for Jay to pick them up for a return caravan."

The air smelled sweeter, of growing things, though still muggy, and it was very warm. Cleo had extended, the better to see out the window, and seemed more interested in the grass and shrubs than she had in salt buttes.

The caravan snaked through waves of grasslike growth that carpeted the vast plain; ahead was Little Dip, truly a mere pond, but surrounded by a grove of scraggly trees. A thin plume of smoke trailed upward from the trees.

"Well, what do you know?" Sonny said.

"Oh, no," Cadiz said.

"What is it?" Delanna asked, staring at the smoke. "Fire monkeys?"

"Fire monkeys!" Cadiz exclaimed. "What would fire monkeys be doing out here?" She hauled her duffel over into the front seat and began rummaging frantically through it. "Where's my comb?"

"It isn't fire monkeys," Sonny said, sounding amused.

"Cadiz wouldn't be combing her hair for a sparkle of fire monkeys."

Delanna leaned forward to peer through the windshield. She could see a solaris parked at the edge of the pond and a man standing next to it, his arms crossed over his chest, calmly watching the caravan approach. "Who is it?"

"Somebody loan me a comb!" Cadiz said, yanking the rearview mirror so she could see herself in it.

Sonny reached lazily into his shirt pocket and pulled out a comb. "You never worried about fixing your hair for us."

"Oh, shut up," Cadiz said, grabbing the comb from him and pulling it through her tangled blond curls.

"Who is it?" Delanna asked. They were close enough for her to be able to see the man's face, if it hadn't been for all the dust. It billowed up along the pond till she couldn't see anything.

"Oh, look at me!" Cadiz wailed to the mirror. "Why didn't I ask Jay if I could use his sonic at camp last night?"

Sonny pulled in at the far end of the caravan next to two solarises that already had their solar panels unfurled from the masts. He stopped, and Cadiz, with a last nervous look in the mirror, jammed her hat down over her head and jumped out.

The man was already walking up from the pond, coming purposively toward them, but Cadiz didn't start toward him. She stood stock-still beside the solaris, biting her lip nervously.

A sudden, frightening thought struck Delanna. "It's not the vet, is it?" she said, reaching instinctively for Cleo.

"The vet?" Sonny said, surprised. "What would he be doing out here? Nah, it's B.T."

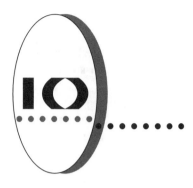

B.T. walked the last few yards, and Delanna thought, I
should have recognized him. He was thinner than Sonny,
and lankier, but he had the same shy smile, the darker hair
brushing his neck, and the way he stopped short of the
solaris and stood there turning his hat in his hands was pure
Tanner.

Delanna scrambled out of the solaris. She wondered
briefly whether she should take Cleo with her, but the
scarab was fully retracted and sound asleep. She left her
lying on the seat and pushed the canopy gently to so the
noise of shutting it wouldn't wake her, and went over to
meet B.T.

In spite of the still-blowing dust, B.T.'s hair was damp
and neatly combed and the whiskers were gone, Delanna
noticed, amused. So Cadiz wasn't the only one who'd
searched frantically for a comb. And from the way he was
looking at Cadiz, there obviously wasn't anything to the
ham's rumors about him and Mary Brigbotham. He had
eyes for Cadiz, and Cadiz alone. He smiled tentatively.

Delanna looked at Cadiz, expecting the same smile, but
she was glaring at B.T. from under her jammed-down hat.
Neither of them said anything.

"What are you doing out here, B.T.?" Sonny said into the uncomfortable silence.

"I got your message the solaris was acting up," B.T. replied, "so I thought I'd come meet you at Spencer's Wagon. I borrowed Flaherty's old solaris. I didn't want you breaking down out on the flats."

"Well, you took your time about it," Sonny said. "Cadiz has been on the ham night and day, trying to find you."

He grinned at Cadiz, and she shot him a look that would have intimidated a fire monkey.

B.T. glanced timidly at Cadiz and then back at Sonny. "I got as far as here and ran into heavy clouds for three days and couldn't go anywhere, but I figured I'd still have plenty of time to find you. What'd you do to make it across so fast? Fly?"

"Practically. Jay's got a new program," Sonny said, "and Delanna here knew how to run it—it was like stepping over a mud puddle."

"We didn't need you anyway," Cadiz chimed in belligerently. "Jay and Sonny fixed the solaris. Jay's wonderful at fixing things."

Delanna gaped at Cadiz, and then at B.T., but he was ignoring Cadiz.

"So this is your new bride, Sonny," he said, nodding at Delanna. "It would have been a real mess if she'd decided not to stay. It's going to be strange for a while to think of you as a married man."

Delanna thought, This is no time to explain about it being an in-name-only marriage, especially if Cadiz had tried to make B.T. jealous of Sonny the way she was trying to make him jealous of Jay now. Delanna stepped forward and took B.T.'s hand. "You probably don't remember me," she said brightly. "You were just a little boy when I went away to school."

"Remember you?" he said, grinning at her. "With Sonny talking about you all the time? He was always—"

"I think maybe you'd better take a look at the solaris," Sonny broke in. "Jay and I worked on the transmission, but it's still sucking sunshine. Need to get the collectors up, too, get the battery recharged."

While Sonny raised the mast, B.T. popped the hood on the chassis of the solaris, still ignoring Cadiz, who was glowering at him, her arms folded.

"Wait," Delanna said. "Let me get Cleo out first." She went around to open the canopy. Sonny had put the boom on and she had to wad the canopy under it.

"Cleo?" B.T. said. "How many women you got traveling with you, Sonny?"

"It's Delanna's pet," Sonny told him. "And she's contraband. Doc Lyle doesn't know about her, so you can't go talking about Cleo on the ham or showing her to people. Nobody knows about her except Cadiz and Jay."

Delanna reached into the back seat. "Cleo's a scarab," she said. "She—"

Cleo wasn't on the seat. Delanna crawled into the back and reached under the seat, feeling for her. "She's not here," she said, emerging. "Cleo's not here." She leaned across the front seat to see if the scarab had wedged herself under the dashboard.

"How'd she get out?" Sonny asked. "The canopy was shut, wasn't it?"

"No," Delanna said defensively. "She was asleep."

"What does it look like?" B.T. said. "How big is it?"

"Cleo probably saw B.T. and got scared," Cadiz put in.

"Maybe she's back with the geese," Sonny said.

"Can it swim?" B.T. asked, peering out at the pond.

"No," Delanna said, and then to Sonny, "Let's check the geese."

But before they could start toward the pen, Jay Madog called out, "Looking for something?" He was holding his coat by the sleeves like a sack, and when Delanna ran up to him, he thrust the coat at her. Delanna pulled the sleeves apart and found Cleo tangled in the lining. Carefully she disengaged the scarab's limbs and toes. When Cleo was free, she immediately extended her forelegs and grabbed her mistress in a hammerlock around the neck. "Where was she?" Delanna asked Jay.

"Over by Tom Toricelli's rig," Jay said.

"He's got chickens," Sonny said. "Did anybody spot her?"

"I don't think so. She was headed toward the wagon, so I threw my coat over her before anyone could see her. What do chickens have to do with it?" Jay asked Sonny, puzzled.

"She keeps trying to hatch out eggs," Sonny explained.

"Are you sure nobody saw her?" Delanna asked anxiously.

"If they had, you'd have heard some yelling," B.T. responded, coming over to look curiously at Cleo. "What is it, a bug?"

"No," Delanna said. "I'd better put her in the solaris." She went over to the still-open canopy and pried Cleo's forelegs from around her neck. She set her gently on the back seat, draped Cadiz's jacket over her so anyone looking in the window wouldn't see her, and backed out of the solaris and practically collided with Jay.

"I was on my way down here to talk to you when I found Cleo," he said in a low voice. "I wanted—"

"Just a minute," Delanna interrupted. "I don't trust her." She leaned in to look at Cleo again and then snapped the canopy shut.

"Jay!" Sonny called. He had the hood up, and B.T. was leaning over the motor. Cadiz was looking daggers at B.T. "Come show B.T. what you think the trouble was."

"In a minute," Jay called back. "We'll get to Flahertys' tomorrow," he said to Delanna, "and I'll be starting back. I wanted to make sure I told you how—"

"Jay!" Cadiz said, as if she'd just noticed him, and came flouncing over. "You said I could come to your rig and take a sonic any time I wanted to, didn't you?" she said, slipping her arm flirtatiously through Jay's. "Is your offer still good?"

"I guess," he told her, looking bewildered.

"Oh, good," Cadiz said, turning to make sure B.T. could see her. "Because there's nothing interesting going on *here*."

"I need to talk to Jay," Delanna broke in, wishing she could take Cadiz over her knee and spank her. "Jay, you're sure Tom Toricelli didn't see Cleo?"

He nodded and tried to disengage himself from Cadiz. She tightened her grip on his arm. "I didn't see anybody, and Cleo was nearly underneath the wagon they've got their chickens in."

"She wanted to sit on their eggs," Delanna explained. "She keeps going broody and wanting to nest. I think she thinks she's a bird."

"You two can talk about the birds and the bugs later," Cadiz said, pulling playfully on Jay's arm. "Now, what about that sonic?"

"Don't you have to get clothes or a towel or something?" Jay said, looking appealingly to Delanna.

"*You* can loan me a robe," Cadiz said, giggling archly.

B.T. slammed the hood of the solaris down hard. "It's getting stuffy around here," he said, pointedly not looking at Cadiz. "I'm going back to get my sails up." He stomped off toward the pond, where the campfire still wisped smoke.

"Come on, Jay," Cadiz pressed, yanking on his arm.

"Delanna, I'd keep Cleo inside the solaris," Jay advised. "It's only another day to Flahertys', but you don't want anybody seeing her."

"I will," Delanna said, but Cadiz had already dragged Jay off, giggling loudly so that B.T., halfway to the pond, could hear her, and hanging on Jay's arm.

Delanna and Sonny stood looking after them. "Well, that was something," Sonny commented.

"It sure was," Delanna agreed, frowning. "I've never seen anything quite like it."

"Somebody needs to take Jay Madog down a peg or two for sticking his nose in where it isn't wanted," Sonny said, making a final knot in the sail rig.

Delanna turned to look at him, astonished. "You're saying this is *Jay*'s fault?"

"No," he said, snapping the solaris hood up with a jerk. "I'm saying it's Cadiz's. She always does this. She used to do it with me. You saw how she acted in Grassedge, carrying on like she was my girlfriend. She's been doing it for two years. I figured she couldn't pull this stuff now that I was married to you, and then in waltzes Jay—"

Delanna should have protested that bit about being married, but she was too angry. "Jay was simply returning Cleo!"

"Who you let out."

"So now it's *my* fault? Along with Jay's and Cadiz's?"

"Well, who else's would it be?"

"What about B.T.? He saunters in here, doesn't even say hello to Cadiz, doesn't even *look* at her!"

"If he'd tried to, she probably would have snapped his head off."

"And as long as we're passing out blame, how about you?" She mimicked Sonny's voice. " 'Where you been, B.T.? Cadiz's been worried *sick* about you. She's been on the ham every day, all day and all night, trying to find you.' "

"Well, she was!"

"But she doesn't want *him* to know that, not when he doesn't act like he's glad to see her!"

"Glad to *see* her!" Sonny shouted. "Why the hell do you think he came all the way out here?"

"Then why didn't he say that? Why didn't he tell her how he feels?"

"With your boyfriend and Cadiz hanging all over each other?"

"Jay is *not* my boyfriend!"

"Yeah, well, all I know is, a guy's gotta have some sign

that the girl won't laugh in his face before he tells her how he feels," Sonny said, "and if she keeps playing games, you can't blame him for keeping his mouth shut." He slammed the solaris's hood down. "I'm gonna go talk to B.T.," he said, and stormed off.

"And we are *not* married," Delanna called after him, but not very loudly.

In spite of the fact that she'd just been defending Cadiz, she knew Sonny was right. B.T. couldn't be expected to tell Cadiz he'd come out here for her if he thought she liked Jay, and Cadiz had laid it on pretty thick.

Delanna wished she could go up to Jay's rig before Cadiz did something really stupid, but she was afraid she'd only make things worse. She remembered how furious she'd been when Sonny'd come up to the rig to rescue her.

And she wasn't eager to hear whatever it was Jay wanted to tell her. His manner had changed when she'd figured out the program for him. He'd stopped turning on the phony charm and she'd been pleased that he seemed to be seeing her as a person instead of merely another conquest. She hoped he didn't plan to go back to trying to seduce her now that they were through the Flats.

Besides, she didn't dare leave Cleo. She turned around and looked at the scarab. She had her forelegs against the side window, peering out like a child with its face to the glass. Delanna hoped Jay was right, and the Toricellis hadn't seen Cleo. B.T. knew what he was talking about— there would have been yelling, or worse, and somebody would have come to report to Jay that there was some kind of big bug loose in the caravan. But there was no noise except for the usual settling down for the night. The sun was almost through setting, and the sky and the lake were a pale yellowish-green.

She took one last peek at Cleo and then sat down against the solaris and thought about what Sonny had said. He was right about Cadiz and her game-playing, but he obviously didn't realize how hurt Cadiz had been when B.T. ignored her.

Or maybe he did. *A guy's gotta have some sign that the girl won't laugh in his face before he tells her how he feels*, he'd said, and she wondered if he was really talking about Cadiz. Or about her. She hadn't laughed in his face when Maggie'd told her they were married. She'd said, *So because of your stupid laws I'm married to a Neanderthal.* And she'd thrown him out in front of everybody at Last Chance. And taken a sonic in Jay's rig. And just now told him again that they weren't married. And he had told her it was no wonder the fire monkeys were crazy about her hair. He had saved Cleo and rescued her from the fire monkeys and the vet.

Twilight gradually descended, and all around she could smell supper cooking, but Sonny and B.T. didn't come back, and neither did Cadiz. Delanna made a fire of sorts, heated up what was left of Cadiz's latest stew, and sat down and waited again.

A little after dark Cadiz came back, looking scrubbed and very subdued. "Where's B.T.?" she asked wistfully.

"I don't know," Delanna told her. "I think he's with Sonny down at the pond."

"Oh," Cadiz said and squatted down next to the fire. She'd discarded her hat, and her blond hair was brushed and clean, Delanna noticed.

Cadiz picked up a dry Red Sea stick and poked at the edges of the fire with it for a while.

"Do you want something to eat?" Delanna asked.

"No," Cadiz said, holding the stick in the flames and watching the twigs shrink away from the fire. "I ate with the Hansens."

"The Hansens?"

"I decided I didn't want to use Jay's sonic after all," she said. The stick caught fire and burned, twisting like a live creature. It was painful to watch. "So I went over to the Hansens and borrowed some water from them so I could get cleaned up.'' She looked at Delanna defiantly. ''They're only half a day from home, and they had plenty.'' She threw the still-writhing stick into the fire. ''Oh, Delanna, he didn't even say hello to me.''

Delanna tried to think of some way to say, You weren't very nice to him, you know, but considering how Cadiz looked, it would be like kicking a dog. She said instead, ''He came all this way.''

''Yeah,'' Cadiz said. ''To fix the solaris. I've liked him since I was *little*,'' she burst out. ''I used to do everything I could think of to make him notice me!''

You still do, Delanna thought, but she didn't say that either. ''Maybe you should tell him how you feel,'' she suggested.

''Right! And have him look at me like I'm not even there and tell me he loves Mary Brigbotham.'' She stood up. ''I'm going to bed. Can I have the back seat?''

''Sure, if you can stand Cleo. I'm afraid if she sleeps out here, she'll go after those chickens again after I'm asleep.''

''I can stand her,'' Cadiz said grimly. ''At least *she* likes me.''

B.T. likes you, too, Delanna thought, and wished he could see Cadiz, her pretty hair that she'd washed for him, and her despairing face. If he could, he'd blurt out the feelings Delanna was sure he had for Cadiz, and she dawdled over getting her bedroll out of the back in the hopes he and Sonny would come back.

They did, but not until the women were asleep, because the next thing Delanna knew, Sonny was bending over her, shaking her and saying, ''Come on. It's time to go.''

It was pitch-dark, and Delanna blinked sleepily at him. ''What is it? What's wrong?''

''Nothing. We're making an early start. The caravan wants to make Flahertys' by noon.''

She sat up, still not awake. B.T. was standing drinking a cup of java next to his borrowed solaris, which he must have driven up there in the night, and Cadiz was stowing her bedroll in the trunk of Sonny's solaris. "I don't understand," Delanna said. "How can the solarises work in the dark?"

"We'll use the batteries till the sun comes up," Sonny said. He straightened up. "Come on. We're eating breakfast on the way."

Delanna got clumsily to her feet, wadded up her bedroll, and took it over to Cadiz. "Where's Cleo?" she asked.

"Asleep in the back seat," Cadiz snapped. "Finally. She spent half the night scrabbling at the window, trying to get away from me." She grabbed Delanna's bedroll away from her and shoved it into the trunk. "She obviously would have preferred to sleep with Mary Bigbottom, too."

There was nothing forlorn about Cadiz this morning. There was no sight of her pretty hair, either—she'd jammed her floppy hat down so far, Delanna couldn't see it—and when B.T. came over with his bedroll, Cadiz said, "*Then*, when Cleo'd finally given up and gone to sleep, some *lunk* drove up his solaris and woke her up again." She snatched the bedroll violently away from him, and Delanna was glad it wasn't a weapon.

"Okay, let's go," Sonny said, handing Delanna cava and a thick slice of bread. "Who's riding with who?"

There was another one of those deadly silences. Delanna looked at B.T. hopefully, but he was studying his cup of cava. Delanna couldn't blame him—Cadiz was looking daggers at him. Even if he did pluck up the courage to ask her to ride with him, Cadiz was in no mood to accept, and if Sonny blundered in and told her to, she and B.T. were liable to kill each other before they got out of sight of Little Dip, let alone all the way to Flaherty's.

"I'll ride with B.T.," Delanna said brightly, and for her pains, got a dark look from Cadiz and a disappointed one from B.T. "Just a minute," she added. "Let me get Cleo." She crawled in the back of the solaris and got the scarab, who gave her a look as baleful as Cadiz's and grabbed onto the seat cushion for dear life. By the time Delanna got her pried loose, half the caravan had pulled out, and B.T. was standing impatiently by his solaris, waiting for her.

"Sorry," Delanna said, and scrambled in on the passenger's side, pried Cleo loose again, and dumped her in the back seat. "Now go to sleep," she admonished the scarab.

B.T. started up the solaris and moved into line with the caravan behind Sonny. Delanna turned around to check on Cleo. The scarab wasn't asleep. She was hanging onto the back of the front seat, pulling herself up. A solaris pulled into line behind them, its lights shining straight onto Cleo.

"Oh, no!" Delanna said, and leaned over and started to work Cleo's claws loose.

The scarab dug in. "Cleo, let *go*. They're going to see you."

"What's the problem?" B.T. asked.

"I'm afraid the solaris behind us will see Cleo," she said, pulling at Cleo's claws. It was no use. Every time she got one loose, Cleo grabbed on with another.

"Here," B.T. said. He handed her his jacket. "Drape that over her." He angled off slightly to the side so the lights weren't shining directly into the back seat. "How's that?"

"Better, thanks," Delanna said. She draped the jacket over the back seat like a tent and anchored it with a flashlight and two empty ambrosia bottles. "Okay," she told B.T., and he pulled back into line.

"How'd you manage to smuggle your bug past Doc Lyle, anyway?" he asked as she turned back around and sat down.

"I didn't. Sonny did." She told him the whole story, how Sonny had smuggled Cleo out of quarantine and tricked Doc Lyle into thinking Cleo'd gone down the garbage disposal at Last Chance. She started yawning halfway through, and kept murmuring, "Sorry."

"Why don't you sleep for an hour or so?" B.T. said finally. "And then you can drive and let me sleep."

"Okay," Delanna said. "I'd better check Cleo first."

She peered under one edge of the jacket. Cleo had retreated to the far corner of the back seat and was curled into a ball. ''She's asleep,'' Delanna said, and she was, too, almost instantly.

She slept for a lot longer than an hour. It was fully light when she awoke, and the flat brown plains had disappeared. They were in rolling hills, and here and there was a patch of gray-green grass.

''What time is it?'' she said, stretching.

''A little past ten.''

''Ten? Oh, gosh, I'm sorry. Do you want me to drive now?''

''Nah. We're stopping for an early lunch in a little while, and I'm wide-awake. You better check on your bug. I heard her rustling around a while back.''

Delanna twisted around to look at Cleo. She had been rustling around, all right. She had pulled down B.T.'s jacket and was lying in the center of it, fully retracted.

''She's made a nest out of your jacket,'' Delanna told B.T. ''I'll get her out of it when we stop.''

''That's okay, if it keeps her out of trouble. It doesn't look like I'm going to need it—it looks like it'll be real warm today.''

Delanna looked out the window. The sky was clear and a brilliant blue, and the ground around the caravan was already shimmering. They wound through the rolling hills, which were less patchy now and a little greener.

''You can see the mountains if you look hard,'' B.T. said, pointing ahead.

Delanna leaned forward and squinted. At first she couldn't see anything but a few white clouds on the horizon, and then she realized it was snow on the peaks of the Greatwalls, still so distant they were almost the same color as the sky. ''I see them,'' she said. ''They're beautiful. I'd forgotten how high the Greatwalls are. I remember when I was a little girl I thought they were how you got into space.''

She glanced at B.T. and saw he was frowning at her. "What is it?" she asked. "What's wrong?"

"Nothing," he said. He yawned largely and shook his head as if to clear it.

"Are you sure you don't want me to drive?" she asked. "I'd be glad to."

"It's not much farther," he said, and she saw he was frowning again. "You're not like what I expected at all."

"What did you expect?"

"I don't know." He shrugged. "You're a been-to, and you went to a fancy school and all. Sonny didn't even get to go to lanzye school. I figured . . ." He hesitated.

That I'd think Sonny was a hick, she finished silently, reflecting uncomfortably that that was exactly what she had thought when she'd seen Sonny in his clunky boots, his flowered shirt and baggy pants, pulling that wagon full of geese.

"I figured you wouldn't have much use for Sonny," he was saying. "I thought you'd take off on the next shuttle."

Me, too, Delanna thought.

"And if you had, I guess me and Sonny would be looking for jobs at the mines. The kind of people who came thinking there was quick money in the mines are a lot different than land settlers." He shook his head. "No place to raise Wilkes and Harry. But we'd of had to do something to hang on for ten years, and I suppose making tile is honest work. Your staying opens up all kinds of possibilities."

But I'm not staying, she thought. Hadn't Sonny told B.T. that she wanted to leave just as soon as Maggie could find a way? Delanna couldn't blame him if he hadn't—news like that out on the ham would have made their trip completely unbearable—but she was surprised Sonny hadn't let B.T. know last night. Unless he thought there was a chance she'd change her mind.

Oddly, that thought didn't infuriate her the way it should have. She thought of his coming to the thicket to rescue her, of his saying, "No wonder the fire monkeys are crazy about your hair." Her cheeks felt hot, and she glanced nervously at B.T., but he hadn't noticed.

"I figured after that fancy school on Rebe Prime you'd hate camping out," he said, "and not being able to take a bath."

"Haven't you heard? I did take a bath. In a salt creek," she said ruefully.

He grinned. "I heard about that. But you were a good sport about the teasing and you've pitched in and helped with the cooking and the driving. I figured you wouldn't do anything except sit around and complain, like—" He stopped, looked embarrassed, and said, "I better check the ham to see what the weather's like up ahead." He began fiddling with the radio.

Like who? Delanna wondered. Not Cadiz, who might do some complaining but who certainly couldn't be accused of sitting around and not pitching in. The legendary Mary Brigbotham? He wouldn't expect Delanna to be like her, would he?

There was nothing but static on the ham. "Must be sunspots or the storms," B.T. said, and his voice sounded defensive. "Sonny may not have gone to a fancy school, but he works like a dog to keep Milleflores going." He fiddled with the set again, and it let out a long, tortured scream.

"Here, let me," Delanna offered, feeling more confused than ever. She had never said Sonny didn't work hard, and B.T. had sounded really angry. At who? Maybe Sonny *had* told him about their marriage-in-name-only, and it was her he was angry with, but she didn't think so.

She messed with the dials, and a man's voice boomed forth. ". . . by day after tomorrow."

"Sorry," Delanna said, lowering the volume, even though she thought B.T. was the one who'd turned it up in his fiddling.

"How's the weather there?" the man's voice went on, less deafening now..

"Cloudy, and the barometer is falling," a woman's voice

said. "You'd better make sure you got something left in your auxiliaries before you start."

The man signed off, and another man cut in before Delanna could ask about the weather.

"This is Tom Toricelli calling Valley View Lanzye. We're almost to the South Road. I'll be home by supper, Sugarbabe."

Sugarbabe's voice said, "You must have had a good trip."

"Sure did," Toricelli said. "I thought when I saw that storm, we were going to be three months getting across the Flats, but we came through as smooth as ambrosia sliding down. Jay's got some new software—"

"Betty wants to say hello," the woman interrupted, and a child's voice said, "Did you bring me something, Daddy?"

"Sure did," he said. "I've got some fine chickens for you to play with, and I'll tell you all about the trip when I get there."

"Did you see any fire monkeys?" Betty asked, and Delanna leaned forward and turned up the volume.

"Not a one," he said. "But I saw the dangdest animal at Little Dip. It was sneaking up on my rig. It looked like a big beetle—"

"Oh, no," Delanna said, clapping her hand over her mouth. "That's Cleo!"

"—bigger than any beetle I ever seen," Tom Toricelli went on.

"Excuse me," Sonny's voice cut in. "Sorry. Caravan priority call. I need to check in with Jay Madog."

"That's okay, Sonny," Tom said. "Betty, Daddy's gotta go. See you at supper."

Sonny started through the motions of the check-in, which Delanna was sure was trumped up.

"At least Sonny stopped him before he got any farther," B.T. noted.

"I know," Delanna said, relieved. "Jay said nobody saw

her. You don't suppose Doc Lyle was listening in, do you?''

''To a bunch of How's-the-weather's and I'll-be-home-for-supper's? Nah. Don't worry. Sonny'll talk to Tom before he gets back on the ham and make sure he doesn't say anything else.''

Delanna nodded, but she listened anxiously to the rest of the morning's transmissions, and as soon as they stopped for lunch, she jumped out of the solaris and ran to talk to Sonny.

He confirmed what B.T. had told her. ''I just talked to Tom. I convinced him what he saw was a pond turtle. I told him last time I was at Little Dip I saw one two feet across.''

''Are you sure he believed you?''

''Yes. Don't worry. Tom's not going to be talking about it on the ham anymore—he's almost home. And Doc Lyle wouldn't have heard the transmission anyway. Today's the day the shuttle comes in. He's got livestock to inspect.''

The shuttle. Delanna thought of when she'd come in on the shuttle and Doc Lyle had impounded Cleo at the cargo warehouse. It seemed like a thousand years ago. And a thousand miles.

Five thousand miles, she reminded herself, and at least a two-week trip across the Salt Flats. Sonny was right. Cleo was safe.

But she kept Cleo in the back of the solaris till they started again, and then made B.T. fall back and stop so she could let her out for a few minutes.

When they caught up again, the solarises had slowed, and three had turned off across the bottom of a hill.

''Where are they going?'' Delanna asked. ''Were we supposed to turn?''

''They're going home. That's the road south to Toricelli's Valley View and Yamomoto's Silvan Springs Lanzye. No point in them going all the way to Flahertys' and then having to backtrack.''

"Are we going to Flahertys'?" she asked, thinking of Jay and wondering if they would suddenly peel off, too, and not so much as a wave from him. She might not want him trying to seduce her, but that didn't mean she didn't want him to say goodbye.

"We've got to. This is Flahertys' solaris. Anyway, the shortcut doesn't take off that much."

She watched the solarises head off, growing smaller and smaller. "Don't they even say goodbye to each other?"

B.T. reached over and turned on the ham. "They're saying goodbye, all right."

"Now, remember, I want that recipe for ambrosia compote," a woman's voice said over the ham, "and tell Maurey he owes me a dance at the harvest-do."

"We'll see you at the harvest." A man's voice.

Another man. "Tell Mort Sanderson to come get his ditcher. And ask down your way if anybody's got a cannonball ricer."

"Goodbye, Ellie," a young man's voice said, so full of emotion it was painful to listen to.

"Goodbye!"

"Don't walk on any salt."

"Drive carefully."

"So long!"

It went on until the solarises were out of sight and the dust they'd thrown up settled, just as if they'd been standing there waving goodbye, and then gone back to business as usual.

The ham came to life again. "I got a whereat for Bruno Stern. And what's this I hear about Jay Madog and the Flaherty girl?"

B.T. reached over and snapped the switch off with such violence Delanna thought he might break it.

"People come up with the most amazing gossip on the ham, don't they?" Delanna said mildly.

"I know where they heard that one," B.T. said grimly.

"Sonny told me you can't believe everything you hear

on the ham. We heard you were off visiting Mary Brig-botham, when you were really on your way to meet us.''

''Mary Brigbotham?!'' he said, outraged. ''I've never said two words to her. You can't believe what you hear on the ham.''

Delanna didn't say anything.

''Mary,'' B.T. said thoughtfully. ''Is that why Cadiz has been so bent out of shape since I got here?''

Delanna nodded. ''The ham said you were off courting her, and Cadiz couldn't find you when she tried a whereat.''

''Mary Brigbotham.'' He shook his head. ''She's one of those meek little things who just stands around and won't even stick up for herself. Why would I want a girl like that? Cadiz—'' He stopped.

''Have you told her how you feel?''

''*Told* her? What does she think I came all the way out here for?''

''To fix Sonny's solaris,'' Delanna said innocently.

''Now why in the hell would she think that?''

Delanna shrugged. ''That's what you told her.''

He mulled that one over for a while. ''Anyway, how can I tell her anything? She wouldn't even talk to me when we stopped back there for lunch. She was busy flirting with Jay.''

Oh, Cadiz, Delanna thought, you are absolutely determined to mess this up. ''She doesn't care anything about Jay,'' Delanna said aloud.

''Well, you sure couldn't prove it by the way she hangs on him. She used to do that with Sonny, too, but I never worried about it, because he never even looked at her. All he did was talk about you. But Jay's different. He's romanced every girl and woman on Keramos, so he must be good at it, and Cadiz looked like she was believing every word.'' B.T. paused briefly, then said, ''There goes another one.''

He pointed at a solaris pulling out of the caravan. There

was no road Delanna could see, but the solaris turned south and started off over the scrub-dotted hills.

"Oshigas and Hansens'll be turning off in a few minutes," he said and picked up the ham mike. "Hey, Hansen," he said into the mike. "It's B.T. Tanner. I've still got that distillation gauge of yours. Want me to run it up?"

"Keep it till the harvest do," Hansen replied. "I got a new one in Grassedge. What's this I hear about Cadiz and Jay Madog getting married? Did she get tired of chasing you and decide she wanted to be the one being chased? Jay—"

B.T. stuck the mike against his mouth and made a sound like static. "Sunspots," he said, and jammed the mike back in its holder, looking glum.

"How far is it to Flahertys' lanzye?" Delanna asked.

B.T. pointed to where the hills were higher and greener. "See that break in the hills there? Flahertys' is just beyond that. Not far."

Not far was two hours. The hills got greener and more rolling, and narrow streams began to trickle down between them. The Hansens and Oshigas turned off along one of the streams, disappearing at once among the hills to the north, and immediately afterward the caravan seemed to stop climbing. The hills became lower and softer-looking, covered with tall, thick blue-green grass.

Delanna leaned forward, trying to catch a glimpse of the Flaherty settlement, wondering if it would be as disappointing as Spencer's Wagon. She had tried to remember Milleflores, but she had only a vague memory of the cabin and a couple of lean-tos roofed with brush. Her father had built the cabin out of rough bricks, but a lot of the lanzyes had only had tents, sided to keep animals out. And Doc Lyle had said Milleflores was "pretty rundown," whatever that meant.

She'd avoided thinking about what Milleflores would be like. "I'll think about that when I get there," she'd told herself, and now they were nearly there, and Flahertys' would be some indication of the kind of place she'd be spending the next two weeks. Or the next year, if Maggie's Circuit Court appeal failed.

"Is Flahertys' nice?" she asked.

"I guess. The people who live there are friendly, if you don't count Cadiz."

Delanna wanted to know if they'd be camping, but she was reluctant to ask B.T. what facilities they had, not when he'd praised her willingness to rough it. At least the streams they were driving through didn't look like they'd burn your skin off. She'd check before she waded in, though.

B.T. was looking even glummer than when Hansen had asked about Cadiz and Jay, and no wonder. Cadiz was almost home, and if Delanna knew her, she'd flounce out of Sonny's solaris and into the tent or cabin or whatever without so much as a goodbye.

"Will we stay long at Flahertys'?" she asked.

"Probably just the night. Sonny'll want to get home to check on Harry and Wilkes. If you weren't with me, I'd cut off right now and send the solaris back with Wilkes in the morning. No sense giving Cadiz another chance to not speak to me."

Then I'm glad I'm riding with you, Delanna thought. She wished there was something she could do to get them together, but they were both so stubborn. If they got there in time for supper . . . "How far did you say it was to Flahertys' lanzye?"

"We've been on it for an hour and a half. And right over this hill," he said as he topped it, "is the ranch. See, what'd I tell you?"

For a minute, she didn't see what he was pointing at in the valley below. She had been so ready for a scattering of lean-tos or a flimsy tent. And the ranch was the same green of the hills. Greener. The sprawling house and array of outbuildings and barns were all built of ceramic brick in a shiny emerald green. They filled nearly the whole valley, glittering like emeralds, lining the stream that flowed through the center and then curving up to meet the house, which was even bigger than the one at Last Chance.

"But—" Delanna gasped. "It's beautiful!"

B.T. started down the hill. "Provided the inhabitants are on speaking terms with you."

"Which it looks like she is," Delanna said, pointing to a figure in pants and a floppy hat heading up the hill at a half run.

"That's not Cadiz," B.T. said, sounding even glummer. "That's her mother."

Mrs. Flaherty waved, and as she got closer, Delanna could see the hat was in even worse shape than Cadiz's. She trotted up to B.T.'s window and motioned to him to open it.

"B.T. Tanner," she said, "what's this about Cadiz and that no-good Jay? I thought you were going out there to propose to her."

"She—" B.T. began.

"And here's the blushing bride!" Cadiz's mother thrust her arm across B.T.'s face and grabbed Delanna's hand. "Last time I saw you, you were knee-high to a cannonball and now look at you! No wonder Sonny's been crazy about you all these years. B.T., what are you stopping up here for? Come on down to the house. We've got a wedding celebration to beat all wedding celebrations ready for you, Delanna."

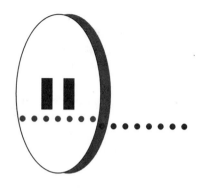

Delanna was afraid the party was going to start the minute they got down the hill, but Cadiz's mother, who'd trotted down ahead of them, was still in the yard greeting everybody when they pulled into the drive, and directing traffic with her hat. B.T. drove down into the driveway and parked next to a tractor with the biggest sail rig Delanna had ever seen. Sonny was nowhere in sight, but Cadiz was standing next to the solaris, scanning the crowd.

"Did she really keep trying to get me on the ham?" B.T. asked Delanna.

"Ask her yourself," Delanna said, tucking her jacket over Cleo so she couldn't be seen. Luckily, the scarab was still asleep. She hoped all the hustle and noise wouldn't wake her up. "Go on, B.T. Now's your chance."

He got out of the solaris and started toward Cadiz, looking determined, but before he'd taken two steps, Cadiz called out, "Jay! Jay Madog!" and flung herself off to meet Jay, who was heading toward them through the maze of solarises and wagons.

Cadiz slipped her arm through his. "Oh, Jay, I was afraid you'd turn off on the South Road," she said flirtatiously, and loudly, so B.T. would be sure to hear, "and I wouldn't get to say goodbye to you."

B.T. looked like he'd like to throttle her, and Delanna wished he would. She checked Cleo again and went to look for Sonny to tell him about Cadiz's mother's plans for a wedding celebration. She didn't think he'd want another shivaree any more than she did. She headed for the glittering emerald ranch house.

Cadiz's mother was standing at the door. "Now you all make yourselves at home," she was saying. "You've got the run of the place, as if you didn't know it. Food's in the kitchen, ambrosia's in the barn," she said, pointing. "Ham's in the house if you've got messages to send." She grabbed Delanna's arm. "You and I have to talk wedding party, Mrs. Tanner, and I want to know what's going on with B.T. and that daughter of mine," she said, pointing at Cadiz, who was standing next to Jay's van, laughing up at him. "I'd like to knock their heads together. It'll have to wait till after the shivaree, though. But I expect you'd like to get cleaned up before we get down to business."

"That would be wonderful," Delanna said, grateful to put off talking about the impending party. And a sonic sounded heavenly after the mud of the Flats. "You wouldn't have a sonic, would you?"

"A sonic? You can have a bath if you want. *Cadiz!*" Cadiz's mother yelled in a voice that would have carried across the Salt Flats.

Cadiz disengaged herself from Jay and started over to them. "Cadiz, get over here and show Sonny's bride where she can get a bath instead of lollygagging with Jay Madog!" her mother said, and left Delanna to go help a woman lift two little girls out of a wagon.

"The bathtub's in the stillhouse," Cadiz said. "Did B.T. say anything about me while you two were in the solaris?"

"He said you wouldn't talk to him," Delanna told her. "Do you know where Sonny is?"

"No, I haven't seen him since we got here."

1 9 6

"Well, go look for him and tell him I need to talk to him while I go get a towel and some clean clothes."

"All right," Cadiz said. "Was he really mad about Jay?"

"Wouldn't you be?" Delanna asked her, and set off through the yard to the Flahertys' solaris for her towel.

Cleo was awake, climbing over the back seat into the front. Delanna coaxed her back into her jacket nest. While she was digging for a clean shirt, B.T. stomped over, yanked open the trunk, and grabbed out his bedroll.

"What are you doing?" Delanna asked.

"I'll tell you what I'm not doing, I'm not sticking around here." He dumped the bedroll in the back of Sonny's solaris.

"But . . ." Delanna began, looking anxiously back at the house.

B.T. was rummaging in the back of Flahertys' solaris. "I know, her mother's having a big shivaree and all for you and Sonny, but I can't take any more of Cadiz hanging all over Jay." He dredged up a boot. "I'm sorry if I'm letting you down."

"You're not, but . . ." Delanna thought frantically, trying to think of something that would convince him to stay.

B.T. found the other boot, tossed both of them across into Sonny's solaris, and slammed down the trunk. The noise scared Cleo, and she began scrabbling against the window.

"Would you do something for me first?" Delanna said, grabbing B.T.'s arm as he started for the cockpit. "It'll only take a few minutes. Cleo needs a walk, and there are so many people here. Do you know of somewhere sheltered she could get some exercise?"

"You could take her in the compost shed." He pointed across the drive at a small building separate from the rest. "Nobody'll be going in there." He got in Sonny's solaris.

A compost shed was hardly a romantic setting. "But she needs water. Isn't there a stream or some trees or something near here? Please. She's been in the solaris all day.''

"There's a little grove of balla bushes down past the drive," he said, pointing in the other direction. "Down that hill. There's a stream at the bottom of it." He slipped the solaris into gear.

"But how will I get her past this crowd? What if someone sees her while I'm carrying her? Couldn't you drive us down there? Please?''

He looked disgusted, but he switched the motor off and got out of Sonny's solaris and into Flahertys'. Delanna hopped in happily beside him. He maneuvered between the haphazardly parked solarises and wagons and drove down the drive. "At least I won't run into Cadiz down here," he said, turning the solaris along the narrow stream. He stopped next to some low bushes flanked by taller trees. The bushes had feathery leaves and little pale yellow blossoms on them.

"This is perfect," Delanna said, picking up Cleo and setting her down next to the meandering stream. The scarab promptly curled into a ball.

"She doesn't look much interested in exercising," B.T. said.

"She'll extend in a minute," Delanna said. "Would you do me one more favor? Please. I haven't had a bath since Last Chance, and Cadiz's mother says they have a bathtub and everything. Would you watch Cleo for just a few minutes while I have a bath? I promise I'll hurry."

"I guess," he said reluctantly, "but then I'm leaving."

"I think that's a good idea," Delanna said. "There's no point in sticking around if you're never going to tell Cadiz how you feel.''

"What do you mean? How am I supposed to tell her when she's always hanging on Jay?''

"She wasn't hanging on Jay when you got to Little Dip, and you didn't so much as say hello to her. Cadiz isn't a mindreader. How's she supposed to know if you don't tell her?''

"I was ready to cross the Salt Flats to see her!''

"And then told her you came to fix the solaris. Do you know what she did when she saw it was you? Had a fit 'cause she hadn't washed her hair. She practically knocked Sonny and me down getting to a comb, and then you didn't even look at her. I don't blame her for going after Jay.''

Delanna picked up her towel and shirt, and a comb for emphasis. "If I were you, I'd tell her the next time I got the chance, or the ham'll be reporting her engagement to Jay for real.'' She pointed at Cleo with the comb. "Don't leave Cleo alone. She's not used to deep water. I'll be back as soon as I can.'' She started up the hill. Okay, she thought, that's one. Now let Cadiz still be at the house.

She was, getting a lecture from her mother. "What took you so long?'' Cadiz asked, dragging Delanna into the still-house.

"I had to take Cleo down the hill,'' Delanna explained. "She'd been in the solaris all day. I left her down the hill by a stream, but now I don't think I should have.'' She looked anxiously in that direction. "What if she comes looking for me and somebody sees her? Would you watch her for me, just while I take my bath?''

"Where is she?''

"I'll show you,'' Delanna said, and led her back out of the stillhouse and across the yard. "B.T.'s going home.''

"Going home? Why?''

"He said he couldn't stand watching you and Jay to-gether—it hurt too much.''

"He did?'' Cadiz stopped and looked back at the solar-ises.

"He's gone by now. He was throwing everything into Sonny's solaris when I went to get Cleo. You have to keep a close eye on Cleo. She wanders off.''

Cadiz looked for a minute more at the solarises, and then started walking again, looking dejected. "I was just trying to make him notice me.''

"I know,'' Delanna said, leading the way down the hill.

She couldn't see the solaris's antenna above the bushes. That was good. "But you can't send out mixed signals like that and expect him to be able to figure out it's him you love." She walked into the first of the trees and into earshot of whoever was in the thicket. "You do love B.T., don't you?"

"Of *course* I do."

"Then you'd better stop playing games and let him know. There's Cleo. Don't let her climb any trees. She keeps trying to sit on birds' eggs."

"I can't let him know," Cadiz said plaintively. "He's already gone. Probably to see Mary Brigbotham."

"Don't let Cleo wander off," Delanna said briskly. "She can move pretty fast if she wants to. And keep her in the thicket so nobody can see her. I'll be back as soon as I can."

Cadiz walked toward Cleo, flapping her hat dejectedly.

"Talk to her," Delanna called after Cadiz, "so she won't get scared and retract. Tell her hello."

"Hi, Bug," Cadiz said unenthusiastically.

Delanna couldn't see B.T. through the concealing thicket, but Cadiz must have. She stopped cold, swept her hat up to jam it on her head, and then let it fall. "B.T.," she said, surprised but at least not belligerent.

"What are you doing here?" B.T. asked, and Delanna thought, Oh, no, if they realize they've been set up, it's all over.

"I came to check on Cleo," Cadiz said. "And to ask you if it's true what they've been saying about you and Mary Brigbotham."

"Mary Brigbotham!" he said in a tone that should have been all the answer she needed.

Delanna crept behind a cannonball trunk, trying to see B.T. It's not bad enough you're matchmaking like Maggie, she told herself, now you're acting like the gossips on the ham, but she leaned out from the tree, trying to get a better view. She could see the tips of B.T.'s booted feet.

"You know better'n to believe what you hear on the ham," he told Cadiz.

"Yeah," she said, turning her hat in her hands. "What about you? You didn't believe that stuff about me and Jay being engaged, did you?"

"I don't know. Are you?"

"Are you kidding?" Cadiz said contemptuously.

So far so good, Delanna thought, watching them. Now if they could just get five minutes of uninterrupted time together . . . which shouldn't be too hard. The thicket screened them from the outbuildings, and everyone was still up near the brewhouse, drinking that terrible ambrosia. And taking baths.

Which reminded Delanna that if she wanted one, she'd better take it while she had the chance. She turned to start back.

"What're you doing way down here?" Jay said.

Delanna jumped like she'd seen a fire monkey. "Jay!" she said, trying to sound pleased instead of panicked. "If you're looking for Cadiz, she's up at the ranch house. I'll walk you back."

"I wasn't looking for Cadiz," he said, leaning his hand on the thick stump of a balla bush.

"Oh." Delana sneaked a glance back at the stream. Cadiz was no longer in sight, but the thicket wasn't that concealing. "Well, *I'm* looking for her," she said. "Cadiz promised she'd show me where I could get a bath." She showed Jay her towel and started past him.

He didn't move his hand from the tree. "It was you I was looking for," he said. "I had something I wanted to tell you."

"You can tell me on the way back," she said, and ducked under his hand. Blessedly, he stopped leaning on the stump and came along beside her.

"I wanted to talk to you last night," he went on, "but Cadiz was playing some kind of game with B.T. She didn't take a sonic in my rig, by the way."

"I know, she told me," Delanna said, leading Jay up the hill at an angle that put the entire width of the thicket between them and the stream. "She said she decided she wanted a real bath, and so do I. Sonics are nice, but I feel like I'm dust from head to foot."

"I didn't want you to think I was encouraging Cadiz," he continued, sounding oddly ill at ease. "I don't know what kind of gossip's been going around, but I wanted to tell you you can't believe everything you hear on the ham. I haven't romanced half the women they say I have."

Even half was quite a few, Delanna thought. She risked another glance over her shoulder as they came into view of the outbuildings. She couldn't see Cadiz or B.T. at all, which meant they were still talking. She hoped.

"I also wanted to tell you thanks for figuring out the program," Jay said. "If you hadn't, we'd have been caught in that storm and still be on the other side of the Flats."

They were coming out of the trees. Delanna, scanning the outbuildings to see if anyone was heading their way, didn't catch what Jay was saying and had to ask.

"I said, I'm sorry we didn't get caught by the storm."

"Why?" Delanna asked absently, watching a couple who were walking hand-in-hand toward one of the solarises. Cadiz's mother waved to them with her hat and trotted over to catch up to them.

"Because—" He stopped walking. "I can't tell you this and walk at the same time." He caught hold of her arms. "Because if you hadn't programmed the computer, we'd still be on the other side of the Flats, and I wouldn't be having to say goodbye to you. Delanna—"

With a shock, she realized what he was going to say. She should have seen it coming, should have realized as soon as he started explaining about Cadiz and the sonic, but she had been so busy matchmaking, she hadn't been paying attention. If she had been, she'd never have let it get this far.

"I wouldn't blame you if you did think I was a ladies'

man," he said, and it was disconcerting to see him so uncomfortable, "the way I came after you at first, but coming across the Flats, watching you at the computer, I . . ."

I had no business letting it get this far, Delanna thought. *"You can't go on sending mixed signals like that without getting in trouble,"* she'd told Cadiz, and she should have taken her own advice.

"I've got to start back tomorrow," Jay went on. His grip on her arms tightened. "I've got another caravan waiting back in Grassedge, and I want to get them across before the rains start. I'll only be gone a few weeks, thanks to your help with the program, but I wanted to tell you something before I left." He leaned toward her.

She said the first thing that popped into her head. "Are you going to bring me my trunk?"

"Your trunk?" he said blankly.

"From the ship. You said you'd have it brought down on the shuttle and bring it to me on the next caravan."

He let go of her arms, and she took advantage of the chance to start walking again. "I'll be so glad to have it. I've been wearing Cadiz's clothes, but I'll be awfully glad to get mine again, especially the shoes. Cadiz's shoes are smaller than mine, and my feet have hurt ever since Spencer's Wagon."

"I'll bring you your trunk," he said. He caught her arms again and turned her around to face him. "I'd bring you anything you wanted. You know that, don't you? Delanna—"

"*There* you are," Cadiz's mother shouted. Delanna turned. She was coming toward them, her hat flapping.

"What are you doing down here with Jay Madog? Didn't anybody ever tell you what a notorious sweet-talker he is?" She hit Jay playfully on the arm with her hat. "Delanna, I can see I'm going to have to warn you about him. He's got an eye for every pretty woman on the planet, whether they're married or not."

Delanna suppressed a smile.

"You just stay away from the bride, Madog, at least till I've had a chance to put on her shivaree. And that goes for Cadiz, too." She whacked him with the hat again. "I heard about you on the ham, enticing her into your fancy rig. Shame on you. How are B.T. and her supposed to get together when you keep meddling?"

"I didn't—" Jay began, looking intensely uncomfortable.

"Now you just come along, Delanna, before this sweet-talker steals you away from Sonny," Mrs. Flaherty said. She grabbed Delanna by the arm. "And I'll tell you what I've got planned for the wedding celebration."

Delanna let herself be led away.

"You probably been a been-to too long to remember what a shivaree is, haven't you?"

"I remember shivarees," Delanna said, afraid she'd gone from the frying pan into the fire. "Miz Flaherty, Cadiz told me where I could get a bath, but I lost my way."

"A bath. Of course you want a bath after coming across the Flats. You just come along and get cleaned up, and we'll talk about the shivaree afterwards." She dragged her briskly toward the stillhouse. "Speaking of Cadiz, where did that girl get to? Probably off fighting with B.T., if I know those two."

Probably so, Delanna thought. All that her attempts at matchmaking had done were to get her in over her head with Jay, and if her plan was working as well for B.T. and Cadiz, they'd probably drowned each other in the creek by now.

"I don't know what it'd take to get those two together," Cadiz's mother said, "especially with Madog always buzzing around, stealing other people's women. There's Sonny. I better ask him if he's seen B.T."

She hailed him with her hat. "Sonny! Sonny Tanner! Where's B.T.?"

"I don't know," Sonny said, coming over. "I've been

looking for him. We need to get loaded, Delanna, so we can get started.''

''Get started?'' Cadiz's mother said. ''For where?''

''Milleflores. I want to get as far as the foothills road by nightfall, so there's enough left in the batteries to get us home.'' He looked at Delanna's towel and clean shirt. ''Sorry, Delanna. Your bath'll have to wait till we get home. You haven't seen B.T., have you?''

''No,'' Delanna said, and just then she did see him, walking up the hill from the stream. Alone.

''You can't start for Milleflores now!'' Cadiz's mother protested. ''Not before the wedding celebration.''

''Can't be helped,'' Sonny told her. ''I've got these geese to get home, and Wilkes and Harry are there alone.''

''They're old enough to take care of themselves,'' she said. ''What about your shivaree? Mel and the boys—'' She caught sight of B.T. ''B.T. Tanner, you get over here and tell your brother he can't leave tonight.''

B.T. ambled over, looking . . . Delanna couldn't tell. He didn't look angry, but he didn't look happy either. His face was carefully noncommittal. Maybe he did kill Cadiz, Delanna thought.

''You're leaving?'' B.T. asked.

''I need to get these geese home and check on the boys. You need to get your things into our solaris.''

''Well, I thought maybe . . .'' B.T. said, looking past Sonny toward the driveway. Cadiz roared up the hill in the Flahertys' solaris, peeled into the driveway, and skidded to a stop in front of them. She had her hat jammed on, which was a bad sign, but she bounced out of the solaris and went straight over to B.T. He put his arm around her.

''I thought maybe I might stick around for a few days,'' he said. ''If that's okay with you, Sonny.''

Sonny didn't say anything. He just stared. Cadiz's mother had dropped her hat.

''B.T. and I thought we'd better check that stand of trees over on the east forty,'' Cadiz said, looking lovingly up at him. "In case they need spraying. Then he can bring you the ditcher, 'cause Daddy will be done with it by then. Don't you think that's a good idea, Sonny?"

Sonny was still staring stupidly. Delanna poked him in the ribs. "Sure. Fine," he stammered.

"Great," B.T. said, grinning broadly. He grabbed his bedroll out of Sonny's solaris and handed Cadiz his boots, and they started off for the ranch house, walking hand in hand.

"Well, will wonders never cease?" Cadiz's mother said softly. She stooped and picked up her hat. "How do you suppose that came about?" she wondered aloud, dusting it off.

"I don't have any idea," Sonny said, but he was looking speculatively at Delanna. "Anyway, I'm glad it happened. Now B.T. can bring the supplies home, and all we'll have to take is the geese."

And Cleo, Delanna thought, looking worriedly after the happy couple. She hoped they hadn't gotten so wrapped up in each other they'd forgotten all about her.

"Cadiz," Delanna called, sorry at having to break things up after all her careful shielding of the pair. She hurried after them.

They stopped but kept hold of each other's hands.

"Where's Cleo?" Delanna asked.

"Cleo?" B.T. echoed, as if he'd never heard the name before.

"My scarab," Delanna said.

B.T. looked anxiously back toward the thicket. "I guess I forgot all about your bug."

"You were *supposed* to watch her," Delanna blurted out, and stopped, but too late.

Cadiz was grinning. "Cleo's in the back of the solaris, wrapped up in B.T.'s jacket," she said to Delanna. "I covered the bug up so you can't see it, and if you think I couldn't figure out you set us up, dragging me off to that thicket and telling me that story about B.T. leaving, you're crazy.''

''I *was* leaving,'' B.T. put in, ''and it's a good thing for you Delanna asked me to watch that bug, or else I'd have been long gone.''

''I always thought Sonny should have put your bug down the disposal,'' Cadiz said, gazing at B.T., ''but now I'm actually starting to like it.''

Sonny came up. ''Delanna, sorry to break this up, but if we want to get to the foothills road by sunset, we've got to go. B.T., I unhooked the supply wagon so you can bring it when you come. We'll save a little sunshine in the batteries if we just have to pull the geese and the crate from Sakawa's.''

Delanna retrieved Cleo from the Flahertys' solaris, still wrapped in B.T.'s jacket, and settled her in the back seat of Sonny's solaris. The wagon with the geese was already hooked up behind the crate wagon, and the geese were complaining loudly about having been moved. Delanna leaned over the back seat, tucking Cleo in.

''You're leaving?'' a voice said, leaning in through the window, and Delanna jumped a foot.

''Oh, Jay, it's you,'' she said. ''I was afraid someone would see Cleo.'' She tucked the towel-tent back in place and turned back around to sit down. It seemed safer than getting out of the solaris.

''You didn't tell me you were leaving this afternoon,'' he said, resting his folded arms on the window.

''She didn't know it,'' Sonny broke in, coming up with a rucksack from the Flaherty's old solaris. ''I've gotta get home and check on the boys.'' He handed Delanna the rucksack, and Jay had to move back from the window, but as soon as Sonny left to get something else, Jay stuck his head in the window again.

''I didn't get to tell you what I wanted to this afternoon, but it can wait. I'll tell you when I bring you your trunk.''

''Can't you talk this no-good groom of yours into at least

staying to supper?'' Cadiz's mother said, elbowing Jay
aside.

''Nope,'' Sonny said. He handed Delanna a bag of geese's feed through the window. ''I've got to get these geese
settled so they can start nesting.''

Cadiz's mother looked knowingly from one to the other.
''They can't fool me,'' she said to Jay. ''Sonny just wants
to be alone with his bride. Well, I don't blame him.'' She
smiled at Delanna. ''A caravan out in the middle of the Salt
Flats isn't much of a place for a honeymoon. But you've
put it off this long, you can surely put it off till morning,
isn't that right, Jay?''

''I'd like to see you stay,'' Jay said to Delanna.

''Nope,'' Sonny said again. He pecked Cadiz's mother
on the cheek.

''It's not fair, doing your bride out of her shivaree,'' she
said. ''Not to mention me. You know how I love wedding
celebrations.''

''Looks like you might get one,'' Sonny said, nodding
at Cadiz and B.T., who were bending head-to-head over
some flowers popping up through the blue-green lawn. He
came around and slid into the driver's seat. ''Cadiz and
B.T. look like they could use one.''

''Cadiz and B.T.?'' Jay said, looking over at the couple.
''How'd that happen?''

''Well, it was no thanks to you, Jay Madog,'' Cadiz's
mother said, and smacked him with her hat again. ''And
now that it's happened, you stay out of it.''

Sonny took advantage of the diversion to pull away.

''Don't think you can get off that easy!'' Cadiz's mother
shouted after them. ''You're going to have a wedding celebration at the harvest-do, and a shivaree to end all shivarees!'' She waved her hat. ''I mean it!''

''Sorry,'' Sonny said to Delanna, maneuvering through
the parked solarises and turning down the long drive. ''This
is the last time you'll have to put up with that. Cadiz'll fill

her family in on the situation, and we'll think of some excuse for the harvest-do.''

He came to where the drive turned into a road. It followed the stream as far as the trees and then turned north. Sonny struck off at an angle to it, down a lane that was scarcely wider than a footpath.

''What did Jay want?'' he asked.

That's the question, Delanna thought. ''He told me he'd bring my trunk with the next caravan.''

''He can leave it at Flahertys', and B.T. can come get it. He'll want excuses to see Cadiz.''

Good, Delanna thought. *Because next time Cadiz's mother might not be there to interrupt Jay when he says he wants to tell me something. I should never have let it get this far, not when I*—She refused to let the thought go any farther.

She concentrated on the scenery. The narrow lane had piddled off into a faint line between fields as they drove across the lanzye. The fields were mostly corn, but beyond them Delanna could see neat rows of cannonball trees, and off to the left a hay pasture as green as the Flahertys' emerald-tiled ranchhouse.

''It's so beautiful,'' she said as they passed into the shade of two columns of first-generation cannonballs, tall and stately as pillars. The late afternoon light turned the gray trunks pale gold.

''The Flahertys are pretty well off,'' Sonny said. ''Cadiz's mother brought been-to money into the farm when she married Mel Flaherty, and they were able to buy up two other lanzyes after the ten-year wait.''

''Oh?'' Delanna said.

''They planted one of the lanzyes in blowwheat,'' Sonny said, his voice sounding oddly belligerent, ''so they don't have to be dependent on the cannonball crop for ambrosia. Three years ago a big hailstorm wiped half of it out.''

She looked curiously at him, wondering why he was telling her all this. He was watching ahead intently, his hands gripping the steering wheel, even though the path looked no narrower or more crooked than when they'd set out. "I remember a little of Milleflores," she said. "It had a lot more flowers than the Flahertys', didn't it?"

"Thousands of flowers. Just like the name," he said. "Not very many of them are in bloom just now, but when we found out you were coming, I had Wilkes get your mother's garden fixed up. I remembered you always liked flowers."

She had loved the flowers. She remembered picking endless bouquets, making Sonny trek through endless weeds to get her some blossom she wanted.

"I got in trouble when I first got to school," she said, remembering something she hadn't thought of in years. "I picked some flowers in the school garden. The monk who tended them was so angry, and I was so surprised. It had never occurred to me there wasn't an endless supply."

Sonny was watching her. "I never thought of you having any trouble on Rebe Prime. I always thought of your life there as perfect."

"So did Mother," Delanna said. "I seem to remember a pool at Milleflores. I used to float flower boats on it. Is it still there?"

"The mineral spring?" he said. "Yeah. I haven't been down there for a while. When B.T. gets home, I'll get him to see if the spring needs cleaning out. If he comes home." He grinned at her. "Funny how he and Cadiz patched it up all of a sudden. You have anything to do with that?"

"Me?" she said innocently, and then smiled back at him. "I was worried Cleo might wander off again. I thought somebody should watch her."

"So you sent Cadiz?"

"And B.T."

"Well, you did everybody a big favor. Poor B.T.'s been moping around over Cadiz for two years."

Moping around. B.T. had used the same words. *Sonny's been moping around over you since as long as I can re-*

member, he'd said. She looked across at Sonny, but he was watching the road intently again, and this time it seemed necessary. They seemed to be heading straight for a dense thicket.

Delanna turned around to check on Cleo. She was still asleep, curled up in the nest she had made of B.T.'s jacket and probably dreaming of hatching a clutch of goslings. Sonny had said not to worry about Tom Toricelli's reference on the ham, and Delanna was certain no one had caught sight of Cleo since, but she still felt nervous.

She tucked the jacket more securely around Cleo and turned back around just in time to see them plow into a wall of gray-green. She gasped before she realized they were Red Sea bushes, the leaves thick on the knobs, the branches bare between.

Sonny drove straight into them without slowing down, and the gray-green leaves and grayer branches parted almost before the hood of the solaris touched them. They were thick on all sides, much denser than they had been in the little grove where she'd seen the fire monkeys, but Sonny maneuvered through them as if the path still existed.

Delanna peered forward, trying to catch some sign of thinning, and caught a glimpse of something moving out of the corner of her eye. "Was that a fire monkey?" she asked, pointing ahead and off to the left.

"Not if Flahertys can help it," Sonny said, glancing briefly where she had pointed and then turning his attention back to the nonexistent road. "You'll see some on Milleflores, though. Doc Lyle says they don't communicate, but they seem to have passed the word about who'll shoot them and who won't." He glanced at Delanna.

"I'm not worried. I'll know to smack them on the nose next time," Delanna said.

"You may have to. If they can communicate like I think they can, you'll have a lot of sightseers."

"Sightseers?"

"Yeah, coming to see your hair. They generally stay

away from your mother's cottage, though, so I doubt if you need to worry.''

The solaris burst suddenly out of the Red Sea thicket and onto a road. It wasn't much of one—it was overgrown in the middle and pocked with mud holes—but Sonny picked up speed as though he had come out onto a straightaway.

They lurched in and out of the mud holes, sending the geese into hysterics, and Delanna, bracing herself against the seat, decided this wasn't the time to ask any more questions, but she wondered why the fire monkeys left her mother's cottage alone, and what Sonny meant by that phrase anyway. The Tanners had had a one-room cabin on their own lanzye, but when Delanna left for school, Mr. Tanner and the boys had been living with them, and her mother hadn't written anything about the Tanners building another cottage.

But if the Flahertys' lanzye was any indication, there were dozens of buildings at Milleflores by now, enough for each of the Tanner boys to have his own cottage.

Now that Delanna thought of it, her mother had sometimes referred to Sonny as if he were a distant neighbor instead of someone who lived with her. Delanna had put that down to her dislike of Sonny, whom she frequently criticized. She had called him ''stubborn and silent and slow-witted'' in her letters, and Delanna had thought the same thing about Sonny when she first met him.

She sneaked a glance at him while he concentrated on the mud holes. He might be silent, but he certainly wasn't slow-witted. He had maneuvered them neatly out of Miz Flaherty's wedding celebration and instantly figured out her part in getting B.T. and Cadiz together.

They had been driving between overgrown fields in which a few stray cannonball trees stuck up like signposts, but now they were back in the wild blue-green grass, and the road was narrowing and getting more rutted. Instead of slowing down, though, Sonny was driving faster and faster. The geese had gone beyond hysteria into a kind of honking whimper, and Cleo climbed into Delanna's lap and put her forelegs around her neck.

"Sorry," Sonny said, his voice jouncing with the solaris. "If we don't make the foothills road by sundown, the batteries will never get us all the way home."

Delanna had assumed this was the foothills road. "How much farther is it?"

"Five, six miles," he said. "We'll make it."

They better than made it. The sun was still shining on the tops of the mountains when they bounced into a thicket, out of it again, and across a nearly dry stream to the crossroads. "Great," Sonny said. "We should be home by moonrise."

The foothills road was no improvement over whatever it was they'd been on, but Sonny slowed down a little, and the scenery improved considerably. The Red Sea thickets gave way to balla bushes, and after a few miles, they were among cannonball orchards again. The trees here were young, not nearly as tall as the first-generation trees, and less evenly planted, but the pink evening light filtered between them in delicate shafts. Under the trees was a tangle of underbrush Delanna didn't think would part if you tried to pass through it, and here and there she could see a clump of some pink flower, almost as rosy as the sunset.

"Are we on Milleflores la—" Delanna started to ask, but just then Sonny jammed on the brakes and brought the solaris to a skidding halt that sent the geese into wild honkings.

"Look!" he said, pointing through the windshield at a bird that was breaking out of the trees. It was huge, with vivid green feathers, but as it cleared the cannonballs, the wings spread into a glory of rainbow colors: a dazzling blue and red and a rich purple.

"What—" Delanna began, and a second bird, just as vividly colored, launched itself after the first rainbow-hued rocket.

Sonny had his door open and was half out of the solaris,

trying to follow the birds as they disappeared flashing into the cannonball orchard. He watched the vacant sky a minute longer and then lowered himself back into the solaris. "Royal Mandarins! A pair of them," he said, sounding excited. "The boys were right! They said they'd seen a Royal Mandarin on Milleflores, but I didn't believe them!"

"They're beautiful," Delanna said. No wonder Doc Lyle had been so enthusiastic about them. She'd told him she couldn't remember having seen one, and she would surely have remembered something as lovely as these, even if she had only been five.

"I'm almost sure that was a nesting pair," Sonny said. "Doc Lyle'll go crazy. They're like his pets. He's been working to bring them back, but I was afraid they were too far gone. Nobody's seen a nesting pair in a couple of years." He reached to switch on the ham. "Wait'll Doc hears about this." He picked up the mike. "Sonny Tanner calling Doc Lyle."

"You're calling the vet?" Delanna said, shooting an alarmed glance at the back seat. "He won't come out here, will he? To see the Royal Mandarins?"

"Nah," Sonny said. "People have been calling in sightings every few months, and all he does is log 'em."

"But you said they were his pets—"

"They are, but sightings are a good sign. He'd come if he thought they were in trouble again, not when they're doing fine. Besides, he's got his hands full in Grassedge. He doesn't have time to come running out here."

"But what if Tom Toricelli says something about Cleo on the ham again? Or Cadiz tells her mother about how she and B.T. got together?"

"Cadiz's mother's got bigger news to spread. She's been trying to get B.T. and Cadiz together for two years." Sonny looked at her seriously. "Don't worry. Doc Lyle's five thousand miles away. He's not going to show up all of a sudden and steal Cleo. Trust me."

She nodded.

Sonny turned back to the ham. "He's not at his office. He must be out at the shuttle. This is Sonny Tanner calling Grassedge. Patch me through to the shuttleport."

There was a crackling of static, and then a voice said, "This is Maggie. What d'you need, Sonny?"

"Doc Lyle."

"He isn't here."

"Where is he?"

"Don't know. He left a message on the ham for me to do the shuttle inspections. Didn't say where he was going."

"Okay, thanks." Sonny looked at Delanna. "He's probably out at the mines. He's not on his way here, if that's what you're thinking. If he was headed out this way, we'd have heard it on the ham. And he wouldn't set out alone. He'd wait for a caravan."

Delanna nodded again, but she reached into the back seat, where Cleo had taken to her jacket nest again, and put her on her lap.

Sonny spoke into the mike again. "I need a whereat for Doc Lyle."

A woman's voice came on. "Sonny, it's Liv Webster. Doc Lyle's down at Harvest Home. Harry Corning's sheep have got the wobblies. You want me to patch a relay?"

"That's okay, Liv. When he comes back, just tell him I sighted a pair of Royal Mandarins on my land."

"I heard you skipped out on your shivaree so you could get your bride to yourself," Liv said. "So what are you doing birdwatching when you could be kissing her?"

"Tell Doc Lyle to call me for particulars," Sonny said, and switched off the ham. "I told you you didn't have to worry, Delanna. Harvest Home's five hundred miles the other side of Grassedge. If it'll make you feel better, though, we'll come up with some kind of hidey-hole for Cleo. Then if Doc Lyle should come, which he won't—not if he's got wobbly sheep to doctor—he won't find her."

"Thank you," Delanna said, smiling at Sonny. "I'd appreciate that."

The sun had gone down while Sonny was on the ham, and the sky had dimmed to a pale, clear yellow-pink. "My pleasure," he said.

"We're on Milleflores land?" Delanna asked, even though she knew the answer from what he'd said on the ham.

"Yeah, I've been seeding these fields the last couple of years, trying out different strains. We don't have enough manpower for more orchards yet, but I figure by the time Wilkes and Harry are old enough to plant, there'll be enough seedlings for three more orchards. We've got four down by the lanzye and an aisle along the road."

His pride as he told her about the orchards was obvious, and she felt a twinge of guilt. It must have hurt Sonny to hear her say she couldn't wait to sell her half of Milleflores.

"You've done a lot," she said. "I can't wait to see it."

"Yeah," he said grimly. He opened his door abruptly, got out, and took off for the cannonball trees.

"What is it?' Delanna asked. "Another Royal Mandarin?"

"I'll be back in a minute," he said, and disappeared into the trees. Delanna opened the window and leaned out, scanning the sky, but she couldn't see anything. She could hear birds twittering, though, settling down for the night. The light was fading fast, from yellow-pink to a clear blue. There was a breeze, and the air smelled wet. It must have rained here.

Cleo crawled out of her lap and up the window, extending her forelegs and stretching. Delanna scanned the grove of cannonballs, but it was already dark between them, and she couldn't see Sonny. Far off to the left, there was a flicker of orange light. A fire monkey bonfire?

There was a thrashing sound, and Sonny emerged from the trees, carrying an armful of something. "Here," he said, and handed a huge spray of pink blossoms through the window to her.

"Rosewillows," Delanna breathed. She buried her face in them. "They're beautiful."

"Yeah," he said, still standing by the solaris. Cleo scrambled up and out the window, and he picked the scarab up and held her, still watching Delanna. "Beautiful."

The evening seemed suddenly to have gone silent, the birds no longer chirping, the breeze stilled. "Thank you," Delanna said. "I'd forgotten how beautiful Milleflores was."

"Yeah. Beautiful," he said, and the birds started up again. He came around the solaris and got in. "I remember how you used to like rosewillows," he told her, "and the ones near the lanzye aren't blooming yet." He switched on the ignition and started down the road again.

"I love them," Delanna said, looking at him.

"I'm glad," he said, watching the road, which was already getting hard to see.

They jounced in and out of several incredible mud holes, terrorizing the geese again and showering them both with rosewillow petals, but he didn't turn on the lights. He simply leaned farther over the steering wheel, peering ahead.

"Don't want to waste the batteries," he said when they fell into a depression that was as deep as a sinkhole. "We've still got quite a ways to go. Try and get some sleep."

Delanna couldn't imagine sleeping through all this upheaval, but she leaned back against the seat and closed her eyes, and she must have fallen asleep because she heard Sonny saying, "Wake up."

She opened her eyes. Sonny was looking down at her, and it came to her that she had snuggled closer to him while she slept. Her head was resting on his shoulder. She had not let go of her bouquet of flowers. She didn't move. The solaris was full of the smell of rosewillows and a silvery light. The moon must have come up.

"Wake up," Sonny said again, and she smiled up at him. He looked seriously down at her. "Delanna—" he said, and unlike when Jay had said her name, she felt no impulse to blurt out something to keep him from speaking. She waited, her arms full of moonlit flowers, for him to finish what he was going to say.

"Delanna," he said again, and shook her shoulder. "We're here."

She sat up. The solaris was stopped under a line of cannonball trees, stark-looking in the moonlight. The road had narrowed to a path again, and next to it, in a tangle of weeds, were a couple of lean-tos. Behind them, even deeper in underbrush, was a ramshackle shed. A place for storing orchard equipment, maybe, or an abandoned still.

"Where are we?" Delanna asked, blinking. "Why did you stop? Did the batteries give out?"

"No," he said. "We're here." He opened his door and got out. "Welcome to Milleflores."

Delanna stepped out, the spray of rosewillows still in the crook of her arm. "I don't remember it looking like this," she said, squinting at the lean-tos.

"Those are new," Sonny said as he shifted the camping gear to get at Delanna's carryit. "Well, new since you left Keramos. Sun-fired ceramic, kind of dull in the moonlight. We had enough left over to coat your mom's cottage, too." He gestured vaguely toward the dense shadow of underbrush. "Get Cleo, and I'll show you the way. The garden kinda overgrew the path."

A light went on in one of the lean-tos and Delanna could see the silhouettes of two boys as they dashed past the windows. The door slammed. "Sonny, that you?" one of them shouted from the stoop in front of the door. "Me and Wilkes was asleep."

"I'll bet," Sonny muttered. "They probably ran all the way from the fishing pond when they saw the solaris moon-flash back on the ridge. They know I don't like them night fishing without me or B.T." He was shaking his head, but he didn't seem too angry at them. "It's me," he said to the boys. He put the carryit on the roof of the solaris and closed the canopy. "As long as you're awake, come on down and get these geese into their pen, and say hello to Delanna, too.''

While the taller boy started toward them in a sauntering gait that Delanna had seen both his older brothers use, the little boy ran at breakneck speed and threw himself at Sonny in a mock tackle, then wholeheartedly hugged him.

"This is Harry," Sonny said, his arms still full of the wriggling boy who had already turned his attention from Sonny to Delanna. He was smiling at her.

"Hello," Delanna said. Harry was all agrin, moon-silvered hair tangled and matted, eyes too bright to have just awakened. She thought he might be about seven years old.

"That's Wilkes," Harry said, pointing to his brother.

Wilkes was thin and very tall, perhaps eleven or twelve years old. His hair was as matted as his little brother's but darker. He extended his hand solemnly, and Delanna shook it.

"Harry, did you take a shower at all while I was gone?" Sonny asked, wrinkling his nose as he put the little boy down.

"Sure I did. B.T. made me," Harry said indignantly.

"So you haven't had a shower since B.T.'s been gone, eh?"

Harry ignored Sonny and turned to Delanna. "Were you really in a space ship?" Harry asked. "Is it cold up there in the dark? I wouldn't like it if it never was morning. I made a picture of the *Gripsholm*. That's the first ship ever to send a shuttle down to Keramos. You want to see it?"

Harry had taken Delanna's hand and she would have let herself be led away, she was so charmed by his friendly chatter, but Sonny grabbed his little brother by his shirt sleeve.

"Help Wilkes with the geese, Harry. You can show Delanna the picture in the morning."

"Aw, Sonny . . ." Harry started to say, but Wilkes had taken the handful of shirt away from Sonny and was dragging Harry toward the wagon. "Goodnight, Delanna," Harry said resignedly. He struggled with his brother's grip on his shirt for a few steps then suddenly let himself go limp. Wilkes kept hold of Harry's sleeve and, without missing a step, dragged him the rest of the way to the wagon. The alarmed geese drowned out the sound of Harry's mischievous giggle.

"This way, Delanna," Sonny said. He had her carryit under one arm and Cleo under the other and was walking through a dark tangle of weeds. She followed close behind, barely able to see the path he was following through the underbrush. Black leafy things brushed her legs and arms, and stems snapped under her feet. They got to a gravel path that was free of brush all the way to a stone stoop in front of the cottage.

Delanna had no memory of a stone stoop in front of her mother's cottage. "I remember a wooden porch," she said, "and I thought there were trellises."

"This is the new addition," Sonny explained. "The trellises are on the other side, the side with the view." He took the two stone steps in one stride, then handed Cleo to Delanna so that he could throw open the door of the cottage. "I'll get the light," he said, stepping inside ahead of her. "Inside isn't going to look the same either, 'cause we added a proper kitchen to the house when we were living with your mother, so it's bigger than it was.

It doesn't look bigger, Delanna thought as the light came on, just strange. Though the kitchen she stepped into was unfamiliar, she recognized the wooden table with the lion's claw feet. It was nearly white from years of bleaching, dented and scarred from endless piles of vegetables being sliced or diced on its thick, utilitarian boards. Behind the table, the chipped blue ceramic shelves that filled the long wall from floor to ceiling were the same ones that she remembered as being over the fireplace, and she recognized her mother's big pots and pans and even the flower pattern on the dishes. The huge fireplace had been opened so that she could see through to what used to be the only room in the cottage. What had been the kitchen area when it was a single-room cottage now had a few chairs and a rug, like a little sitting area in front of the fireplace, and her mother's bed and trunk were along the far wall by the door. No doubt the porch she remembered just beyond.

"It's pretty much the way your mother left it," Sonny said. "The boys and I just cleaned it up a bit."

It was spotless. They'd even used bleach on the floor, and the rug in front of the fireplace, though quite worn, looked as if it had been fluffed. It didn't smell as if it had been closed up for nearly a year, either. "Is there a bath?" Delanna asked hopefully. She could see that the old dry sink had been jerry-rigged with a pump and drain. Maybe the outhouse had been replaced, too.

"Well, yeah, kinda," Sonny said, showing her a little room off the kitchen that was lined with the same blue ceramic as the shelves in the kitchen, except that most of these were broken pieces cemented together. "Just a gravity shower, but you can get the water nice and hot with this little stove."

The stove was a mound of soot-stained ceramic, and it was quite cold to the touch. The shower was nothing but a curtained circle with a drain in the floor. The toilet was of a kind she'd only seen in pictures, but considering the alternative, Delanna was grateful.

Sonny was frowning at the shower, as if he disapproved of it. But when he noticed Delanna looking at him, he said quickly, "I can get a fire started in the stove before I go. I know how much you wanted a bath, but maybe a shower will do for tonight. Tomorrow I'll try to figure something out." He'd stepped into the tiny bathroom, eyeing the shower as if he were measuring. "I've got an old vat I could clean up, maybe fit it . . ."

Delanna touched Sonny's shoulder to get his attention. "I'll be fine, Sonny. I'll worry about a shower tomorrow. Everything's fine."

"Your mother reused everything to save money when we built on the addition," he said. "I think she . . . Well, I guess she was entitled to reuse whatever she wanted to."

Delanna nodded uncertainly. Her mother had written about a disagreement with Sonny over his not wanting to reuse perfectly good ceramic, just because a few pieces were cracked. But it wasn't just a few pieces. Nearly every one was broken. It must have taken a lot of patience to piece them together, then lay the pieces and cement them in place. A lot of patience.

"A lot more hodgepodge than you're used to," Sonny said.

"I'll be just fine with my mother's things," she assured him.

Sonny looked relieved. Delanna smiled and expected him to say good night and leave, but he just stood there, looking at her.

"What?" she asked. "Is something wrong?"

"Wrong? No. Um, the nights are chilly. I'll build a fire for you before I go." He brushed past her to the firewood box and started laying a fire in the big fireplace that separated the two rooms.

Delanna put the rosewillows on the table, then wandered into the other room to tuck Cleo into a pillow. The scarab didn't even open an eye; she was getting so used to being stashed in odd places, anywhere from under a floppy hat to on top of a feather-filled pillow. Her mother's old space-trunk was at the foot of the bed, a flimsy thing compared to the one Delanna had, but the latches still worked and the lid opened easily enough. There were linens stacked neatly on one side and ledgers piled on the other, with a few wrapped packages in between. She started to close the trunk, thinking that she'd go through it in the daylight, when she realized that among the ledger binders were several books. She pulled them out, eager to see what kind of writing her mother had owned in book form. Most people used hand-held readers or even their vegas for reading entertainment, so hardcopies in genuine perfect bound-book form were reserved for keepsakes and collectibles. She picked up the top one. Its cover was plain red, no pretty gold lettering, just a hand-written title in black ink that read *Serena Milleflores, Her Journal.*

"My mother kept a journal?" Delanna said, opening the book randomly to the center. The paper was as thin as tissue, but slick and opaque.

"They're in her spacer trunk," Sonny said, poking his face through the fireplace. "Oh, I see you found them."

"I didn't know my mother kept a journal," she said, sitting down on the edge of the bed. She opened it to the middle. It was written in the small, cramped hand of the letters she'd sent to Delanna.

Oh, Mother, she thought, with a sudden ache in her heart. She closed the journal and sat there with it in her lap, thinking about her mother's letters and then the letter from the attorney on Rebe Prime. "We regret to inform you of your mother's death . . ."

"I think I'll read these a little later," she said, fighting back tears.

Sonny looked at her, but didn't say anything. He'd gotten a fire burning nicely in the fireplace, and come around to the sitting area side to draw the screen. The lights flickered.

"You don't have a very big power reservoir here," he said apologetically. It's going to be lights out whether you like it or not in about ten minutes. There's a good lantern over there by the ham, and both of them will switch automatically to the backup battery if you need them during the night. But everything else runs off the main energy storage cells."

"Everything else?" Delanna said, looking around the cottage. Aside from the ham and the lights, she didn't see anything that would use energy, no vega terminal, no clothes freshener, no room monitors. Even the quilt on the bed was just scraps of flannel sewn together, not a real sleep-keeper with temperature sensors and response units.

"The water pump," Sonny said. "If you're thirsty, you might want to get a drink now. Although there's always water in the hot water reservoir, and there's a faucet on it."

"Well, maybe I ought to just fill a pitcher with water," Delanna said, heading for the kitchen. She took a white pitcher off the shelf and went to the converted dry sink to fill it so that Sonny would know that it was done before he left. She also wanted to make sure she could figure out how to turn on the water. She was pretty sure there wasn't a household monitor around to tell her if she couldn't figure it out.

"Just push the faucet," Sonny said after watching her squeeze and then press the levers at the dry sink.

Delanna pushed. Water fell from the spigot. It worked pretty much like a picnic canteen. She filled the pitcher, then took it to the table and put the spray of rosewillows in it. She filled another pitcher for herself.

"Are you hungry?" Sonny asked. He had opened the cupboard behind the table. It was stocked with ceramic canning jars and freeze crocks. "These grain crackers are really good with cheese," he said, taking the lid from a crock.

"No, I'm not hungry. But I'm very tired," Delanna said, almost regretfully. She didn't really want him to leave, especially with his trying so hard to make her feel at home and her really not knowing her way around yet. But she was beginning to feel so tired that she thought that if she sat down at the table for a snack, she would end up snoring in the cheese.

Sonny fished out a few of the crackers before he put the lid back on. "Well, I guess I better go check on the geese, make sure Harry and Wilkes closed the door on the poultry shed." He closed the cupboard and went to the door. She saw him glance at the rosewillows and smile before he stepped out into the night.

The lights flickered again. Maybe a five-minute warning? Delanna wondered. She hurried into the other room where she'd seen her mother's dresser. In the second drawer she found some nightgowns. At least, they looked like night-gowns—long shapeless shifts in pastel colors. They didn't feel cuddly, though, the way that nightgowns should. She pulled the softest one out just as the lights went out. Whether it was a nightgown or not, tonight it was going to be. The light from the fireplace was adequate to find her way to the bed. She left Cadiz's clothes in a heap on the floor, slipped the worn garment over her head, and pulled back the covers on the bed. She could hear Cleo purring contentedly on the pillow. It would have been nice to have a bath, but after weeks of camping, the thought of a real bed was even more enticing. She nudged Cleo over a bit and put her face on the pillow. The last thing she remembered was hearing the geese honking.

• • • • • • •

Honking was also the first thing she heard on awaking, followed by Harry's shouts, all directly under her bedroom window. Sunlight was streaming in the window and Cleo wasn't on the pillow anymore. Delanna got out of bed, certain she was going to have to rescue the geese from Cleo, though how the scarab had gotten out of the cottage, she didn't know. But Cleo was on the kitchen table, nib-bling rosewillow leaves, and a note that Cleo had also sam-pled but apparently found distasteful told Delanna that Sonny had slipped in earlier to build a fire in the hot-water heater.

She looked out the kitchen window, up toward where rows of cannonball trees lined the road for as far as the eye could see, which was to the top of a ridge that had to be miles distant. It surprised her that the plantings would be that vast, though it made sense to have them accessible right along the road for picking equipment. If there was picking equipment.

Closer in, where the road dead-ended above the cottage, someone had unfurled the solar collection panels on the

solaris, and she could see feet underneath it, so she assumed
Sonny was trying to fix it again. Little Harry was trying to
herd the geese from the poultry shed to the pond, and they
were going the wrong way just now. The geese were almost
all the way back to the shed, and Harry was trying to get
there before them, no doubt to close the door before they
got in and refused to come out again. Delanna was tempted
to go out and help him, but that lasted only until she
glanced at the note in her hand again. She didn't need to
read it again to decide to take a shower first thing. Her
fingernails and knuckles were filthy and her hair was so
dirty her scalp itched, and the geese would be no happier
with two people chasing them. She went back into the bedroom to find towels and something to wear besides Cadiz's
dirty clothes.

The towels were in the linen closet, right where she remembered they'd be, and she found a short-sleeved shift
hanging among the roughies and shirts, all of which looked
too big for her. She grabbed the shift anyhow, pulled the
belt off Cadiz's skirt, and headed for the shower. The water
was nice and hot at first, but she'd just lathered her hair for
a second time when it started to cool down. She rinsed right
away, but not quickly enough to avoid a final rinse in icy
cold water. She still had goose bumps after she'd toweled
off and slipped into the shift, so she took a comb and went
to sit in the sunshine to dry her hair. Cleo scampered after
her.

There was a proper porch off the bedroom, one with a
bench and table for working outdoors. The garden grew
right up to the steps and onto the trellises, where Cleo had
already spotted a profusion of tight pink buds that she could
pull apart. Delanna looked around to see where the geese
were and spotted them swimming contentedly in the pond.
They were unlikely to attract Cleo's attention at this distance, so she just called to the scarab instead of scooping
her up.

They went down into the garden, where Delanna could

look more closely at what was blooming and what was about to bloom while she fluffed her hair in the sun. There were lots of monkey candles and a cluster of pumpkin-faces just budding. The garden looked well-tended up close to the cottage, the rows cultivated and the plants staked. But the farther Delanna got from the cottage, the more tangled and dense the growth became. She tried to comb her hair as she walked, but it wasn't long before she tucked the comb under her belt so that she could use both hands to lift a drooping blossom, the better to see its orange petals and smell the sweet perfume.

"Can you smell that, Cleo?" she asked as the little scarab extended to see what Delanna had found so interesting. They were near the corner of the garden where a thick hedge bordered the tangled rows. Here flowers and vegetables grew side by side. Whatever plan there had been to this intermingling was no longer discernible. The bushy plant Delanna had found looked like a fountain of leaves in a turnip bed, but the blossoms were lovely. "I think it's a peony, though I've never seen one this large before."

"Who you talking to?" she heard Harry say, startling her to her feet.

She whirled around, and saw him only ten feet away, sitting cross-legged among the greenery, ripe orangey-red fruit dripping down his hand and chin. He had a silver bowl in his lap. "Hello, Harry," she said. "I see you got the geese to the pond."

"Is it the bug?" Harry was saying as he scrambled to his feet. "I didn't think you'd bring her out here 'cause of what Sonny said about our having to be careful about Doc Lyle and everything." Harry jumped nimbly around plants with his bare feet, balancing the big bowl and the half-eaten fruit in his hands.

"She's not a—"

"Bug," Harry finished for her when he spied Cleo crouched at Delanna's feet. "Sonny said you said that all the time. But she sure looks like one, a real *big* bug." He thrust the bowl and dripping fruit into Delanna's hands and scooped Cleo up. The scarab retracted completely, and Harry laughed, delighted. "You hiding in there, Cleo girl?" he said, tapping gently on her thorax plate. "Oh, feel how smooth." He was smearing juice from the fruit on Cleo's plates, and the moisture caught the sunlight. "Ohh," Harry breathed, turning her, the better to catch the sunlight on her plates. "Look at that. She's beautiful."

Cleo's carapace perked a bit; the scarab knew when she was being admired. Harry was staring at her, mouth agape, waiting for something more to happen. Delanna put the fruit in the bowl and reached over to stroke Cleo's carapace. The scarab tucked it in tightly, and Harry looked at Delanna, as if he thought she could make Cleo do something she didn't want to do. "It's going to take her a while to get used to you, Harry," Delanna said kindly. "Probably the best thing you can do to hurry her is to put her down and let her come to you."

Harry put Cleo down beside the peony and squatted next to her, his nose no more than fifteen inches away. The scarab stayed in a tight ball as Harry stared expectantly.

"Let's just go about our business, Harry," Delanna suggested, reaching for his hand. Cleo was not going to approach Harry in the next fifteen seconds, which Delanna figured was about the maximum time that seven-year-olds could remain patient. "What were you doing, weeding?" Delanna asked, looking at the stuff in the bowl.

"No, having breakfast," Harry said, reaching into the bowl for the half-eaten fruit. "And I'm supposed to bring some to Wilkes and Sonny, too. Just because they have to fix the solaris, I have to pick *their* breakfast, too. They wouldn't even help me with the geese! It's not fair."

"I used to have to take care of the geese, when I was little," Delanna said.

"Did they run away from you, too?" Harry asked.

"Yes, they did. But only until I learned how to trick them," Delanna said. They'd moved about ten feet away from Cleo, who was still tightly wadded up in a ball. "What are you supposed to be picking, Harry?"

"Picking," Harry repeated, swallowing the last of the fruit. "Oh, you know. Breakfast. Whatever is ready. Timarines, mostly," he said, holding up the orange-red fruit. So that was what it was. It looked like a cross between a tomato and an orange.

"How did you trick the geese, Delanna?" Harry asked.

Delanna realized that this part of the garden had changed from flowers to vegetables, and that she didn't recognize many of them. "You pick, and I'll hold the bowl," Delanna said. "And while we're doing that, I'll tell you how I tricked the geese."

The trick, of course, wouldn't take more than a few sentences to explain. But the plan was to keep Harry occupied with something other than Cleo—who was just now cautiously extending and watching them warily—stay in the sun so that her hair would dry, and figure out which parts of these plants were edible by watching Harry pick them first. That called for a fairly long story, so she started with holding the geese for Doc Lyle at the spaceport.

Harry listened, while both of them scooted along on their hands and knees until Harry would pause to pull one plant out by the roots or snap the leaves off another. He'd toss them in the bowl, where Delanna broke off pieces to sample. Sometimes Harry would get engrossed in the story and Delanna would have to motion to him to keep picking. They were in the far corner of the garden, where the vines and leaves were thicker and taller, probably the section of the garden that sprouted earliest in the year. Harry was more selective here, bypassing the larger and probably tougher fruits. Cleo was following more closely now; Delanna caught enough glimpses of her to know she was doing some exploring on her own, sometimes a row or two over, sometimes so close, Delanna could feel the scarab's little claw touch her hair.

"Think we have enough now, Harry?" she asked, finishing the story. "The bowl is almost full."

Harry scooted back to look in the bowl and shrugged. "B.T. is gone, so we don't need any for him, but Sonny is back, and you're here, too."

"Did you fill this bowl while Sonny was gone?" Delanna asked, figuring that B.T. and Sonny probably ate about equal portions, so all they'd need was a little extra for herself.

Harry shook his head. "Didn't use a bowl," he said. "B.T., Wilkes, and me would just stop here and eat as much as we wanted."

"Well," Delanna said, eyeing the volume of greens critically, "if we had some goose eggs, I think we have enough to make a nice omelette."

"We have eggs!" Harry said brightly. "There's two in the poultry house. I'll go get them." He leaped to his feet, getting ready to make a dash for it, and then looked at Delanna. His eyes widened. "You aren't still afraid of fire monkeys, are you?"

"Why do you ask?" Delanna said, certain she didn't want to know. "Please don't tell me there's a fire monkey behind me. It's Cleo touching my hair, isn't it?" She turned.

It *was* Cleo, pulling a claw through Delanna's hair as she retracted into a ball that was nestled in the leathery palm of a fire monkey. Instinctively, Delanna reached for the scarab, and the fire monkey flung Cleo aside, its eyes fixed on the movement of Delanna's hair, dancing just out of her reach. Another fire monkey caught Cleo.

"Just bop him on the nose," Harry said.

"You bop him," Delanna said. There were four fire monkeys now, and she couldn't imagine how creatures that big had gotten so close without being seen or heard.

"I can't," Harry said. "I'm not tall enough. My clapping doesn't work either."

"Don't scare them away while they've got Cleo," Delanna warned. The fire monkey that had Cleo was rubbing her plates, apparently intrigued by the glitter. It probably looked like fire to the monkey, the way Delanna's hair did. Delanna grabbed the comb from under her belt and began running it through her hair. The monkey stopped stroking Cleo to watch. The others—there were seven now, and more just outside the garden—took jerky steps toward her, but the one holding Cleo just stood there, its orange-yellow eyes unblinking.

"Boy, they really do like your hair," Harry said. "They never come that close to me."

Delanna took a half-step toward the one holding Cleo, and it took a half-step backwards. She pulled the comb through her hair, combing it forward, hoping to get the monkey to reach for the comb. Its arm twitched, and the next time the comb came forward it reached out. At the same time Delanna made a grab for Cleo, but the fire monkey popped the scarab into the air, far above Delanna's reach. Delanna shrieked. Another fire monkey caught Cleo before she hit the ground.

"Did you see that? What a great catch," Harry said admiringly.

"Harry, I don't think you're taking this seriously enough. I know they don't mean any harm, but Cleo could get hurt if they drop her."

"When they throw burning sticks, they don't drop them," Harry told Delanna. "And those have only one safe end to catch."

"Harry, you're not helping," she said. "I want Cleo back, and I want her now. I'm going to walk right up to that fire monkey . . ." She began marching as she spoke, trying to keep her resolve up with the sound of her own voice. "And if he doesn't give Cleo to me, I'm going to . . ."

The fire monkey flicked Cleo into the air and backed up a few steps. Delanna lunged, trying to catch Cleo herself, but a pebbly hand snatched the scarab out of the air. Delanna lunged again, hoping to catch this new monkey off guard, but it merely threw Cleo before Delanna got anywhere near as close as she'd gotten to the others. Before she could change direction, Cleo was in the air again, tossed to yet another monkey, and another.

The fire monkeys were still in a semicircle around Delanna, but they seemed to have lost interest in her hair. Cleo's glittering form was their new fixation. Delanna stopped and stood still, because each time she moved toward one of them, they threw Cleo again, just like in a game of keepaway. But the fire monkeys kept on tossing Cleo. The sun glinted like metallic rainbows on her plates.

''They probably like the way the sun gleams on Cleo's plates,'' Delanna said, wishing that she'd never polished them. What was she going to do? The fire monkeys were in complete control. If she tried clapping, what would she do if they just dropped Cleo, or maybe ran off with her? She couldn't take the risk. She'd just have to outwait them.

''What's Cleo doing?'' Harry asked.

Harry was still outside the semicircle, his hand shielding his eyes from the sun as he watched Cleo being thrown from monkey to monkey. Delanna, inside the semicircle, had to blink each time Cleo passed between her eyes and the sun, but now she saw what Harry was asking about. Each time Cleo was tossed, at about the top of the arc, she extended fully, legs swimming, but her carapace remained folded, as if she knew that her skinny little legs wouldn't distort her trajectory very much. For a moment Delanna thought the scarab was panicking, but then she heard her purring as she whirred overhead, her legs treading air.

''That little imp!'' Delanna exclaimed. ''She's enjoying herself! Cleo, you come here this minute.'' And of course Cleo did not obey; she never did, at least not right away. But in a few minutes, she was no longer a ball when one of the fire monkeys caught her, or Cleo caught its hand. Whoever caught who, Cleo skittered down the fire monkey as if it were a scratching post, and flung herself into Delanna's arms. Delanna clapped at the fire monkeys, and they bolted a few steps. "Go on, go away," she said, clapping again. She hugged Cleo, and when she looked up again, only two of the fire monkeys were in sight. Delanna sighed with relief.

"That sure was neat," Harry said, coming over and touching Cleo before Delanna could say anything. The scarab did not retract. Delanna supposed that after playing ball for the fire monkeys, the scarab could endure the admiration of a little boy.

"Little minx scared me half to death," Delanna said.

"I think they only eat cooked meat," Harry said, "stuff they find in the fires. But I've never seen them take anything and actually cook it themselves."

"Hear that, Cleo? You could have been roasted," Delanna said, nuzzling the scarab. "You naughty girl, cooperating with them like that."

"Oh, speaking of food. Will you still make that omelette?" Harry asked, ready to break away.

Delanna nodded, and looked around for the bowl of greens, half certain the fire monkeys had taken it with them. But the bowl was right where they'd left it, not even upset. She scooped it up and started to follow Harry. He was already racing up the hill toward the poultry shed.

Harry had collected the two goose eggs by the time Delanna got to the cottage. Cleo took one look at the eggs, and extended fully so that she could transfer herself to Harry.

"Hey, she likes me," Harry said, trying to balance the eggs and Cleo, too. He would have dropped one of the eggs but for Cleo's quick grab. She chittered at him. "She wants both of them," he said, and handed her the other egg. She wrapped her claws protectively around them.

In the kitchen, Delanna was rinsing the greens when Sonny came in. "You all right?" he asked. "Wilkes and I saw a sparkle of fire monkeys coming up from behind the cottage."

"Oh, Sonny, you should have seen them," Harry said, and while the little boy went on talking, Delanna cut the vegetables for the omelette and put them in the skillet.

Sonny, uh-huh-ing Harry, raised a ceramic tile on the counter to reveal a power cell for the skillet, and he pulled some spices out of the cabinet. Delanna sniffed them one by one, recognized two of them as oregano and pepper, and rejected the others, even though several of them smelled quite nice. She didn't want to ruin the omelette with some native spice she didn't understand. But Sonny took one of the rejects back out of the cabinet and added a pinch to the vegetables.

"And Cleo goes . . . *wrrrr, wrrrr,*" Harry said. He was aping Cleo's flight between the fire monkeys. The scarab was on the table, hiding under the drooping rosewillows with her two eggs.

Delanna stirred the vegetables, uncertain with some of the fleshier ones of when they were cooked enough. Sonny came over and stabbed some of the roots with a fork, taking a tidbit to taste. He nodded, indicating they were ready, and would have gotten the eggs, but Delanna stopped him. "Better let me do this. Cleo will never forgive anyone else," she said.

"Hey, what's Cleo doing?" Harry said, finally noticing Cleo hiding with the eggs. He'd finished his story and now seemed to be thinking out loud, telling them what they could plainly see for themselves, that Cleo was hiding with the goose eggs.

It was easy enough to snatch the eggs from Cleo, for they were much too large for her to get into her pouch, but she chittered at having them taken away and squeaked loudly when Delanna cracked them into the pan. Delanna handed her back the empty shells, which the scarab sniffed at. Then, with what could only be interpreted as complete disdain, she stepped down from the tabletop to the chair, slid down to the floor, and skittered into the other room. Harry followed her on his hands and knees.

"Hey, Cleo," he said. "Do you want to help me make a goose pole?"

"A what?" Sonny asked, but Harry didn't hear him.

"I told him about tying a piece of bread on the line of a fishing pole," Delanna said. "The geese run after it, and you can lead them almost anywhere. It's easier than shooing them."

"I never would have thought of that," Sonny said.

"I didn't either. I learned how in an animal behavior class."

Sonny had fetched some plates out of the cupboard and was setting the table. He moved the rosewillows, and Delanna thought of how nice it had been to get them, and how nice the hot shower had been this morning, too, not to mention that her mother's flower garden had been weeded and everything was so clean. Milleflores didn't have the luxurious buildings of the Flahertys', but the people sure were every bit as nice.

Harry came back in, carrying Cleo, who was curled up into a ball, sulking. Harry didn't seem to care. He seemed just to like holding her. "Sonny," he added, "are we going out to the orchard today, or are you and Wilkes going to work on the solaris?"

"Wilkes has already found the problem with the solaris," Sonny said.

Delanna stirred the eggs again. "Well, that was lucky," she commented.

"He's got it fixed so it'll hold till we can get the motor fixed," Harry said. "It was a piece of bent metal in the transmission, wasn't it, Sonny?"

"Well, as a matter of fact, it was," Sonny said, looking sourly at his little brother. "And if Wilkes knew what the problem was, why didn't he send me a here's-what-you-need? We were slowing down the whole caravan for days!"

Harry shrugged. "You kept asking for B.T."

"Cadiz kept asking for B.T." Sonny threw an exasperated look at Delanna.

Delanna smiled. Sonny even seemed to have trouble talking to his own brothers. Maybe she shouldn't have been so hard on him for not being perfectly clear in his communication with her all the time.

"So we're going out to the orchard?" Harry asked.

"Wilkes and I are going out to the orchard," Sonny said. "You're staying here and doing your chores and helping Delanna." He turned apologetically to Delanna. "The orchards have got to be ditched before the rains get here, so we won't get around to cleaning the hot spring for a while."

"That's okay. I don't have a sandshift to wear in swimming anyway. It's in my trunk, and that's either still in orbit or waiting for Jay Madog to pick it up at the spaceport." She pulled the omelette off the power unit. It was ready. "Get your brother, Harry. Breakfast is ready."

"Wilkes!" Harry shouted, not even moving near the door. Then, in a normal voice, he said to Delanna, "Well, if you don't have any clothes, is that why you're wearing your mother's nightgown?"

"Nightgown?" Delanna glanced down at the shift. She had thought it too brightly colored to be a nightgown, and besides, it was hanging next to the roughies, like outerwear. She sighed. She supposed now that those pastel-colored things in the drawer were her mother's dresses, though how she was supposed to have guessed, she didn't know. She sighed again. "I guess I should be grateful that I didn't find that out on the ham."

The door slammed as Wilkes came in. He washed his hands and sat at the table, his eyes coming to rest on Delanna. He didn't exactly gape, but Delanna could see that he, too, was surprised to find her wearing a nightgown. Was nightwear considered as intimate as underwear? From the look on Wilkes face, she thought it must be.

"Yes, it's a nightgown, Wilkes. I thought it was a dress, and I made a mistake," she said, and he half-smiled at her, as if to say he didn't care. "You," she said to Sonny, "should have told me right away instead of letting me cook breakfast in a nightgown, probably embarrassing your brothers half to death." Delanna slammed the omelette pan on the table in front of them.

Sonny went to sit down. "I don't think they're all that embarrassed, even if they haven't seen a nightgown without a wrapover before," he said. "Besides, they know you don't have your trunk and that you're having to make do. And as for me not telling you right away, well . . ."

He was just going to remind her that he'd tried to warn her about the salt creek, and not to wander off, and she never listened to him anyway and at least half the time she snapped his head off, so why would he want to tell her she was wearing a nightgown?

But Sonny didn't say those things. He grinned at her and said, "I thought you looked nice."

Delanna was almost sorry Harry had told her she was wearing a nightgown, her mother's day clothes were so long and cumbersome, and the pale colors were dirty the instant she stepped into the garden or picked up the bucket of feed for the geese. She wondered how her mother had managed to get any work done wearing such clothes.

If only she had her trunk. She tried to calculate how long it would take for Jay to bring it to her. Almost two weeks each way, if the caravan had as much luck on the Salt Flats as they had had and there weren't any storms, so three weeks to a month, even if he'd started back to Grassedge immediately, and in the meantime she was stuck in these draggy pink things she could hardly walk in. A month!

I hope Jay hurries, she thought, and then instantly retracted the wish. She didn't want him to hurry. She didn't even want him to come. "When I come back, I have something I want to tell you," he'd said, and she was afraid she knew exactly what it was.

She should have set Jay straight right away. *You can't go on sending mixed signals like that without getting in trouble*, she'd told Cadiz. She should have taken her own advice. Instead, she'd flirted with Jay, gone to his van, tried to attract his attention.

Only I don't want it now . . . she thought, and wouldn't let herself finish the thought. Well, maybe he wouldn't come back. Grassedge was a long way away, and the summer rains were due in a few weeks. With luck, he'd be stuck on the other side of the Salt Flats for a month or longer, and by that time he'd have found some widow or farmer's daughter to pursue.

In the meantime, though, she had to have something to wear. She found a pair of scissors and hacked off one of the dresses to knee-length, which helped, but it didn't solve the color problem, and when she tried to wash out the ti-marine stains she'd gotten all down her front fixing dinner, the shift turned into an intractable mass of wrinkles.

She didn't know if Sonny had a smoother, and he wasn't there to ask. His trip to Grassedge and back had apparently put him far behind schedule, and for the next week and a half she scarcely saw him. When she did, he was busy setting up the still, or digging muddy trenches in the orchard, or snapping out orders to Harry and Wilkes, whom he kept working almost as hard as he did.

"What can I do to help?" Delanna asked whenever she saw him, and he'd say, out of breath and covered in mud, "If it's not too much trouble, you could make up some vegetable rolls for us to take with us. Wilkes and me've gotta go check the north orchard."

A few vegetable rolls were hardly her share of the work, and Delanna felt guilty sitting around when there was obviously more work than the three of them could do, and poor Harry was hauling heavy buckets of water and weeding the garden.

One morning she caught Wilkes before he left with Sonny, and asked if she could borrow a pair of trousers and a shirt, and then helped Harry carry the water to the vegetable garden, glad to be at least a little useful.

"Harry," she asked him while they were picking the

supper vegetables, "what did my mother do around here?"

Harry straightened up, looking so bewildered, Delanna wondered if it was possible no one had told him she was Serena's daughter.

"I mean, Serena, Miz Millesflores," she said. "I want to do my share around here, and I thought I could start by doing the jobs Mother—Serena—did. What were they?"

Harry ducked his head. "I dunno," he mumbled. "These timarines are going to be ripe in another couple of days."

"Did she take care of the garden?" Delanna persisted. "Or brew the ambrosia?"

Now he looked uncomfortable, embarrassed. "I gotta go listen to the ham. Sonny says I'm supposed to find out what the weather is," he said, and fled into the cottage.

Now, what was that all about? Delanna wondered. Had Sonny told the boys they weren't to ask her to do any chores? He certainly didn't ask her to do any himself. When she'd asked him this morning about what she could do while he was gone, he'd said, "Just rest. You've had a hard trip."

But he'd had a hard trip, too, and that didn't stop him from getting up at the crack of dawn and working in the orchards till after dark. The least she could do was take over her mother's jobs.

The next day Sonny took Harry with him, so Delanna did Harry's around-the-house chores, gathering in the ripe vegetables and washing out the boys' muddy shirts and feeding the geese. Sonny had built a makeshift pen out of sticks and wire mesh for them near the pond. Delanna assumed that once they got used to their surroundings the geese could roam free in the yard, but she hadn't had a chance to ask Sonny if there were any predators around that might attack them—or her—so she decided to leave them in the pen till she could find out, and went in the cottage to listen to the ham. That was Harry's job, too. He was supposed to listen for weather reports from the surrounding lanzyes and report them to Sonny.

These reports didn't come at any particular time or in any particular order, but were sandwiched in among a hodgepodge of news, recipes, farming advice, whereats, and gossip. Delanna was afraid they'd still be discussing her encounter with the Red Sea bushes, but she was old news. The new gossip centered on an outbreak of the sheep virus down south, a brawl at Maggie's saloon, and B.T. and Cadiz's romance.

Mixed in with all this, and hard to separate from it, was the weather. ''Barometer's high this morning,'' a gruff-sounding man from North Cutting would report. ''I've got a chicken with some kind of mange on its comb. I tried bag salve and antibiotic, and neither one worked. Anybody out there got any idea what this is? Eighty-one and a few cirrus clouds.''

The sweet-voiced woman who called in from Rambaugh's Corner was even worse. She interspersed the weather so haphazardly with instructions on how to set in a sleeve, Delanna wasn't sure which was which, and wound up her report with a highly colored version of B.T. and Cadiz's courtship.

''So then he says to her, 'Cadiz, stop flirting with Jay Madog,' '' the woman related, '' 'You're my girl, Cadiz,' he says. Oh, Bob says to tell you this morning he saw a fire monkey with a beard. That means the rains will be bad this year. So, anyway, B.T. must have told Madog what was what, too, 'cause Jay took off for the Flats and not even a goodbye to that Collins girl he kept hanging around at the Flahertys'.''

Good, Delanna thought. Jay had obviously forgotten about her the minute she and Sonny drove out of the yard.

''Don't worry about pulling the gathering stitches out till you're all done,'' the woman said on the ham, and Delanna realized they were back to the set-in sleeve. ''Cooler than usual this morning, a couple of cumulus down by Sugarbowl.''

Delanna had no idea where Sugarbowl was, or North

Cutting, or any of the other lanzyes that called in. They could be fifty miles to the south or five thousand. She wrote everything down, including the reporters' names when they gave them, which they usually didn't. Obviously they assumed everyone would recognize their voices. Sometimes they didn't even bother to say where they were calling from, and Delanna would have to write, "Woman with an older-sounding voice, talks fast, lots of static. Mentioned someone named Lonell."

"That'd be Livvy Cameron up at Trickle," Sonny said when she read him her notes. "Anybody report muggy heat or a falling barometer?"

"Just Hardscrabble. He said the temperature was over a hundred."

Sonny shook his head dismissively. "He's out by Spencer's Wagon. It's always hot out there. Looks like the rains might hold off at least till I get the north orchard ditched." He stood up tiredly to go back outside. "Thank you for taking down the reports. I'll see Harry's here to do it tomorrow."

"You've got plenty of other work for Harry, and I don't mind. Is there anything I can do to help with the ditching?"

Sonny looked surprised and pleased, but all he said was, "If you could make up some vegetable rolls for tomorrow. We'll be out in the back orchard pretty much all day."

Vegetable rolls. At least after that he took Harry with him every day, but Delanna still felt as if she wasn't pulling her weight. She knew there were all sorts of things that needed doing, but she had no way of knowing what they were.

She tried calling Cadiz for suggestions, but couldn't raise anybody. Because they're all out getting ready for the harvest, Delanna thought disgustedly. She put out a whereat for Cadiz, finished writing down the weather reports, and went out to the garden to pick the vegetables and some timarines for supper.

Quite a few of the timarines were ripe and soft to the

touch, and the rest looked like they'd be ready for picking within a few days. And obviously something had to be done with them, but what? Irradiating? Flash sealing? Delanna had no idea how to do either, and she hadn't seen any equipment in the cottage. She would have to ask Cadiz, if and when the whereat found her.

On her way back into the cottage, laden with timarines, she glanced into the bedroom and saw her mother's trunk, and thought, Maybe there's something in Mother's journals about it. She washed and sliced the vegetables and put them on to cook and then went into the bedroom and opened the trunk. She sat down on the floor and took the journals out, somehow reluctant to open them. There were no dates on the covers. She opened the top one. She couldn't find any dates on the inside either, and she didn't see anything that was written like a recipe or instructions. The journals were written edge to edge with no spaces between sections and almost no paragraphs.

She felt a pang again at the sight of the familiar handwriting and her mother's obvious attempt to conserve paper, but she tried to ignore it. She needed to help Sonny, and surely her mother had written about the harvest and how she put up food.

She glanced through the pages, finally finding abbreviated dates for the right time of year. Her mother had only recorded the day and month, so she didn't know which year the entries had been written, but it didn't matter. All she had to do was find the right month.

The word ''harvest'' caught her eye, and she read: ''The harvest-do is finally over, thank God. Eaten nearly out of house and home. The Tanner boy would have passed out every drop of ambrosia if I hadn't locked it up. Two of the bumpkins had what passes for a wedding—and the Tanner boy said we had to open at least enough ambrosia for the shivaree-ers, but I wasn't about to see Delanna's future drunk up by a lot of drunken, reeking peasants.''

Delanna bit her lip, thinking of the high-spirited shivaree-ers at Last Chance singing carols and laughing outside her window, and of Cadiz and B.T. She wondered if her mother would have classified them as bumpkins, too, or if there was more to it that she hadn't recorded—some other worry that had made her sound so angry and unforgiving.

Whatever it was, these entries weren't helping her find out what to do with those rapidly ripening vegetables. They were too late. She flipped back to the month before.

"It looks like it will be a passable harvest this year, so I should be able to send Delanna money for new clothes. I so want her to be in style."

Oh, Mother, Delanna thought wryly, if you could see me now.

"We would have had a bigger crop if the Tanner boys had cleared that patch of woods to the north, but they were too lazy to do it. I think I'll tell Delanna to buy some of those new highup shoes."

"Lazy," Delanna murmured, thinking uncomfortably of the expensive shoes and glitter skirts in her trunk.

The back door banged. "Hi, Delanna," Harry called. "We're home!"

"I'm in the bedroom. I'll be out in a minute," she called, glad the bedroom door was partly shut. She scooped up the journals.

"What was the weather today?" Sonny called out.

She dumped the journals hastily into the trunk and shut the lid. "My notes are right there by the ham. I'll be right out." She shut the trunk, lowering the lid slowly so it wouldn't make any noise, put her folded nightdress on top of it, and opened the door.

Harry met her outside the bedroom door. "We finished ditching the north orchard," he told her, "and Sonny said we didn't have to start on the next one till tomorrow."

"Did you find my notes?" Delanna asked Sonny. He was sitting at the table, looking exhausted. "I'll get them," she said hastily.

She fetched the notes and sat down across from him.

"Clear weather and the barometer's thirty point six at Hernandez's Holding. Ditto Rambaugh's Corner," she reported, reading from the list. "Ultima Thule had a rain shower yesterday—"

Sonny looked up. "What time?"

"Mid-afternoon."

"Just a thunderhead, then. Any temperatures over ninety?"

"No," she said, scanning the list. "Wait." Sonny had looked up again with interest. "Ninety-three degrees at Diehard." He shook his head.

"That's out on the edge of the Salt Flats."

She read through the rest of the list, pleased that she'd been able to identify almost every voice this time. "And eighty-two degrees and cirrus at West Wall," she finished. "North Cutting didn't call in."

"Good," Sonny said. "Sounds like I'll be able to finish the ditching before the rains hit." He stood up stiffly. "I guess I'd better go out and take a look at the outlying orchards."

"Can't you eat first?" Delanna asked. "Supper's all ready."

He shook his head. "I want to see how much ditching needs to be done, before dark. You and the boys go ahead and eat. Don't wait supper for me."

He started for the door and Delanna followed him. "Wait a minute, and I'll make you something to take."

"No, that's okay," he said. "I'll have something when I get back." He reached out suddenly and grabbed her hand. "Thank you for listening for the weather, and for supper and everything."

"I just wish I could do more," Delanna said. "I know, I know," she went on before Sonny could speak, "you need vegetable rolls for tomorrow."

He grinned, gave her hand a little squeeze, and went outside and around the corner of the cottage. She stood in the door a minute, watching him. The lazy Tanner boy, working all day and then going back out to check on the outlying orchards.

She wondered suddenly if Sonny had read the journals. He was the one who'd put everything in her mother's trunk, folding the linens and neatly stacking the pile of journals. I hope not, she thought, and vowed not to let him see her reading them.

Sonny didn't get back from the orchard till long after dark, his boots caked with mud, and in the morning he and the boys left for the south orchard before Delanna had a chance to ask him what needed doing, so she went on with her usual jobs—weeding the garden, coaxing the geese to lay, writing down the weather reports. In between, with the bedroom door shut and the trunk pushed in front of the door, she read her mother's journals.

Not for advice on what to do with the ripe timarines, or to find out what jobs her mother had done, because after reading only a few entries it became obvious she hadn't done anything.

She had been ill—the entries, especially in the last journal, were full of references to medicines and "bad" days— but even in the early journals, it was clear she hadn't helped with the harvest or the garden or the cottage. No wonder Delanna had spooked Harry when she asked him what her mother's jobs were. Her mother hadn't had any.

All she had done was complain about Keramos, the weather, the lack of civilized amenities, and above all, about Sonny.

"I talked to the Tanner boy about why he hasn't gotten the vegetables put up yet," she had written, and "Told the Tanner boy *again* to fix the roof," and "demanded to know why the shower isn't done yet."

She always referred to him as the Tanner boy, never by name, as if he were a stranger or a servant, and lazy was the least of the things she called him. "He's a stupid, dirty rustic," she wrote. "Thank God I got Delanna away from him, and from here.'' He was ''horribly rude'' and ''ignorant'' and ''a sullen lout.''

I'd be sullen, too, Delanna thought, if someone was calling me stupid and issuing orders like a queen. And that wasn't the worst of it. ''I told the Tanner boy I'm sending Delanna the money from the ambrosia. Of course he said *he* needed the money, wanted to hire the south woods cleared. And now he claims the solaris needs a new transmission, but I know that's just an excuse. He begrudges every penny I send Delanna. I intend to see that she has the best of everything. He can clear the woods himself.''

But the solaris did need a new transmission, Delanna knew. Parts of it were breaking loose and catching in the gears. She wondered exactly how much of the lanzye's profits her mother had sent her. Was that why Millesflores was so shabby-looking and the Flahertys' so prosperous?

She looked up at the light coming through the bedroom window. It was getting on toward noon, and today Sonny and the boys were out in the back orchard and she had volunteered to take lunch out to them. ''*No* vegetable rolls,'' she'd told Sonny.

She put the books away, thinking about the clothes and jewelry and spending money she'd had, and went to get the sack of food and the water jug.

Three fire monkeys were clustered by the door when she went outside. ''Cleo can't play right now,'' she said, waving her free hand at them. ''Shoo.''

Two of the fire monkeys began to shuffle away obediently. The third, a pudgy one she hadn't seen before, began to gesture excitedly at her hair.

''I don't have time for this,'' Delanna told him, setting the jug and sack down between her knees while she tied a scarf over her hair. ''I have to take Sonny his lunch. Go home. I mean it. Shoo.''

She clapped her hands together sharply, and the pudgy one stepped back to let her pass, looking awed. The other two waited till she'd gone out into the yard and then took up their positions by the door again. The pudgy one sat down on the step. Well, at least they weren't following her.

She went around behind the cottage, looking for Cleo. "Cleo!" she started to call and then bit the word off. She didn't want the fire monkeys to hear her and come looking for their playmate—or their ball—she wasn't sure how they viewed Cleo.

Whichever she was, Cleo was out at the goose pen, clinging halfway up the wire mesh and poking one of her fuzzy forelegs through the fence, trying to reach the box nest. The geese, particularly the one in the corner sitting on the nest, were hissing furiously.

"Come on, Cleo," Delanna said. "We're going for a walk."

The scarab turned and looked at Delanna and then turned back to the nest.

"You're going to make me late with the lunch," Delanna said, setting the sack and jug down again. "Come *on*." She pried Cleo loose from the cage, having to unhook the last foot toenail by toenail, and set her down in front of the sack.

"Come on," she said, picking the sack up again. "We're going for a nice walk in the orchard."

Cleo followed reluctantly, casting longing looks back at the geese, who were honking a noisy good riddance at her.

"That's a good girl," Delanna said. "There'll be lots of birds. You might even find a nice abandoned nest with an egg in it you can sit on." And stop giving the geese heart attacks, she thought.

The path to the back orchard was really just a trail of mashed-down weeds. It led through a little copse of monkey candles and past the clearing where Delanna remembered the hot spring as being.

She walked around it twice, trying to spot the spring, but the floor of the clearing was completely covered with a thick accumulation of dry leaves.

She wondered if it had dried up. Even if it was still there, it was getting late. She'd have to look for it after she'd taken Sonny's lunch to him.

"Let's go, Cleo," she said and looked around. The scarab was nowhere to be seen. "Cleo!" she called, peering through the trees.

There was a horrible squawk, and a bird flapped out of the underbrush straight at Delanna, rising sharply in a rainbow of spreading wings. Cleo emerged from the underbrush, scuttling rapidly toward her mistress. There was another squawk and a sound of wild flapping, like one of the geese, and a second bird flew out of the underbrush spreading its wings in a sudden rainbow of red and indigo and dazzling green feathers. Cleo tightened into a ball, which was a good thing because the Royal Mandarin dived straight at her head, skimmed over her, and flapped gorgeously out of the clearing.

"Is there a Royal Mandarin's nest in there? You shouldn't mess with their nests," Delanna scolded, "even if they are on the ground. They're an endangered species."

Cleo peeped one eye out from under her shell.

"*And* they're liable to clobber you. Now, come *on*."

Cleo followed her docilely the rest of the way, not even casting a glance up at the trees. Sonny and the boys were on the far side of the orchard, digging deep trenches at the foot of the cannonball trees. The ground looked as hard as a rock, and all three of were clearly exhausted. Sonny was dripping with sweat as he forced the spade into the granite-hard dirt, and he stopped periodically to rub his neck and his shoulders as if they were sore.

Delanna stopped, watching him struggle with the unyielding soil, and feeling ashamed at the money she'd spent on clothes, money that could have gone for a ditcher so Sonny wouldn't have had to dig the whole lanzye by hand.

Sonny tossed a spadeful of dirt aside wearily, but when she said, "I brought your lunch," he looked up eagerly and propped the spade against a cannonball tree.

"Lunchtime, Harry, Wilkes," he said, starting across the

narrow ditches to Delanna, rubbing his shoulders. "What is it?" he asked, looking anxiously at her. "Is something the matter?"

Yes, she thought. I pranced around Gay Paree buying glitter skirts and highups that I didn't need, with money that should have gone for farm equipment.

"No," she said, opening the lunch sack and handing Wilkes and Harry a cup of soup and a piece of catchbread.

The boys sat down under the nearest cannonball tree with their food, but Sonny ate his standing up, gulping the soup and immediately going back to his digging.

"Thanks for lunch," he said, putting his weight on the spade. "Are you sure nothing's wrong?"

"It's just . . . you're all working so hard," she said. "Isn't there anything I can do?"

"You're doing it,' Sonny said. He wiped at the sweat on his forehead with the back of his hand. "Coming all the way out here with lunch." He took out an already damp handkerchief and wiped at his forehead with it.

Delanna took her scarf off and handed it to him. He took it gratefully and swabbed at his face. "You shouldn't do that, you know," he said, looking at her hair. "Might blind somebody."

He grinned at her, and her heart seemed to turn over.

She put her hand awkwardly up to her hair. "I put the scarf on so the fire monkeys wouldn't follow me."

"Didn't work," Harry said, and pointed behind her.

She turned around. The three fire monkeys who'd been at the door were all standing at the edge of the orchard, staring at her hair.

"Looks like you've got a whole passel of admirers," Sonny commented.

"They probably followed Cleo. They're always wanting to play ball with her."

"I don't think Cleo's the attraction," Sonny said, and her heart did that peculiar flip-flop again.

But he probably hadn't meant anything by it, she

thought, walking back through the woods, because he'd immediately turned his back on her and begun digging again and hadn't even noticed when she left, followed by Cleo and the fire monkeys. But he'd kept her scarf. He'd put it in his shirt pocket.

She stopped to look for the hot spring again. Sonny's back and shoulders were obviously sore—a warm bath might ease his aching muscles. It sounded heavenly to her, too. The shower that never stayed hot wasn't making a dent in the dirt she picked up daily from the garden.

She stood for a long minute on the path, trying to envision where the spring had been. Over there, she thought, at the far side of the clearing, just below a large flat rock where a thicket of rosewillows was swollen with buds. She broke a branch off one of the bushes and began picking her way through the clearing, using the branch like a broom. Cleo followed her, picking her way through the thick leaves, and behind her, on the path, the three fire monkeys watched the proceedings with interest.

"We'll probably both fall in," Delanna said to Cleo, "and they'll really have something to watch." She swept at the leaves, trying to catch a glimpse of bare rock, but under the leaves there was nothing but more leaves. She swept at those leaves, and blackish water pooled up in the depression.

She dug into the mass of wet leaves with the branch, but it wasn't strong enough. It broke off with a loud snap, and two of the fire monkeys dived for cover in the rosewillows.

She bent down and scooped up a double handful of sodden leaves. The water was cold. It's probably just rain water, she thought, but she scooped up another handful of leaves and was rewarded by more water welling up in the hole she'd made. It was only slightly less cold, but after a couple more handfuls it got clearer and began to feel somewhat warm. Cleo dabbled a claw in the water.

"I need a spade or something," Delanna said, "but at

least it's still here. Come on, Cleo. Let's go back to the cottage.''

The scarab obediently followed Delanna back to the path, through the copse, and almost to the geese's pen. Then she abruptly stopped, turned around to the fire monkeys, who were following at a discreet distance, and held her forelegs up to them. The closest monkey raced forward, scooped Cleo up, and flung her wildly through the air. The closest monkey faded back, like a kickballer, caught the scarab with one paw, and tossed her to the third monkey. Cleo squealed in delight.

Delanna shook her head, checked on the geese, who were standing by the fence keeping an eye on Cleo, and went in the cottage. She should probably get the shovel and go back to the spring now, but it was hot, and she hadn't had any lunch. She dished herself up some soup, put out another whereat for Cadiz, and ate her meal listening to the ham.

The woman at Rambaugh's Corner had finished with the sleeve and had moved on to bound buttonholes, and the sheep virus outbreak had spread east. There was a whereat for Doc Lyle, and one for Jay.

''This is Clinton Manzilla. Anybody know where Jay Madog is?''

He should be out on the Salt Flats, Delanna thought, and another voice came on, saying, ''He's leading a caravan across the Salt Flats.''

''The hell he is. We've been at Last Chance for four days, waiting for him to show up.''

A young woman's voice cut in. ''Try Hashknife Lanzye. I'll bet you anything he's up there with Miriam Takahashi.'' She sounded disgusted, and Delanna wondered if she was the ''Collins girl'' he'd been ''hanging around'' at Flahertys'.

Sam Noakes of West Canyon came on. ''I saw him two days ago, heading south with a wagon and in a hell of a hurry. My guess is he's down at Meridian with Carolina Goldstein.''

"I thought she was promised to Dig Perry."

"That wouldn't stop him," the woman said derisively. "Jay Madog makes a specialty of brides-to-be."

And brides, Delanna said to herself, smiling ruefully. She thought of Jay saying, "Don't believe everything you hear on the ham." Even if she only believed a tenth of it, it was fairly clear she shouldn't count on getting her trunk any time soon. Which was a relief, even if she had to wear Wilkes's trousers and shirt a few more weeks.

"This is a whereat for Sonny Tanner," said a voice Delanna immediately recognized.

"Cadiz," Delanna said, snatching up the mike. "Sonny's not here. This is Delanna."

"Oh, good. It was you I wanted to talk to. I got to thinking, I'll bet you don't have anything to wear down there."

"The clothes I borrowed from you," Delanna told Cadiz, "but I didn't want to ruin them. I've been wearing a pair of Wilkes's old grubs."

"I knew the clothes Serena used to wear would be useless, and I meant to send you some work clothes, but I"— a smile crept into Cadiz's voice—"I forgot . . . oh, Delanna, I'm so happy!"

She burst forth in a monologue of praise for B.T., which should silence the old biddies on the ham who'd been talking about her getting engaged on the rebound, and Delanna could hardly shut her up to ask her about the timarines.

"They're nearly all ripe," she told her when Cadiz finally paused for breath. "What am I supposed to do with them? Irradiate them?"

"*Irradiate* them?" Cadiz hooted. "Oh, by all means. And then we'll flash-pack them and tie them up with pink ribbons and set up an electronic market, just like on Rebe Prime, so you can go shopping. *Irradiate* them!?"

Delanna had a sinking feeling this would be the talk of the ham for the next few days, but she persisted, "Well, then, tell me what to do with them. And don't tell me to ask Sonny. He's too busy for me to bother him."

"I know. It's my fault for keeping B.T. How are you doing? B.T. asked me to find out if you need him right away. Our ditcher's broken, and B.T. thinks it'll take him another two days to fix it."

At least you *have* a ditcher, Delanna thought. "I don't know. Sonny's awfully busy, and he's got the boys working really long days with him. I'll ask him."

"Tell him at the most we'll be there in four days. As for the timarines, they can get a little ripe and no harm done, but the ground cherries will start to mildew if you don't get them out from under those big leaves as soon as they go sweet, and they usually do that just about the same time timarines ripen."

"They're sweet," Delanna said. Ripe ground cherries *and* timarines to deal with. "What do I do with the ground cherries?"

"You dry them." Cadiz gave Delanna instructions for slicing and pitting the ground cherries and spreading them on drying racks, interrupted by corrections from the sweet-voiced woman from Rambaugh's Corner.

"Do I dry the vegetables, too?"

"No, you can them in glass jars. I'll show you how when I get there. And I'll bring you down some clothes. You can't have Sonny seeing you in grubs."

"Cadiz, I have another question. What can you tell me about my mother?"

There was a long, static-punctuated pause. Like Harry, Delanna thought, and wondered if Cadiz was looking uneasy, too, and would make up some excuse why she had to go.

"I didn't really know her very well."

This didn't sound at all like Cadiz, who knew everybody, and had decided opinions about them.

"Was she . . ." Delanna began, and realized she couldn't ask what she wanted to on the ham. "What was she like?" she finished lamely.

There was another silence. "She kept pretty much to

Milleflores. And for the last couple of years she was sick. I have to go. B.T.'s calling me. We'll be down in a few days.''

Cadiz wasn't talking, and even if she was, Delanna couldn't bring herself to ask, Was she as bossy and bitter as she sounds in the journals? Was she mean to Harry? Is her sending me money for fancy clothes the reason Milleflores is so run down?

Oh, Mother, Delanna thought, and went out to look for the drying racks Cadiz had told her about.

For the next two days she picked, washed, pitted, and sliced ground cherries. Sonny had told her to tell B.T. to go ahead and stay and fix the ditcher, and it was a good thing he hadn't asked to have him come home right away, because the ham was out.

"Sunspots," North Cutting said when the static let up for a few minutes. "I've got whereats for—"It cut out again.

Delanna left the ham on all day while she worked so she could pick up the snatches of messages and weather that came through, but by the second day there was nothing but a steady, irritating static.

She worked on the ground cherries till mid-afternoon and then went out and worked on the spring. With an audience of fire monkeys and Cleo (when the scarab wasn't stalking birds who might have a nest), she cleared away the matted leaves that covered the spring and then waded into the tepid water and began to dig out the shovelfuls of mud that were choking the flow. The water roiled up muddy and foul-smelling, but after what felt like a thousand spadefuls of muck, it began to clear and the water temperature became warm and then hot. The fire monkeys sat in a circle around the edges watching her, almost as fascinated by her muddy exertions as they had been by her hair. From time to time, one of them dipped a tentative paw into the water and then yanked it out hastily and stuck it in his mouth.

Good, Delanna thought, that means they'll stay out of it.

But the next afternoon when she came out armed with a broom handle for getting at the packed mud inside the spring, two of the monkeys were sitting in the water up to their chests, languorously trickling water over their heads.

"Out!" Delanna said, wading in and smacking them with the business end of the broom. "You didn't lift a finger to help me, so you don't get to bathe in it. It's my spring."

They scurried out, holding their heads and looking properly intimidated, but as soon as they reached the edge they sat down and dangled their feet in the spring.

"I cleaned it. I should at least get the first bath," she said.

One of them scooped up a handful of water and poured it over his head.

Delanna shook her head. It was useless. They loved warmth, and the spring was deliciously warm. She'd just have to bring the broom with her when she bathed. Or take her bath when they weren't around.

She cleaned out the spring's source with the broom handle and swept the bottom for good measure. The water drifted muddily and then ran clear again. She rinsed the broom in the water and swept the flat rocks in the center of the pool.

"It's ready," she said to the fire monkeys, "and tomorrow after Sonny and the boys go out to the orchard, I'm coming back out here to have a bath." She waved the broom at them. "Alone."

She didn't get the chance. Sonny and the boys worked in the orchard closest to the cottage the next day, and Harry ran in and out all afternoon, fetching water and a shovel and the eternal vegetable rolls. And the remainder of the ground cherries had all turned ripe at once. She worked on them all the next day, picking and washing and pitting and slicing till she was covered with juice.

When she carried the wide trays of ground cherries out to the racks in the back yard, the fire monkeys trailed after her and peered under the netting and into the geese's pen, obviously looking for Cleo.

"I don't know where she is," Delanna told them, stringing up the netting over the racks. "In the woods probably."

Cleo had apparently liked their little walk in the woods—when she wasn't at the spring, she was in the copse, looking for nests, which the geese would have appreciated if the fire monkeys hadn't kept peering through their pen, looking for the scarab. They were protesting loudly right now.

Delanna shoved the fire monkeys away from the pen and finished tying the netting to the corner posts of the drying racks, hoping she was doing it right. She couldn't call Cadiz to find out. The ham was still having sunspot problems.

The static died down just after noon, but it was obvious everyone expected it to start up again. They confined themselves to brief weather reports and messages: "Barometer's thirty point eight and steady at West Wall, eighty-eight and cirrus clouds at Salazar's Gap, a thundershower last night at Diablo Lanzye."

The caravan leader apparently hadn't found Jay. There was a whereat for him, and one for Delanna from Maggie Barlow. "Clear and eighty-four at Stillwater. Eighty-six and—" The ham blurred to static again. She'd have to try answering Maggie later.

Delanna finished slicing the last of the ground cherries and carried the tray out to the racks. She was sticky with juice. When she walked into the front yard to the pump to wash her hands, Harry was there, out of breath from running.

"Sonny said to tell you," he said, panting, "we finished ditching the front orchard and we're going out to the east orchard." He took off at a run down the driveway.

As Delanna sluiced her hands under the pump, she heard a loud squeal and glanced up, thinking the fire monkeys must have found her—and Cleo came soaring through the air straight at her head. Delanna ducked, and a fire monkey caught Cleo neatly and raised his arm to throw her back. The scarab squeaked with delight.

Delanna clapped her hands sharply. "Go play somewhere else," she ordered. The monkey who'd caught Cleo hugged her protectively to his chest. "You can play with her," Delanna said. "Just not here. Go on."

She shooed them into the side yard and went back in the cottage. It was hot inside, and the wash under the pump hadn't helped. She felt gummy all over. I need a bath, she thought, and realized this was the perfect time to go to the spring.

Sonny and the boys were out at the east orchard, the fire monkeys were busy with Cleo, and the ham was out, so she wasn't obliged to stick around and listen for the weather. It was the perfect opportunity.

She snatched a towel and soap out of the shower and started out, thought better of it and went back into the bedroom to get one of her mother's nightgowns. There was no one around, but if the boys finished early or Cleo and the fire monkeys tired of their game, she didn't want to be caught skinny-dipping.

She put on the short nightgown, wishing she had one of the sandshifts from her trunk, criss-crossed the sash around it under the ribs, tied the ends around her waist, and sneaked out of the cottage.

She needn't have bothered. The fire monkeys, delighted to have found Cleo, were playing some elaborate version of dodgeball over by the geese. Cleo was squealing, the geese were having conniptions. They wouldn't have noticed Delanna if she'd walked right through them.

She hurried down the path and through the copse. When she got to the spring she stopped and looked back toward the cottage, but the fire monkeys were still busy with their game. She could hear faint squeals.

She slipped off Cadiz's shoes and stepped into the water. Oh, this was wonderful. The water was deliciously warm.

She took another step and then sank into it, the skirt of her shift billowing up around her like some floating flower.

It was better than wonderful. It was heaven. She felt clean for the first time since her ill-fated dip in Salt Creek, and she could actually feel the soreness and fatigue floating away into the warm water. This would be wonderful for Sonny's aching muscles, for his sore neck. She'd make him come out here with her as soon as he got home tonight. He wouldn't want to—he'd say he was too tired—but he'd be so pleased when he saw it.

She wondered if he had any clothes to go swimming in. Not sandskivs, that was certain, not when he didn't even have two changes of clothes, not when there wasn't any money for a ditcher or a solaris transmission. She thought guiltily again of the clothes she'd bought on Rebe Prime.

There was nothing she could do about that, but the spring would at least show him she was willing to do her part. She thought about how delighted he'd be with her surprise. He'd smile that slow smile of his . . .

She lay back in the warm water and floated, her arms out. She closed her eyes. It sounded like the fire monkeys had moved their game into the geese's cage. She could hear them clear out here.

She ignored the sounds, turned over and swam a few strokes and then floated on her back again, her hair trailing out behind her, looking up at the blue sky through the trees overhead. Clear and eighty-eight, she thought.

How could her mother have hated this place? It was beautiful—the warm spring, the sky, the wildflowers. She thought of Sonny handing her the armful of rosewillow, smiling at her in the twilight, saying, "Yeah. Beautiful."

You were wrong about Keramos, Mother, she thought. And wrong about Sonny. He's hard-working and steady and always there. She thought about him rescuing her from the fire monkeys in the clearing, about his saying, "It's no wonder the fire monkeys are crazy about you." Wonderful, she thought, closing her eyes and drifting, wonderful, wonderful, wonderful.

"Well, if it isn't a mermaid," a voice above her said.

Delanna opened her eyes and tried to stand up. Her foot went out from under her and she went under, splashed wildly, and swallowed half the spring. She choked and began to cough.

"So, mermaid, what were you thinking about that was making you smile like that? Was it me?"

She struggled to get her footing in the waist-deep water. "Jay!" she said, still coughing. "What are you doing here?"

14

"You asked me to come, remember?" Jay said, stooping to test the water with his hand. He was wearing tan shorts, no shirt or shoes, and he was grinning at her. "You begged me to come."

"I asked you to bring my trunk," Delanna said as her feet finally found bottom. She put her hands on her hips, puzzled because she knew he hadn't had enough time to make a round trip with a caravan from Grassedge.

"I brought it," he said easily, "along with some amenities of civilization."

He cupped his hands to squirt water at her, but Delanna put her hand out to deflect the spray. She felt something hit her shoulder and heard a *plop* that sounded nothing like water. Looking down, she saw a bar of ruby-red soap floating at her hip.

"It's been a long, hot drive," Jay said. "I could use a nice soak."

He'd come ready for one, wearing only a pair of shorts and bringing along a bar of soap. He must have arrived shortly after she left the cottage, discovered her alone in the pool, and gone back to shed his shirt and shoes and get the soap. No ordinary soap either. The aromatic oils were already forming a colored film as they dissolved in the warm water. She wondered how long he'd been watching her before he made his presence known. Probably long enough to be certain Sonny or the boys weren't going to come in from the fields any time soon to join her. Jay Madog was getting out of hand, and she had to do something about it.

"Jay," she began. "I really appreciate your bringing my trunk so quickly . . ."

"I couldn't have done it without having the soundings data properly integrated into the probability program. I think I set a record for round trips," he said as he sat down on the rocky ledge at the edge of the pool. "You really are something, Delanna. Part cyber-genius and part mermaid. What other surprises do you have for me?"

"You aren't going to like the next one," she said as he put his feet into the water, and found himself standing on another rocky ledge. It looked as if he were getting ready to dive toward her, and Delanna didn't want to play water games with Jay Madog alone in a secluded pool. She threw the bar of soap in his direction. He reached out and caught it smartly, grinning as he opened his other hand to show that he had a second bar.

"What's my surprise?" he asked, nonchalantly tossing one bar of soap back to her and the other onto the ledge at the edge of the pool.

Jay couldn't have seen the fire monkey that stepped through the shrubs just in time to snatch the soap out of the sunlight where it had flashed like a gem, but he saw Delanna's face turn to shocked horror when she realized the fire monkey had the soap in both hands and that Cleo had come hurtling over the bush, chittering gaily as she pulled in her legs and extended her carapace like a rudder, fully expecting to be caught.

"No!" Delanna shouted, half-leaping, half-diving to make the impossible catch herself.

Jay turned just in time to see the rest of the sparkle

emerge from the bushes. He stumbled backwards into the water as Delanna thrashed past him. She was certain Cleo was going to crash onto the rocks before her eyes, exoskeleton cracked or worse, when the fire monkey with the bar of soap in his hands calmly stuck out its foot, scooped Cleo out of the air and, with a circular motion as graceful as a ballerina's, propelled her to another set of outstretched hands.

"Get back!" Jay shouted. "Let them have it."

He grabbed her hand, but it was soapy and she slipped through. She scrambled up the rock ledge at the bank to grab the broom out of the niche she'd left it in, just in time to protect herself from the grasping fingers of fire monkeys so fascinated with her hair and so brazen today that only the broom discouraged them.

"Cleo, heel!" she said sharply over the *whump! whump!* of the broom. "And you," she said to the culprit with the soap, "put that down and don't you *ever* catch anything else when you're playing ball with Cleo!" *Whump! Whump!!*

The monkey with the soap grunted and dropped back into the bushes, the others following, though not before making a half-hearted grab for Cleo, who was—amazingly—standing at Delanna's left heel. Delanna gave another swipe of the broom but it only *whooshed* through the air. The fire monkeys were gone. Delanna flung down the broom and picked up Cleo, cuddling her. The scarab was clutching the other bar of soap, which was about the size and shape of a goose egg. "Your naughty friends scared me to death. Look at this—you've broken another scale," she scolded mindlessly, the adrenalin from Cleo's near miss still rushing through her. She took a deep breath, felt some relief, and at last remembered to look around for Jay.

He was wading in from the center of the pool. "Those fire monkeys are too bold," he said, sounding unnerved.

Cleo's claws were caked with soft soap by now. She tasted it and, finding it not to her liking, wiped it off on

Delanna's hair. Delanna stepped back into the pool, trying to pry the soap bar out of Cleo's claws as she walked out to the waist-deep part. Getting it loose at last, she tossed it back to the ledge as Cleo wiped her claws again on her hair.

"I should get my gun," Jay said. He'd been reaching out for Delanna, but stopped when he realized she had Cleo in her arms.

"It's just my hair," she said. "They like the color." And her hair was now streaked with blobs of melted soap. She rinsed Cleo's claws and by the time she got all the dust off her scales, she was sure that the scarab was fine.

"A sparkle of fire monkeys that big so close to the cottage could get dangerous," Jay said in an angry tone.

Delanna perched Cleo like a pendant at her neck and quickly lathered up the soap in her hair. "Your red soap was the big attention-getter this time," she told Jay.

"I have more soap," he said, his voice still sounding angry. "Sonny should know better than to let that many hang around."

"Sonny likes the fire monkeys," Delanna said, bending over to quickly rinse the lather out of her hair, then whipping it up with a spray that made Cleo blink and contract as tight as she could without letting go.

"Damn things are vermin," Jay insisted.

Delanna could tell that Jay was shaken—overreacting, in her opinion—upset because he obviously wanted to hold her close and make sure she was all right, but was repelled enough by Cleo that he couldn't. Surely he knew that his repulsion for Cleo was enough to keep them apart. But she guessed he didn't, because he just stood there, as if he were waiting for her to put Cleo down, never thinking that Cleo's legs were not long enough to wade in from here.

"Do you live with a broom at your side all day long?" he asked.

"This really has gone too far," Delanna said. She took a deep breath, taken aback by his continued vehemence, and worse because she was sure it had less to do with monkeys and more to do with his fear for her. "I told you you weren't going to like my surprise," she said, turning to wade back to the edge of the pool while she steeled her courage to tell him—what? That she liked fire monkeys when they weren't scaring the spit out of her, and that Sonny would never talk about shooting them, not to mention that Sonny would want to know that Cleo was all right, too. That was *what*, but *how* to say it was another matter.

"No, I don't like meeting a sparkle of fire monkeys with nothing but a woman with a broom between them and me," Jay said. He was right behind her, sounding a trifle calmer. "But I can't help admiring how you handled the broom."

Say it straight out is how, Delanna told herself sternly. She grabbed her towel and wrapped it around her head. The afternoon was still warm enough that she didn't mind drying off in the air. "Jay . . ."

"Delanna!" It was Harry shouting. "Delanna, there's a big rig at the cottage. Delanna!"

Jay was standing on the ledge, dripping on the rocks and shaking his head bemusedly. "I knew I shouldn't have taken the time to go back for soap."

"Delanna!" Harry burst through the bushes, took one look at the pool and said, "Wow! You cleaned it. Hi, Mister Madog." Cutting between them, Harry stepped onto the top ledge in the pool, wetting his trousers to the knees. "You got a new rig, huh, Mister Madog?" And to Delanna, "Sonny says B.T. and Cadiz will be here in a few minutes and you should come home." He splashed some water on his face, the dust at the edges forming muddy rivulets as he climbed out. "We saw a sparkle of fire monkeys . . . Oh, no!"

Delanna whirled around, groping for the broom, but it wasn't fire monkeys. It was Wilkes, who, in a rare burst of speed, dived past her, one outstretched arm catching his brother under the armpits, dragging the smaller boy into the deeper part of the pool. Wilkes popped up like a cork, grabbed Harry by his trousers and dunked him up and down in the water, agitating the younger boy like laundry until Harry threw his arms around Wilkes's neck and hung on for dear life. Wilkes sank beneath the surface, taking his brother down with him, and then paddled toward the shallow ledge a little ways from where Delanna and Jay were standing. When Wilkes stood up and climbed out of the pool, Harry was still wrapped around him, hanging on.

"I think we have to go now," Harry said, rubbing his eyes with what was now a clean fist. "Come on, Delanna. Hey, Mister Madog, where'd you get the new rig? How come the sail boom is so fat? Do you have two batteries? Bet Sonny's gonna be surprised that he doesn't have to tell me to take a shower."

Jay sighed and Delanna shrugged as they followed the boys through the bushes up toward the cottage, Harry's nonstop chatter filling the copse.

They found Sonny in the kitchen filling the big ten-gallon kettle with water. He was shirtless like Jay, his skin red-brown and nearly as dirty as Harry's and Wilkes's had been before their impetuous dip in the hot spring, which Harry was babbling on about, barely pausing long enough for Sonny and Jay to greet each other.

Soon Sonny put his hand over Harry's mouth and sat down in a chair, announcing through his playful wrestling with the boy in his lap that when he'd seen B.T.'s scooter off in the distance he'd decided to take the afternoon off and fix a big dinner, in which he invited Jay to participate. When Jay had accepted graciously and they started talking about the sail size in Madog's new rig, Delanna stepped into the bedroom to slip on a robe over the almost dry shift she was wearing. When she returned, the flame was still on under the kettle and there was a sack of sun dumplings on the counter, but everyone was gone. A glance out the window told her they'd gone up to Jay's rig, probably to get her trunk. Delanna hurried back into the bedroom. With Jay already here and Cadiz and B.T. on their way and a big dinner already on the stove, she might not get another chance to try answering Maggie's whereat. Amazingly, Maggie was standing by the ham.

"Where are you?" she demanded.

"In the bedroom," Delanna said, startled.

"I mean, which lanzye?"

"Milleflores, of course."

"Well, that's a relief. When you didn't answer my whereat I got worried that maybe you'd thrown in the towel and gone to Flahertys' to wait for Mad Dog. They've been sunspotted out for two days, too, and when I didn't hear any new-bride stories, I thought sure that—just when things were starting to look good—you'd gone and blown it."

"Blown what?"

"You do remember how important it is for you to be at Milleflores, don't you?"

"Of course I do, the residency requirement."

"Good. Because it's here."

The ham crackled, and new voice came on. "Since when have you started giving newlyweds advice, Maggie?" That could only be Mrs. Siddons.

"Sara Siddons, when it comes to being a newlywed, we all know you have more experience than wedding licenses."

"What's that supposed to mean?"

"There have been sunspots here, too," Delanna broke in, "and unless you count standing in the shower so long that the hot water runs out, there aren't any new-bride stories to tell."

"Leastways, none for the air!" someone said with a howl of laughter. It wasn't Miz Siddons.

"Look, honey, there isn't a private channel available right now," Maggie was saying. "The sunspots have backed up emergency traffic, so the public bands will have to do until . . ." There was a pause, but no crackle to indicate interference. "There! I've got a reservation on one-oh-seven for a week from today. Meanwhile, you just stay put, if you get my meaning."

"I'm not going anywhere."

"Good. Oh, yes. That crazy Mad Dog is bringing your trunk."

"He's already here."

"In the bedroom?" It was Mrs. Siddons again.

"Sonny's helping him bring the trunk in from the rig," Delanna added smoothly.

Someone chuckled. It might have been Maggie, who then said, "You don't want to know how he got it, okay?"

"Why's that, Maggie?"

"Let's just say it's better not to know. You can take the refund for the unused portion of your fare, though. I doubt the *Scoville*'s management will bother filing a lawsuit, but if they do, you might as well have the use of the credit until they catch up with it."

"Maybe it will be enough for a new ditcher," came Grandpa Maitz's voice. "Sonny needs one."

"She'll probably spend it on a bathtub," a woman's voice interjected, "and bath salts!"

Delanna groaned.

"Now, about the condition of the trunk," Maggie was saying. "Did you want to press charges? I've got the letters now, and Frank Fuller is in jail, but I told the sheriff not to book him until I talked to you."

"What letters?"

"The ones you told everyone in the train station about. It was mean, but really the joke's on Frank. He said he thought they were Sonny's love letters and that they'd be a howl at the bars, but it was only your mother's letters. I think they're all here. First guy he sold one to went looking for Frank with a twitcher, raving about being cheated. I think the twitcher was punishment enough, but if the trunk is badly damaged, maybe you'll want to press charges so you can get compensation. Didn't Mad Dog tell you about this?"

"I guess he didn't have a chance," Delanna said, thinking, *because I thought he was going to say something else* and didn't let him. Jay Madog was a harmless flirt who didn't want anything more from her than a handling fee for rescuing her trunk. What a relief.

She heard the screen door bang shut.

"Delanna? Where are you? It's me, Cadiz. I've brought you some clothes."

"In here, Cadiz," she shouted. And to Maggie, said, "I've got to go now. Cadiz is here."

"Has B.T. proposed yet?" Mrs. Siddons asked.

"None of your business, you old cat," Cadiz said.

"Sounds like you have a house full of company," Maggie remarked. "You call me, okay, honey?"

"Okay. Bye, Maggie. Bye, Mister Maitz. Thanks for telling me about the ditcher." She put down the microphone.

"How'd you know we brought the ditcher? We've been sunspotted out since yesterday, but Daddy said if we'd come right back and bring Wilkes to help B.T. with the bucking, we could just go ahead and load the ditcher and go. Daddy's done ditching this year, and with B.T. scouting building sites, Sonny's got to be getting behind."

"*Has* B.T. proposed yet?" Delanna asked.

"As a matter of fact, yes," Cadiz said, grinning from ear to ear. She flung herself down on the bed. "Oh, those Tanner boys are so good-looking!"

They are, Delanna thought, thinking of Sonny's dark hair, his slow smile.

"I *knew* it," Cadiz said, sitting up. "I knew if you two were alone together something would happen. So what did?"

"Nothing," Delanna said, smiling in spite of herself.

"But you like him. And you like Milleflores."

"I'd forgotten how beautiful it was," Delanna said simply.

"I *knew* it," Cadiz said. "Here." She tossed a sack at Delanna. "Wear this. Sonny'll love it. Wilkes is bringing the rest."

"You mean my clothes?"

"No. These are loaners. I made Jay put all the stuff from your trunk in his chem cleaner. It was all full of grease and gunk from Frank Fuller pawing through it. No brains at all."

"You mean Frank Fuller?"

"No, I mean Jay Madog. Just hope the stains haven't had time to set. If he'd had any brains he'd have put everything in the chem cleaner while the stains were fresh instead of waiting till they'd had a chance to bake all through the Salt Flats."

Delanna opened the sack and took out a dress. A real dress, one with a waist over a gathered skirt, made of soft challis that had mauve and gray-blue flowers along the hem. There was also a mauve petticoat and a pair of gray stretchies.

"This is lovely," Delanna said. "But won't you need it for your wedding?"

"That's a long way off," Cadiz said, lolling on the bed. "We're not even engaged yet."

"But I thought he asked you to marry him," Delanna said, letting the shift drop to her ankles and stepping into the petticoat.

"He did. Or I asked him. We sort of asked each other. But that doesn't mean we're engaged. We still have to do all the negotiations."

"What negotiations?" Delanna put the dress on.

"Keramos. Marriage laws. Remember? The laws that married you to Sonny? B.T. and I weren't betrothed, so we have to work out what each of us is bringing to the marriage. My dad has to dower me with part of our lanzye, and B.T. has to bring property of his own, and there's the will to do. We'll be lucky if we're engaged by harvest. I wish I'd been betrothed, like you."

Delanna ignored that. She looked in the mirror and adjusted her petticoat. "This is so pretty," she said. "Are you sure you want to loan it to me?"

"B.T.'s already proposed to me. You're the one with a man to impress."

Someone knocked on the door. "Dinner's almost ready," Sonny announced.

Delanna opened the door. Sonny's pants were still dusty, but he'd washed up and put on a fresh shirt. He stared at her. "Something wrong?" she asked.

"No. You just look . . ."

"Beautiful," Jay said, stepping up behind Sonny to take Delanna's hand and pull her into the kitchen. "Sorry about the trunk, but I doubt if anything in it could have been lovelier than this. Isn't she a pretty picture, B.T.?"

B.T. was pouring sun dumplings into the kettle. He smiled but didn't say anything.

Cadiz stepped past Delanna and took a stack of plates out of Wilkes's hands and began setting the table, B.T.'s gaze on her so fast that Delanna was almost positive it was Cadiz he'd been smiling at in the first place.

"Where's Cleo?" Harry asked, poking his head around so he could see into the bedroom.

"I left her on the counter," Delanna said.

"She probably slipped out with all the coming and going," Sonny said.

"I'll find her," Harry shouted as he dashed for the door.

"Where do you keep the salt, Delanna?" B.T. asked, looking in a cabinet she'd rearranged only days ago. "Or do you just dip a finger in?"

"Cadiz has been telling saltwater bath stories, I see," Delanna said, slipping out of Jay's reach to find the salt for B.T.

Harry burst back in. "Come see!" he shouted. "There's a Royal Mandarin out here." And the screen door slammed before Wilkes could get through, and slammed again before B.T. could catch it. The rest of the adults didn't slam the door, but they did crowd onto the stone stoop just in time to see a flash of green and purple disappear under the dense shrubbery.

"I told you we'd seen one on Milleflores," B.T. said to Sonny.

"It was dragging a wing," Harry put in solemnly, "like it was hurt."

"Birds do that to lead you away from their nest," B.T. said excitedly. "You don't suppose there's a Royal Mandarin nest around here, do you?"

"I bet there is," Harry said, darting off into the bushes.

"I'd better go take a look," B.T. said, taking off after him.

"I'll go with you," Cadiz called, and she and Wilkes followed B.T. and Harry.

"Find Cleo, too!" Delanna shouted after them.

"They won't find anything with the four of them crashing around out there," Sonny said, shielding his eyes against the afternoon sun. He was looking at a thin line of clouds against the mountains to the east. "What's the satellite reading on those clouds, Jay?"

"Just a squall, Sonny," Jay responded easily. "The big stuff is still on the eastern slopes, and not enough pressure to push it over the divide. The south gap is still clear. If the forecasts are right, it'll stay that way until harvest. No rain to speak of."

"I trust forecasts about as far as my eyes can see," Sonny said.

Jay smiled. "Terrible life out here on the lanzye; first you worry about rain, then you worry about no rain."

"Cannonball rinds are so hard and the stems so sturdy that I wouldn't have thought rain could hurt them," Delanna said. "Do they start to rot or something?"

"It's not the cannonballs," Sonny explained. "Once the blossoms set, not much of anything can hurt them. It's the garden crops and washouts I'm worried about. I've got one more orchard to ditch before I can ditch the fields."

And nothing but a loaner for five days to do it with, Delanna thought. Which reminded her of the refund money

Maggie had mentioned. "Jay, don't I have a refund coming from the *Scoville*?"

"Not from their point of view. They say you abandoned your berth, but when they realized they were risking alienating their biggest customer on Keramos, Mad Dog Prairie Caravans, I was so sure they'd reconsider that I just tacked what I thought was the right amount onto my last invoice."

"And they paid it?" Delanna asked.

"Well, the payment is subject to their homeport accounting guru's approval, which they probably won't get, but notice of that will be too late for them to traipse all the way across the planet to collect after I tell them I already paid it out to you."

"I'd take it while you can, Delanna," Sonny said, "that is, if there's anything left of it after Jay's handling fee."

Jay smiled gallantly. "The lady can decide if the fee is appropriate or not."

"Whatever it is, Jay, I'll be thanking you to take it in cash," Sonny said darkly, "and not in services, like another lesson in running your computer program or whatever excuse you're going to dream up to get Delanna up to your rig."

"Ladies make their own excuses," Jay said, smiling smugly.

"Oh, let's hear about the one you and Amanda Rhathborn used when her daddy came back early because the fish weren't biting." It was Cadiz, who had come around the corner of the cottage with Cleo in one hand and a ripe timarine in the other. She climbed the steps and shoved Cleo at Delanna. "Someone gonna answer that boil? Or are we gonna have sun dumpling mush for dinner?"

Sonny dashed for the kitchen.

"I caught your bug headed for the woods," Cadiz said. "Now B.T. is convinced the Mandarin circled around. Cleo spotted it just before I caught her, so now he's poking around in the copse. The dinner bell was the one thing I could think of that could keep him from searching the entire wood.'' She bit into the timarine.

''Then let's see what we can do to help Sonny hurry dinner along,'' Delanna said, reaching for the screen door and holding it open for Jay and Cadiz.

''Hey, these are ripe,'' Cadiz said, wiping pink timarine juice from the corner of her mouth with the back of her hand.

''You said to dry the ground cherries first,'' Delanna reminded her.

Cadiz nodded. ''I just meant that we can dice some up. Timarines are good with sun dumplings.''

''There's a basketful on the counter,'' Delanna said. ''You slice them. Jay, why don't you get a sack of ground cherries out of the ice cave for me? I think that with some crushed grain crackers I can put together a nice cobbler pretty quickly.'' And to Sonny, she said, ''Did you remember the salt?''

He gave her an ''oh, yeah'' look and took the salt shaker off the counter where Delanna had left it. Jay reached for the trapdoor in the kitchen floor and disappeared down the ladder to the ice cave.

The flame under the kettle was just tiny blue beads now, and the sun dumplings were turning yellow as they cooked. In a minute or two they'd be saffron-colored, ready to eat, not enough time to crush the grain crackers. Hastily Delanna put a layer of the crackers on the bottom of a flat pan.

''I'd better get the boys in,'' Sonny said, ''or these dumplings will go orange on us and start falling apart.''

Jay popped back into the kitchen and let the trapdoor fall shut.

''Do you have any more timarines in the cottage?'' Cadiz asked. ''Some of these are already overripe and only fit for drycake.''

''Sackful on the back porch,'' Delanna said, trying to guide the fall of ground cherries into the pan with her hands as Jay poured. "And I need you to tell me what to do with them before you leave. I think there's a lot of them ripe, and I don't know if I should be boiling them up or throwing them in the ice cave or what."

"Sack them and hang them in the attic from the turning hooks," Cadiz said. "Just make sure . . ." The *gong* of the dinner bell drowned her words, and Cadiz was gone.

"What did she say?" Delanna asked Jay as she threw another layer of grain crackers into the cobbler. She turned to get some sugar from the canister.

"She said to forget the timarines and head back to Grassedge with me," Jay said.

"But then how would Sonny and the boys get through the winter?" Delanna asked him brightly. "Without the timarines, I mean."

"I don't think you mean timarines at all," Jay said. "I thought that Otherside rustic living would have made you miserable by now, and I have to tell you, it's a big disappointment to me that you're not. I thought I'd find you ready to abandon everything."

"Well, you sure figured me wrong, didn't you?" Delanna swooped the cobbler off the countertop.

"I don't know," he said, sticking a finger in the cobbler and putting it in his mouth. "You haven't been here very long. You might change your mind after the rains come. Or after you've been up to your elbows in timarine juice for two weeks."

"I doubt it," she said, shoving the cobbler into the oven. She started for the cupboard.

He blocked her way. "What I do know," he said, "is that if you do change your mind, all you have to do is say the word, and I'll come and get you. From Last Chance. From Grassedge. You call me on the ham and tell me you want me to come, and I'll fly that rig across the Salt Flats."

"If you're not busy with Amanda Rhathborn."

"Ham gossip," he said, leaning lazily toward her. "I haven't looked at another woman since that day at the shuttleport. I haven't wanted to. Since I met you . . . We could make a great team. With your soundings program reading, we could take caravans across the Salt Flats in record time, maybe even open up other routes, and there'd be no reason to spend time on one side or the other. Not when I had what I wanted right there with me all the time. I mean it. You say the word, and wherever I am, I'll be in Milleflores before you can pack that trunk of yours.''

''And it'll be all over the ham before you get your rig in gear,'' she replied, trying to return their conversation to its earlier lightness. ''Call you on the ham. I'm sure Sara Siddons would love to listen in on that conversation. Not to mention Amanda Rhathborn. And the Spellegny twins.''

He was steadily backing her into the pantry. She glanced toward the door, wishing Cadiz would hurry.

''We could use a code,'' he said. ''You could say you've got the program ready. Everybody on the ham knows you set up the soundings program. You send the message 'Delanna needs Madog to pick up the program,' and I'll know what it means. You send it to me any time, anyplace, and I'll come so fast—''

''You can stuff those sacks a little fuller before you hang them,'' Cadiz said, coming back into the kitchen with her arms full of timarines, which she dumped on the counter.

Delanna ducked under Jay's arm and started sorting them.

''The idea is to get a timarine cake when they're done drying,'' Cadiz explained, ''and you just slice off what you need.''

''Then shouldn't I wash them first?''

''Of course you wash them first,'' Cadiz said, and with a distasteful glance at the ones she'd just dumped, rolled them over to the sink and started pumping water over them. ''Just do everyone a favor and use fresh water, not salt.''

''I already put salt in,'' Sonny said, coming back through the screen door.

Delanna peeked into the kettle and saw the first blush of

orange. "Get the big colander," she said, grabbing the kettle handles with dishrags. Sonny fumbled in the cabinet until he found the colander, but he couldn't put it in the sink until Cadiz had finished fishing out the timarines.

Some of the sun dumplings broke open, the nuggets of spiced meat the color of burnt orange but still solid; only the spongy dough had given way, and the aroma was heavenly.

Harry, Wilkes, and B.T. came in and lined up at the sink to wash their hands. "We saw *two* of them," Harry announced excitedly.

"A nesting pair?" Cadiz asked.

"Maybe," B.T. said. "I was thinking we should call Doc Lyle."

"Doc Lyle?" Delanna said anxiously. "The vet? Shouldn't you wait to make sure it's a nesting pair?"

"He'll want to know just that we saw two," B.T. told her. "He's liable to come out to see them himself, he's so crazy about the silly things." He started for the ham.

"Don't—" Delanna began.

Sonny interrupted. "No point in trying to get Doc Lyle. There's been sunspot activity all day. And he's got his hands full with a red virus epidemic down south. Besides, you don't want to get him all excited about a nesting pair till we're sure."

"You're right," B.T. agreed, and went back to the sink. Delanna sent a look of silent gratitude to Sonny.

"I'll bet they've got a nest near the spring," B.T. said. "I've got half a mind to stay and look again in the morning."

"The other half better win," Cadiz said warningly. "You know I have to get back to help Mama with the canning. And Daddy's counting on you and Wilkes to fell that stand of trees so they can get to the kiln before the rains."

"I could help drag branches," Harry piped up as Wilkes pumped water over his little brother's grubby hands. The timarines were safely in a bowl with paring knives set atop them, and the sun dumplings were on the table. "They have riding pokos and swings. I don't see why I can't go if Wilkes gets to go."

"Because you have to take care of the geese," Sonny said.

"And bad enough I'm taking Wilkes away," B.T. put in.

"Don't want you or anyone else bucking logs alone," Sonny told him. "Bringing me the ditcher will get more than me and Wilkes could do by hand."

"They have a riding poko that's just my size," Harry said wistfully.

"I told you, you need to take care of the geese," Sonny said.

"I can do that," Delanna offered, wondering why they hadn't thought to ask her when they first discussed their plans. Obviously going to Flahertys' was a special treat for the boys.

"Well, I suppose that if I'm going to have one, I might as well have the other," Cadiz said.

"Are you sure?" Delanna asked, thinking belatedly that the last thing Cadiz needed was another person around. She and B.T. would never get time to work out their marriage negotiations with the boys there.

"It's okay," Cadiz assured her.

Harry was begging Sonny to let him go, and Sonny thought out loud that he supposed it would be all right if Delanna didn't mind looking after the geese, and Harry whooped with joy.

"Let's eat," Delanna said.

Harry bolted his food while everyone else savored the hearty sun dumplings, leisurely dicing timarines over the top of each helping and talking about crop yields, then Harry asked to be excused so he could pack some clothes. The yields, from what B.T. was saying, were going to be low nearly everywhere in Otherside except here, where the gap had brought warm winds last spring when the late frost hit so much of the blossom set.

"Weather's been good here all year," he said. "Hope it holds till harvest."

"Tell me about harvest," Delanna said. "I don't remember much about them except that there was a lot of food."

"Cannonball ice," Harry said, having returned with his duffel, "and timarine pie and races and fireworks."

"All that's after the harvest," Sonny explained. "All the lanzyes around come to help, and afterwards there's a big do."

"And fallberries," Harry added.

Everybody laughed.

"I seem to remember somebody getting married," Delanna said. "Under a big arch of flowers. Or is that a memory of something else?"

"There *are* weddings at harvest," Jay said, looking meaningfully at her.

"And engagements and baptisms," Sonny added. "The circuit judge travels up and down with the harvest."

"And dancing in the orchard under a double moon," Jay put in, still looking at Delanna.

"And hogseed cobbler," Harry said.

"The cobbler!" Delanna exclaimed, and got up to check the oven. The edges of the deep-dish pie were just starting to get too dark. "This needs to cool down a minute."

"Good, then we have time to go up to my rig and get your clothes out of the chemmer," Jay said.

"I'll go with you and transfer my things from the scooter to the rig," Cadiz said, just as Sonny started to frown. "B.T. can help."

B.T. seemed surprised. "There's just the picnic basket."

"You need to look for my sunshades. I dropped them into that black hole you call a carryit. I can help Delanna fold her clothes."

"Guess I might just as well stay here and watch the

cobbler cool,'' Jay said, hardly trying to conceal his annoyance.

"Probably so,'' Cadiz agreed brightly.

"Except for my refund,'' Delanna said. "Where is it?''

"In the rig,'' Jay said, getting up after all. "You won't find it without me.''

"Why is that, Jay?'' Cadiz asked. "You hide it under the pillow?''

"No, Cadiz. You have a suspicious mind, you know that?'' Jay and B.T. walked out the door, Cadiz close on their heels, speculating aloud on where else the refund chit might be.

"I'll make the cava,'' Sonny said when Delanna looked questioningly at him. He seemed both amused and pleased. "Go ahead with them.''

The refund chit was in a built-in safe, which so disappointed Cadiz that she went to the chem cleaner without comment and started folding clothes.

And when Delanna looked at the chit, she was momentarily speechless, too. "I don't understand,'' she said. "This can't be right.''

"Jay's handling fees can be brutal,'' Cadiz said, "in more ways than one. Oh, can I borrow this?'' She held up a yellow skirt that was embroidered with purple flowers.

"Sure. Find the same blouse that goes with it and take that, too,'' Delanna said, still staring at the chit. "But, Jay, I don't understand this chit.''

"Let's just say I think everyone should have options, and that gives you one you didn't know you had,'' he said, walking over the thick carpeting as he headed for the door. He paused there a moment, holding the shiny balance pole, half out the door. "When I come back at harvest time, I'll have another option for you.''

The door slammed, and Jay was gone, leaving Delanna still staring at the refund chit.

"How much did he charge you?'' Cadiz asked. She already had the clothes in a neat stack, from which she scooped the top half and thrust it into Delanna's hands. Picking up the other half, she gestured for Delanna to get the door. "You gonna tell me?"

"Nothing," Delanna replied, carefully balancing the pile of clothes while she slipped the chit into her pocket and then opened the door. "The chit is for the full amount of the fare I paid, not just the unused portion. He didn't charge me anything at all."

Maggie had said she could accept the refund chit. Had she known what was in it? Delanna supposed that if Jay wanted to waive his handling fee, she needn't feel any obligation, but how could he hope to get the full fare back from the *Scoville* when she'd used part of it getting from Rebe Prime to Keramos, and probably hadn't really been entitled to any refund at all? Unless he'd made up the balance with his own funds, and if he'd done that, he'd gone far beyond the friendly business arrangement she'd expected.

"You're awfully quiet, even for you," Cadiz commented as they walked through the sun-drenched shrubs that crackled with their passing. The sun was a blob of fierce gold on the horizon, and the dust sparkled on the foliage. "You aren't thinking of chucking everything and buying a new ticket to Carthage or somewhere, are you? I mean, with a full refund you'd have enough to live on for a while almost anywhere."

"Or enough for a ditcher," Delanna mused.

"Are you serious? You'd spend it on a ditcher? That'd be great! I mean, B.T. is so worried about leaving Sonny in the lurch for manpower and he's got all these ideas about him and Sonny forming a partnership that he'll never get around to talking to Sonny about because he doesn't know what will happen to Milleflores if you take off or your part gets sold, and he doesn't want Daddy to dower me with more than he's bringing. But if Sonny had a ditcher, they could plant that far north orchard, and Daddy could give us the meadow next to it for a house, and we might be able to get everything negotiated before the harvest.''

Harry and Wilkes came running up from behind the cottage, Wilkes carrying Cleo, and Harry with his duffel bag of clothes under his arm, a sock dangling from the drawstring where it was snared. Silently, Wilkes handed Cleo to Delanna.

"We caught her heading up to the woods again," Harry said. "I've already put the geese into the poultry shed for the night, and Wilkes remembered to feed them, too."

"Cava and cobbler's on the table," B.T. called from the stone stoop. "Wilkes, did you check to make sure Harry packed both his shoes?"

"They're both packed," Harry shouted. "Come on, Wilkes. Cobbler!" Both boys dashed for the cottage.

"Wilkes is so quiet," Delanna said, shifting Cleo to cling to her neck to that she could keep both hands on the stack of clothes. "Harry does all the talking, even answering for Wilkes."

"Harry's got a mouth on him, all right," Cadiz agreed, "and Wilkes is so easygoing, kinda like Sonny, that he just can't get a word in."

"Sonny does talk, though," Delanna said. "I don't think I've ever heard Wilkes say a word. He can talk, can't he?"

"Of course he can," Cadiz said. "He's just shy." She frowned. "Come to think of it . . ." She charged up the steps and through the door B.T. was still holding open. "Sonny, Wilkes can talk, can't he?"

Whatever Sonny's answer was, Delanna didn't hear it because the screen door slammed with a bang, and by the time she reached the table, Jay and B.T. were in a heated argument about the higher success rate for cannonball saplings transplanted in early fall over those transplanted at any other time.

The cobbler was consumed and the cavapot drained, but when Jay seemed to be the only one nursing the dregs, Cadiz snatched his cup away along with the dirty cobbler plates, got the boys organized, and herded them toward the door.

"Come on, B.T.," she said. "Come on, Jay. We've got a long way to go. We'll be back in a few days to get the ditcher," she said to Delanna. "If Mama doesn't need me, I'll stay and help you with those timarines. Harry, do you have your jacket?"

Harry ran out to get it and B.T. put his own jacket on.

"You sure you can manage without me awhile longer?" he asked Sonny.

"Only one person can operate a ditcher at a time," Sonny said.

"We should get that new still up and running," B.T. went on, still worried.

"That's what was in the crate from Sakawa's," Cadiz said to Delanna. "B.T. says Milleflores ambrosia will sell off-world, too, if they ever get the still set up in time to distill some of the harvest."

"We can do it after the ditching's done," Sonny said, going out with them. "You heard Jay. We've got plenty of time before the rains hit."

"But *not* plenty of daylight left," Cadiz said. "Come *on*, you two. Get moving." She disappeared.

B.T. and Sonny went out together. Jay took a swallow of cava from what Delanna would have sworn was an empty cup and stood up.

"If you *do* change your mind—"

"Come *on*," Cadiz said from the doorway. "Let's *go*."

"I'm coming,' Jay said, looking at Delanna. "Any time."

"Thank you for bringing my trunk," Delanna said. "And thanks for the refund."

"Come *on*," Cadiz said for the third time.

"I'll be right there," he said, still looking at Delanna. "I mean it. Any time."

15

Sonny spent the next two days ditching the orchards. De-lanna hardly saw him at all. He came in late for supper, ate quickly, and then went back out. "To take advantage of the light," he told Delanna.

"Can't I help?" she asked him the first night when he dragged himself in dead tired.

"No, that's okay," he said. "Only one person can op-erate a ditcher at a time."

"But there must be *something* I can do," she persisted, and almost added, I'm not my mother. I'm willing to work.

"Just look after the geese," he said, "and write down the weather reports for me."

She did, even though it took most of the morning, and she had to listen to an enormous amount of gossip in be-tween the weather reports. Mary Rees's baby had heat rash. Neder Gustafson's son had tipped over his solaris and sprained his arm. Jay Madog was trying to steal Cadiz Flah-erty away from B.T. Tanner.

"More ground cherries than we have sacks for . . ."

". . . the only honest crop buyer on the planet, at least I thought he was until he offered prices that would be an insult for stunted cannonballs with rind blight."

"Mel Flaherty's bucking logs with the Tanner boys . . ."

"Barometer's down a bit here at Blue Rug, but no clouds to speak of. And what are they doing bucking logs when Sonny don't have his ditching done?"

". . . don't think it had anything to do with using ground cherry pits as mulch last fall, do you?"

Mrs. Siddons said Neder Gustafson's son had been driving too fast and B.T. had no business taking little boys out bucking logs, suggested Mary Rees try cornstarch for the rash, and gave her daughter a new recipe for timarine pie that her daughter just had to try.

It was impossible to just sit there and listen. Delanna washed and bagged the timarines Cadiz had brought in, waited for Mrs. Siddons to start on another recipe, and then darted out for one more bushel.

Mrs. Siddons was still listing ingredients when Delanna came back in, so she went out again and fed the geese, who were honking hungrily.

They were easily led to the pen, where Cleo, who knew just where to wait, nearly sneaked in with them. Delanna caught her in time, only to have a couple of fire monkeys snatch her away, which at least got Cleo's mind off the geese and left Delanna free to deal with the timarines.

She picked another bushel while Mrs. Siddons told her daughter how to make pintucks, and washed and bagged the timarines to a discussion of how hot it was. "I've never seen the clothes I hung out on the line dry faster. I started taking the first towel down as soon as I had the last one hung up."

Delanna waited a few minutes, hoping Mrs. Siddons would give more of a weather report than that, and then went out for more fruit.

She got into a routine of picking a bushelful in between weather reports, lugging it into the cottage, and bagging the fruit right away, which gave her back a rest from stooping to do the picking.

The weather reports trickled in, and she wrote them

down, though she could easily have remembered them. They were all the same. Hot. Dry. Not a breath of air moving anywhere.

By midday the fire monkeys had come back to annoy her by lurking among the timarine plants and startling her when they touched her hair. Cleo was nowhere around. She brought a broom back to the garden after about the tenth bushelful was washed and bagged, but the fire monkeys were so persistent she finally returned to the cottage to figure out how to get into the attic so she could hang the sacks that were ready.

She found a trapdoor in the kitchen ceiling, and hooks in the attic that snapped over the necks of the sacks. It was stiflingly hot and she was dripping with sweat before she realized there was a fan at one end of the attic and some wires that she followed to a solar connector. She patched in the wires and the fan came on, moving air that had become almost sickeningly sweet with timarine aroma.

By mid-afternoon it was too hot to work. Delanna went out on the porch and sat down, but there wasn't a breath of air moving there either, and her hair was so full of timarine juice and flour, the flies came buzzing around immediately.

The flies were going to eat her alive if she didn't get cleaned up, and she didn't have the strength to heat the water for a shower. She changed out of her sticky clothes and into her sandshift, grabbed a towel and Jay's soap, checked on Cleo, who was watching the geese, and walked down to the spring.

It was a little cooler in the woods, but not much, and there wasn't a sign of life, not even a lurking fire monkey. She wondered where they'd gone. Someplace cool and shady, probably, or did they like this weather?

When she got to the spring, she found out where some of them had gone. Three of them were sitting in the water, up to their necks, perfectly still. They weren't asleep, but they didn't move, not even when Delanna stepped into the spring.

She washed her hair hastily with the soap, keeping a wary eye on the monkeys the whole time, but they didn't move. When she'd wrapped a towel around her hair and started back, they were still sitting there motionless.

She hadn't bothered to dry off, and Mrs. Siddons hadn't been exaggerating—Delanna's shift was nearly dry by the time she got back to the cottage. But the evaporation had made her at least momentarily cooler, and she took advantage of it to clean up the kitchen and get dinner started. Then she changed into a cool dress from her trunk, sat down on the porch with her mother's journals, and read them with a kind of sick fascination. She had to know just how bad it was, whether what she was afraid of was true: that her mother had stripped Milleflores in order to send her to school.

It was worse even than she'd feared. Her mother had prevented Sonny from going to the lanzye school, convincing him that ham school was all he needed, that there wasn't enough credit after Delanna's school bills were paid. And it was true. The account ledgers showed that every penny from the cash crops had gone to Delanna and none to the Tanners. There was a complicated accounting of bartering for cannonball saplings for the far north orchard and one particularly awful entry: ''I sold the ditcher to Emil Vanderson so Delanna can have the sixteenth birthday she deserves.''

She remembered that birthday. She had had a party for all of the girls in her dormitory and then taken them on a ride all around Gay Paree in a K-chopter. And while she was spending money on parties and gee-gaws and sneaking out of her school at night, Sonny had been struggling to keep the lanzye going on almost nothing.

She put the diary in the trunk, wishing she could throw it away, and went in to check on dinner. Sonny came in while she was setting the table, looking less worried than he had. "I got a lot done today," he said. "The ditcher really helped," but as soon as he'd finished eating, he got up to go out again. "I've still got a lot to do. I've got to ditch the west orchard and cut saplings for the north orchard before the rains come." He started out the door.

Cleo would have followed, a glint atop rapidly churning sticklike legs that would have made it through the door before it slammed if Sonny hadn't scooped her up with one hand. She chittered loudly as he cradled her against his chest.

"Naughty girl. Whatever has gotten into you with all this sneaking out and disappearing?" Delanna scolded, trying to take her from Sonny. The tips of Cleo's toes were locked so tightly in the fabric of Sonny's shirt that it took both of them to get her untangled.

"Your hair smells nice," Sonny said when Cleo finally was free.

"It's that soap I got from . . . from my mother's trunk," Delanna said, cuddling Cleo. "I used it in the hot spring this afternoon."

"The hot spring," Sonny said, rubbing his shoulder as if it ached. "Sounds nice."

"Then what are we waiting for?" Delanna said. "I actually have a sandshift again. Two, in fact!"

He shook his head. "It's late, and I ought to help you with these dishes."

"I can do the dishes tomorrow."

"It's getting dark."

"Not for at least half an hour."

"I have to—"

"Ditch the west orchard, hook up the still, and fix the roof before the rains come. You can do it tomorrow."

Sonny glanced out the window at the sky, then back at Delanna, and she thought he was going to refuse. Then he grinned. "I'll get my shorts and meet you at the spring. Last one in is a soggy cannonball."

He dashed out the door and slammed it behind him so

fast Delanna didn't even have time to shout, "Don't let Cleo out!" and it took her another five seconds to comprehend his sudden playfulness and realize *she* was going to be the soggy cannonball.

Delanna yelped and ran for the bedroom. She stashed Cleo on a pillow, tore through the pile of clean clothes, grabbing her sandshift, and changed as fast as she could. She was out the door—careful only not to let Cleo out— and running at breakneck speed through the garden toward the spring when she realized she'd forgotten towel and soap. She started back and then caught sight of Sonny coming down the hill from the lean-to at a dead run. She could tell he was faster than she was, but she'd had enough of a head start that she thought if she tried very hard she just might beat him to the copse, and if she could do that and get on the path ahead of him, he'd have a difficult time getting around her.

Once past the garden, the uneven ground forced her to be more careful where she was putting her bare feet, but she was still ahead when she got to the path in the copse. Sonny caught up quickly, but couldn't get past her without veering off the path and risking stepping on rocks or bumping into bushes and trees. For the minute that it took them to race to the spring, she was sure she had won and had already started whooping in triumph, but she hadn't counted on his passing her in the three strides it took him to get through the clearing at the bank. He dove headlong off the same rocks Wilkes had dragged Harry from a few days earlier. With a squeal she jumped in after him, and sank beneath the heavenly warmth, head and all.

Only to feel herself being hauled up by two strong arms.

"Are you okay?" Sonny asked, his hands still gripping her shoulders.

"Of course I'm okay," she said, pushing her hair back from her forehead.

"You're also last," he said and heaved her out into the middle of the spring.

She surfaced, laughing.

"Are you okay?" Sonny asked again, sounding worried this time.

"No thanks to you."

"Sorry," he said contritely, paddling over to her. "But you don't look soggy enough yet." He dove suddenly for her ankles and pulled her under.

She came up gasping and choking. "I thought your shoulders hurt," she coughed, "and, no, I'm not okay. I swallowed about half the spring."

"Don't worry," he said, grinning. "It's fresh water, not salt.

"Ooh!" she cried, and struck her hands flat against the water, splattering him. "I've heard enough salt-water jokes to last me a lifetime," she said, splashing him with every other word.

He put his hands up defensively.

"And I don't want to hear any more from you!"

He grabbed for her, but she dove away from him and swam for the shore.

She could feel him diving after her, so she doubled back underwater in time to catch him without his feet under him and kept him under a second or two longer than would be comfortable by wrapping her arms and legs around his body. When he finally stood up in the chest-high water, she was clinging to his back like Harry had clung to Wilkes.

"No more salt-water jokes?" she said, gripping him tighter.

"No more jokes," he said.

"Truce?" she said.

"Truce," he agreed, and she let go.

"When you're the last one in, you're going to feel like a sack of cannonballs," she said, swimming warily away from him.

He didn't try to follow her. He was looking upward. The sky was a pale pink, the first stars already coming out, but he wasn't looking at them. He was looking toward the northeast, at the Greatwalls.

She swam over to one of the rocks and pulled herself up onto it. Sonny was still looking at the mountains, though there was nothing interesting there except a narrow line of golden-pink cloud. She kicked lazily at the water, looking at the reflections of the pink sky in the water.

Sonny paddled over to the rocks.

"Looking for rain clouds?" she said.

He shook his head, frowning a little. "The rains aren't due for another couple of weeks. Did you listen to the ham today?"

She nodded.

"What kind of weather were they reporting at Blue Rug?"

Blue Rug was northeast of Milleflores. "Hot and dry," she said, and that seemed to satisfy him until she added, "and the barometer had dropped a bit." He crawled up onto the rock and sat down beside her, dangling his feet in the water and looking at the sky, which had deepened to a rose color.

After a minute, he said, "What about North Cutting?"

She wasn't sure where that was, but it didn't matter. "Hot and dry. Every lanzye reported the same weather."

"And they all reported in? In spite of the sunspots?"

"Except Hatton Creek," she said.

He shook his head dismissively. "That's down south," but he was watching the line of cloud, which had darkened to grayish-rose.

"Are you worried about the rains arriving early?" she asked.

He shook his head. "Those aren't stratus clouds."

He didn't say what kind of clouds they were, and Delanna didn't ask. They sat there, dangling their feet in the warm water and watching the early moon come up. Whatever had been bothering him, he didn't seem worried anymore. He leaned back on his hands and watched the rest of the stars come out one by one. A stray breeze kicked up, ruffling the leaves and drying Delanna's hair. It smelled of rosewillow blossoms and something faint and spicy.

"I love it here," she said.

Sonny nodded, looking around at the spring. "I haven't been here since we were kids."

"Really? I would have thought you'd come here all the time after working all day. It's so relaxing."

"The trees drop a lot of leaves and branches," Sonny said.

"It didn't take long to clean it," she said.

"Quicker to take a shower," he said.

Delanna nodded. After working in the fields all day, cleaning the spring, even if it only took a few minutes, would be one more chore too many.

"We had a spring in the garden of my school on Rebe Prime," she said. "Not a natural one like this. Artificial. And it didn't smell as nice as this, but we used to go swimming there at night. We weren't supposed to. They locked the gates at nine o'clock because we were supposed to be in our rooms studying. But sometimes . . ." She told him about tiptoeing down the marble staircase with their shifts and towels, about tricking the lock to the garden with an override password she'd overheard one of the monks use.

"Later on, one of the girls figured out that the password to the gardens also worked on the side door that opened onto the street. The only problem was that the lock didn't have any ears on the street side, so we couldn't use the password to get back in and we had to stay out until the monks opened the front gate in the morning."

She prattled on, telling him about where they'd gone and what they'd done, about the story they'd come up with to tell the monk when he opened the gate, a story he hadn't believed for a nanosecond.

Sonny sat silently beside her as she talked, not commenting or asking any questions, not even laughing when she told him what the monk had said about their all-night escapade, and finally she fell still.

"What's the matter?" Sonny asked her. "Why'd you stop?"

"I was afraid I was starting to bore you."

He shook his head. "I like listening to you."

"I shouldn't do all the talking," she said. "Tell me about growing up here on Milleflores."

He looked uncomfortable. "Nothing much to tell," he said, and then was silent again.

"What did you and B.T. do for fun?"

"Nothing much."

So much for trying to get Sonny to talk. It certainly wasn't anything like being here with Jay that afternoon. Jay, who never needed any encouragement to talk. Who never needed encouragement, period.

But that was what was nice, that it wasn't anything like being here with Jay. She could never have sat quietly beside Jay like this, dangling her feet in the water and drinking in the evening. She would have been too busy fending off his compliments and his passes.

She didn't have to do that with Sonny. She felt safe sitting here next to him in the near-dark, and almost glad he was so quiet. The breeze murmured, cool against her wet shoulders, and night things started to call softly like music on the water, almost like a lullaby. The early moon was up now, and they watched its reflection ripple silver around their toes.

"Tell me some more about your school," Sonny said after a long time. "It was big, wasn't it?"

It had actually been comparatively small, only two thousand students. But that was bigger than the entire population of the lanzyes, let alone the one-teacher schools. "It was pretty big," she told him.

"I had this idea it was little," Sonny said, "like the one in Grassedge, till Ser . . . your mother set me straight."

Delanna could imagine. She'd read that entry in her

mother's journal. "Read Delanna's letter to the Tanner boys. Why do I bother? Sonny asked what her *teacher's* name was. As if The Abbey were a common lanzye school. Too ignorant to even imagine a *real* school!"

Was it any wonder Sonny was so quiet, Delanna reflected, when for years her mother had pounced on everything he said, ridiculing him and making him feel stupid and uneducated? She shivered.

"Getting cold?" Sonny asked.

"A little," she said, rubbing her arms. It had grown darker, and the breeze on her shoulders was chilly.

"We should be going back," he said.

"I know," she agreed regretfully. "I've got to put those dishes to soak."

"And I've got to ditch the west orchard," he said.

He slid down the rock into the water and extended his hands to Delanna. She took them and slipped down into the water, too. It felt blessedly warm.

Sonny hadn't let go of her hands. He drifted toward the bank, facing her, though it was too dark to see his face, the water buoying them like soft clouds, suspending them in time, in the fragrant darkness.

"Ohhh," Delanna sighed. "This is wonderful."

"Wonderful," Sonny said, and she wished she could see his face.

Her foot touched bottom, and she stood up, half out of the water, still holding Sonny's hands. He stood up, too. They were in the path of the early moon, its silver trail lighting the water and their wet bodies.

"Should be getting back," Sonny said again, but he didn't move.

"Dishes," Delanna said.

"Ditcher," he said, but he still didn't move. They stood motionless, the moon rippling around them.

Delanna had trouble catching her breath, as if Sonny had ducked her under the water again. "We should . . ." she stammered.

Sonny was looking past her shoulder at something. He frowned and tugged on her hands, pulling her over beside him.

"What—" she said.

"Shh," he whispered and nodded toward the far end of the spring. "We've got company."

She peered into the darkness beyond the moon's wake. Near the bank was the fire monkey she'd christened Big Guy, up to his neck in the water. She could see his scales glinting in the moonlight.

"It's only a fire monkey," she said.

"I know," Sonny replied, but he didn't stop frowning.

"They just sit there," she said. "They were like that earlier today."

"They?" he said. "More than one?"

"Yes," she said, frowning herself now and wondering what this was all about. "Three of them were in the spring this afternoon."

"Like that? Up to their necks?"

"Yes. Why? Is something wrong with them? Are they sick or something?"

"No," Sonny said. "They probably like the spring at night as much as humans." He crawled out onto the bank. "We should be—"

"Getting back," she finished for him, wading toward the edge.

He grinned at her when she said that and stooped to get her towel, but he was still frowning, and he was silent all the way back to the cottage.

Which was just as well. Things tended to get out of hand at the spring, especially on a night that smelled like rose-willows. And this was hardly the time to complicate things any more than they already were, with the Circuit Court here and her case coming up before it next week. "Sit tight," Maggie had said. Not hold hands in the moonlight.

She expected Sonny to leave her at the door and hurry off to his ditching, but instead he came in and looked at the ham records. "West Wall," he muttered, going down the list, "thirty-one inches, Far Reach, twenty-nine," but apparently he did find what he wanted. He put the book down and started out.

At the door he turned, as if suddenly remembering Delanna, and her breath caught chokingly the way it had at the spring.

"Did you notice the fire monkeys sitting in the spring before today?" he said.

She shook her head. "Wait, once when I thought they were busy playing with Cleo, I saw one monkey in the water. I don't know where Cleo had gone . . . or where she thinks she's going now." Cleo was heading for the door this minute, with a stealthy sideways scuttle that had nearly worked.

"No, you don't," she said, and made a lunge for the scarab. Cleo grabbed for her towel and Delanna's tangled hair, and by the time she got free, Sonny'd shut the door behind him.

Delanna held the scarab out in front of her and shook her. "You're not going anywhere tonight," she said and pulled Cleo close. "And neither am I."

16

Delanna got up at the first honk of the geese to cook breakfast for Sonny, but he was already gone when she went out to the lean-to. When she came back, the Big Guy was at the front door, along with three others, waiting for Cleo. Delanna went in and woke her up, and the scarab literally leaped outside and into their arms.

Delanna went into the kitchen. Sonny had left a note: "Ditching the west orchard all day. Please write down weather reports from Salazar's Gap and Teapot Lanzye, especially the barometer readings."

Delanna duly jotted them down, though they were no different than the reports from any of the other lanzyes: hot and dry. Clear Ridge said, "Couple of clouds to the south. Don't think it's anything but a shower," and Delanna wondered, writing it down, if it was the line of cloud Sonny had kept watching at the spring the night before. She smiled at the thought of the hot spring, and of Sonny, and set to work on the tamarines, singing as she washed and bagged them.

By mid-morning all the weather reports were in, along with the day's ration of gossip. Apparently Jay had wasted no time after he left Milleflores. There was a whereat for him, and Evan Brigbotham came on to say, "He's headed up north to deliver a load to Trickle."

"And stop in to see Lorita Rees."

"I thought he was romancing Cadiz Flaherty."

"She's engaged to B.T. Tanner."

"Since when has that ever stopped him? Remember that time the Carm girl got engaged to Miguel Sandros?" They'd gone on to tell the story in great detail, which Delanna, hauling sacks of timarines to the attic, only half listened to.

There was also a piece of good news. The epidemic of red virus had spread to two other lanzyes in the south, and Doc Lyle had headed down there to vaccinate the flocks. Delanna knew she shouldn't be glad about an epidemic spreading, but she was. It meant Lyle wouldn't be showing up at Milleflores.

In the late morning, she stopped working with the timarines and made a picnic lunch that included a fresh cobbler, after which she was so coated with timarine juice and flour that she had to take a shower. She put on fresh clothes, her own green shortpants, lace blouse, and matching ankle boots. The fire monkeys had carried Cleo off somewhere to play with her, so Delanna was able to let her hair dry in the sun on her way to the orchard.

It was farther than she'd realized, and the sun was well overhead by the time she heard the ditcher. As soon as she came over the hill, the noise stopped, and she realized that Sonny must have spotted her. He met her halfway up the hill, filthy and sunburned, but glad to see her.

"I've only seen people dressed like that in the holos," he said, and then almost as if he were embarrassed, he took the basket from her and looked away. "There's a sort of flat spot right over here," he said, leading her along the side of the hill.

Cannonball trees lined the hill in neat concentric rings, a quarter of which were now edged by meter-deep ditches for catching water and soaking roots, encouraging them to go deep instead of growing sideways and close to the surface, where there wasn't always sufficient moisture to sustain them.

They settled in the shade of a cannonball tree that had a generous canopy, its trunk bulging with fruit. The trees had been too young to bear when Delanna had last been on Keramos, and she left Sonny to spread the blanket so she could look at the mottled fruit more closely. They were bigger than a man's fist, growing straight out of the trunk on tough, thick stems. Above her, branches formed a nearly perfect spiral to the top, each branch clustered with fruit for the first meter or two where branching and foliage occurred.

''The cannonballs look almost ripe,'' she said.

''They are,'' Sonny agreed, frowning as he joined her. ''I wish they were a little farther behind. The harvesters won't get to us for another two weeks.''

''Can't you call them on the ham and have them come earlier?''

He shook his head. ''There's a schedule for harvesting the lanzyes. It rotates every year.''

''But can't it be changed?''

''Not unless the rains come early and bring the cannonballs down. Otherwise, the schedule's set by law so no one lanzye gets an advantage over another.''

Even though one crop might ripen sooner than another, Delanna thought. ''Doesn't it ever occur to you lanzye owners to revolt against all these laws of yours?'' she said, and then realized Sonny would think she was talking about the marriage laws. ''I don't remember the cannonballs growing so close together like that,'' she said hastily.

''This is the first year we have branch fruit,'' Sonny said.

''You trimmed out the growth so the branches would bear, too,'' she said.

Sonny nodded. ''They teach cannonball culturing along with programming in that fancy school?'' He'd unwrapped a sandwich and bit into it now.

"Mother's letters. She said she argued for two years before you'd try it." *Dim-witted Tanner boy can't see a designed experiment if it bit him on the nose.*

Sonny swallowed hard and nodded. "Your mama wasn't always right, but I admit she was right about pruning out from the trunk and encouraging thick branches. And I admit that at first I only did it to . . . well, to appease her. We're getting half again what other growers get."

"What else didn't you and my mother agree on?" Delanna asked.

Sonny took another bite of the sandwich, mumbled something, and walked back to the picnic blanket to find a drink. He poured some juice for both of them and handed her the other half of his sandwich.

"You going to tell me?"

"Tell you what?" he asked.

"What else you and my mother didn't agree on."

Sonny shook his head.

"Why not?"

"Rather eat." He bit into the sandwich. "Tell me some more about your school. What did you do between the time the parties were over and the monks opened the gates in the morning?"

"Different things," Delanna said. "If any of us had any tokens, we'd go to one of the all-night pancake kiosks by the portways or walk along the streets." While he ate, she told him about the brightly lit streets of Gay Paree and the busy skies.

He finished the cobbler and leaned back against the cannonball tree. "You walked all night?"

"Sometimes. If it was summer, we'd sit under the bushes in the park and talk until we fell asleep."

"Weren't you afraid you'd sleep too long?"

"Traffic noise in the morning awakened us. We could count on that, just like you can count on the birds in the morning here. Birds are sweeter than turbo whines, and the K-chopters were positively deafening. The school wasn't more than a half mile from where they emerged from the tunnel.''

She looked at him. He'd closed his eyes, and she thought she might have put him to sleep, but as soon as she stopped talking, he said, ''Tell me about the K-chopters.''

She explained how they moved efficiently and silently through thin-atmosphere tunnels that catacombed Gay Paree and how there were always booming and banging noises from the egresses at the portways. She told him where the K-chopters went, and how to sneak on board if you didn't have a token, watching him, half-hoping he was asleep. He looked exhausted, and why wouldn't he be? Working all day and half the night. If she kept talking, maybe he could rest a few minutes.

But he sat up abruptly and said, ''Sorry. It's so hot. Did you get the weather reports from Salazar's Gap and Teapot?''

She took her notes out of the basket and showed them to him. ''Hot and dry on all the lanzyes,'' she said.

He nodded absently, looking through them. He stood up, his eyes searching the blue sky. There was nothing but a low-flying bird to see. He handed the reports back to her. ''Thanks for bringing me lunch,'' he said. ''Don't bother about fixing supper. I'll be late,'' and started for the ditcher.

''I could bring you supper,'' she said, but he was already gone. Before she'd finished repacking the basket, she heard the ditcher snarl to life, and he was back at work.

''Back to the timarines,'' she muttered, and started the return trek back to the cottage, but by the time she got there she was too hot to face them.

She sat down instead with her mother's diaries. For a change, her mother wasn't complaining about Sonny. She was complaining about the weather. ''The rains hit yesterday, two weeks early and with no warning at all. Barbaric weather. One day it's ninety-five degrees and not a leaf moving, and the next day wind and hail as big as goose eggs! We lost half the timarine crop. I told the Tanner boy he should have gotten them in last week. The hail broke most of the tiles on the front of the cottage. Where we'll get the money to replace them I don't know, what with tuition and Delanna's needing new clothes for the fall term.''

Delanna snapped the book shut and set it on the trunk that held those new clothes. She changed out of her short-pants and into her grubbies and went out to the kitchen. The least she could do was make sure the timarine crop got in before the rains came, especially if they were likely to come, as her mother said, without any warning.

She worked on the timarines the rest of the afternoon, took a shower when she started to stick to the sacks, fixed supper in spite of what Sonny had said, and started in again. She worked until dark, showered again, and went out on the porch to sit and wait for him, wondering when it was going to cool off.

It didn't, even when she gave up and went in to bed, and the next morning it was even hotter. Sonny had left another note. ''I took a lunch with me.'' He didn't say which orchard he was working in or when he'd be back. Or when he had come in. She had an idea it had been this morning, that he'd come in to write the note and gone straight out again.

It was so hot, and sultry, though the sky had a thin haze to it. Too hot for the fire monkeys, who had all disappeared. When Delanna went out to pick more timarines, Cleo was wandering around the yard, looking for them.

''Lose your playmates?'' Delanna asked her. ''I think it's too hot to play.''

Too hot to even gossip on the ham. Mrs. Siddons came on, gave the weather report, and signed off without even a comment about Jay. Or Delanna's salt-water bath. ''Ninety-seven degrees and not a breath of air moving here,'' she said. ''Overcast.'' Delanna wrote it down, and the other reports, with sticky fingers. Twenty-nine inches and haze at Ultima Thule. Ninety-five degrees and clear at Yamomoto's Sylvan Springs. Ninety-four degrees and haze at Deepcut. She washed and sacked the rest of the timarines and hung them in the attic, which was stifling even with the fan. "A hundred and fifty degrees at Milleflores," she muttered and went outside to stick to the porch.

The haze had disappeared, and there wasn't a breath of air moving. Cleo had disappeared, too, probably seeking refuge under one of the bushes or out at the spring. Delanna thought about taking a bath in the spring, but the idea of even warm water was too hot. She took a shower instead, leaving her hair wet, and went out on the porch again.

Cleo was still gone. Delanna checked the geese's pen. The scarab wasn't there, but the geese were, looking wilted and too hot to even honk. She let them out into the yard and filled the water trough, which usually brought Cleo immediately, and decided she'd better go look for her.

She walked down to the spring, expecting it to be even hotter and more airless on the path among the bushes, but there was a breeze blowing from the southeast, and when she came out of the thicket she could see, above the mountains, a line of clouds like the one Sonny had been so interested in that night at the spring, only closer. And darker.

Cleo was nowhere to be seen, and neither were the fire monkeys. The surface of the spring looked still and hot. She stepped out on the rocks at the edge of the spring to get a better view of the clouds, and nearly fell in.

The fire monkeys were there after all, on the far side of the spring, the same place she and Sonny had seen Big Guy the other night. They were all here now, the whole sparkle, sitting in the water up to their necks.

Delanna looked at them and then at the line of cloud, and went straight back to the cottage and the ham. "Valley View Lanzye," someone was saying. "Sixty-eight degrees."

Delanna riffled through the weather reports she'd written down, looking for Valley View. "Ninety-three degrees and dry," they'd reported this morning. A drop of twenty-five degrees in a couple of hours. She switched frequencies. "Eighty-four degrees," Mrs. Siddons said, "and windy. Clouds in the southwest," she added, and signed off.

Delanna stared at the ham, wondering what to do. She'd go get Sonny if she knew where he was working, but he hadn't said, and a screech from the solaris wouldn't do any good. He probably wasn't anywhere near it.

She went back out on the porch. She couldn't see the line of clouds from there, and there certainly wasn't any temperature drop in Milleflores. It looked and felt exactly the same as it had yesterday. And the day before that. And maybe the fire monkeys did this all the time when they weren't playing ball with Cleo.

But she went into the house and got a basket and began harvesting the rest of the timarines and dumping them in the sink, not bothering to take the time to wash them. She emptied the basket and went out to the kitchen garden to bring in the vegetables and greens, picking everything that was remotely ripe and some mimkins and tomatoes that weren't.

By the time she was finished, she could see the clouds over the orchard treetops, and a breeze had sprung up, ruffling the leaves and the water in the geese's trough. There was still no sign of Sonny. Or Cleo. If the weather got worse, Delanna thought, the last thing she needed was to be out looking for a wayward scarab. She set the last of the near-ripe longpeas on the counter and headed for the spring again.

The breeze had turned into a wind, and the clouds were halfway up the sky, dark and menacing-looking. "Cleo!" she called. "Come on, Cleo! I'll let you help feed the geese!"

Halfway to the spring, she caught sight of the scarab at the base of a tree, chittering at something in the brush. She scurried off into a Red Sea bush as soon as she caught sight of Delanna, but Delanna dived for her and caught a corner of her shell. "What are you doing out here, Cleo?" she said. "Making some poor bird's life miserable?"

Cleo struggled wildly, but Delanna managed to hold on and get her back to the house. "This is no time to be naughty," she scolded, carrying her into the bedroom. "A storm's coming." She dumped Cleo on the bed and switched on the ham, dialing through the frequencies.

". . . Hashknife. Dust clouds so tall they look like moving mountains . . ."

". . . rains are here. Never seen them come in so fast."

"Dotted Line. Sixty-eight degrees and rain . . ."

". . . stock in before it . . ."

". . . not a shower. This is it."

"Stay there," she told Cleo, shutting the bedroom door, and ran back outside. What else should she be doing? The woodbox. She filled it from the pile out behind the cottage. The still was sitting next to it, not yet taken off its cart. She pulled it, cart and all, into the holding shed, barred the door, and went to get the clothes, flapping wildly, off the line.

A goose honked at her as she started back to the cottage, her arms full of clothes, and she dumped the clothes on the bed next to Cleo and ran out to collect them. She began herding the geese away from the trough and into the pen, thinking that at least this was easier than rounding up Cleo, when a blast of wind came up, raising a howl through the copse and scattering the geese, fading back just as soon as they'd scattered. Of course they hadn't scurried back into their pen. All of them were out now.

"Great," Delanna muttered, hurrying after them, counting heads as soon as they were gathered. The gander was missing and the others not cooperating at all. She'd have to get some grain to tempt them, or all that bread in the kitchen would do, and the cottage was closer. She ran into the cottage, grabbed the bread, turned to go out, and ran smack into Sonny.

"The rains are coming!" he shouted over the wind, which was howling in earnest now.

"I know!" she shouted back and started past him. "The geese! They're out and scattered."

He snatched the bread from her, and she ran out after him. It was sprinkling, large splattering drops that added to the geese's terror. They honked and ran in circles, not even noticing the bread Sonny was holding out to them. In desperation, Delanna threw her arms around the closest goose, caught it, and started running for the poultry shed.

"We'll have to take them one at a time," she shouted to Sonny, but he wasn't nimble enough to catch them. She shoved the honking goose into the shed and ran back for another. Sonny had corraled two of them up against the wire pen and she was able to get one under each arm. It was the last time two were close enough together, and after that she ran back and forth, one goose at a time, Sonny herding the rest until she could return. She caught one more, and Sonny took it from her, urging her to catch another, which she did, and he took that one, too.

Rain had started to come down in earnest now, and the wind drove it sideways through the dust clouds until it was virtually raining mud. Delanna dove for the last goose, and came up with muddy tail feathers.

"Let it go," Sonny shouted.

She could feel the sting of something more than rain on her bare hands, and so could the goose. It ran in a panic, wings spread, which was its undoing, for the wind caught the outspread wings and Delanna snagged the goose's feet midair. She turned and saw Sonny's mud-spattered grin, and then, battling the wind, they started for the poultry shed. The temperature had dropped radically. Delanna was freezing.

Inside they quickly checked their count. "All here," Sonny announced. "I'll get them food," he shouted. "You get inside. There's hail in those clouds."

"Will it damage the cannonballs?"

"No, but it can sure damage us. Go!"

Delanna dashed for the cottage through the rain, now

coming down in huge, icy drops. The kitchen door was open and banging, and she pulled it shut and began closing the shutters.

The bedroom door was open. For a second she couldn't remember if she'd left it open when she brought in the clothes, and then, with a sinking feeling, knew she had. "Cleo!" she shouted, but she wasn't on the bed, or under it.

She darted back out onto the porch, nearly colliding with Sonny again. "Cleo's out," she said breathlessly.

"You didn't put her in the cottage?" Sonny said, a look of amazement on his face.

"Of course I put her in the cottage. She got out!" Delanna tore out the door, and the wind ripped it from her hands. She'd never have gotten it closed alone, but Sonny was right behind her. Together they shut the door.

"I think I know where she went," Delanna said and started along the path to the spring.

The rain had turned to icy pellets that were accumulating in rivulets as she slip-slided along the path. She looked frantically in the bushes on either side, and then caught sight of a moving clump of mud just ahead that could only be Cleo, plodding through the puddles. "Cleo!" she shouted.

The scarab didn't even turn. She took off at full speed in the opposite direction, heading for the tree Delanna had found her under earlier. Delanna started after her, slipped in the mud, and nearly went down. She steadied herself, cursing her stupidity, and looked up to see Sonny, holding Cleo triumphantly up by a hindleg.

"Got her!" he said, laughing, and the heavens opened up.

"**Run!**" Sonny said, wrapping Cleo in his jacket, and they took off down the path, ducking as if they were under fire.

They were. The hail was as hard as bullets and as big. Bigger. Delanna felt a thud on her shoulder as if somebody'd thrown a rock and looked down to see hailstones as big as ground cherry seeds on the path. She ducked down farther and put her hands up over her head.

Sonny couldn't. He had his hands full of Cleo, who was, amazingly, still struggling, and Delanna saw a pebble-sized hailstone strike him on the forehead. She reached for Cleo, but Sonny shook his head. "Get the door open!" he shouted.

She ran ahead and up onto the porch, slipping on the layer of hail that covered it. She braced both feet against the door and got it open, and Sonny ran past her into the cottage. She darted in after him, the door almost slamming on her, and stood breathless and dripping on the floor.

Sonny let go of Cleo, who lunged for the door and began scrabbling at it. Sonny began pulling the shutters closed. His shirt was spotted with big patches of wetness, and blood trickled from a cut on his forehead.

"You're bleeding," Delanna said.

He rubbed it with his hand. "It's just a nick. Take Cleo," he said, picking the scarab up again and thrusting her at Delanna, and reached for the door.

"What are you doing?" Delanna said, almost letting go of Cleo. "It's hailing out there."

"I've got to get the timarines in."

"They're in," she said. "Everything that was ripe."

He opened the door. "Then I'd better see if I can salvage any of the vegetables."

"They're in, too. And the still's in the shed."

He let go of the door, and looked at her. "You're wonderful," he said.

"And you're drenched. And bleeding." She set Cleo down and went to get the medikit.

"I'll be fine as soon as I get a fire started. How much wood is there in the woodbox?"

"I filled it this afternoon. And there are two more loads in the pantry. I had Wilkes bring them in before he left."

"You *are* wonderful," Sonny said. "You thought of everything."

"Hold still," Delanna told him. She swabbed at his cut with disinfectant, then put a press-bandage over it. "Are you hurt anywhere else?"

"I don't think so," he said, his teeth chattering. "I got a bump on my noggin from one hailstone, and I do mean stone."

He knelt by the fireplace and started piling sticks into a pyramid. Delanna handed him the match. He struck it and held it to the wood curls, and the fire caught and flared up into a satisfying blaze.

He put a log on and held out his sleeve for inspection. "See," he shouted over the din. "Dry already."

She had to look at his lips to make out what he was saying. The patter of hail had suddenly turned into a bombardment. "It's getting worse," she shouted back into a sudden silence that surprised her so much, she started to laugh.

"No need to shout," Sonny said with a grin, over the patter of rain.

"Is the hail over?" she asked, opening one of the shutters a crack to look out the window. Rain was sheeting down with a few hailstones mixed in, careening off the white layer of hail in the yard.

"It comes and goes," Sonny said. "The hail can start again any time. Without any warning. Which is why it's a good thing we don't have to go out in this again."

There was a crash of thunder and a banging.

"Like that?" Delanna said, looking up at the ceiling. It sounded worse than ever, a steady cacophony of sound punctuated by crashing noises.

Sonny was frowning. "That's not hail," he said, and stood up. "It sounds like the geese. Did you fasten the shed door?"

"Yes," she said. It did sound like the geese, but they seemed completely hysterical, the way they'd been when Cleo tried to get into their cage, only much worse.

"The roof must have blown off," Sonny said. "We'll have to bring them in. Are there any sacks in here?"

She hadn't thought of everything after all. "There are some out by the drying racks," she said. But that was an open shed. The sacks would be drenched by now, and how would they get frantic geese into sodden gunnysacks?

Sonny was apparently thinking the same thing. He was looking around the kitchen for something else to put the geese in. Rope for leashes? No, they'd never get it tied properly in the wet. The cooking pots were too small, and it might start hailing again any second.

"The gunnysacks will have to do," he said, which was exactly what Delanna was thinking. He started for the door.

Cleo scuttled madly across the floor, claws skittering, and beat Sonny to the door by a good five feet.

"Oh, no, you don't," Delanna said, scooping the scarab up. "You're not going anywhere." She put Cleo in the bedroom and grabbed her coat. "Do you want a jacket,

Sonny?'' she called to him, pulling hers on and shutting the bedroom door tightly so Cleo couldn't get out, but he was already gone. She pulled the hood up over her head and dived into the storm after him.

The rain was almost worse than the hail had been. It came down in deafening, icy sheets that stabbed like needles. And it made the hailstone-covered ground slippery and almost impossible to walk on. It was blinding, too, and she had to feel her way around the side of the cottage to the drying racks.

Sonny, his shirt soaked through and his wet hair in his eyes, was already there, trying to find the sacks. Delanna pulled them out from under a drying rack. The rack had protected them; they were wet but not sodden. She jammed them inside her coat and started for the geese's pen with Sonny.

It was raining harder now, clattering onto the tiled roofs so loudly he could no longer hear the geese. The barnyard was a lake, full of white hailstones, and they edged their way around it to the geese's pen.

The roof was on the poultry shed, but the wooden gate was open and banging wildly as the rain buffeted it. Oh, no, Delanna thought, they've gotten out—and she looked wildly at the pond and the outbuildings. There was no sign of the geese.

Sonny grabbed her arm. ''They're in here,'' he shouted into her ear over the din, and pushed her ahead of him into the low-ceilinged shed. ''See?'' He pointed at the back corner.

The geese were huddled—no, crammed—into the corner as if they thought the banging gate were alive and coming after them. They gabbled wildly every time it banged shut and backed farther into the corner.

Sonny pulled the gate shut and held it so it wouldn't bang, but the geese paid no attention. They didn't look at Delanna, who approached them, cooing softly, ''It's all right. It's all right.'' Panic-stricken, they continued to gabble and push themselves hysterically against the walls of the shed.

"The sound of the hail must have scared them," Delanna shouted.

"How could they even hear it over that din?" Sonny shouted back.

She handed him all but one sack and held the other one open, advancing slowly on the geese. They honked and backed away.

Sonny grabbed her arm again. "I think I've found the problem," he yelled and pointed into the opposite corner, where the food pans and solar heater stood.

Huddled awkwardly over the heater, looking about as terrified as the geese, was a fire monkey. Big Guy, Delanna thought, though he was hunched over too much for her to be sure. His skin looked pale and mottled.

"I thought you said the fire monkeys were in the hot spring," she said to Sonny.

"He must have come back for something."

Cleo, Delanna thought. He'd come back to get his favorite plaything and gotten caught in the storm. A potentially deadly storm for a cold-blooded creature like a fire monkey.

"Should we try to take him to the spring?" she asked doubtfully.

Sonny shook his head. "It's too far. He'd never make it. That whitish color means he's already stiffening up. What about the outbuilding?"

"There's no heater in there," she said. And he couldn't stay here. The geese would die of fright. "We'd better bring him in the cottage, then," she said, and was surprised and warmed by Sonny's pleased look.

But not warm enough to keep from freezing if they stayed out here much longer. "Come on, Big Guy," she said, going over to the monkey. "Let's go in where it's warm." She touched his paw and drew back, alarmed. It felt hard, like stone, and icy cold. "Come on," she said, taking his arm. "Warm. Fire."

He clutched the heater, looking up at her with panicked eyes.

Sonny moved to his other side. "Come on, old fellow. Let's go," he said, and lifted him up by main force, one hand under the monkey's armpit and the other around his back, and got him out the gate and into the yard, but he refused to go any farther.

Delanna fastened the gate shut and came around to the other side to help, but Big Guy flailed out at her wildly, his eyes rolling.

"He doesn't know us," Sonny shouted, struggling to keep hold of him.

Delanna pushed back her hood. "Look, Big Guy, it's me," she said, holding out a strand of her red hair. "See. Fire. Warm."

The monkey didn't grab for it—he just stared dully—but when she put her hand under his elbow he didn't resist. They started across the yard.

It was no longer a puddle. It was a lake, with little floes of drifting ice. But there wasn't time to try to get the monkey around it. They waded in up to Sonny's boot tops and across. The water was like ice. It sent a shudder through Delanna, and Sonny's teeth started chattering.

Big Guy showed no sign he even felt it, not even when halfway across there was a huge crash of thunder, and hail started splattering into the lake, mixed with the needlelike rain. But his walk slowed and became stiffer, and by the time they got him to the cottage, they were practically carrying him.

Delanna left Sonny supporting him and opened the door, hitting Cleo in the process. The scarab dived out and halfway across the stone stoop before Delanna snatched her. "Oh, no, you don't," she said, catching hold of her foreclaw and standing back against the open door for Sonny and Big Guy to pass.

Sonny half-carried, half-dragged the monkey in and dumped him in front of the fire, and Delanna whisked Cleo back to the bedroom. "What do you think you're trying to do?" she scolded. "Get yourself killed? It's hailing out there!"

It was, and not mixed with rain. There were two more crashes of thunder and then the sharp patter of hail on the roof. "You stay in here or I'll put you in Mother's trunk."

She shut the door and pulled an empty ambrosia crate in front of it, saying without turning, "We got inside just in time. How's Big Guy doing?"

Sonny was gone. She ran to the door and opened it, but she couldn't see much past the stoop. Pebble-sized hail was racketing down, bouncing off the dirt and bushes, splashing into the puddles. "Sonny!" she yelled. "Sonny!"

Cleo was scrabbling at the bedroom door, and Big Guy, slumped in front of the fire, looked half dead. Delanna hesitated, biting her lip, and then pulled her hood forward over her wet hair, and started out the door.

She collided with Sonny at the bottom of the stoop. He shoved her back up in the door and shut and barred it behind them.

"Where did you *go*?" Delanna said, her voice shaky with relief.

"Out to check on the geese," he said through chattering teeth.

He was completely drenched, the bandage on his forehead sopping, his shirt and pants clinging wetly to him, and water from his hair dripping onto his face. And there was blood trickling down his cheek and onto the sodden collar of his shirt.

"You're hurt!" Delanna said. "Let me see!"

He felt the top of his head and his hand came away pink. "I'm fine." He could hardly get the words out, his teeth were chattering so hard. "Those hailstones are like rocks."

"Here," Delanna said. "Come over by the fire, and get

out of those clothes. You'll catch pneumonia. Do you have pneumonia on Keramos?''

''Y-y-y—'' he stammered, his teeth chattering, and then gave up and nodded.

''Get out of that shirt,'' she said. ''I'll get you a towel and something to wrap up in.''

She pushed the crate away from the bedroom door and opened it. Cleo shot through, straight for the back door, and began scrabbling at it. She couldn't get out with the bar on, so Delanna ignored her. She grabbed the quilt off the bed, a towel, and a pair of trousers and went back into the main room.

Sonny was standing where she'd left him, trying to unbutton the cuffs of his shirt. His hands were shaking so hard he couldn't get the button through the hole.

''I'll do that,'' Delanna said. ''Here, come over by the fire.'' She stepped over Big Guy, who was still slumped in front of the fire, and started unbuttoning the cuff. ''You had no business going out in that again,'' she said, freeing the button from the sodden cloth. She reached for his other sleeve.

''I w-wanted to make sure B-b-big Guy hadn't s-switched off the heater or s-s-something.''

She unbuttoned the last button and turned to get one of the towels. ''You could've gotten killed,'' she said, turning back to him. ''The geese would've been—''

He was pulling his shirt off, wrestling with the wet sleeves.

''Would've been what?'' he said, shivering.

''What?'' she said blankly. The fire lit up his bare chest, coloring it with that same orange-gold color. He pulled the sleeve free of his arm.

''You said, 'The geese would have been—' ''

''Fine,'' she said, and handed him the quilt. ''The geese would've been fine. Do you think Big Guy will be all right?'' she went on rapidly. ''Should I get him a quilt, too?''

"I'll get it," Sonny said.

"No. Here," she said, handing him the trousers. "These are a pair of B.T.'s that you loaned me. You wrap up and sit down by the fire. I don't want two frozen monkeys."

"J-just one," Sonny said, obeying her. He pointed at the monkey's legs, which were looking less mottled. "He's thawing out already."

She fetched a quilt anyway, an old pink one, and draped it over the monkey. He stirred, as if in protest, but didn't try to kick it off. Cleo came over and looked curiously at him.

"See," Delanna said. "Your playmate's right here. You don't have to go outside to look for him."

She went and got the medikit and some strips of cloth and knelt down beside Sonny to doctor his cuts.

"Y-you should g-get out of those w-wet things, too," he said.

"In a minute," she told him, parting his wet hair to find the wound. "You've got a goose egg."

He grinned at her. "That's appropriate, I guess. Since I was checking on the geese."

She dabbed at the cut. "It's the only egg we'll get for weeks, probably, after the scare Big Guy gave them." She put a folded square of cloth over the cut and said, "Hold this on it for a minute," and stood up.

She put the kettle on, picked up the sodden wad of Sonny's shirt and pants and put them in the sink, then went into the bedroom and took off her own clothes. They weren't nearly as wet as Sonny's, except for the hems of her trousers and her socks. The coat had kept her pretty much dry.

She put on a pair of dry socks and then opened her mother's trunk and put on the nightgown she'd mistakenly worn that first morning here. She tied her robe from school over it and went back into the other room.

The kettle was boiling. She made Sonny a cup of tea, which he took with still shaking hands, added another log to the fire, and went back to the bedroom to get another quilt out of her mother's trunk.

"Th-thank you," Sonny said when she put it around his shoulders. "Are you sure you d-don't need this? You must be freezing."

Actually, all her moving around had warmed her up; it was Sonny who looked chilled to the bone. But when she sat down next to him, he took one of the quilts off his shoulders and offered it to her.

"I'm fine," she said, scooting closer to the fire. "Or I will be as soon as my hair dries." She ran her fingers through it, looking at Big Guy, who had lost his mottled look and was stretching his arms and legs in front of the fire like a cat. "Do you think the other fire monkeys are okay?" she said, thinking of the hail piling up in the hot spring.

Sonny might have been reading her mind. "The spring's hot enough to melt any ice. And if it starts to hail again, they'll just duck under the water. They can stay under a long time."

"How long will the storm last?"

"A day. Maybe two," he said. "Which might turn out to be a good thing."

She looked at the fire, thinking about the two of them together here for two days, safe, warm, alone.

"A good thing?" she asked.

"For the harvest," he said. "This hail'll bring down the cannonballs, and they'll move the harvest up. So I hope it hails all night."

As if in answer to his wish, a fresh onslaught of hail rattled down loudly on the roof. They both looked up.

"You got your wish," Delanna shouted, and Sonny shouted back something she couldn't hear.

"Drink your tea," she yelled, pointing at the mug, and Sonny obeyed, taking it in huge gulps, but it didn't seem to be having any effect. He hadn't stopped shivering, even though the fire was putting out plenty of heat now, so much that Big Guy had fallen asleep curled up in front of it. He pulled both quilts tighter around himself, but every few seconds his whole body was racked by a huge shudder. What if he'd caught a chill and was getting sick?

"Do you want some more tea?" Delanna asked, frowning.

"I j-just can't seem to get warm," he said apologetically.

She tried to think what might help. "Do you have any alcohol?"

"Some ambrosia," he said. "I'll get it," and unwrapped himself from the quilts and started for the door in his bare feet.

"You're not going outside again?" Delanna said, aghast. She started to scramble up.

"Nope. Stay there," he said, and knelt beside the hand-woven rug just inside the door. He pushed it back, uncovering a trapdoor, and lifted it up. Inside were several rows of green ceramic bottles. He hauled one up, shut the trap-door, got a mug out of the cupboard, and came back over to the fire.

He sat down by Delanna, uncorked the bottle, and poured the mug half full of ambrosia. He handed it to Delanna.

"No, thank you," she said, thinking of that one vile sip she'd had at Maggie's. She could still taste it. "It's too bitter for me."

"Not my ambrosia," he said. He offered it to her again, but she shook her head, so he took it himself, drinking it in gulps, the way he'd swallowed the tea. She wondered how he could stand the taste.

He poured more of the clear liquid into the mug. "That helped," he said, taking another gulp, and it obviously had. His hand was steady, and his teeth had stopped chattering. "You sure you don't want some? This is Milleflores ambrosia."

"I'm sure," she said.

"It's not bitter," he coaxed. "It's my own special recipe. Smooth as silk." He lifted the mug in a toast to Big Guy, who had moved again and was squarely in front of the fireplace, Cleo perched on his hip. "That's why I kind of have a soft spot for the fire monkeys, because they were responsible."

He took another swallow. "That's always been the biggest problem with the ambrosia. The way it tastes. Otherwise, it's a perfect crop for export off-planet. Lower mass and lower volume than cannonballs, and bigger profit. The lanzyes could stop eking out a living, with a cash crop like ambrosia. But none of the off-planet traders'll even touch if because of the bitterness."

He sipped at the ambrosia. "And ambrosia's a perfect drink—none of the liver damage you get with whisky, no hangover, and you can't get falling-down drunk no matter how much you drink. *And* it metabolizes in your system so you're sober enough to handle a ditcher two hours later." He took another sip. "Not a single side effect."

Well, maybe one, Delanna thought, watching him. Ambrosia might not make a person drunk, but it was certainly making Sonny talkative. He'd said more in the last five minutes than he had on the entire trip across the Salt Flats.

"A lot of the lanzyes think the fire monkeys should be wiped out because of their starting fires. They started one in my barn three years ago." He drained the mug. "Everybody's got a theory about how to get rid of the bitterness—adding honey, adding herbs, distilling it, straining it, adding bark. I had an idea that we were making the mash too soon after picking, so three years ago I saved out some cannonballs and set 'em on straw to ripen for a while."

"And the fire monkeys set the straw on fire," Delanna guessed.

"Burned the cannonballs to a crisp," he said. "Right through the rind. I tried to cut away the charred parts, but the insides were singed, too. I was so mad!"

"Didn't you have some others you could have ripened?"

He shook his head. "I'd had to sell the whole crop to the traders just to make enough—"

He stopped short, and Delanna knew he'd intended to say, just to make enough to pay your tuition.

"Well, anyway, I was going to throw the whole mess away," Sonny said, "but then I figured it might be good enough for home if I distilled it instead of brewing, so I cut off the burned parts and made some mash. It was a lot less bitter than mash usually is. I laid it to the cannonballs being riper, but the next day when I saw the fire monkeys slinking away—" He grinned. "I'd really yelled at them. When I saw them, I got to wondering if maybe it was the scorching that had done it, so I made a mash out of the burned parts I'd thrown away, and that was it!" He held up the ceramic mug. "Smooth as silk. I took one drink and started saving up right then for a real still."

And it took you three years to get the money for a still, Delanna thought, because every penny was going toward tuition and birthday parties and highups for me. She wondered if he had told Serena about his plan. She hadn't gotten that far in the journals, and she didn't think she wanted to. She could imagine what her mother would have said.

Sonny was saying, "That's why when I found you in the thicket that day I didn't want to raise the alarm and maybe get one of the monkeys shot. I owe them a lot."

He grinned at Delanna. "I'll never forget how you looked that day, standing there in the middle of that sparkle of monkeys with Cleo and fending them off even though you didn't have any way of knowing they weren't dangerous. All they wanted was to touch your hair. It was so bright, it looked like it was made out of flames. I knew how they felt."

He extended his hand to touch her hair and then let it drop. "So anyway, I bought the still right before your mother died, and that's why I didn't have any money when you got here."

"And why you were in Grassedge," Delanna said.

He didn't answer, and she wondered if the ambrosia had run its course.

"You were in Grassedge to pick the still up," she said.

He looked down at the mug. "Yeah. Actually, it worked out great, your being on the shuttle at the same time Sakawa had the still ready. I hadn't told anybody about the scorched ambrosia or ordering the still, but keeping a secret on Keramos is pretty much impossible."

"I know," Delanna said, only too aware.

"But they were all so busy gossiping about you, nobody even noticed the still."

"I'm glad my salt bath served some useful purpose," she said wryly. "So you're going to distill ambrosia out of all of this year's crop and sell it to off-planet traders?"

"The still's not big enough for that, and it takes most of the crop just to keep the lanzye going and pay off the debts your—" He stopped. "After B.T. and I get the far north orchard planted, things'll be easier, and I can think about saving out part of the crop for ambrosia."

"If the fire monkeys don't set fire to somebody else's cannonballs first," Delanna said.

"They won't. We got a deal. They work for me, and I let 'em look at your hair."

She smiled. "And play ball with Cleo," she added, looking over at the scarab, who'd gone over to the window and was trying to pry the shutters open.

"Maybe she's hungry," Delanna said. "Are you?"

"I'll help," he said and started to get up.

"No, stay there and keep warm," she said. "I'll fix us some supper."

She heated soup and sliced bread, thinking about what Sonny'd said. And not said. *I had to pay off the debts your mother ran up*, he'd started to say and then stopped himself. Apparently the ambrosia hadn't completely loosened his tongue. He still wouldn't say anything bad about her mother.

And if Delanna took her half of the estate and left him, once again mired in debt and scrabbling to keep the lanzye going on too little, he wouldn't say anything bad about her either. She wondered if her mother had had any inkling of his loyalty, his quiet faithfulness.

She fed Cleo, who ate about three bites and then went back over to the shutters. The rain had let up a little, subsiding to a dull roar, but as Delanna dished up the soup, it started up again. Cleo skittered away from the window and back over to Big Guy, who was still asleep.

"Are you sure we won't wash away?" she asked Sonny, handing him his bowl.

"Nah. The geese might end up swimming in their pen, but they'd probably like that."

He talked the whole time they ate, telling her about rains he could remember from other years, hail as big as goose eggs and one time when the orchards flooded and they'd gone out to find cannonballs floating past the front door. "This isn't bad at all," he shouted over the din. "All we have to worry about's staying put and staying warm. Speaking of which, I'd better put some more wood on that fire."

He shrugged off the quilts and stood up, still talking. Big Guy was squarely in front of the fire and he had to push the monkey out of the way to get to the wood pile. Big Guy grunted and rolled over.

Sonny piled on logs and came back, rubbing his hands to warm them. "That should do it for a while," he said, sitting down next to Delanna. "It's cold in here." He offered her one of the quilts again. "How about you? Are you warm enough?"

"I'll get another quilt," she said. She went in the bedroom. It was freezing in there. She took another quilt out of the trunk, grabbed the pillows off the bed, and took them back out to the fire. Sonny had draped his own quilts over his shoulders. "I think we're going to have to sleep out here tonight," she said. 'It's freezing in the bedroom."

She handed him the pillows and sat down beside him, wrapping herself in the quilt.

"Tell me some more about your school," he said. "Was it a big building?"

"It was lots of buildings, all connected by portways and tunnels." She described it to him, telling him about the dormitories and labs and eating halls.

Big Guy turned over and then turned over again, like a piece of meat on a spit, but each time moving closer to the fire till he was completely blocking it. Delanna shivered and wrapped the quilt more tightly around her.

"Hey, you're stealing all the heat," Sonny said to Big Guy. He stood up and tried to shove the fire monkey out of the way, but it wouldn't budge.

"He's not moving," Sonny said. "Here. I've got an idea." He took the quilt from Delanna's shoulders and sat down next to her, draping it over both of them, and then added his quilts on top. "How's that?" he said. "Better?"

She nodded, very aware of his closeness, of his bare chest. "Better."

He looked at her for a long moment and then turned back to the fire. It leapt up, filling the room with warmth and a soft golden light.

"I never imagined your school as a lot of buildings," he said. "Your mother told me it was big, but I always imagined it as being in a big field with all kinds of flowers and you sitting in the middle of it studying, with your hair blowing. That was the only thing I didn't remember about you, how bright your hair was. I remembered it was red, because I used to call you Timarine Rind, but—" He reached his hand up to her hair again, and this time he touched it, gently, twirling a lock of it around his fingers.

"I'm surprised you remembered me at all," Delanna said, blushing. "I was only five when I left."

"Of course I remembered you," Sonny said. "Your mother used to tell me all about you and what you were doing."

I can imagine, she thought.

"She used to read me all your letters. The whole time I was growing up I kept thinking what it would be like when you came back from school. I imagined it like this, sitting together in front of the fire.''

There was a sudden rat-a-tat of hail on the roof, and Cleo began to scrabble at the door again. The fire monkey stretched and gave out a long, rumbling belch.

''Well, maybe not exactly like this,'' Sonny said, and smiled at her. Her heart turned over. ''Your mother said you were never coming back, that you were going to stay on Rebe Prime, and I guess I pretty much believed her. When Maggie told me you were coming, I got so excited I took off for Grassedge in the solaris without even letting Wilkes overhaul the transmission. It's a wonder I'm not still out in the Salt Flats someplace. . . .'' His voice trailed off.

He *hadn't* come into town for the still, Delanna thought. Or the geese. He'd come into town to meet her.

''Of course, as soon as I saw you at the shuttleport, all dressed up and so educated and all, I knew your mother was right, that you didn't belong here.''

He stared into the fire. ''I knew it was impossible, but I couldn't give it up. That's why I didn't tell you on the way into town. I wanted to pretend it was true, that you were really my wife, even if it was only till we got to Maggie's.''

''I don't see why,'' Delanna said, remembering that long walk into town with the cart and the geese. ''I acted like a spoiled brat the whole way into town.'' And later. Throwing temper tantrums. Flirting with Jay Madog—

He grinned. ''I didn't mind. You were so pretty—'' He looked away from her to the fire. ''I kept thinking if I could just get you to Milleflores,'' he went on, and his voice was softer, drowsier, ''and you could remember how beautiful it was, you'd change your mind and stay. . . .'' His voice trailed off again.

She hugged her knees. ''It worked,'' she murmured.

He didn't say anything, and she thought maybe he hadn't heard her.

''I want to stay,'' she said, turning her head to look at him.

He was asleep. His dark hair tumbled over his forehead,

and he looked like the boy Delanna remembered, the boy who'd let her tag after him. She tucked her hand under her cheek and lay there watching him, thinking, oddly enough, about the ditcher. If we bought a used one, she thought, we could buy some more geese with what was left over and sell the eggs to the other lanzyes.

"I do. I want to stay," she whispered, and fell asleep.

When she woke up, it was pitch-dark in the room, and chilly. She wondered if the cold had wakened her and then realized it was the silence. The rain, and the hail, and the wind, had stopped, and the only sound was the faint hum of the ham.

The fire was nearly out; there were only a few reddish embers, and Big Guy was practically lying in them, his arms wrapped tightly around Cleo. Delanna slid carefully out of the quilts, so as not to waken Sonny, and stood up. The fire wasn't giving off enough light to see by, and she was sure to trip over the woodpile or Sonny's foot or Big Guy, or all three, if she didn't turn on a light. She crept carefully over to the window and opened the shutters.

It was nearly morning, the sky a faint lavender-gray with a few wisps of tattered cloud in it. There were a couple of puddles in the yard, reflecting the clear pale sky, and a pair of twinkling stars. The air smelled heavenly, wet with the fragrance of balla blossoms and rosewillow, and if it hadn't been for the rime of white hail along the porch, and a flattened, twitching Red Sea bush, she might have thought it was the aftermath of a spring shower.

Milleflores was beautiful, even in the wake of a terrible storm. No wonder Sonny loved it.

I love it, too, she thought, and said aloud, "I want to stay."

The air from the window was chilly, and after a minute Delanna reluctantly pulled the shutters to, leaving them open just far enough so she could see her way, and went to fix the fire.

Big Guy was still stretched out in front of the hearth, his backside close to the embers, his arms squeezing Cleo tightly. He snored gently. She tried pushing him to one side, but he was too heavy. She had to straddle him to get at the wood and then stand with her bare feet in the ashes to put it on the fire.

It blazed up nicely, and she stood and watched it a minute till her toes got too warm. The ham was sputtering, little bursts of sharp static that meant the storm was still going on somewhere. She stepped back over Big Guy, went to the ham and turned it off, and then returned to their makeshift bed.

Sonny had turned on his side, and kicked the covers off in doing so. He lay sprawled like a child, his head and chest faintly flushed in the reddish light from the fire. Delanna's foot hit the ceramic bottle of ambrosia, and it went over with a thunk, but it didn't wake him. It was as if he, as if all of them—Big Guy and Cleo, too—were under a spell, a spell of warmth and silence and gray morning light, and nothing could wake them.

She pulled the quilts up over Sonny's shoulders and crawled in beside him, and was instantly asleep.

When she woke again, sun was pouring in through the opening in the shutters and slanting in long yellow bars between the slats. There was a terrible pounding sound, and she thought drowsily that the hail must have started again, and then realized not even cannonball-sized hail could make a sound like that.

Big Guy was alternately yanking and pounding on the door, trying to get it open. Cleo was helping, scrabbling at the latch with her claws. Neither was getting anywhere.

Nor were they likely to, since the bar was still in place, and figuring out how to remove it apparently wasn't a skill the fire monkeys had mastered.

I should let them out, Delanna thought drowsily. Before Big Guy sets the door on fire. But she was too sleepy to move, and too comfortable.

She was snuggled up against Sonny, and his arm was flung over her. She raised her head a little to look at him. He was asleep, his mouth open and his breathing even. He won't be for long, she thought. That pounding would wake the dead.

But until he did wake up, she wanted to stay where she was, noise or no noise. She lay her head back down and nestled into the curve of his arm. She closed her eyes.

There was a grunt and the clatter of something heavy hitting the floor, which had to mean Big Guy'd figured out the door. And that probably meant no barn or outbuilding or geese pen would be safe from the fire monkeys again. She opened her eyes, worried suddenly that she'd been responsible for a fire monkey technological revolution.

Sonny was looking down at her. He'd propped himself up on his elbow, and the quilt had fallen away from his chest. His dark hair was tousled, boyish, but with his eyes open he didn't look like a boy at all.

"Good morning," he said. "The children have gone out to play."

"Cleo, too?" she said, making a motion to get up.

His arm tightened around her. "Cleo, too. Don't worry. The storm's over." He cocked his head toward the door. "And it doesn't sound like they're going very far." He smiled down at her.

Outside, there were more grunts, and splashing, and a delighted squeal from Cleo. There was the rustle of leaves, too, from the open door, and the sound of a grass thrush singing. But it was as if there was no sound at all, except the thudding of her own heart.

"About last night," Sonny said, looking down at her again.

She waited for him to say he'd had too much to drink, that it was the ambrosia talking.

"I meant every word," he said, and bent down to kiss her.

She disentangled her arms from the quilts and wrapped them around his neck. "So did I," she said.

"Well," Cadiz said from the doorway. "It looks like we got here just in the nick of time."

Sonny smiled lazily. "It's always a pleasure to see you, Cadiz."

"I'll bet," she said, slapping her hat down on the sideboard. "Do you realize that while you've been storm huddling, the fire monkeys have been looting the place? They made off with one of the quilts and they're using it as a trampoline."

Delanna sat up and could see enough through the window to know that it was only Cleo bouncing as four fire monkeys held the corners of the pink quilt. She sank back down. "When they make a sack out of the quilt and start hauling timarines with it, we'll know for sure we're in the midst of a technological revolution."

"Huh?" Cadiz said.

"It's all right, Cadiz," Sonny told her. "They didn't come looting. The big one spent the night in here with us. He probably got tangled in the quilt when he lit for the door."

"I didn't open the door," Delanna said. "Did you?"

Sonny shook his head. "Smart kid. Gets it from Mama."

Cadiz frowned. "I don't think a fire monkey qualifies as a chaperone," she said.

"How about some breakfast?" Sonny suggested, getting to his feet. He headed for the fireplace, where Delanna had hung his wet clothes the night before.

"Breakfast? Oh, no," Cadiz said. "We gotta hurry. There's an all-help out on the ham from Stillwater Canyon. The dam is leaking. When we couldn't raise you on the ham, B.T. and I decided we'd better swing by to get you. When the melt from the hail pushes that water level up, it will be more than the Mainwarings can do to keep plugging that dam. And if it goes, Stillwater and Trickle Lanzyes are going, too."

"Why didn't you wake us with the screamer?" Sonny said as he grabbed his shirt from the hook.

"We tried to, but . . ."

"I turned the ham off during the night," Delanna cut in. "It was crackling."

Hastily Sonny thrust his arms into his shirt. "I'll come right away," he said. "Delanna, you'll need to check the geese." He sat down on the quilts next to Delanna to pull on his socks and boots. When he'd drawn the laces tight and snapped them in place, he jumped to his feet and extended a hand to her to help her up. "Next time leave the ham on even if it's crackling, sweetlove," he said, his fingers lingering in her hand just a few seconds longer than was needed. "Sometimes a bad storm will circle back."

He'd said 'bad storm' as if it were one word, and he hadn't mentioned that sometimes in a *badstorm* people needed to get a call through, like now, and they couldn't if the ham was off. Delanna felt a little sheepish.

"I'll turn it back on right away," she was saying when she caught Cadiz screwing up her face to mouth, "sweetlove," at her from behind Sonny's back. The look was gone when Sonny turned to rush past her through the door.

"You coming, Cadiz?" he shouted over his shoulder.

"Maybe that fire monkey was just the right kind of chaperone, after all," Cadiz said, "sweetlove."

"He doesn't even know he said that," Delanna protested.

"I know. That's what makes it so nice. If fire monkeys can loosen a Tanner's tongue, I'm gonna get me some."

"All they do is block all the heat from the fireplace," Delanna said. She picked up one of the quilts from the floor and started to fold it.

"Nothing like a nip in the air to turn a huddle into a cuddle."

"Cadiz?" Sonny was practically all the way to the road and Cadiz tore out after him, running at full speed to catch up. The solaris started moving as soon as she was safely inside.

Delanna stood at the window with the quilt in her hands watching the solaris until it turned out of sight at the bend in the road. Sunlight glared off a layer of hail that covered nearly everything, and vapor was rising now, too, as the morning air warmed. Cleo and the fire monkeys had tired of their trampoline game, and were headed into the copse playing catch-ball with Cleo, Big Guy bringing up the rear, trailing the now very bedraggled quilt. She should try to rescue it.

Quickly she put down the quilt in her hands to get dressed. Remembering to first turn on the ham, she went down through the copse, looking for Cleo and the monkeys. Leaves left on the trees and bushes were shredded and pockmarked. Hail was ankle-deep in most places but quickly melting as the sun climbed steadily in the sky. The fire monkey footprints turned into a maze of rivulets. Delanna gave up, not even sorry that she hadn't found the quilt, and went to tend the geese.

Some of the shingles had come off the poultry shed; nothing Sonny couldn't fix in a few minutes. She'd hold nails for him and hand him the hammer and keep the geese out from underfoot. She hummed the goose girl song as she strewed grain for their breakfast, and the geese honked at all the appropriate phrases, it seemed to Delanna, one or more in perfect rhythm.

She went back to the cottage. The garden had been battered to green slime by the hail, but some of the flowers had been protected from the worst of the onslaught by the cottage, and Delanna thought she might get another bloom from them if she trimmed smashed flower heads. She bent over, shears in hand, snipping and singing, thinking of how sweet the cottage would look when the harvesters came and of how proud of their lanzye Sonny would feel. And she would feel proud, too.

There. She was finished. The saffron fallbabies and bright pumpkin-faces would be setting new blooms in days. Even the monkey candles looked like they might come back, though they wouldn't be so tall this time. Pleased with herself, she went inside.

Her jacket and Sonny's pants were still by the fireplace and they were thick with goose down and the feathers that had stuck to the damp fabric last night. As she took them out to the porch to shake them, they left a trail of down and feathers in the living room. When the clothes were safe to bring back in again, she began sweeping. The slightest breeze had scattered down under chairs and into the farthest corners of the room. She had to move everything to clean; even the kitchen table and her mother's trunk in the other room harbored the white fluff. The temperature was rising and the air was moist from the melting hail, making the down cling now instead of floating off every time she took a step. By the time she was finished, she was sweating.

She flopped down in a chair, wishing she'd thought to get herself a glass of water first, when she heard someone in the front yard.

"Sonny," she said, and flew through the door to greet him. "Did you get the dam . . ."

But it wasn't Sonny. It was Doc Lyle. He was holding Cleo in one hand and two bedraggled, very dead Royal Mandarins in the other.

"I have two dead Royal Mandarins and a specimen of outlaw animal life," he said angrily. "We have laws about not introducing alien species into Keramos for a reason."

"You don't think Cleo killed—"

"I can't prove that she did—"

"That's ridiculous. Scarabs aren't predators. Cleo wouldn't kill anything," Delanna protested. She started to reach for the scarab, who was squirming now in Doc Lyle's grip.

"And you can't prove she didn't."

"They look drowned to me," Delanna said, and they did. Their bright feathers were sopping wet and streaked with mud. "The storm . . ." She started to explain how bad the hail had been, when he cut her off again.

"The law," he said, "is very clear on these matters. Introduce nothing that hasn't been subjected to compatibility studies under the Domestic or Feral Animal Act. These two Mandarins may have been the last breeding pair on the planet and your scarab may have killed them. I just banded the female last spring and came back to check, hoping she'd found a mate. And she had. And now this."

"Cleo wouldn't hurt anything," Delanna insisted. The scarab was chittering now and once again Delanna reached for her. Doc Lyle pulled away. "She's frightened."

"She's contraband. We don't know what diseases she may have."

"She's had all her shots," Delanna protested. "You know that. You saw her health certificate."

"Parasites, habitat infestation, ecological ruin. We have laws on Keramos to prevent such disasters and you have broken the law. She'll have to be destroyed."

"Destroyed!" Delanna started crying. "No. Sonny won't let you destroy her. He'll . . ."

"He'll lose Milleflores. I'll condemn this lanzye and everything on it if Sonny Tanner interferes with the law again. And don't try to tell me he wasn't involved the last time. Those jeweled scales around the garbage disposal has Tanner cunning written all over it," Doc Lyle said. "Now run up and get an isolette out of my solaris."

"No!" Delanna said through a hot stream of tears. "Cleo is my friend. I won't let you hurt her."

"I'm going to put her down humanely," the vet said, as if that mattered. But when Delanna cried all the harder, he shook his head and started walking back up toward the road. The sparkle of fire monkeys scattered out of the bushes where they'd been lurking, waiting for Cleo. The vet hardly noticed them. He kept glancing down at the dead Royal Mandarins and shaking his head.

Delanna ran alongside, promising she'd keep Cleo locked up in the house forever, if only he'd spare her life. Doc Lyle's lips just thinned all the more and he walked even faster. Delanna was breathless from tears and panic, but she made another grab for Cleo. Doc Lyle brushed her off with an elbow.

At the solaris, he tossed the dead birds into the cab and pulled out an isolette. He opened the hatch.

"Please," Delanna begged. "Please, at least let me say goodbye to her."

"You can say goodbye to her when she's safely in the isolette," he said, popping Cleo inside.

Still chittering, Cleo started to claw pitifully at the sides of the isolette. Doc Lyle turned to get the Royal Mandarins off the seat, finding a sack from somewhere inside. Delanna stood by, dumbly watching him stuff the dead birds into the sack. She wondered if she could dive for the isolette, pick it up and run away before he could stop her. But she knew she wouldn't be able to run fast enough. And where could she go?

The fire monkeys were creeping back, Big Guy still dragging his quilt. Doc Lyle had had to open the sack again to check the band on a pathetically stiff little bird leg; then he put the dead birds into the back of the solaris and started writing something on his vega tablet. He glanced up at the fire monkeys, and some of them dropped onto all fours and crawled under bushes. Apparently unconcerned, the vet returned to what he was doing.

Delanna wiped her tears on her sleeve, trying to think. There must be something she could do. She wondered if she should call Maggie. She might have found a loophole.

But even as the thought crossed her mind, Delanna realized that Maggie would have stopped looking for a legal loophole the moment she thought Cleo had been ground up in the garbage disposal. Doc Lyle turned to put the vega tablet inside the solaris and closed the canopy.

"I'll feed her a good meal with a sedative in it before I put her down," Doc Lyle said, not unkindly. He turned to pick up the isolette, and found Big Guy looming over it. "Shoo," the vet said, with a clap of his hands.

Big Guy shied a few steps and the quilt caught on the corner of the isolette and pulled it over with a clatter, making Cleo chitter indignantly. The increased noise made Big Guy try to jump away but now the quilt was firmly snagged on the isolette, which clanked along after him as he hopped through the bushes in a complete panic. The isolette hit a rock and bounced, the crashing noise spooking the other fire monkeys out of hiding. The jolt knocked open the door. Cleo gave out a startled roar and rolled free. One of the monkeys scooped her up and tossed her to the front runner. Big Guy gave a final tug on the quilt and it came free. He loped after the sparkle, still dragging the tattered quilt, eager to join the catch-ball game.

Doc Lyle reached for his gun and Delanna sucked in her breath in renewed panic. "Don't," she said.

"Can't," he said, shaking his head angrily. "Season isn't open yet, and I used up all my anesthetic darts on a wounded poko. But if I don't do something, those fire monkeys might leave with the scarab."

"They live around here. They play ball with Cleo all the time," Delanna said, hastily adding, "for hours at a time, even days."

"So now I have to worry about a scarab-wrought plague among Keramos' fire monkeys, too," the vet muttered. "And they may live around here now, but fire monkeys migrate south right after the first big storm, and that was last night.'' He walked over to the battered isolette and picked it up. Some of the wires were bent and a corner bashed in, but the door still worked. He brought the isolette back to Delanna. ''I tell you what I'm going to do. You get that scarab back from those fire monkeys before they take off; they tend to linger if there's a hot spring available to them and I know Tanner has one down in the copse. So you get her back and get her secured in this isolette and I'll come back for her in a few days. I've got to go check on the other Royal Mandarin I banded last fall.''

''But . . .''

''No buts about it. And you tell Sonny Tanner that if he tries any of his tricks again like telling me the fire monkeys took the scarab with them on their migration, or presenting me with anything except that scarab safely in the isolette, I will confiscate Milleflores. Have I made myself perfectly clear? Nothing except the scarab in the isolette.''

''Yes,'' Delanna said miserably.

Doc Lyle put down the isolette at her feet, climbed into the solaris, and drove off, leaving Delanna standing numbly in the road.

After a while, she walked back to the cottage, carrying the battered isolette. The way was very muddy now; nearly all the hail had melted except where it lay in shadow. The cottage was hot and stuffy. She tried to think of what to do. It was useless to try to get Cleo away from the fire monkeys before they were finished with their game. But they'd tire of it soon enough, and even if Cleo took off as she'd been wont to do these last few weeks, she'd come home when she got hungry.

The ham was noisy.

''. . . had a crack big enough to drive a solaris through,'' Grandpa Maitz was saying, ''but they rolled one of them big boulders in and now they're hand-packing the rest with stones and mud.''

''They gonna get done before the water level rises?''

Delanna recognized Tom Toricelli's voice, from Valley View, which she knew now was high on the mountain slopes. "It's awfully warm up here at Valley View and the melt's gotta be putting a lot of runoff into the streams."

"Sonny and B.T. Tanner arrived a while back with the Flaherty girl," another voice came on. "Mel Flaherty brought his whole crew and a couple of winches at first light. I think the younger Tanner boys were with him, too. Emil, the Hansens, and Mort Sanderson took off at the first alarm, so they're probably there by now, too."

"Maurey and Edgar left just as soon as they dug Edgar's solaris out of a mudslide," Kaylee added. "Edgar blocked a drift of hail and mud from pouring into his basement by driving the solaris into its path. I guess it was a mess, but it fired up after a good wash with the hose."

They were going to go on forever, Delanna thought, and she needed to get through to Maggie. Maybe Maggie would know what to do about Cleo. She picked up the microphone.

"Can I break in to call Maggie Barlow?" Delanna asked.

"Well, you sure could," Kaylee said pleasantly, "but Circuit Court is in session. All the lawyers shuttled up to the *Justice* yesterday. Court's in session now, so you can't even get a relay to her. You could leave a whereat, though."

"Oh," Delanna said dully. She'd forgotten how close her court date was.

"Wasn't there a whereat message for Tanners' from Maggie?" Mrs. Siddons asked.

"There was indeed," Grandpa Maitz said. "I'd all but forgotten with all the storm traffic. I wrote it down . . ." It sounded like he was shuffling through papers. "Here it is. It just says 'All's well. Sale is possible. A few minor restrictions. Sit tight.' That make any sense to you?"

"What's Sonny selling?" Mrs. Siddons asked.

"It makes sense," Delanna said. A few weeks ago news that a sale of her interest in Milleflores was possible would have made her happy. Ecstatic, if she'd learned this around the time of her salt bath. Now she only knew that she loved Milleflores and she could never sell it. And all the legal ramifications about Milleflores paled with the knowledge that Doc Lyle was coming in a few days to take Cleo.

"What's Sonny selling?" Mrs. Siddons asked again.

None of that matters anymore, Delanna thought, but she knew Mrs. Siddons would keep asking until she got an answer. "Just . . . an old clock," she said.

"A clock?" said Mrs. Siddons. "Why would Sonny need a lawyer to help him sell a clock?"

It was a stupid answer, one that would only make Mrs. Siddons all the more curious. "It's not important," Delanna said, trying to sound breezy. And then she added, "Grandpa Maitz, do you know when they'll be done with the dam?"

"Oh, they're sure to be working through the night. Even if all goes well, and I think it is, they'll wait for the reservoir to crest from the melt before heading home."

Delanna nodded to herself. It was just as well. Her eyes were red from tears and Sonny would want to know what was wrong, and she didn't want to tell him. She hadn't known the last time he'd helped her save Cleo that he might have been putting Milleflores at risk. He hadn't told her, though he must have realized it. And she knew that since he'd done it once, he'd do it again. She had to solve this problem on her own.

"Do you have a message for Sonny?" Grandpa Maitz was saying. "I'll be driving some supper over pretty soon. Have to start early enough to make the round trip before sundown. My battery isn't what it ought to be."

"Maybe you ought to get a clock instead," Mrs. Siddons said. "One that's so fancy a lawyer has to help you sell it probably won't ever run down. And maybe Mrs. Tanner wants to leave a whereat message about the clock for Maggie."

The clock was definitely a mistake, Delanna thought. But

she'd deal with that later. "Just tell Sonny that I'm fine and that all the geese are fine, too."

"I'll do that," Grandpa Maitz promised. "What word do you want to leave for Maggie?"

Yes, Delanna thought. An injunction or something. "Tell Maggie I need—"

"I've got an emergency whereat for Doc Lyle," a male voice cut in. Delanna had heard the voice before, but she couldn't immediately put a name to it.

"This is O'Hara at Winterset Lanzye," the man said. "I need Doc Lyle. I heard he was in the neighborhood."

"This is Doc Lyle; I'm listening."

"I've got some mighty sick sheep here," O'Hara said.

"You haven't been grazing them on Milleflores land, have you?"

"Of course not," O'Hara said sounding just a little indignant. "Why do you ask?"

Because he's trying to make Cleo out to be a Typhoid Mary, Delanna thought sadly.

"Never mind," Doc Lyle said grumpily. "I'll head over there now. Be there before nightfall."

The air waves were silent for just a moment, then Mrs. Siddons broke in again. "Salty Tanner, are you still there? Did you want to finish your whereat for Maggie Barlow about the clock?"

Delanna clicked on the microphone. "Just tell Maggie I no longer want to sell the clock," Delanna said, and she clicked off. The message would confuse Maggie, but it might stop her from proceeding with further negotiations, if that's what she was doing. It didn't get her the injunction she needed, if one were possible. But at least nosy Mrs. Siddons had kept chatting long enough that O'Hara had cut in with his emergency call. Delanna had forgotten that Doc Lyle would do what everyone did while driving in his solaris; he'd listen to the ham. And if he knew Delanna was trying to get an injunction to save Cleo, he might decide not to wait to destroy Cleo humanely when he came back for her. He might decide to shoot her on sight.

Delanna tried to eat, but the food just stuck in her throat. She went to look for Cleo and found nothing but fire monkeys, including Big Guy, sleeping in the sun. She tried to roll him off the quilt, but he wouldn't budge. Cleo was nowhere to be found. Poor thing. She was probably scared out of her wits after bouncing around in the isolette.

Delanna swept out the poultry shed, mindless mechanical work while she tried to think of what to do. Call Maggie. No, Doc Lyle would hear and come back and shoot Cleo. Take Cleo and run away. Right. She'd be lucky to get as far as the Salt Flats on her own, and if she tried crossing those on foot, she and Cleo would both die, and soon there would be nothing but a few bones dressed in whatever she was wearing and what would look like a jeweled purse lying next to her, Cleo's dessicated body. If only she could get across the Salt Flats, and then make it onto the shuttle with Cleo. She still had the refund money.

She put the geese up early, which seemed to suit them just fine. Then she went to the cottage to take a shower, which she desperately needed now. Cleo was sitting on the stoop, having a conniption.

"I knew you'd be back when you got hungry," Delanna said, picking her up. The scarab broke loose as soon as they were in the cottage, raced for the table, swiped Delanna's uneaten sandwich from lunch, and started back for the door almost before Delanna could get it closed again. Delanna picked her up again and tried to cuddle her, but Cleo squirmed. Delanna sighed. The smell of geese was overpowering, even to her. She popped the scarab into the isolette, sandwich and all. Cleo fiddled with the door, then went back to the sandwich and started eating it.

Delanna dumped her clothes into the hamper and stepped into the shower, her dismal options preying on her mind. Maybe she could get a secret message to Maggie, but Delanna knew that was impossible with the airwaves closely monitored by Mrs. Siddons and the other busybodies. Maybe Sonny could think of something. Of course he could, and he could lose Milleflores, too. Or maybe she could get Wilkes or Harry to hide Cleo somewhere, which was just as disastrous as Sonny helping her, since Wilkes and Harry were Tanners, too. Jump on a shuttle before Doc Lyle knew she was gone with Cleo, and die in the Salt Flats getting there. Could she take the solaris and get across the Salt Flats before Doc Lyle *and* Sonny knew she was gone? Probably not. She didn't have a good map, let alone soundings, and the floods from the hail would have washed away any trace of previous caravans. And Sonny's transmission still needed to be rebuilt. It might break down halfway there. Besides, she didn't even know how to spread the solar collectors.

When she realized she'd been standing in the shower so long that the water was getting cool, she started to lather her hair. The ruby red soap had practically disintegrated in the running water, the soap Jay had brought for her. She stared at it. Jay had said he'd come get her. She shook her head and started to rinse her hair. Jay might get her across the Salt Flats, but his expectations if he got a call from her had nothing to do with rescuing her scarab. The water turned very cold. She stepped out of the shower.

While she ate dinner and listened to the ham, she let Cleo out of the isolette. The dam had been saved, and everyone was tired and hungry, but no one had been hurt and no property damaged. Now the workers were just waiting for the reservoir to crest, which would happen in a few hours. Cleo scratched at the door the entire time Delanna ate her cold timarine cakes. And after Delanna went to bed, lying there awake, still trying to think of what to do, Cleo left her pillow and went to the door to check if it was open yet.

In the morning, Delanna knew the fire monkeys were gone. She thought it was strange that none of them were waiting for Cleo when she finished her breakfast. A little while later she heard on the ham that the workers had all left Stillwater Dam, and she started watching the distant patch of road that was visible to her between the south orchard and a series of hillocks that came out from the Greatwall Mountains like an overgrown rib. She never did see the solaris, but she thought she saw a sparkle of fire monkeys trudging along the road. When she saw one dragging a bright pink spot, the quilt, over the emerald-green landscape, she was certain the Milleflores fire monkeys were on their way south.

She took Cleo with her to let the geese out, and when she tried to close her into the poultry shed for a while, the scarab got away. Delanna went back to the cottage to try to make up a coded message for Maggie, something so clever that she could safely say it over the airwaves and Maggie would know to exhaust every effort to find a way to keep Cleo alive. She'd just crumpled about the hundredth piece of paper, certain now that a coded message for Maggie was hopeless, when she heard her name on the ham amidst the storm traffic still going on.

"Mrs. Tanner, are you around?"

She walked over to the set and snapped on the microphone. "I'm here," she said tiredly.

"Sonny and the boys back yet?"

"N . . ."

Harry burst through the door. "We're home," he shouted as he ran past her to the kitchen. "Sonny and B.T. are driving down to the east orchard, and Wilkes and I are supposed to bring them some lunch right away."

"Yes, they're here," Delanna said, "but they're out in the field."

"You should have seen the size of the boulder, Delanna, and we moved it with just . . ."

The rest of what Harry was saying was muffled because he'd ducked down into the root cellar.

"Well, you tell Sonny that the harvesters have moved him up in the schedule because of the hail. They'll finish

Stillwater and Blue Rug, and head right on to Milleflores, following the path of the storm.''

''I'll tell him,'' she said. Wilkes had just walked in and was looking around for Harry, then heard his voice from the cellar. He got a sack, and sauntered after his brother, down into the root cellar. They couldn't hide Cleo for her, not any more than Sonny could do anything for Cleo. She glanced at the crumpled paper. A coded message for Maggie was useless; Maggie didn't have the key to any code Delanna could come up with. She had to get across the Salt Flats with Cleo.

''Does anyone know where Jay Madog is?'' she said softly into the mike.

''Could be anywhere,'' Grandpa Maitz responded. ''You need to whereat him?''

''Yes, please,'' she said, still softly. ''Just tell him Delanna said the program's ready.''

19

Jay had said he'd be there before she had her bag packed. He wasn't. What was worse, she couldn't even risk asking if he'd gotten her message. Especially not with Doc Lyle possibly listening in. He would realize instantly what she was up to and head straight back to Milleflores. So Delanna had to wait, and hope, and try to keep tabs on Cleo.

She had put her in the isolette at first, but the scarab had nearly done herself an injury trying to get out of the confined space, and she'd made so much noise Delanna was afraid Sonny would hear her and ask why she was shut up. She closed her in the bedroom next, but Cleo still struggled and scrabbled incessantly to get out, leaving long, desperate claw marks down the door.

"Your friends the fire monkeys aren't here," Delanna explained. "They went south to where it's warmer. And you can't go out. You have to be here when Jay comes," and she shut her ears to Cleo's pitiful chittering.

The scarab got out in spite of the barricaded doors, the shuttered windows. The second time, Delanna searched frantically for her for a full day, during which she became convinced the scarab had gone to find the fire monkeys and almost wished she had. She'd be safe with them at least, but Doc Lyle would blame Sonny, and Delanna couldn't let that happen. When she finally did find her, it was at the foot of the same tree where she'd found her the day of the storm, and Cleo came quite docilely, ate, and allowed herself to be put back in the bedroom. From which she immediately escaped out the window.

Delanna put her back in the isolette and put the isolette out in the geese's shed, where Sonny couldn't hear her. He was scarcely ever there anyway, and neither were the boys. They were busier than before the storm, cleaning up after it and getting the windfall cannonballs in, and they came in well after dark, ate, and went straight to bed, hardly saying anything. For which Delanna was grateful.

She was even more grateful that Cadiz wasn't there. B.T. had had to take her home to help put Flahertys' lanzye back together again. She called on the ham twice daily, and just getting through that conversation without Cadiz finding out something was wrong was difficult enough. She could never have pulled it off in person. And she could never have pulled it off if Cadiz hadn't been preoccupied with her engagement negotiations and the harvest.

The storm had done what Sonny'd hoped—brought the harvesters to Milleflores sooner. They were coming in four days, which was barely time to get ready for them. Cadiz and Delanna's conversations on the ham sounded like Mrs. Siddons'—they were almost entirely recipes—and now Delanna understood the importance of her having gotten in the timarine crop. They were going to feed the harvesters. Timarine cobbler, timarine bread, timarine stew, even roast leg of timarine. Cadiz gave instructions on how much to make and how to serve them and promised to come to help as soon as she could. "We've got everything settled except the will. Daddy wants us to put in a betrothal provision for our kids, and B.T. and I are saying no."

Delanna was glad there was so much to do. It kept her from thinking about Sonny, what her leaving would do to him, to Milleflores. About what it would do to her. Now that she was leaving Milleflores, it seemed unbearably beautiful to her. The hail had destroyed most of the flowers that weren't right next to the cottage, but others, encouraged by the wetness and the cool temperatures, had sprung up. Goldbells and archangels and violet-hearted firrioles. They blossomed between the outbuildings, at the corners of the porch, in a cranny of the geese's pen.

She tried not to notice them, and concentrated on baking timarine spice cake and pudding and listening anxiously to the ham for news of Jay and Doc Lyle. There was nothing. Everyone, from Spencer's Wagon to Ultima Thule, was too busy reporting storm damage to even gossip. Roads were washed out all over, and a bridge was out on the north road, which was either good news, if Doc Lyle had gone that direction, or bad news if it was up by Carmodys', where Jay was delivering his load.

Teapot Lanzye had lost an outbuilding and five chickens. Sylvan View had lost part of an orchard from wind damage. Carmodys' had flooding.

The rains hadn't hit the Salt Flats yet, and there was a good deal of speculation about when they would. Delanna refused to think about what would happen if they couldn't get across. She concentrated on figuring out what to do when they got to Grassedge. She had her ticket refund, and she could sign an indentured-servitude contract with the shuttle or borrow the difference from Maggie. Not from Jay. He'd already rescued her trunk and gotten her refund chit, and she'd owe him her passage to Grassedge. She didn't want to be any more in debt to him. The shuttle was due in two weeks, and the next one after that in a month. If Jay came today, they could make it easily. And if she missed it, she'd simply get a job at one of the saloons till the next shuttle. Or hide in the mines if she had to.

She hadn't thought any further than that. She supposed she'd go back to Rebe Prime, though she didn't have any idea what she'd do there. It didn't much matter. All that mattered was Jay coming today.

But he didn't come that day, or the next. Cadiz called to say they were starting down from Flahertys', and Sonny sent Harry in to help Delanna get the cottage ready for the harvesters. "Some of them might be here as soon as tonight, depending on the roads. They'll camp out in the orchard, but they'll want to use the shower."

There wouldn't be more than a few hot showers even if the harvesters kept them brief, but there would be plenty of warm towels. Harry brought yet another armload down from the Tanner lean-to, and she put them in the bathroom drybox that kept its solar heat through the night.

"I'm going to sleep out in the orchard tonight with the harvesters," Harry announced. He was struggling with the latch on the drybox, which wouldn't fasten because towel hems were caught in the door. "Sonny said I could."

"Could what?" Delanna asked as she opened the door to free the towels. They were in a heap, and Delanna started folding them.

"Sleep in the orchard," Harry said eagerly. "Sometimes they build a campfire and roast timarine puffs on a stick. And they tell stories, even scary ones. You could come, too, Delanna. You tell real good stories."

Harry's eyes were so bright with anticipation that Delanna's heart ached to see him. What kind of campfire stories would the harvesters tell next year? Would Harry be so eager to listen to the story of the runaway bride? Could he possibly understand that she *had* to save Cleo?

"I hope the harvesters come real soon," Harry said.

What if Jay doesn't get here before the harvesters start to arrive? Delanna thought desperately. How will he get Cleo and me out of here? She switched on the ham, wondering if she should ask for a whereat on Jay. Iron Lick was on, reporting storm damage. "Four trees down, and I found the other Royal Mandarin today. A female. It was dead. There's a chick, but it can't survive without the mother. Tell Doc Lyle I've got it in an incubator anyway." Iron Lick was on the other side of the Greatwalls. Please,

please, Delanna prayed, let him go get the chick.

The harvesters started to arrive, bearing huge quantities of food, ambrosia, and good will. "So this is Sonny's bride," they all said, handing her cloth-covered baskets full of timarine puffs. "You're even prettier than they said. And you don't look near as salty as I expected."

More people from the nearby lanzyes arrived, and Delanna had her hands full carrying food out to the long trestle tables in the orchard. She ran to see who it was every time she heard a solaris pull in, hoping it was Jay, but it never was. It was Mort Sanderson, Bruno Stern, Sugarbabe Toricelli, all the people Delanna'd been listening to for weeks on the ham.

None of them looked at all like she'd expected. Mary "Big Bottom" Brigbotham was a dazzlingly pretty girl with a perfect figure, Tom Toricelli was tall and thin and had coal-black skin, Old Man Morelli was no older than Sonny. Only Mrs. Siddons looked exactly like she sounded, a plump, middle-aged woman with shrewd little eyes that took in everything. She arrived wearing a smocked shift Delanna'd heard her tell her daughter how to make, and carrying a huge pot of the fabled green stew.

"There's timarine surprise and blue-carrot cake out in the solaris," she said, looking Delanna up and down. "This stew's cooked. It just needs hotting up. You look peaked. Sonny not treating you right?"

Delanna took the stew from her and set it on the stove. "Sonny's wonderful," she said.

Mrs. Siddons looked dissatisfied, obviously wishing there was something she could take back to the ham to gossip about. "Well, I must say," she declared finally, "you don't look much like a been-to to me."

But Delanna was a been-to, and she was going to be again. And in a few days Mrs. Siddons would have plenty of gossip to dispense—about how Delanna Tanner had left her husband and run off with Jay Madog, about how she couldn't stand the lanzye life and had gone off to Carthage, how they had always thought it was a mistake for Sonny to have married her in the first place, a been-to like that with all her airs and fancy clothes. And just like her mother.

It doesn't matter, Delanna told herself. I won't be around to hear it. But Sonny would. He'd have to listen to it all, the speculation, the well-meaning advice, the pitying remarks.

Cadiz arrived, with extra chairs and news about her engagement. "I think we're actually going to get everything negotiated in time to announce our engagement at the harvest," she said, bubbling over with excitement. "Anyway, Mother made me bring a dress. So, how are things coming with you and Sonny?"

"I've got to go bring in some dried mimkins," Delanna said, and started out.

"I'll finish bringing in the things from the solaris," Cadiz said. "And then I want to hear all about it."

Delanna went out to the drying shed, glad to escape for the moment. And what was she going to say to Cadiz when she went back in? How was she going to work with her in the same kitchen? *Oh, please, Jay, please come.*

She reached up for a tray, and a man grabbed her arm and spun her around and kissed her. "Jay!" she said when he released her.

He put a warning finger to his lips. "I figured it'd be easier if nobody saw me, so I came in the back way. The rig's parked on the road by the path to the spring." He looked at her eagerly. "I came as soon as I got your message."

The excitement in his eyes was hard to look at. Delanna averted her head. "Thank you."

"I couldn't believe you sent it," he said, his grip tightening on her arm. "I never thought you'd do it." He started to pull her close.

"We'd better go before anybody sees us," she said, pulling away. "I just have to get my carryit and Cleo. My bag's in the cottage."

She ducked free of him and ran into the cottage, hoping Cadiz was still out at the solaris.

She was. Delanna rushed into the bedroom, opened her mother's trunk, and grabbed the carryit. The dried bunch of rosewillows that Sonny had given her was lying under it. Don't think about that, she told herself. Don't think about anything. Just get Cleo and go. She opened the door a crack to make sure there was no one there, and then ran back behind the cottage to Jay.

"You're sure in a hurry to go with me," Jay said, reaching for her. "It's very flattering."

She shoved the carryit at him. "Cleo's in with the geese," she said, and started for their pen.

"Jay Madog!" Cadiz called out.

Delanna froze. She turned around, to see Cadiz standing next to the cottage, her hands on her hips.

"What on earth are you doing here?" Cadiz said heartily. "I thought you were up north. The Spellegny twins too much for you? Or did you hear I was getting engaged and couldn't stand it?"

She sauntered toward Jay, grinning, her hands still on her hips. "What'd you come back for?" she asked. "Mary Brigbotham or—" She stopped short at the sight of the carryit. She looked at Jay, the grin gone, then looked at Delanna for a long moment.

Delanna looked away.

"Never mind," Cadiz said to Jay. "It's obvious what you came back for. And it's obvious you got it." She started for the front of the cottage.

"Cadiz, you don't understand—" Delanna said.

Cadiz turned. "What don't I understand?" she said furiously. "It isn't what it looks like? Your carryit's full of dried mimkins? *What*?"

Delanna raised her head to look at her. "Please don't tell Sonny. Not till we're gone. Please."

"Don't tell Sonny—? Why not? You don't want to hurt his feelings? You think he won't notice till the harvest is over that you're not here?'' Cadiz said savagely. ''You think maybe he's too dumb to notice at all?'' She stopped, breathing hard. ''How could you do this to him? B.T. and I were going to build on the north meadow so we could all live close to each other.'' She looked like she was going to cry. ''How *could* you?''

Don't cry, Delanna thought, *I couldn't take that.*

''Delanna was never Sonny's wife, you know that,'' Jay said. ''It was a marriage in name only. A business arrangement.''

''Is that true, Delanna? It was just a business arrangement? Nothing else?''

''You don't understand,'' Delanna said.

''Fine,'' Cadiz said. ''Explain it to me.''

''I don't have time. I have to go get Cleo.'' She brushed past Cadiz and ran over to the poultry shed, blinking back tears. *There's no time to cry. Just get Cleo and go*, she thought. And stood there blinking at the empty isolette. Its door had been forced open.

There was no way Cleo could have gotten it open, or the door of the shed either, but she had. They were both standing open, and there was nothing in the shed except an irate goose. Delanna picked the isolette up and looked in it anyway, unable to take in the fact that Cleo was gone, and then looked around wildly. What if Doc Lyle had already come back and taken the scarab without telling her?

''No,'' she said aloud, trying to stay calm. ''He would have unlocked the isolette, not broken it open.'' Cleo had gotten herself out. But what if, free, she'd wandered out into the orchard and into the middle of the harvest? Delanna dropped the isolette and ran back to Jay and Cadiz.

''Cleo's missing!'' she cried. ''We've got to find her!''

''Maybe she ran off without telling anybody. Like her owner,'' Cadiz said.

''She's probably just wandered off,'' Jay said. ''Wasn't she hanging around the fire monkeys?''

''They've gone south,'' Dellana told him. ''You have to

help me find her!'' She grabbed Jay's arm. ''Jay, go see if she's in the outbuildings. Cadiz, look in the cottage. Sometimes she crawls under the bed.'' She started off at a run down the path to the spring. She'd caught Cleo many times at the base of the same tree. Maybe she'd gone there again.

She wasn't there. The tree had been felled by the storm and lay half in the spring, its roots across the Red Sea bush Cleo had tried to escape into when Delanna caught her before. ''Cleo!'' she called, trying frantically to think where else she could be. She turned to go back to the path and met Cadiz before she had gone five steps.

''I want to know what's going on,'' Cadiz said. ''And don't tell me you're in love with Jay Madog. I saw you and Sonny together after the storm. Why are you really leaving? What's happened?''

Delanna started past her. ''I have to find Cleo.''

Cadiz blocked her way. ''Why? Cleo's run off before, and you never got this worked up.''

Delanna plunged into the Red Sea bushes and around Cadiz to the edge of the spring. Cleo wasn't there either. The spring was clogged with leaves and fallen branches, the way it had been the first time she saw it. She leaned out over the rocks, looking for the fire monkeys, but they had gone south and there was nothing by the rocks but mud.

''You can't fool me, Delanna Tanner. Something's happened. What is it?''

Jay came up, still holding onto Delanna's carryit. ''She wasn't in the outbuildings. Did you find her?''

''No,'' Delanna said, looking frantically around. Where else could she have gone if not to the tree and not to the fire monkeys? Maybe she'd found an egg to hatch. Maybe one of the geese—''We need to go back to the cottage,'' she said to Jay. ''She may have made a nest under the cottage.''

''No,'' Cadiz said, standing in Delanna's path. ''I'm not letting you do this.''

''You don't understand,'' Delanna said.

"You're right. I don't. Explain to me exactly why you're running off with Jay Mad—'' Cadiz stopped at the expression on Delanna's face.

Sonny had come up behind Cadiz. He was carrying one of the long hooks used to bring the cannonballs down, and he'd arrived just in time to hear her say, "Explain to me exactly why you're running off with Jay," not that she'd needed to. Jay was standing there with Delanna's carryit. But Sonny wasn't looking at Jay. He was looking at Delanna, like a man who'd been slugged in the jaw.

She had thought she couldn't stand the sight of tough, brazen Cadiz near tears. It was nothing compared to this. *I've spent weeks blaming my mother for what she did to Sonny*, Delanna thought despairingly, *but she never made him look like this.*

The moment seemed to go on forever, him looking so stunned, so *beaten*, and Delanna unable to speak, even to say, Sonny—

Jay started forward. "Now, look, Tanner, Delanna sent for me—"

Sonny ignored him. "Where's Cleo?" he asked, and his voice was steady, but the beaten look hadn't left his face.

"I don't know," Delanna said. "She ran off."

"You've got to find her and hide her," Sonny said. "Doc Lyle's here."

"Here?" Delanna repeated blankly.

"Here," Doc Lyle said and stepped into the clearing. He had a gun and the mangled isolette. "Where is the specimen?"

"I don't know," Delanna said, taking a protective step backward.

"Turn the scarab over now to be destroyed, or I will have to place you under arrest."

"Now wait just a minute," Jay broke in. "You can't—"

"Harboring a contraband species is a violation of Keramos law, carrying with it very serious consequences,"

Doc Lyle said. "I informed Mrs. Tanner of those consequences when I was here before."

Sonny jerked his head around to look at Delanna. "Doc Lyle was here before?"

She nodded.

"I *knew* it," Cadiz said. "I knew there had to be something going on to make Delanna run off with Jay."

Sonny turned to the vet. "And you told Delanna you were going to destroy Cleo when you came back."

"I told her she was guilty of introducing a contraband species onto Keramos, thereby exposing other species to the threat of disease. I told her the specimen had to be destroyed. The law is very clear."

"There has to be some reasonable way to settle this," Sonny said. "Cleo's no danger to anyone. Scarabs don't carry any cross-species diseases, and she's had all her shots. The only reason you didn't clear her in the first place was because Delanna hadn't filled out the proper paperwork before she left Rebe Prime. And now Cleo's been on Keramos for two more weeks than the quarantine period, and she hasn't infected anybody or anything. She's harmless."

"You don't know that," Doc Lyle said. "What if the specimen destroys another species' habitat? Or eats their eggs? Keramos is down to one Royal Mandarin chick, and it has almost no chance of survival. Do you want to see other species destroyed?" He raised his gun. "I was prevented from taking the specimen last time by fire monkeys," he went on, glaring at Delanna.

"That's two I owe them," Sonny muttered.

"I don't intend to be prevented again. Turn over the specimen immediately."

"I don't know where she is," Delanna said stolidly— and Cleo walked into the clearing.

Delanna dived for the scarab, scooped her up, and backed away. "No!" she said. "I won't let you kill her."

"I hereby place you under arrest," Doc Lyle said. He reached for Cleo.

"Get behind me, Delanna," Sonny said, brandishing the cannonball hook at Doc Lyle.

She stepped behind Sonny, clutching Cleo to her chest.

"Put her in the bushes," Sonny told Delanna.

"I'll confiscate your lanzye for this, Tanner," Doc Lyle said, backing off.

Delanna hesitated. "I can't let you do this, Sonny," she said. "Not Milleflores. Not when you've worked so hard to keep it going."

Jay said, "Sonny, you can't give up your lanzye for a—"

"Put her in the thicket, Delanna," Sonny said again, holding the cannonball hook between her and Doc Lyle.

She stooped and set Cleo down. "Go," she whispered, shoving the scarab as far into the Red Sea thicket as she could reach, wishing it were really as impenetrable as it looked. Cleo promptly scuttled off, the thorny branches closing protectively behind her. Delanna stood up.

"I hereby place the two of you under arrest," Doc Lyle declared, eying the cannonball hook warily. "Keramos' laws—"

"Are the reason Delanna couldn't go back on the shuttle," Sonny said angrily. "If it weren't for Keramos's laws, Delanna would never have had to bring Cleo to Keramos in the first place. If it weren't for Keramos' laws, she wouldn't have had to travel five thousand miles to a broken-down lanzye, and she wouldn't have had to put up with being married to an uneducated hick—Keramos' laws are what *caused* this damned mess in the first place!" He flung down the cannonball hook at Doc Lyle's feet. "Go ahead. Arrest me for breaking Keramos' laws."

"You're under arrest," Doc Lyle said, stepping forward and kicking the hook out of reach. "The charges are harboring an illegal species, resisting arrest, threatening—" He stopped.

Cleo scuttled out of the thicket and up to Doc Lyle's feet. He raised the gun.

"You shoot Cleo," Sonny said, "and I'll have your hide."

"Please—" Delanna said in the same instant, but he'd already lowered the gun.

Behind Cleo, in a straggling line, waddled nine Royal Mandarin chicks. One of them, running to catch up, spread its tiny wings, and there was a flash of blue and green and purple.

"Those are Royal Mandarins!" Cadiz said unnecessarily. "I thought the storm killed them all."

"Cleo must have hatched the eggs," Delanna said. "That's why she was trying to get out during the storm."

Doc Lyle seemed stunned. He stared at the Mandarin chicks as if he couldn't believe his eyes.

"It was a nesting pair," Sonny said. "And this contraband species has been illegally harboring them since the storm. So you've got a problem, don't you, Doc Lyle? Cleo's a contraband species, and the law's the law. So you have to shoot her."

"No!" Delanna cried.

"But if you do, you're going to have an extinct species. These chicks can't possibly survive on their own, can they?"

"No," Lyle admitted numbly.

Cleo chittered, and the chicks ran to her, scurrying under her carapace. She gathered them in gently with her forelegs, clucking softly.

"The law is very clear," Sonny went on. "Seems to me the only thing to do is to declare Cleo a Royal Mandarin. That way she's not contraband, and you've got nine Royal Mandarins instead of none."

"Ten," Doc Lyle murmured. "I've got a chick in my solaris."

"Ten," Sonny said. "Bound to be a couple of nesting pairs with ten chicks. How about it?"

"Cadiz!" B.T. called, and strode into the clearing.

"There you are! What have you been doing? I thought we were getting engaged."

"We are, we are," Cadiz said, motioning him to be quiet. "I just wanta see how this turns out first."

Doc Lyle knelt next to Cleo and reached for one of the chicks. It skittered to safety underneath her. Cleo slapped him sharply with a foreleg. He stood up. "I'll go get the other chick," he said.

"And you won't press charges against Sonny or Delanna?" Jay asked.

"I won't press charges."

"And you won't shoot the scarab," Sonny asked, "even after the chicks are full-grown?"

"It's not a scarab," Doc Lyle said, looking wonderingly at the chicks huddling close to Cleo. "You're right. It's a Royal Mandarin. They're a protected species. No one can shoot them." He started toward his solaris.

"Come on, Cadiz. Everybody's waiting," B.T. said. "Come on, Jay. I want you to see this. You coming, Delanna?"

"In a minute," she said. B.T. dragged Cadiz off down the path, Jay in their wake.

"Sonny—" Delanna said, turning to thank him, but he was gone. She stood there a minute, looking at the cannonball hook and at Cleo and her chirping brood, and then sank down on one of the rocks at the edge of the spring, weak with reaction. After a while she started to cry.

Someone was coming. She looked up, hoping it was Sonny, but was only Jay. He handed her the carryit. "I figured you'd want this back."

"Thank you," she said, sniffing back tears. "Jay—"

"Yeah, I know, I know. If it hadn't been for Keramos's laws, a certain bride never would have sent for me."

"I'm sorry I used you," she said. "I was so afraid for Cleo. She's helpless. She depends on me—"

He cut her off. "It's okay. As Mary Brigbotham said to

me the other day, it's only fair I should be the one who gets used for once."

Delanna smiled a little at that.

He turned to leave and then stopped. "My offer still holds, you know."

"Jay—"

"I mean, about transportation. To Grassedge, the shuttle, wherever you want to go. No strings attached, no invitations to my rig."

"Thank you," she said solemnly.

He started out of the clearing, brushing past Sonny. Delanna stood up. "Thank you for saving Cleo's life," she said to Sonny.

"You're welcome," Sonny said stiffly. "I talked to Doc Lyle. He says it'll be about six weeks before the baby Mandarins can survive on their own. The Circuit Court should have granted our divorce by then. Until it's final you can stay in the cottage, or if you want to, you can go on ahead to Grassedge and I'll bring Cleo in when she's done raising the chicks."

Delanna nodded bleakly.

"Cadiz's father is willing to buy the still from me," he went on, looking away from her. "That and the refund will pay your passage to Carthage and give you living expenses for a while. Is that all right with you?"

"It's all right," Delanna managed. "Sonny—"

"I've got to go watch Cadiz and my brother get engaged," he said, and turned to leave the copse.

"Just where do you think you're going?" Cadiz said. She was standing in the middle of the path slapping her hat against her knee, and in spite of her dress and the flowers on the hat, she looked the way she had that first day in Grassedge, standing in the middle of the street. And about as mad.

"Let me by, Cadiz," Sonny said.

"Not a chance," Cadiz told him. "You're staying right here."

"What are you doing here?" Delanna asked. "I thought you and B.T. were announcing your engagement."

"We were. Thanks to a little matchmaking and some good advice. If it hadn't been for you, Delanna, B.T. and I would never have gotten together. We were both too stubborn. And too dumb. Like a couple of other people I know." She looked from one to the other. "I would've let him walk right out of my life without telling him how I felt." She crossed her arms. "I'm here to see that doesn't happen with you two."

"Cadiz, this is none of your business," Delanna said.

"It isn't? If it wasn't for you, I'd still be moping over B.T. and biting his head off every time I saw him. What was it you said to me in the solaris—'If you love him, you'd better let him know.' Good advice. So. Who wants to start?"

Delanna looked at Sonny, remembering B.T. and Cadiz in the camp at Little Dip, both of them miserable and defiant and clearly in love with each other, neither of them willing to say how they really felt. *A guy's gotta have some sign that the girl won't laugh in his face before he tells her how he feels*, Sonny had said, and it applied to him even more than to B.T. Her mother had spent years laughing in his face, and then she'd come along and called him a Neanderthal, told him she'd rather die than be married to him, flirted with Jay Madog. And called Jay to come and get her when she was in trouble.

"Sonny—"

"*Here* you are," Mrs. Siddons said, taking them by surprise. "Everybody's been looking for you everywhere, Cadiz. I thought you'd run off with Jay Madog." She looked around as if she thought he might be hiding in the bushes.

"We had some business to finish up," Cadiz told her, looking at Delanna.

"You can finish it later," Mrs. Siddons said. "Put your hat on."

Cadiz jammed her flowered hat down on her head.

"Oh, no, you can't get engaged looking like that," Mrs. Siddons said. "Delanna, do something with that hat. Sonny, you've got to come do something about B.T.'s boots. Come on!"

She propelled the three of them bodily down the path, shouting, "It's all right. I've found her!" and into the center of the crowd in the yard. "Harry and Wilkes, you get over here."

Harry and Wilkes sidled up. "I heard your bug—" Harry said.

"It's not a bug," Delanna said. "It's a Royal Mandarin." Someone pushed Delanna up next to Cadiz and Mrs. Siddons, who was fussing with her hat. Cadiz looked about ready to take it off and throw it on the ground.

"Here. Let me do that," Delanna offered, and stepped in front of Mrs. Siddons. She tipped the hat back slightly and smoothed Cadiz's hair.

"To quote a friend of mine," Cadiz said, " 'If you love him, you'd better let him know.' " She leaned forward and kissed Delanna on the cheek. "Or I'll throttle you."

"Me, too," Wilkes said.

They all turned to look at Wilkes.

"You *can* talk," Delanna said.

"I told you I thought he could," Cadiz said.

"All right, now, Cadiz and B.T., you stand here." Mrs. Siddons shoved Delanna aside, positioning B.T. and Cadiz. "And her brothers need to be here, and then Mr. and Mrs. Flaherty." She pushed them all into place. "You stand here, Delanna," she instructed, moving her over to the far edge. "And, Sonny, you stand next to her, and the boys next to you. Where's Jay Madog?" He was on the porch, flirting with Mary Brigbotham. Mrs. Siddons grabbed him and made him stand next to Mrs. Flaherty.

Somebody pressed a mug of ambrosia into Delanna's hand. "For the toast," he said.

"Where's Mr. Flaherty? You stand here," Mrs. Siddons

said. "No, no, Cadiz . . . all right. Judge, you can begin any time."

"Thank you," the judge said dryly. "In accordance with the laws of Keramos . . ." He began droning through the marriage regulations.

Delanna looked at the crowd listening dutifully to the judge, then stared at the mug of ambrosia for a long minute before taking a determined gulp. It was like fine wine going down, like silk, like heaven. "It tastes wonderful," she whispered to Sonny.

"I told you," he said. "The night of the storm."

The ambrosia might have loosened Sonny's tongue, but it wasn't helping Delanna. She felt as tongue-tied and silent as the Tanner boys. "Sonny," she began, and took a deep breath. "Cadiz was right," she went on. "The only reason I called Jay was because I was trying to save Cleo. I thought he could get us to the shuttle before Doc Lyle caught up with us."

"Why didn't you tell me Doc Lyle had come around?"

"Because he said he'd take Milleflores away from you, and I couldn't let that happen, not after you'd worked so hard to make something of it, not after everything I'd done, bankrupting you so I could go to school—"

"What makes you think Milleflores would mean anything to me without you?"

". . . to be delivered upon the marriage of . . ." the judge read.

"I don't want to go," Delanna said.

"I don't want you to go," Sonny said, and bent to kiss her. There was a cheer, and Cadiz threw her hat in the air, scattering flowers.

"Wait a minute," Sonny said into the cheering. "Quiet down. I've got an announcement to make." He took Delanna's hand. "Cadiz and B.T. aren't the only two announcing their engagement. Delanna Milleflores and I—" He stopped and looked down at her. "You sure you want to be stuck on a lanzye with a Neanderthal—?"

She kissed him, hard.

"Delanna Milleflores and I want to get married. We hereby announce our engagement according—"

There was a burst of laughter, and Tom Toricelli called out, "You've had too much ambrosia, Tanner. You can't get engaged to her."

If this is another one of Keramos's idiotic laws, Delanna thought, I'll—

"Why not?" Sonny said belligerently.

"Because she's already married to you, you idiot," Mel Flaherty said.

Sonny looked at Delanna.

"He's right," she said breathlessly. "I am."